ISBN-13:
ISBN-10:
Cover design by:
Library of Congress Control Number:
Printed in the United States of America

I0663081

# THE FIRST TO FALL
*A Fallen Novel*

**By**
**Tanisha D Jones**

TANISHA D. JONES

*For:*
*A.H., W.W., C.J. M.T.*
*& those who believed in me*
*When I no longer believed in myself*

# PROLOGUE

He attempted to sit up and slowly realized that he was not in the comfortable California King sized bed in his luxurious penthouse suite; he was on the floor of the suite's living area. It took a moment before he could focus. The room was dark and empty, and he supposed his bandmates had gone back to their rooms with their groupies. The room smelled of stale cigarettes, old liquor, sex, marijuana, and a faint hint of electricity. He smelled rain somewhere far off but coming soon. As he thought it, lightning cracked the night sky in two.

There was an uncomfortable feeling of damp warmth beneath him. Groggily, he rolled over, expecting to find- he didn't know what. Perhaps the beautiful young groupie he'd enticed into his room had too much to drink and had relieved herself in her sleep. It wouldn't be the first time something like that had happened. He preferred urine to some of the other fluids and pseudo fluids he'd woken up in.

He stared out over the penthouse's patio. On his back, the dampness was still there, making his white t-shirt stick to his skin. There was no acrid smell of urine, he noticed. This was something else, something sweetly metallic and sticky. His first thought was the little tramp vomited on him. It wouldn't be the first time, he thought. As he moved, he felt stiffness in his neck, a slow burn started when he touched the spot, and felt a small raised welt just above his jugular.

"Shit," he mumbled to himself. What had he done tonight?

Slowly, he moved to the bathroom, stripping off his clothes as he went. As he passed the bedroom, he noticed a body on the bed. She was tall, tanned, and lean, her perfect nakedness exposed. Her hair was long and startlingly blond against her dark skin.

"Brittney," he mumbled as he stripped off his pants. The name fit her, he thought. She was an enthusiastic and creative girl, with bright emerald green eyes and a full pink mouth. He could forgive her for a little vomit, he thought as he turned on the bathroom lights and started the shower.

He walked into the shower, taking a seat on the bench at the back of the marble and glass stall. When he reached for the shampoo, he noticed his hand was caked with dried blood. A little panicked, he stood and looked at both hands. A scream of nervous horror stopped in his throat. He inspected himself, running his hands over his chest in search of a wound, but found nothing.

Around his feet, rivulets of blood ran and swirled down the drain. His heart raced as he stumbled out of the shower and screamed when he saw the bloody footprints leading to the shower stall. Wet and naked, he immediately lost his footing and began sliding on the white marble floor. He reached out to save himself from the inevitable and painful fall but landed with a thud on his back, his right ankle snapping loudly.

He screeched as the pain ricocheted through his body. Through his pain, he saw something move in the darkness of the bedroom. Brittney. He had woken her.

"Babe, call 911. I think I broke my fucking ankle," he groaned in a slight southern accent. The form moved again, in the shadows but never answering.

"Britt?"

The figure darted quickly to the right and then back to the left. He felt a chill right down to his bones. The pain in his ankle was forgotten for now as fear took over. He focused on the darting thing. There was no way a person could move at such rapid speeds and such an odd angle. Whatever it was, it moved closer, a soft skittering sound accompanying its erratic approach.

"Who's there?" He croaked; his throat suddenly dry.

"Nicholas." It spoke in a whisper and in a voice that was neither male nor female and heavily accented. The hair on his arms rose, his body was covered with goosebumps. He would run if he could; the pain in his ankle had subsided to a dull throbbing ache.

The figure moved closer, slowing its erratic pace as it neared the open door.

"What do you want?" Nicholas screeched in a voice he barely recognized as his own. He reached for the vanity counter and slowly pulled himself to his feet, placing all the weight on his left foot. As he did, he looked at himself in the mirror for the first time. His naked muscular body was slick with blood and water, his crisp blue eyes were wide, and his suntanned face was pale, lips tight and drawn into razor-thin lines. His spiked platinum hair was matted with blood, water, and soap.

The creature moved into the room, its long blond hair shrinking into an angelic heart-shaped face, darkening into a spiked pixie cut as did the sweet blond thatch of hair between its thighs. He watched in something close to shock as startling emerald eyes turned an unexpected shade of silver-gray. The large voluminous breasts deflated to a young girl's firm pert breasts, natural and surprisingly womanly. There was a sickly sound of cracking bones, and he could do nothing but stare in paralyzing terror as the once five-foot-seven beauty Brittney morphed into a four foot eleven elfin – thing. He glanced lower and realized that this girl thing also had a huge and very erect – penis, and he groaned in confusion.

It had large cat-like eyes that studied him as he tried to pull himself away from its approach. It smiled, wrinkling a small upturned nose. Its natural rosy blush and skin as white as pure alabaster made it seem beautiful in a stomach-turning way. Nicholas found himself staring into those large eyes, and calm, sensual warmth came over him. It touched his cheek with feather-soft fingers, and Nicholas' own body went rigid. He closed his eyes and was bombarded with images of so many lives taken before him.

"You are one of ours, Nicolai." Its soft breath caressed his neck, and he became erect. "You are mine." Its lips touched the skin just beneath his ear, and he jerked as his body reacted. He groaned as he exploded his seed onto the floor.

* * *

His housekeeper found him the next morning, alone, lying in a pool of his blood on the bathroom floor. She shrieked at the sight of his pale naked body, the strange angle at which his ankle was turned, and the gaping wound in his neck. The bright blue eyes that had graced many magazines were now clouded and dull, staring endlessly at nothing.

By 10:00 a.m., the news hit. At 10:01 a.m., the world began to grieve one of its biggest pop stars. The coroner ruled it a freak accident; that he'd slipped getting out of the shower, broke his ankle, and bled to death from an injury to his neck. There were no signs of foul play, just a sad, simple accident. Other than the gash in his neck, which the coroner attributed to a broken beer bottle found in the living room near a blood-stained carpet, and a broken ankle, his body exhibited no other injuries.

Nicholas Skylar, or Nicky Sky, as he was more popularly known, was dead. He was twenty-nine years old.

Three days after his death, a public memorial service was held to honor him. The streets outside of the St. Louis Cathedral were packed with sobbing, somber fans, and curious onlookers, most donning his signature color, red. Inside was a who's who of the rich, famous, and fabulous. As his coffin exited the sanctuary, the cathedral bells rang, and two dozen snow-white doves were released over the crowd. A brass band led a second line processional through the city streets as hundreds celebrated his life.

Four days after his untimely death, Nicky Sky woke up.

# CHAPTER ONE

T he silence was overpowering, almost claustropho-
bically so. People in white lab coats moved
through the foyer of the funeral home like the spec-
ters of ancient souls, drifting in and out of his line of vision,
blurring at the edges. There seemed to be an absence of
color to coincide with the complete silence. Everything was
painted in sepia tones that seem to bleed at the edges, making everything surreal. Detective Elijah Cain felt as if he were
moving through oatmeal as he forced his way across the foyer
to the only spot of bright color in the place.

Standing at the far end of the foyer, beneath an ornate
archway, a speck of bright red waved to him. As he shuffled
closer to the dot, he realized that it was a redshirt he was
seeing, worn by his partner and best friend of ten years, Riley
Quinn. While the rest of the room was devoid of color, Riley
was an over-saturated Day-Glo rainbow. His eyes were vibrant
electric blue, his tanned skin glowing a vibrant golden brown,
his shirt a shock of candied red, and his hair a halo of gold ring-
lets. When Riley opened his mouth to speak, the sound was
distorted and muted, and Eli couldn't help but stare at the unbearable whiteness of his perfect teeth.

Riley took Eli's arm, and suddenly, they were speeding
through the house, their surroundings becoming a haze of
blurred colors and sounds. He didn't feel as if he were walking
or even running. It was more of a swift glide as if they weren't
touching the ground at all.

They came to a sudden stop in a room that didn't
quite fit. For a split second, everyone in the room appeared
frozen before suddenly bursting to life, moving and speaking

in hushed tones, in a large white space, at the center of which sat a bed on a platform. People hovered near the bed, taking photo after photo. The only splash of color in the stark whiteness, aside from Riley, whose colors vibrated, were the bright turquoise drapes hung at tall windows on either side of the bed.

"Here," Riley said and motioned towards the bed. Anxiously, Eli approached to see the body. She lay perfectly still in the center of the bed, the plush comforter laid impeccably across her, as if she'd been tucked in. Her skin was the color of caramel, smooth and opulent, her face heart-shaped with flawless full lips. Long jet-black hair was pulled over one shoulder in shiny perfect waves laced with tiny purple flowers. She appeared to be asleep, except for the gaping laceration in her neck.

With a wound that deep, she should've been soaked in blood, but there was none. Not a single drop marred anything in the pristine room. As Eli moved closer, Cain could smell the lavender, from the flowers, he assumed. He stared at her for a long, silent moment. She was stunning, a beauty who had died far too young. The light caught a chain around her neck with a silver pendant that lay between her breasts. He stared at the unique jewelry, and a shiver went through him. The charm was a heart encircled by stylized tribal wings. It was a very distinct, unique design. As Eli leaned closer to look at the necklace and the jagged wound at her neck, her hand grasped his wrist with surprising strength. Startled, he took a nervous step back as her eyes opened. They were the same vibrant turquoise shade as the curtains, the same shade, he thought, as his own.

"Elijah," she called in a disembodied, almost hoarse voice.

\* \* \*

Startled, Eli hit the polished hardwood floor with a resounding thud. Immediately, he sprang to his feet, taking a defensive stance. As he scanned the room for, he didn't know what, he exhaled and shook his head warily. He could feel his heart hammering against his ribs, and he was dripping in sweat. He touched the oddly shaped birthmark on his chest absently as the room around him came into focus. He was in his bedroom, the early morning sunlight streaming in through the blinds at the windows. Sighing, he ran a hand over his wet face and grimaced ruefully.

He heard his name being yelled from the doorway, and he spun on his heel, prepared to strike, as Riley entered the room. Riley stopped. Eli was formidable, standing a full eight inches over Riley's 6-foot frame, even in his underwear.

"Calm down, underwear Ninja. I've been outside yelling your name and banging on the door for like five minutes. What's up? And put some pants on." Riley moved further into the room. Slightly irritated by his own body, Eli stalked into the bathroom.

"Grab the phone," he mumbled as he closed the bathroom door. Riley looked down at the black cordless phone, resting silently in its cradle.

"Phone's not ring-" As he spoke, the phone sprang to life with a nice singsong ring.

* * *

Eli jumped into the shower, letting cold water hit him a full blast. Lathering himself quickly, he felt his wrist. Her touch was there, like a brand on his skin. He could still smell the lavender and see eyes he'd never seen in anyone else. Except, of course, when he looked in the mirror.

He jumped out of the shower and looked at himself in the mirror. Her eyes. That was what was bothering him; she had his eyes. The same bright turquoise eyes lined with thick, overly long dark lashes. The face was different. Her face was heart-shaped and feminine; he had a distinctively square masculine jawline. They both had dark hair, and his skin was more of deep chocolate. But the eyes. He looked down at his wrist, half expecting to see a handprint there. But there was nothing.

He stared at his reflection in the mirror. More to the point, he stared at the raised mark on his chest, the one that looked like the pendant he'd seen around the dead woman's neck in his dreams. It was as long and as wide as his thumb, and at first glance, it looked like a tattoo. He'd tried several times to have it removed, but it always remained. Shaking his head, he slipped on his shirt; it was just a birthmark, he'd been assured. Just an oddly shaped birthmark.

"Just a dream Elijah," he said to himself as he dressed. "Just a very wild dream."

"Are you talking to yourself again?" Riley called from the other side of the bathroom door.

He was standing with his ear pressed to the door, and when the door swung open, he had to jump back. Eli stood in his usual uniform of charcoal gray slacks, a crisp white shirt, and a burgundy tie. A furrowed brow replaced his usually jovial smile.

"E, are you okay?" Riley asked his friend.

"Another dream," Eli mumbled. "Same dream, same girl, only this time, she opens her eyes."

"Really?" Riley's curiosity was piqued. For nearly a year, Eli had been haunted by dreams of Angel, as they had dubbed her. "How did they look? Were they gross and bloody?"

"No," Eli looked at his friend with a pained expression. "They were exactly like mine. And she spoke, and she reached out and grabbed me. I swear I can still feel her fingers around my wrist."

"What did she say?" Riley seemed to hum in anticipation. Eli sat on the edge of the bed and put on his shoes.

"She said my name."

"That's it?" Riley tried but failed to keep the disappointment out of his voice.

"Yep." Eli shrugged and sighed. Once he finished putting his shoes on, he looked at Riley and noticed what he was wearing for the first time, a bright red shirt and blue jeans. He found it a bit odd since Riley hated the color red. He'd once told Eli that since he'd become a homicide detective, red always made him slightly nauseous. Yet, there he stood, wearing the brightest candy red shirt Eli had ever seen.

"New shirt?" He ventured. Riley looked down at the shirt and made a face.

"I know what you're thinking. I still hate the color red. But Adam came over last night with a gift, and red is his favorite color. It was a peace offering after our last fight and-"

"And you'd wear a pink tutu and fairy wings up and down Bourbon Street if it guaranteed you a little piece of ass," Eli quipped.

"Not like you haven't seen it before." Riley laughed before following Eli out of the bedroom and down the stairs to his modest kitchen. It was bright and airy, thanks to Eli's grandmother's decorator. He'd refused the floral wallpaper and marble floors but had succumbed to the granite countertops and stainless-steel appliances.

Though Riley wasn't flamboyant or feminine in any way, he was out and proud. He never made excuses or hid who he was, even in the academy where the other recruits had given him hell, isolating him, bullying him whenever they could. Eli had been singled out as well, being taller and broader than everyone else. He also never smiled or joined in on the jokes or games. He was intimidating. Some had tried to become friendly with him once they realized that Eli had a photographic memory and was a crack shot, but that had been short-lived. The first and only person to make the stone-faced recruit laugh out loud had been Riley Quinn. Riley had not been afraid to approach him and had balked when Eli had grumbled for him to go away.

"Not gonna happen, big guy," Riley said as he plowed into

his lunch. "I would like actually to eat my lunch today, not wear it. And nobody is going to mess with me if I'm sitting here," Riley said around a mouth full of chili. Eli had looked at Riley, then at the group of burly young men staring at Riley with open disdain.

"You haven't been eating?" Eli asked in a low voice.

"You see those jackasses staring at me; they have made sure that I haven't completed a meal in a week. I'm running on fumes at this point, and if I fall asleep in one more class, I'm outta here. So, excuse me if I don't care about your sulky brooding act. I need to eat, and you're the only one they won't mess with, so until we graduate, I'm your shadow, handsome. You now have a little, blond, white mini-me. Where you go, I go." Eli had looked at the skinny little man with big blue eyes and smiled. Riley had finished his chili and dug into a piece of cardboard cornbread like an animal.

"You gonna eat that?" He pointed to Eli's half-eaten food once his tray was licked clean. Sighing, Eli shoved his tray over to him.

"Eat." He said simply. That had been the start of it, and they had remained best friends for ten years. And in those ten years, he had seen Riley go through a dozen boyfriends, his party boy phase in which he wore day glow neon almost daily, and finally his current state of self-acceptance.

"Why are you here so early?" Eli asked, laughing off Riley's comments. Knowing Riley as long as he did, his sexual innuendo and crudeness were part of his charm. Riley could charm both men and women with his easy good ol' boy southern charisma.

"You don't know? We've got a high-profile case. Missing Body." Riley grinned.

Eli groaned and shook his head. "We're homicide, not missing persons."

"I said a high profile. The rock star, Nicky Sky, his body is missing." Riley was about to burst from excitement. One of the perks of being a homicide detective was that they always got a high profile and celebrity cases, not just murders. The death of Nicky Sky had been the only thing Riley had talked about for the past few days. He had spoken ad nauseum about the death, the memorial, and the celebrities floating through the city for the said memorial, an avid fan. Now they had been assigned to the case, Eli would never hear the end of it

\* \* \*

"Missing?! How can a dead body be missing? Did someone steal it?" Eli grumbled. Riley squinted at Eli, waiting as if he knew Eli had the answer. He always had the answer. There was something about Eli Cain that not many people knew. He was a telepath. A very controlled and regimented telepath, but he was one, among other things Riley had discovered. Eli never got sick, rarely slept more than two hours a night, and hardly, if ever, ate more than one meal per day. And that meal could consist of something as insubstantial as a milkshake or a glass of wine. He was just hard-wired differently, always alert, and decisive. But Riley accepted him for whatever he was; Eli was his best friend, after all.

If there were one-word Riley would use to describe Eli, it would be intense. Everything about his posture, his demeanor, his no-nonsense attitude was fierce. The one word their fellow officers would use to describe Eli would be bastard. Because the other thing about Elijah Cain was the pure unadulterated beauty of the man, he was movie-star gorgeous but paid absolutely no attention to his appearance. Riley had been sure that Eli had never been an awkward teenager. He had never had a blemish or a crack in his thick baritone. Eli was perfection in a tailored suit. Being a gay man, he was the only one confident enough to be Eli's best friend. After all, he could care less if women threw themselves at Eli and completely ignored him. Not many men could handle being the wingman to a freaking sex god with a bullshit filter. Cops were known bullshit artists, and being called on it had made Eli less than popular. Riley, on the other hand, found it amusing. Not just the brazen attempts, but the sheer volume and creativity utilized. They mostly failed, and those failures were pure comic fodder for Riley.

"No," Riley started cautiously. "It wasn't stolen."

Eli squinted at the menu board as he waited in line with Riley at the small coffee shop on the corner of St. Charles Ave. and Canal Street. Riley noticed two women in their mid-to-late-fifties, staring at Eli as they moved up in line. One was tall and sleek, a cougar if Riley had ever seen one. The other was more soccer mom than sexpot, but she was the one who fascinated him.

This is going to get interesting, he thought. The soccer mom was staring at Eli raptly, running a nervous hand over her stylishly coiffed hair with perfectly manicured nails. She looked like the part of the society housewife in her perfectly accessorized outfit. She did a double, then a triple take when she'd spotted him; now she approached, slowly, cautiously. Eli placed his order as she approached, and Riley held his breath and waited for the inevitable.

"Excuse me." She touched his arm, and when he looked at her, she gasped.

"Yes," he said, giving her a pleasant smile.

"My God, you are the spitting image of someone I used to know when I was younger. You have the same eyes same dimples. I swear you look exactly like him. Maybe he's a relative. His name was Elijah." She said breathlessly.

"That's my name," he said. His smile never faltered, but his brow furrowed in confusion.

"Is he your father?" She asked, a smile spreading across her lips as she gave her friend a shake. She took a step back.

"I'm sorry; my father's name was Gabriel. He died years ago." His tone was gentle, almost apologetic.

"Oh," she looked crestfallen, but her eyes pleaded with him. "But you look just like- you can't be-" She reached

14

up to touch his cheek, her face softening at the memories of the boy she knew in college in the 1960s. She remembered him holding her hands and taking her to dances, and she remembered kissing him under the willow trees on campus. Eli felt a pang of guilt and sadness over the memories that flooded into his mind. This man she remembered, the one who'd loved her, and then he was gone. She had moved on but never had she completely recovered from his loss.

"Come on, suga. It's not him," the cougar said, escorting her away. She gave Eli a tight sad smile as she led the other woman away. "You know what they say; everyone has a double." She offered as they moved away.

"He just looks so much like him." she was saying. Eli stared after them until the barista handed him his coffee. He shook his head. He'd become accustomed to scenes like this over the years, that hadn't affected him before. But something about the sadness in her eyes touched him. Sighing heavily, he turned on his heel and walked out of the coffee shop. Riley silently followed. This exact scenario had occurred at least once a week. Someone always thought Eli was someone they had known or was the son of some friend they had twenty or thirty years ago.

"I guess I just have that kind of face." Eli would say. This encounter had unnerved him. This was the first time someone had used his name.

* * *

Riding in silence, Riley glanced at Eli and could just about see the wheels turning in his head. Eli's brow was creased as he sped through the heavy traffic that led to Uptown. Eli's intensity was beginning to unnerve Riley as the standard-issue sedan hopped the curb and landed in the jogger and bike path that ran the length of St. Charles Avenue.

"Okay, what's up? You're driving like a fucking lunatic,"

Riley finally asked in terrified exasperation. He wasn't sure if Eli was being affected by the dream, the coffee shop encounter, or the rock star's missing body.

"Just thinking," Eli mumbled. Riley knew that was an understatement. Elijah Cain was always thinking. He never stopped thinking.

"About?" Riley pressed. They breezed past pedestrians before swerving back into the flow of traffic.

Eli was thinking about ten things at once. He was thinking about this dream and the mysterious blue-eyed beauty; he was thinking about the poor disillusioned woman who'd approached him in the coffee shop. He chose the least distracting thing he could think of, though, something that would get Riley's rapt attention off him.

"He walked out. How does a dead man walk away?" Eli began mumbling as if he were trying to wrap his mind around the image of a dead body walking.

Riley shook his head. "No, they had a public viewing and memorial service. But because of all the rain the other night, his tomb wasn't ready, so he was at the funeral home. They were going to bury him today, but the Funeral Director got a call at five this morning because the alarm had been triggered. When he got there, he and the police found that no one had broken in; someone had broken out. They searched to clear the building and found the coffin empty, and the body is gone. Security video was a little blurred but witnesses' say that they saw a thin blond man hopping the fence." Eli frowned as a thought occurred to him.

"Wasn't he embalmed?" He asked Riley.

Riley ran a finger over his tablet and typed for a minute. "No- he wasn't. Not at the funeral home anyway. The report says that he was given an autopsy by- his physician."

"Wait -the coroner-" Eli attempted to view the screen, momentarily swerving into the next lane. Riley, never flinching, shook his head vigorously. Eli's distracted driving had become as familiar to him as breathing. The only thing that amazed him is that they had never had an actual accident. Not so much as a scratch.

"Never examined him, other than to pronounce him dead on at the scene. Do you think this was all some elaborate publicity stunt? Nicky Sky did have a movie about to be released and a new album coming out; rising from the dead would be-"

"Stupid," Eli said. "Wouldn't he wait until the movie came out to show himself? It would make a better impact. Then he could come up with some elaborate story of his disappearance. No- this is something else." Eli could feel the familiar itching in the tips of his fingers as he drove. This was different. It was all sorts of wrong.

The dark, unglamorous sedan that was their work vehicle came to a stop in front of the massive gates of St. Pierre Brothers Funeral Home in the Garden District. The building resembled a Tuscan villa, all red roof tiles, and putty-colored stucco walls. Eli leaned out of the driver's side and pushed the call button on the intercom. After a loud buzzing, a high-pitched nervous voice crackled through the silver box.

"Yes?" Came a shrill voice followed by static as the speaker left the line open for a response.

"N.O.P.D." There was a moment of silence before the massive gate began sliding open.

"That's odd," Riley commented as the car rolled onto the grounds.

"What? The gate?" Eli asked, slowly steering the car up the garden lined path.

"Yes, they locked the gate during business hours. Who are they trying to keep out?" Riley looked out of the window at the massive lawn.

"Maybe now," Eli teased, "It's about keeping them *in*."

\* \* \*

Walter St. Pierre was a small, nervous man with watery

blue eyes and deeply tan skin. He seemed to be in his early to mid-forties, with thick dark hair. He stood on the threshold of the building, his hands shoved deep in the pockets of his khakis. Around him was a swirl of activity as the forensics team mulled around, and police officers questioned witnesses and staff members. Walter stood in the center of the action, the anxious eye of the storm.

"Detectives?"

Riley raised an eyebrow, staring at the little man. "I'm Detective Quinn. This is Detective Cain."

"Walter St. Pierre." Keeping his hands fisted in his pockets, he offered them a bow in greeting. Eli felt wave after wave of anxiety coming from the man, worry, and terror.

"Germophobic," Walter muttered as he hurried off a bit embarrassed. Riley gave Eli a quizzical glance.

"How can a mortician be a germaphobe?" Riley whispered. Eli shrugged and followed the jittery little man.

❋ ❋ ❋

They followed the jumpy, twitchy Walter St. Pierre into the main foyer, and an immediate feeling of déjà vu overwhelmed Eli. He paused, falling behind the others as everything seemed to fade into sepia tones and blurred around the edges. The busy, bustling bodies of the forensics teams seemed to move as though they were underwater. Eli felt as if he, too, had been submerged in a vat of ice-cold water, and his breath left him. He froze, paralyzed as the day slowly rewound before his eyes. The bodies moved awkwardly backward, out of the room, gradually speeding up until they were wraith-like balls of colored light. Walter St. Pierre was no longer leading him and Riley through the halls of the funeral home. He was alone in the silent solemnity of the foyer.

Finally, the hallways were dark. Only the soft dim lights from the security system illuminated the halls. As if pushed,

Eli found himself moving forward through the halls, coming to an abrupt halt in one of the viewing rooms. There were soft lights and a vast array of bouquets filling the room with overpowering and conflicting floral scents. In the corner, on an easel, was a promotional photo of Nicky Sky. Nicky stared at him from the picture; his piercing cyan eyes stared blankly into oblivion, a much-photographed smile frozen on his lips. Eli stared at the photo, feeling as if he were being drawn into the image, almost hypnotized by the young man's boyish beauty, and he felt anguish over the loss.

A muffled cough caught Eli's attention. He turned to see a red lacquer casket with steel trim, surrounded by flowers, cards, and stuffed animals that had been placed on and around the altar. Even though the casket was closed, Eli knew Nicky had made that noise. The room was silent, and then the choking cough came again. Only this time, the lid of the casket was thrown open as Nicky sat upright, pulling wads of cotton from his nose before clutching at his lips as if in agony. He struggled to lean over the side of the open casket, making deep throated gagging noises that seemed to ring in Eli's head as the coffin slid from its mount with a muted thud, tossing Nicky to the floor.

He bounced to his feet, pulling at his lips with one hand, and searched blindly around the room with the other. Finally, his hand landed on something small and metallic, which shone silver when it caught the light. A letter opener, Eli realized. A cheap giveaway with the name and number of the funeral home printed on the side.

Nicky used the razor-like edge of the letter opener and slashed at his mouth several times. Each time, blood poured from newly opened wounds, until finally, he was able to pry a thin wire from his lips and open his mouth. Instantly, he began to cough and, reaching into his mouth. He pulled a cloying amount of cotton from his throat before throwing up what looked to Eli like a mixture of cotton and bile. Nicky inhaled deeply, gulping air, and started clawing at his eyes. He wheezed and gasped for air, his breathing ragged and labored, his fingers digging until the eye caps holding his eyes closed were removed. Finally, Nicky opened his eyes, tears of blood streaming down his cheeks as his breathing regulated itself. Slowly, he opened eyes that glowed like white ice in the dimly lit room.

He wore an expensive dark suit tailored perfectly to his body. His blond hair stood in defiant spikes, and he smiled, the wounds around his mouth and eyes rapidly healing

Eli stared, unable to breathe, when Nicky slowly turned toward him. Eli frowned, confused as to whether Nicky saw him or not when he winked, then began walking awkwardly toward the door. He paused in front of Eli, who hadn't moved from the doorway, his face twisted in discomfort. Eli was a bit startled as Nicky reached into the back of his pants and began digging most unpleasantly before pulling out another bloody wad of cotton. Shaking his head, Nicky tossed the cotton to the floor and exited the room by passing through Eli's body.

The moment Nicky stepped into him, an icy chill rattled Eli, and he could feel himself falling backward as the room went dark.

* * *

He opened his eyes and found Riley hovering above him, his face tight with concern as he watched his friend being helped to his feet. All activity in the foyer paused as the nearly seven-foot-tall detective was being helped to his feet. Eli straightened his clothes and ran a hand over his hair. Graciously, he took the bottle of water being silently offered by an attentive female officer. As usual, Eli was oblivious to her fluttering eyelashes and coy smile.

"E, you okay? How many fingers am I holding up?" Riley held up his hand, and Eli brushed it away. He, in turn, raised his hand in an obscene gesture.

THE FIRST TO FALL


"How many am I holding up?" He smirked, and Riley exhaled in relief.

"He's fine," Riley assured the approaching EMT. "Mr. St. Pierre?" Riley motioned for the little man to continue leading them towards the crime scene, the scene Eli had just visited. He shook his head, trying to focus. As they walked, Riley and Eli stayed back, just out of Walter's earshot.

"How long was I out?" Eli asked between sips of water. His throat was suddenly parched.

"Couple of minutes, and you hit the ground pretty fast and hard. I've never seen you pass out like that. Is that the first time that ever happened? Are you sure you're okay?" Riley spoke in a low voice so their escort wouldn't overhear. Eli nodded.

"I'm fine, but that was... new," Eli mumbled.

* * *

They entered the room where Nicky had been kept, and it was exactly as Eli had seen it in his vision. The bright red casket lay overturned on the floor; flower petals smashed beneath it. There were wads of bloody and damp cotton on the floor, and the room smelled of vomit and mums.

"Just like I left it," Eli mumbled.

"What?" Riley stared at him and then the colossal poster of Nicky Sky.

"This is what I saw," Eli whispered to Riley. "When I was out, I was in this room. I saw that poster. I saw Nicky Sky get up from that coffin and walk out of here."

"What's with all of the cotton?" Riley knelt and poked at a pile of bloody cotton with an ink pen.

"He pulled that out of his ass," Eli spoke in a strange, hollow monotone. Riley looked up at him with concern.

"Are you sure you're okay?" He asked, and Eli nodded.

"We block all of the orifices with cotton to prevent leakage," Walter said, and Riley's face twisted comically in disgust before dropping the ink pen to the floor.

"I thought you didn't embalm him." Riley moved slowly away from the cotton and spotted the bloody letter opener on the floor. He motioned to another officer in the room to come and bag the evidence.

"Well, we didn't, but- the rest- it's standard procedure for all of our guests." Walter nervously stepped back until he was standing at the entrance of the room, shifting anxiously from one foot to the other.

"Well? What happened?" Riley asked, an immobile Eli.

"He just got up and walked out. I don't know how more people didn't spot a dead rock star in a shiny suit, but he walked out of here.  What does the surveillance tape show?" Eli grumbled, rubbing his suddenly irritated eyes; they burned, and his head was starting to throb.

"Nothing. There was some sort of distortion on the tapes, just a dark blur, and then nothing. If that's all, I think I should get back- the reports and he-" He was gone before the sentence was finished, nearly sprinting down the hall. They watched the little man leave, disappearing around a corner. Shaking his head, Riley turned back to Eli.

"So," Riley started with a smile. "I was right. He wasn't dead. It's some sort of stunt." He folded his arms across his chest and rocked back and forth on his heels the way he did when he thought he was right. He was usually wrong.

Eli shook his head, prepared to burst his friend's bubble yet again.

"Nope." Eli sighed heavily, his mind trying to grasp the reality of the situation. "When he walked out of here, Nicky Sky was most definitely dead."

# CHAPTER TWO

In detail, Eli recounted the events he had witnessed regarding the rise of Nicky Sky. As he spoke, he occasionally took a sip from his bottle of water but never took his eyes from the overturned casket on the floor. Once he finished, Riley exhaled for him.

"So, he wasn't dead?" Riley asked, confused by the story Eli recounted.

"No, he was dead, as dead as a person can get. But that smile and wink, it was like he knew I was there and he could see me. Like he knew I was watching, he wanted me to watch."

"Okay- okay, so he got up and left. But he couldn't have just walked away, and no one notices a presumed dead rock star wandering around. Someone knew he was waking up and waited for him, someone like-"

"His doctor." Eli completed Riley's thought for him.

✳ ✳ ✳

Once out of the funeral home, Eli became himself again. The fresh air rejuvenated him, clearing his mind and shaking the cobwebs free. He drove down the winding path to the gate as Riley typed away on his computer.

"Doctor C. Keegan Kent. Whoa, check out the pedigree. Doctor Kent has been practicing medicine since 1996. Has been the Director of Advanced Medical Research for Medi-Corp for nine years, graduated Magna Cum Laude from Princeton, graduated from Tulane Medical School, top of the class, a pioneer in genetics, created a synthetic material that acts as skin replacement for burn victims. Holds honorary degrees from Oxford, Yale, Stanford, and Duke; spent a semester at the Sorbonne as a guest lecturer. Expert on Japanese culture- lived there for a year studying technological advances in robotics and medicine. Fluent in French, Japanese, Dutch, Spanish, Farsi, Italian, Afrikaans, German, Portuguese, Greek, Cantonese, and Mandarin. Is it me, or is this guy too smart to be a rock star doctor?" Riley asked.

"Money can get you a lot in this world," Eli mumbled as he tried to fight his mounting headache.

❊ ❊ ❊

Eli pulled the car to a bone-jolting stop in the parking lot of the MediCorp building, a green glass and silver chrome building three blocks from the Mercedes-Benz Superdome in downtown New Orleans. The main lobby resembled a terrarium with a large glass reception desk near two elevator banks. The greenery in the lobby flourished in the constant sunlight from the floor to ceiling windows. There was a slight mist in the air, Eli assumed, from the sprinklers that sprayed the foliage occasionally throughout the day, giving the place a tropical feel. Behind the desk sat a pretty blond girl in a tailored red suit and impossibly high heels. She stood as they approached, her smile widening as she greeted them.

"Good morning, welcome to MediCorp. How may I help you?" She practically sang.

"Good morning, I'm Detective Quinn, and this is Detective Cain." Her smile faltered only slightly as she inspected Riley's presented badge. She looked at him with large brown eyes, her smile spreading.

"I'm Bianca. What can I do for you, gentlemen?" She never lost eye contact with Riley. Eli stared at them in amusement. Little did she know; she was barking up the wrong tree.

"We are looking for Doctor Keegan Kent," Eli interjected.

"Doctor K? Doctor K's labs are on the fourth floor. I'll have to escort you up. That floor is secure, and sometimes the noise is-" She trailed off as she came from behind the desk to lead them to the elevator. She pushed the call button, and the doors of the glass elevator slid open smoothly. Once inside, Eli noticed that there was no button for the fourth floor. He also saw that Bianca had just about drowned herself in rather expensive perfume. The smell filled the elevator and burned his nostril when the petite woman stood next to him. As the doors closed, Bianca touched a hidden panel in the elevator wall. A door slid open, and she inserted a key, turned it slightly, and punched several numbers in a keypad before removing the key. The panel slid closed, and the elevator lurched to life.

"Nice perfume." Riley just about choked, wiping his watery eyes.

"Thanks. It's French. Doctor K gave it to me for Christmas, all the way from Paris." She gushed.

"What's the big secret?" Riley asked, sidling up to the striking blond. She looked at him; her face seemed to be frozen in a permanent smile.

"Doctor Kent is very private." It was a well-rehearsed response, and the only answer she gave, remaining silent until the elevator stopped. The door opened directly into a large space full of computers, stainless steel and glass tables, and polarized windows. Several men and women in lab coats milled from station to station taking notes and staring at unreadable screens. Eli and Riley stepped into the room behind Bianca, who was walking at an advanced clip. She walked through the room into a smaller windowless, more tightly packed room that housed several small machines resembling robotic arms, and smaller half-constructed devices were strewn everywhere. There was a large bank of printers spewing paper at a constant clip. Music blared from unseen speakers into the room as a kid wearing a lab coat lay on a table near a bay of printers, his eyes closed.

When she shut the music off, the kid jumped up, startled and slightly dazed. He was tall and thin, all knees and elbows with hair that hung to his shoulders in dark waves. He had olive skin and dark piercing eyes that seemed to bore into a person with the slightest glance. He towered above Bianca, who stood all of five foot three, even in the heels. He lumbered toward her angrily.

"Bianca, what the fuck-" He spoke in a clipped tone that made every word seem an unfinished question. She smiled and strolled past him.

"Good morning to you too, Sunshine. This is Xander Felder. Xander, these are Detectives Quinn and Cain. They are looking for Doctor Kent. Xander is the doctor's lapdog."

"Research assistant." He corrected. For a moment, as he looked at them, Eli saw a dark cloud of foreboding in the young man's eyes and got the distinct impression that he was not long for this world. He realized young Xander would be dead within a week. The thought sent a chill down his spine, and he quickly shook off the feeling.

Bianca ignored his violent outburst and pushed the call button for the elevator.

"Any way you say it, you're still the bitch." She spoke in sugary sweet tones as she stepped into the elevator. As the doors closed, she gave Xander a satisfied smirk and teasing little finger wave.

* * *

Eli smelled her before he saw her or heard her heels on the tiles of the floor. The smell of jasmine and lavender overpowered him, and his knees went weak, his stomach twisted into a knot of nervous anticipation.

"What happened to the music?" A female voice called from somewhere unseen. Immediate warmth spread low in his belly as she spoke, her voice rich and husky and melodic. Eli swallowed hard and slowly turned as she appeared, and the whole world fell away.   She was tall, near six three, wearing black stilettos and curve-hugging blue jeans, a snug black turtleneck, and a lab coat. Her hair was so dark it looked blue under the fluorescent lights, and her skin was the color of caramel. She had an exotic otherworldly look, ethereal, and she was gorgeous. Looking at her, she couldn't be older than twenty-five or twenty-six years old, but he knew that she was older.

As she came closer, Eli could only hear his heartbeat thumping in his ears, matching each of her footfalls as she came towards him, her head down. She was engrossed in paperwork attached to a clipboard.  He knew right away that when she looked up, her eyes would mirror his own, pure, clear turquoise with large dark lashes.

"*Angel,*" he whispered in a sluggish voice. He felt intoxicated woozy, for lack of a better term, His body tensed with the immediate need to be with her, in her. The need for her was raw and vicious, so much, so his knees buckled.

"Pardon?" She looked at him with those eyes, his eyes, and it was as if someone had punched him in the gut. His breath caught in his throat. Her expression of surprise matched his. Startled, she audibly gasped and stared at him. Curiously, she tilted her head to the side, staring with a cute little smile playing at the corners of her full lips.  She bit her bottom lip, and everything in his body became tense and hot. The room crackled with the sexually charged electricity that was generated between the two of them.

Never in his life had Eli wanted anyone as much as he wanted this woman this moment. His hands itched to touch her face, to see if it was as smooth and soft as he'd dreamed, to see if she was quite simply, real. He licked his suddenly dry lips and tried to speak, but nothing would come out.  His throat had sealed shut.

She looked intrigued and slightly amused by Eli, a small, almost unperceivable smile forming on her full lips. She cleared her throat and stood a little straighter.

"May I help you?" She spoke again, and he found himself focusing on her lips. Her voice poured over him like warm butter, and his heart jumped. He etched every part of her into his mind. He noticed the slight hint of her bubblegum pink tongue. He studied the way her eyes danced in her confused amusement, the flicks of silver in those vibrant eyes. He focused on the curve of those perfectly formed lips and the way her nose twitched slightly. Again, he attempted to speak, his mouth opened, but again he said nothing, so Riley stepped forward.

"Hi, I'm Detective Quinn, and my mute friend is Detective Elijah Cain. We are looking for Doctor Kent. We have questions regarding Nicky Sky-"

"What about Nicky?" She asked, her hand immediately going to her throat.

"I think we should talk to Doctor Kent about that. Is *he* in?" She smirked and looked past them at Xander.

"They didn't ask," Xander answered without looking up from the billows of paper pouring from the printers.

"Come with me," She spun around and led them in the direction from which she'd emerged.

"It's her," Eli finally managed in hushed tones as they followed her. "The girl- from my dream." Riley slapped him on the back.

"She is a hottie. I say go for it."

"No," Eli corrected. "Not the girl *of* my dreams, the girl *from* my dreams. "

\* \* \*

They followed her into a small, neatly organized, and expensively decorated office. The walls were painted a pale gold shade, which seemed to complement the gold tones in her skin and made the place feel warm. Three of the walls were home to shelves of books on every subject, art, literature, history, science, finance. The fourth wall was all windows. Her desk was antique mahogany with ornately carved legs and gleamed like glass. Her chair was a high back Victorian, with elegant red satin cushions. The two armchairs facing her deck were covered in the same expensive fabric. On the bookshelf behind them was a fish tank, home to the most vibrantly colored fish he'd ever seen up close. The wall nearest the door was covered in plaques, diplomas, and accolades for Doctor Kent. He stared at her as realization dawned on him.

"So, you're-" He groaned.

"Doctor Kent." She nodded, finishing his sentence, with a devious glint in her beautiful eyes.

"Of course, you are. But how?"

"I'm smart. I graduated from medical school at fifteen. I started practicing at seventeen. I took a year off," She stated simply. Eli calculated in his mind that it would make her about thirty years old.

She stared at Eli, unmoving; her eyes bore into him as if she were trying to decide if he were real or not. He was uncomfortable, not only due to her scrutiny but also because his knees were wedged against her desk's front panel. He tried pushing the chair back, but the chair's heavy legs seemed to be glued to the rug beneath them. He braced himself, and with some effort, he moved the chair. He pushed it so well, the front legs went up, and before he knew it, Eli was on his back, staring that the ceiling, his legs in the air. He stared at his stocking foot before tilting his head to see his right shoe had come off and was floating in the fish tank.

She was standing over him in a minute, looking at him upside down. "Are you okay?" She asked. He nodded dumbly. She and Riley helped him up, and Riley fished his shoe out of the fish tank, making sure that none of the fish had stowed away.

"Bathroom?" Riley asked, holding the dripping leather loafer with his thumb and index finger.

As Eli regained his composure, she directed Riley down the hall. He was embarrassed by his ineptitude.

"Are you sure you're okay?" She asked, once again behind the desk. As he sat thinking, he realized that he hadn't seen her move. She was at his side one moment directing Riley to the restroom; the next moment, she was seated calmly behind her desk.

He stared at her, examining her, trying to get a read on her, but there was something not quite right about her. She was something he'd never encountered before, but there was something about her- something familiar. As a police officer, his added ability to see what people were thinking made him indispensable. Yes, the images were sometimes mottled and incoherent, but all it took was one image, one thought, and he had them. He could get a read anyone-but this woman- all he seemed to get from her was an echo of his thoughts. It took a minute before he realized it wasn't an echo. She was trying to read him as well. The realization almost made him fall back in the chair again. Instead, he leaned forward. His eyes narrowed as he stared at her and tried to reread her. It was as if they were canceling each other out, bouncing his thoughts back at him. Finally, something broke through. *'What are you?'* she was thinking quite clearly. Then there was great clarity as her eyes widened in realization.

*'You can hear me.'* The thought was just as bold and clear as if she'd said it out loud. The realization hit her quite suddenly, and her mind closed to him like a vault. That was a neat little trick, he thought.

"Okay, what did you need to ask me about Nicky?" She asked matter-of-factly, avoiding gazing directly into his eyes. Instead, she focused on his left shoulder or a point just above it.

"I wanted to know why someone with your background and your expertise was hired as a private physician to a rock star."

"It was a favor. Nicky and I have been friends since childhood."

"Really?" His brow lifted until they nearly touched his hairline.

"Yes." She affirmed. "We went to the same boarding school, a special school for arts and sciences after Jonas Kent adopted me. Then we remained good friends. Nicky didn't trust a lot of people, Detective, but he trusted me with his life. And I trusted him with mine." She didn't seem to blink as she spoke.

The name Jonas Kent rang all sorts of bells in his head. Jonas Kent was rich, powerful, and mysterious. For him to have taken this girl in seemed entirely uncharacteristic of the man known to the media as the Black Baron of Business. Jonas Kent had come from Europe in the late eighties. Already a shipping magnate in France, he'd come to conquer America. He'd started in real estate in New York, adding to his already massive fortune. By the turn of the century, he'd owned businesses in most fifty states and had a home in New Orleans. He'd helped rebuild the riverfront and had made a name for himself by organizing and sponsoring charities in the city. He was a ruthless and cunning businessman who never seemed to do anything that didn't benefit him somehow.

"Why wasn't he autopsied?" Eli was trying to keep on task, but she seemed to bombard him with mental notes, but only what she wanted him to see. There were things that she kept locked away, safe from his prying. Something told him that Doctor C. Keegan Kent was a very dangerous woman.

"It was a request he'd made specifically in his living will. There was no autopsy, no embalming, and a DNR order. He had this thing about becoming a part of the earth, ashes to ashes, dust to dust. He filed the papers no more than a month before he died. Ironic. It was like he knew ahead of time." She visibly shivered at the memory of her friend lying prone on the bathroom floor, the deep red of his drying blood in stark contrast to the pristine white of the marble floor.

"You don't seem all that torn up about the death of such a *good* friend."

"Detective Cain, I've been surrounded by death my entire life. It's the reason I became a doctor. I have also learned
that with life comes death, and I have mourned Nicky in my
way, both publicly at his memorial service and privately. Just
because I'm not sobbing inconsolably at the mention of his
name doesn't mean anything. I feel his loss in every aspect of
every moment of my life." She whispered the last part, her
eyes low.

"You and he were more than friends," he asserted. She
looked at him, her eyes finally locking onto his—a slow smile
tickling the corners of her mouth.

"No. But wouldn't that be a lascivious story for the tabloids?" She had a mischievous glint in her eye as she spoke; her
smile was decidedly predatory. She watched him as he shifted
uncomfortably in his chair.

"What are you?" She finally asked.

❋ ❋ ❋

"I'm a Dete-" He started, and she shook her head, narrowing
her eyes as she searched his face.

"No- *what* are you?" She repeated more deliberately. He pon-
dered this question for a moment, his stare matching hers, his
brows arched in confusion. The room seemed to fill with electrical energy; the already warm room temperature rose ten
degrees as they maintained their silence, their gazes locked.
The lights on the entire floor flickered momentarily, and the
water in her fish tank began to bubble. His body burned with
the need for her. He wanted to bury himself deep inside of her,
sink his fingers into her hair, and hold her tight against him.
He wanted to kiss her, to feel her beneath him, be inside of
her, feel those long legs wrapped around his waist. He could
imagine the sweet warmth of her, imagined she'd taste like
honeysuckle.

Her breath caught in her throat under his steady gaze. She

squirmed in her chair, her body trembling for the sheer presence of him. She could feel him, the heat rolling from him, they want, and her heart raced. The thought of his hands on her made her skin prickle, and her chest tightened as she exhaled sharply. He was going to kiss her, she thought. He was going to get up in a second, come around the desk, and kiss her. If he did that, if she let him kiss her, it wouldn't end there.

Unable to take anymore, she broke their gaze, turning her face away as she tried to compose herself. The room slowly regained its normal temperature, and the hair on his arms stood on end with the residual power in the air.

"Detective-" she began, her voice thick with longing and anticipation.

"Eli. I think you can call me Eli," he whispered, his voice heavy.

"Eli." She repeated his name in a low, breathy sigh. He longed to hear her say his name over and over, her mouth close to his. "This is real, right? I'm not imagining this? I didn't imagine you. What are you doing to me?" She asked breathlessly. The question hung in the air between them, echoing in his head. What had she done to him?

"I'm very real. Can't you -feel me?" His words had a seductive undertone that he hadn't intended but seemed to flow from him naturally. Now it was her turn to be speechless.

"I had to restart the hand dryer five times, but I think I got it mostly dry-" Riley entered the room, holding Eli's shoe. He paused, taking in the two as they guiltily avoided his gaze. They were both flushed and nearly panting. He glanced at Eli as he attempted to conceal the apparent nuisance of his rigid erection. If he didn't know better and if they weren't completely dressed, Riley would have sworn he'd walked in on them having sex. Shaking his head, he did a quick double-take; the fish that had been swimming so prettily before had all floated to the surface, dead.

\* \* \*

Riley said nothing as he took his seat, handing Eli his shoe as he did. Eli took his shoe, mumbling a thank you, reading Riley's confused and suspicious thoughts loud and clear. He cleared his throat and continued to look at the little leather notebook in his hand. Without looking, he could feel Riley's eyes on him, a knowing smile on his face.

"Back to your questions, E-, Detective Cain." She cleared her throat and absently shuffled and stacked papers on her desk.

"Do you believe that there could have been a mistake? Pronouncing Nicky dead." Eli asked.

"No mistake. Why do you ask?" She asked, trying to avoid his eyes. She was blocking him again; he could feel a pressure in his head as if she were physically pushing him away. There was something that she was hiding, something serious. He pushed harder and felt a sharp pain behind his eyes and relented. She glanced at him, her eyes narrowed in a warning, and his brow rose in surprise. That was new.

"Nicky Sky walked out of the St. Pierre Brothers Funeral home sometime after midnight last night." Her head swiveled quickly to Riley.

"What?" She asked incredulously. "There must be some mistake. Or some sort of joke. Nicky was dead," she said.

"Are you sure?" Riley asked.

"I assure you, I checked. Nicky was dead. There is no mistaking when you find your best friend dead." Her gaze was steely, the bright turquoise seemed to deepen until they were a deep midnight blue, and her lips pulled in a tight hard line. She looked fierce, like a warrior.

"I think that's all we need. For now." Eli spoke up, his voice still thick. Her anger reignited his need for her, and he needed to get as far away from her as possible. "If you have any questions or you remember something that may be significant, please call us." Eli rose, handing her his business card with ease. He buttoned the bottom button on his suit jacket to hide his evident arousal in the same movement.

"Call anytime." There was an obvious intention behind his words when he spoke, which caused Riley's brow to shoot up in alarm. Their fingers brushed as she took the card. Her expression softened at his touch.

As the doors of the elevator opened into the lobby, Eli's cell phone rang. He looked at it and made a face at the name brandished across the display.

"Grace," he mumbled. "I promised I'd have lunch with her today."

\* \* \*

Riley remained silent until they were in the car and heading downtown.

"Drop me off at the station," he said, referring to the eighth district police station in the heart of the French Quarter. That was where Adam Forrester, Riley's current boyfriend, was stationed as a patrolman. Eli nodded but said nothing. He couldn't stop thinking of Doctor Kent and what had transpired in that office. Just the thought of it sent a luscious shiver of anticipation through him. He would make love to her, that he knew; the rest was confusing to him. He'd never encountered someone like her; from the second he'd seen her, she had made an imprint on him. Everything about her seemed to be branded on his skin. He frowned and rubbed his right temple as the dull ache in his head subsided.

"Are you going to tell me what happened?" Riley asked, breaking into his reverie.

"I don't know what happened. It was like- electricity. I've never felt such a strong pull to someone before in my life, and I couldn't read her at first. Even with concentrated effort, it was hard to do. It's because she - she could read me. But once we realized- she was so- and I wanted- I felt like I needed to-"

"You needed to fuck her." Riley intervened. His bluntness was right on point as usual. Suddenly it was pouring out of Eli like a flood.

"More than I have ever wanted to fuck anyone in my entire life, but it kind of felt like I did. In here." He pointed to his temple. He shrugged, unable to explain it without going into graphic detail.

"The ultimate mind fuck," Riley said in complete awe. "Talk about safe sex."

* * *

Doctor Kent waited, watching from the windows in her office as they drove away. She watched Detective Cain with a growing curiosity, her arms crossed protectively over her chest. She felt a shiver go through her at the thought of his eyes on her. There was one thing she knew for sure; Elijah Cain was a dangerous man on the trail of something probably not prepared to handle. She sighed heavily and picked up the telephone and dialed, her mind racing.

"Ello," was the gruff response when the line was picked up.

"We have a problem." She said quickly and quietly.

"What kind of a problem?" The voice, deep and hoarse, with a thick, almost undecipherable Irish brogue, was suddenly more alert. "The police were just here. It seems that someone has turned Nicky. Someone who was not there for his rebirth. He's loose." She said.

"Jesus- do you know who did it?" The voice asked.

"No, but the cop who was here is not the type to let this go. You better do something before this gets to the media. The Collective will have a fit if this becomes public knowledge."

"Does Jonas know?"

"I'm trying to keep him out of this for as long as I can. Find him, find his maker, and make this go away. Get the police and the media to drop it. Now."

"I don't know if he's out there are people who've seen

him. There are probably humans involved. This could be a big job..." The voice trailed off, and her anger rose suddenly.

"Your job is to handle these things, Briar. Remember the last time something like this happened. It took nearly a decade for your skin to grow back. This time would be much, much worse. If you can't, then the Collective will make *YOU* go away. You know how they are." There was silence on the other end.

"Get the situation contained. The cop who's on this- he's not normal. He's something different. I need him to let this go. And I need you to get on it as soon as the sun goes down, Briar."

"Sure thing, Sarge." He relented and hung up.

As she disconnected, she noticed her fish floating like colorful driftwood across the surface of the freshwater tank and sighed heavily. She crossed the room and looked down at them in frustration before holding one hand open, palm down over the fishy corpses. Exhaling, she waited, watching as they slowly drifted below the surface and began swimming again. Smiling, she leaned down to peer at them through the glass, and they all moved closer to her, lining the side of the tank. "I am so sorry, my babies." She cooed and gently tapped the glass with a fingertip. They all migrated towards her finger.

"Go play," She whispered, and they dispersed almost immediately.

She returned to her seat and squeezed her eyes shut, hoping that the headache trying to start behind her eyes would go away. She immediately opened her eyes; closing them only brought images of Elijah Cain to the forefront of her mind; he was so large and intense. She could just imagine him as a lover, his body writhing against hers in a tangle of sheets, his naked body hard and muscled, slick with sweat. She could just about feel his hands on her breasts, his mouth on hers, his throbbing hard-

"*Damn.*" She exhaled and let her head rest in her hands. "*Trouble thy name is Elijah Cain.*"

# CHAPTER THREE

Grace Corazon Babineaux lived in a two-story mansion hidden from the street by a brick fence and a large wooden gate on Ursulines Avenue in the French Quarter. As Eli pulled up to the gate, he rang the buzzer announcing his arrival.

"Come on in," came the voice of the housekeeper as the gate swung open to reveal a cobblestone driveway lined with palm trees and elephant-eared plants that hung over the fence. Eli pulled into his regular spot in the garage next to Grace's rarely driven but very well-maintained Rolls Royce. The house was large and white, built in a French chateau, with hardwood floors and high ceilings. Grace had taken great care to maintain the upkeep of this house. It had been in her family since her great-grandfather had built it when he'd come over from France as a *gens de couleur libre( free person of color)* in the 1700's. She loved to boast to anyone who'd listen that the chandeliers and floors were all original to the house. Not to mention the many fireplaces' restoration and the elaborate tile work recently done to the pool.

He entered through the back door as he always did and spotted Boogie, Grace's live-in housekeeper and a good friend. Boogie, whose real name was Marcella Roché, was a short woman with a figure that could still stop traffic, even at her advanced age of seventy-three. Her short hair was dyed a vibrant shade of red that she wore in feathery spikes all over her head. Her makeup was always perfect, accenting the smattering of freckles across her cheeks and her alabaster skin. Born and raised in Chalmette, she had the distinct "yat" accent of St. Bernard Parish and the sassy attitude to match. She wore a pair of tailored Capri pants in a deep blue shade that empha-sized her slim hips and well-rounded ass. As usual, she wore a low-cut blue and white striped top that showed of her rather impressive bosom. She was putting the finishing touches on the salad. She would be serving for lunch as he kissed her on the cheek.

"Hey, Boogie."

She smiled and patted his cheek.

"Hey, Baby. How you been?" She looked at him, her eyes narrowing. "And who have you been boning this morning?" She asked bluntly, holding his face and staring into his eyes.

Eli blushed and pulled away. He glanced down at the tray on which she'd placed Grace's pristine Wedgewood china serv-ing bowl. He glanced at the food Boogie was preparing and raised a questioning brow. There was a fresh salad with wal-nuts and fresh grapes, Shrimp Creole over fluffy white rice, and was that bread pudding he smelled in the oven? Rolling his eyes, he glanced at Boogie, who didn't bother looking up from her cooking.

"Where's Grace?"

"In the salon." Boogie gave him a knowing look, and Eli's face dropped. "And this one is a piece of work." Boogie snorted

* * *

Grace was Eli's maternal grandmother. After his par-ents had died in a car accident when he was twelve, Grace had been the one to raise him. And for the past seven years or so, she had been on a mission to get him married off. As he en-tered the room, she rose to greet him. Grace was a gorgeous and graceful woman of seventy but could easily pass for her late forties. Her skin was smooth and unlined, the color of café au lait. Her eyes were the most unmistakable green he'd ever seen. She wore her usual uniform of neatly tailored chocolate brown slacks, a pink cashmere twin set, and low heels in the exact shade of chocolate as her slacks. Her hair, neatly curled in a stylish bob, was the color of spun silver, and she dripped in gold. She was an old school southern elegant.

"Elijah, sweetie, so glad that you're here." She kissed his cheek. A short, thin woman with obviously surgically altered breasts stood smiling nervously. She had volumes of long brown hair that cascaded over her shoulders and eyes that seemed too large and too dark to be natural. She wore a straight black skirt that clung to her narrow curves and a beige twin set similar to Grace's. Except for her nearly cartoonish breasts, she and Grace could have been twins. As he approached, she nervously toyed with a strand of pearls around her neck. She was pretty, but then they were all pretty. They were all elegant, all well dressed, well educated, and all dull as dishwater. Every week Eli had lunch with his grandmother, and at least once a month, he would find a relatively attractive woman of the same make and model as this one waiting for him. They were always some debutante or society friend's daughter, niece, granddaughter, or cousin that Grace was sure would be perfect for him. They weren't.

They were all too polite, too dull, too uninteresting. After a moment with them, he would receive the clear impression that they were after a ring, a prominent society wedding, and this house or one very close to its like. A few times, he received the impression that they were after money to help save the family business, get their daddies out of debt or simply shop, and live a life of leisure. A couple had just wanted to brag that she was the one who managed to snag the notoriously stealthy Elijah Cain. To marry Elijah Cain was to marry old money. He didn't know how old, Grace had never been completely clear where the money came from, but there was plenty of it. Grace liked to say that she was recession-proof. And she'd proven that she was.

"Elijah," she was saying, steering him closer to this newest young woman. "This is Hannah Freeman. Hannah, this gorgeous hunk of muscle is my grandson Elijah."

Being polite, Eli took her hand to give it a shake when Hannah curtsied and positioned her hand for a kiss. Eli looked at Grace before reluctantly kissing the back of Hannah's hand. It tasted like perfumed lotion and seemed to coat his lips. Suppressing a grimace, he nodded.

"Nice to meet you, Hannah." She smiled wider, exposing a mouth full of sparkling white veneers.

"Good lord, listen to that voice. Like melted chocolate, it's so smooth," she gushed. Eli smiled politely and stood aside, motioning for the women to head into the dining room.

"Shall we?" As Grace passed, he gave her a menacing look that she purposely ignored.

❋ ❋ ❋

Lunch went as it did on these occasions. He listened with little interest as his grandmother, and his fix up du jour spoke of society events, charities, and what hobby held the young lady's interest at that time. This year there seemed to be a growing affinity for flower gardens and Zumba. Every year or so, it changed, he noticed. One year it had been scrap-booking and Tae Bo, another it had been cupcakes and yoga. Hannah had graduated from Loyola with a degree in Art History. She used that degree as the head of several historical societies and charities in the area. He feigned interest but drifted off, listening to her mind instead.

He had to like her, she thought. He was the platinum standard in New Orleans society, and if she could land Grace Babineaux's grandson, she would be the envy of all her friends. He was as sexy as hell, she had to admit. Polite, courteous, he'd held out chairs for her and Grace before being seated. Who does that anymore, she thought? And those eyes were gorgeous- a pure, clear turquoise that seemed to shimmer in the afternoon sunlight. He had laugh lines around his mouth and eyes that made him even better looking if that were possible.

And he was so large. She thought that he was delicious and that she would screw him three ways 'til Sunday. She thought he would have a massive dick and that he would fuck like an animal. She imagined herself doing a sexy striptease. It was sexy to her, but to his mind, it was quite comical. Yes, she liked them thick, dumb, and rough. The stupider, the better. The dumb ones made the best husbands.

He glanced at her, an amused smile on his lips. She took this as a signal and seductively ran a shrimp across her overly glossed lips before biting it in half in what she assumed, incorrectly, was a sensual way. Eli nearly choked on his iced tea as he tried to stifle a laugh.

Hannah left after the excruciating lunch and the equally agonizing coffee and dessert session on the patio. She'd slipped Eli her phone number and a wink before she pulled away from the curb in her little white Mercedes, which seemed to be the norm for these women. They all had a Mercedes or BMW or some other cutesy little sports car. Shaking his head, Eli went back into his grandmother's house, feeling lighter than he had earlier that morning.

❋ ❋ ❋

"So?" Grace asked, expectantly clapping her hands together in excitement.

"So why do you keep doing that, Grace? She's nice enough, but she's not my type."

"And what exactly is your type, Elijah? You never bring any women around. You are nearly forty."

"I'm thirty-two." He corrected.

"And," she continued as if he hadn't spoken, "the only person you see consistently is Riley. If I didn't know you better, I would think that he and you were of the same persuasion." He shook his head.

"Riley would never have me." he joked, giving Boogie a

teasing wink as he poured himself another glass of iced tea.

"Why don't you ask him about the person he was boning this morning?" Boogie threw out casually as she put the dishes away. Again, Eli sputtered iced tea as he nearly choked.

"Really?" His grandmother's eyes sparkled with interest. The doorbell rang, and Boogie dashed out of sight to get the door after stirring up trouble. Eli went about cleaning up the spilled iced tea, his cheeks burning from embarrassment.

"I wasn't fuc- having sex with anyone this morning, Grace. Boogie is just messing with you."

As if on cue, Boogie and Riley entered the kitchen. Riley gave Grace a bear hug and a loud smacking kiss on the cheek before getting his glass of tea and settling on a stool at the island in the center of the room. "Tell her, Boog. Tell Grace that you were just messing with her," Eli coaxed.

"I was not messing with your grandmother. When you came in here, your eyes were of a man who had gotten him some. I know that look very well." And she would know. Boogie had lain to rest five husbands by the time she was forty-five, four of whom expired after a vigorous night of lovemaking. Or so she said. Eli tended to believe it was partly due to Boogie's skill in the kitchen rather than the bedroom.

"Well, it wasn't actual sex. But I bet if I hadn't walked in when I had- it would have been," Riley said before taking a sip of his drink with a sly smirk. He let it hang out there in the air as they all focused on Eli. After what felt like an hour of silent stares, he cleared his throat and gave in. They weren't going to breathe until he spoke up.

"It wasn't sex. It was- something else. And anyway, we were working a case-" There was a collective exhale at that, and Eli blushed.

"Whatever." Boogie dismissed him, turning her attention to Riley.

"Who is she?" Grace asked, sitting on the edge of her seat, her hands clasped together under her chin like an excited teenager.

Riley mimicked her posture, his eyes dancing with conspiratorial glee. "Her name is Doctor C. Keegan Kent. We were talking to her about one of our cases, the Case of the Missing Rock Star." He said it as if it were the title of a Nancy Drew mystery, and Eli rolled his eyes. Grace patted his arm and moved closer.

"You're working that case?" Boogie squealed excitedly. "I heard about it on the news. Is he dead?"

"Yeah, he's dead. According to Eli, who did his – thing," he waggled his fingers at his temples and rolled his eyes back into his head. "He got out of the coffin and walked right out. So, we needed to talk to his doctor, you know, to see why he hadn't been embalmed, and the doc, who we thought was a he, turned out to be a she. And she is a freaking supermodel. The most beautiful woman I have ever seen. Tall, legs for years, long jet-black hair, skin like silk, the color of caramel. She has an amazing body, eyes the same shade as Eli's. She looks like she could be a movie star or a princess. And she is a brilliant doctor. When they met, it was like electricity. You could feel the air go out of the room. It was so strong; the attraction was obvious. Seeing them together- amazing. I mean --when I say gorgeous-- she's like a female version of Eli. They look like bookends, like someone carved them out of the same marble. Perfection. I swear I could hear angels singing." Riley held the women enthralled as he spoke. They turned slowly to look at Eli, who nervously cleared his throat and shook his head.

"It wasn't that serious," Eli began, only to be waved off by Riley, who wasn't done just yet.

"He couldn't even speak to her for a few minutes. He was so in lust. That was the first time since I've known him that I can say a woman has left Eli Cain speechless. He was so discombobulated; he flipped his chair in her office. His shoe even landed in the fish tank." The three of them looked at him with huge grins on their faces.

"You talk too much," he mumbled to Riley, unable to hide the blush that warmed his cheeks. And the three burst into giddy, girlish laughter.

"I'm leaving now." Eli groaned and walked out of the room, followed by a new gale of laughter.

* * *

Eli lay on his living room floor, listening to his iPod and absently clicking the switch for a lamp off and on as the light faded outside. It had been two days since he'd met the beautiful Doctor Kent, and for 48 hours, she had been the only thing on his mind. She ranked higher than investigating the missing body of the rock star. As he and Riley searched every lead for the body of Nicky Sky, whose sightings rivaled Elvis, Tupac, and little green men, she was the only thing that had his focus. Her eyes, her smile, and the way she smelled. The way she could read his mind just as clearly as he could read hers. The way the room filled with electric energy when she entered it. He couldn't stop thinking of the way she licked her lips and bit her lip when she was nervous. He wanted to know if her lips were as soft as they looked, her skin as silky as he imagined. He wanted to know what her body felt like against his.

He sighed and rolled onto his stomach to try to change his train of thought. He'd tried Googling her, but most of the information was the same information Riley had found. There were no pictures of her and only a few brief mentions of her in articles regarding the Kents. She was always referred to as Jonas's youngest daughter, Doctor C. Keegan Kent.

He wondered what the C in C. Keegan Kent stood for, something romantic like Charlotte, Chloe, or Camille, or exotic like Chiara. Maybe it was Cynthia or Christina. She didn't look like a Christy to him. Christian maybe. He frowned and shook his head; warning signs were going off in his head, big flashing neon lights that said *DANGER*. But he couldn't help wanting to know more about the mysterious Doctor Kent. Like, why he'd been dreaming about her for the better part of ten years now.

He hadn't even let Riley know it had been that long. Ten long years and he'd finally seen her in the actual flesh.

He was brought back to the world by the persistent ringing of his telephone. Slowly he rose to his knees and answered.

"Ello," he grumbled into the receiver.

"Hello, Elijah. This is Hannah Freeman. We met at your grandmother's a few days ago." He nodded at the memory of the nervous, ultra-thin woman who wondered about his sexual prowess. Rolling his eyes, he sat on the sofa.

"Yes, of course. How are you, Hannah?" He ran a hand over his forehead as if that would clear his mind. It didn't. He glanced around the room and realized that while he lay on the floor daydreaming, it had gotten dark, casting a gloom over the dimly lit living room. He leaned over and flicked on a lamp and nearly jumped out of his skin as something moved near the front window. Standing, he slowly crept to the picture window that looked out onto the tree-lined street and peeked past the curtains. There was nothing there except an old grey cat that looked back at him before loping off through the hedge that separated his yard from his neighbor's.

"Eli, did you hear me?" Hannah's voice brought him back to the conversation. She'd called to invite him for a drink, and since he had nothing better to do, other than sit in his living room thinking of the Doc, he agreed to meet her. She was persistent, and he needed to get out of the house. Besides, what harm could it do? As he changed into jeans and a lightweight sweater, his mind once again floated toward images of Doctor Kent.

"Get a hold of yourself, man," he told his reflection in the mirror.

* * *

He slowly pulled his black Lexus LX SUV out of the carport onto the narrow cobblestone street. The one expensive gift he'd accepted from Grace was his new car. He could have bought it himself, but she insisted on gifting it to him the previous Christmas. Declining would have hurt her feelings. She had spent weeks agonizing over the car, and she was more excited than he was when she'd presented it. As he rolled through Algiers Point, his cell phone rang. "Hey, Ri, what's going on?"

"Just checking in. I did some follow up on some of those leads, in the Nicky Sky case, came up with nothing. What are you up to? Let me guess, obsessing over one raven-haired beauty? Again?" Eli snorted but didn't bother to deny it.

"I'm meeting Hannah Freeman for a drink at Whiskey Blue, just to get out of the house. I need to burn off some energy."

"You could always burn off energy with Hannah, just until you hook up with the Doc again. I mean, you know you will. I know you will. Hell, even she knows you will-"

"Goodbye, Riley." He hung up before Riley could continue down a road they had traveled many times over the past couple of days. Listening to Riley simply brought him back to her again. Candice. That would be something fitting, or maybe Claudia.

"Crazy." He mumbled to himself.

❖ ❖ ❖

The Whiskey Blue was an upscale lounge located in the W Hotel on Poydras Street, about two blocks from the Riverfront. It took Eli only a moment to find a parking spot, and with a feeling of dread tugging at him, he entered. The darkened bar was crowded with wannabe hipsters hanging at the bar and lounging on leather sofas, and the modestly roped-off VIP area was packed full of fedora-wearing young men with long shaggy hair and skinny jeans. The women were all in tiny dresses and high heels, their lips lacquered with pastel glosses. As he entered, a few of them looked his way, but he paid no attention. He was always oblivious to his appeal to others, but both men and women were drawn to him.

Hannah sat at the bar in a short skirt and too high heels. She stood when she saw him approach, a giddy smile on her face. She was pretty, in a conventional debutante way. Her brown hair was pulled into a high ponytail and lay over one shoulder in an attempt to be sexy. The skirt was black. The low top cut to expose optimal cleavage was a shade of emerald that seemed to match her sparkling earrings. There was something sexy about her, he supposed. She had caught the eyes of several men in the room he noticed, but she seemed to have her laser-like focus on him.

She greeted him with a kiss on the cheek that was sticky with a gloss that smelled of fruit. It took all that was in him not to wipe like a bratty kid when she moved away. He sat with her at the bar and ordered a vodka gimlet, which he was sure he would nurse for the duration of the evening. She ordered some sort of pink frothy thing served in a martini glass with a slice of fruit on the rim. He didn't drink much; he'd never had a very high tolerance for it. From what Grace had told him of the few occasions he'd had one to many, a drunken Eli was a completely uninhibited Eli. And that was not a good thing.

"So glad you could make it. I hope I wasn't disturbing you," Hannah said. But he knew she really couldn't care less if she were disturbing him. All she cared about was sitting across from him right now, making suggestive statements and flirting outrageously.

"No." He tried to smile at her, but it felt tight and forced. She nodded and sipped her drink. She batted her false eyelashes and touched his thigh as she talked to him about her hobbies, which came down to shopping. She tried bringing up her favorite television shows, which all consisted of fluffy reality shows about bland socialites. Her taste in music ran towards the bubble gum pop variety, and her taste in movies was strictly romantic comedies.

"I just love, love, loved the Twilight series," she gushed.

"Did you read the books?" Eli asked, and she snorted.

"Who has time to read, especially when there are perfectly good movies available." He suppressed his urge to roll his eyes. She spoke of her charity work, which sounded to Eli more like an excuse to have lunch with her friends and have parties. There was a lot to the outside of Hannah, perfect make-up, impeccably dressed; she knew what to say and what to do, but that was it. There was nothing underneath the pretty packaging. In his estimation, Hannah Freeman was about as deep and exciting as wading in a puddle. His mind wandered until she began coming on to him. Hannah moved closer, speaking in a whisper so he would have to lean in to hear what she was saying. More than once, she mentioned how drunk she was and touched her décolletage, drawing his eye to her cleavage. She crossed and uncrossed her legs, licked her lips, and moved her hand higher and higher up his thigh.

"I have a room upstairs," she whispered into his ear before nipping his earlobe with her teeth. Eli pulled away quickly, his eyes wide. Another reason he didn't drink much; it dulled his senses and made his "*special talent*" nearly inoperable.

"Well, yeah, you should go up and sleep it off. I have to go, early morning. This was nice; we'll have to do it again." He tossed some money on the bar and backed away, waving to her as he did. He backed out of the bar and onto the street before she could react. He knew it was a cowardly and rather douchey way to handle things, but he needed to get away from her. He needed an escape.

❋ ❋ ❋

Once the night air hit him, he felt refreshed, too wired to go home, and it was too late to go hang out at Riley's. Standing on the corner, he looked towards the riverfront and the flashing lights of Harrah's Casino. A steamboat whistle blew somewhere on the river, and Eli decided a walk would do him fine.

As he strolled past the bustling casino and headed toward the river, his mind went back to Doctor Kent. He wondered what it was about her that drew him to her. Sure, she was gorgeous, but Grace had introduced him to any number of attractive women. He inhaled the fresh cold November air and shook his head. Yes, they were gorgeous, but they were interchangeable insipid airheads that cared more about their shoes than the charities they all seemed to champion. Not Doctor Kent. She was beautiful, no doubt, but was surrounded by an air of intelligence and natural poise. There was also a slightly mischievous glint in her eye, an amusement like she had a secret, and she could read his mind. It was a significant point in her favor that she was like him.

He'd just crossed the base of Canal Street, rounding a corner in front of the Aquarium of the Americas to walk along the riverfront, when a jogger came out of nowhere and plowed into him. He didn't hit the ground, but his knees did buckle, and he took a steadying step backward. He reached out, the wind knocked out of him, and steadied his assailant. She had her head down, earbuds in her ears and an iPod strapped to her bicep. She stepped back.

"I'm so sorry. I didn't see you when I came around the corner." She looked up and smiled with recognition.

"Detective Cain?" She popped the buds from her ears and moved further into the light. She had pale blue velour shorts that sat high on her thighs and a white tank top that clung to her taut frame. Her hair was pulled back in a thick braid; sweat-stained her shirt under her armpits and ample breasts and trickled down her temples, making her hair curl in tendrils around her face.

"Doctor Kent?" He stared at her as if she were a dream. "What are you doing out here?" He asked, surprised by her sudden appearance.

"I don't usually run at night, but I got a late start tonight. Did I hurt you? I did come barreling around that corner pretty quickly," she breathed, an excited smile on her full lips. She pulled the iPod off her arm, wrapping the cord to the buds around it as quickly as possible.

It took him a moment to realize that she was there. "No, no, I'm fine. How about you?" He mumbled. "Aren't you cold?" He couldn't help noticing that she was wearing next to nothing and white puffs appeared between her lips as she breathed.

"Umm, no. Adrenaline gets going, keeps me pretty warm." She bounced from foot to foot, keeping her body temperature up. "What are you doing out here?" She repeated. They fell into a leisurely stroll along the river, her breathing slowing as they crossed the street to the bustling nightlife on North Peters Street.

"I had a date." He mumbled, and her brow went up in surprise.

"And done at-" She looked at her watch. "Nine fifteen. She must have been one hot number." She whistled.

"She was about as hot as deadwood. Real turn on."

She laughed, and right then and there, he decided that her laugh was his new favorite sound. She touched his arm as they strolled, and he felt the electricity pulsing through her. She must have felt it too because she pulled away quickly, avoiding his eyes.

"Don't get me wrong, she's a sweet girl, but just not my type." He shoved his hands deep in his pockets to fight the urge to grab her hand. His mind wandered as he tried in vain to probe her thoughts. She was keeping him out again. He snuck a sideways glance at her, half expecting her to be looking away. Instead, he found her studying his profile. He turned to face her, and she smiled.

"And apparently a lover of lip gloss." She stopped and used her thumb to wipe the sticky smear of gloss off his cheek. Instinctively, he held her hand to his cheek, his eyes hooded by shadows. He didn't say anything, but she knew what he was thinking. He took a step closer, closing the space between them; his warm alcohol-laced breath tickled her nose. He was going to kiss her; she knew it, and her heart began to race. She chewed her bottom lip, and he made a noise deep in his throat and stepped even closer. His closeness made her stomach do somersaults, and she could barely breathe. When he moved in, lowering his mouth to hers, she pulled away slightly.

"That would be a mistake, wouldn't it?" He said, his eyes closed, his mouth still deliciously close to hers. He gently touched his forehead to hers and exhaled. She could feel him bulging against his jeans, grazing her bare skin just above her waistband. She swallowed hard, and slowly she pulled her hand away and averted her eyes, wrapping her arms around her suddenly cold body.

"I think it could be." She shivered, but not from the cold; she wanted him to kiss her.

"You're freezing." He quickly stripped his rich brown suede jacket off and draped it around her shoulders, tugging it closed over her chest. She stared up at him; his mouth was so close to hers. She could smell the sweet musk of his cologne and wanted to lean closer, press her body to his, but that would be a mistake.

"And why would it be a mistake?" He asked. A small smile started at the corners of his mouth, and she looked away, frustrated with herself. She'd forgotten. He could read her thoughts.

She cleared her throat and continued to walk; he matched her pace, strolling quietly through the city. People bustled past the couple, some stopping to smile at them. They were a striking couple, imposing, walking down the street together, both over six feet tall, with dark hair and bright blue eyes. He in jeans and a cream sweater that looked wonderful against his chocolate brown skin, she in her running gear, swallowed in Eli's jacket, her hair pulled away from her heart-shaped face, her golden bronze legs on display. He wanted to hold her hand, to reach up and tuck a wisp of hair behind her ear. But this wasn't a date; he reminded himself. She was still involved in his case, and just being with her, like this, could be deemed inappropriate.

"Have you found out anything about Nicky?" She asked, not knowing what else to say but needing to speak. She was sure he could hear her heart slamming against her ribs. Maybe this line of conversation would curb her urge to jump on him right there on the street. If he touched her or just looked at her with those smoldering eyes, she would give in.

"We've had a couple of leads, but none that amounted to much. My partner, Riley- Detective Quinn, thinks it's a hoax since he had a new album coming out."

"I could understand that. But believe me, when I say, I saw Nicky, and he was dead, definitely, dead." She closed her eyes as the memories came flooding back and gave a shaky exhale. When she was near tears, Eli suddenly changed the direction of the conversation. "Why don't we get out of the cool night air? Come have a drink with me." She smiled and snuggled deeper into his jacket before nodding her agreement.

❋ ❋ ❋

When they entered Doctor Dark's VooDoo Lounge on the corner of Decatur and Conti Streets, a couple of people took notice. The lounge was just a small bar that sat on the corner, with dim lighting and a long cherry wood bar polished to perfection with black leather stools lining it. There was a flat-screen television at the far end, large enough that whatever was playing was visible from the street. The wall opposite the bar was lined with booths with oxblood colored benches and high backs, which gave them an intimate feel. The few tables in the place were all dark wood pub tables with high-backed stools that gave way to a small dance floor. When they entered, it was as if the room froze for a moment before they averted their eyes. As he followed her to the bar, he took note of the men's heads as they swiveled to follow those long bare legs. He found himself ready to pounce on a few. Moving closer to her, he placed a hand on the small of her back possessively to let it be known that she was with him.

When the bartender approached for their orders, she stared at Eli for a long moment. "Don't I know you?" The bartender asked with her deep whiskey-soaked voice.

"Sorry, no," Eli mumbled. She took the unlit cigarette from her lips and pointed at him.

"You sure? You look so familiar." He shook his head.

"Sorry." She eyed him curiously before shrugging it off and taking their order. Eli ordered a beer and waited for her to order the girlie drink du jour, but when she ordered a beer and a shot of Tequila, he couldn't help raising an eyebrow. "I have two older brothers, and my best friend was a rock star. What did you think I would order? A Cosmo? Some kind of fruitini? I'm not that type of girl, Detective." She winked and downed the shot before taking a healthy swig of her beer.

"So, what kind of girl are you?" He asked, taking a sip from his bottle. She smiled brightly and motioned for another shot.

"I am truly one of a kind." She threw back the second shot.

"That you are." He sipped his beer, and they sat in companionable silence for a moment before she turned to him, her hand out palm up.

"Gimme a dollar."

"What?" He stood and began to pat his pockets.

"They have a jukebox, and I don't have any pockets. Give me a dollar." He managed to pull four quarters from his back pocket and handed them to her. She slipped from her stool and headed to the neon juke in the back of the room. She turned to look at him when the first distinctive notes of Al Green's *Let's Stay Together* began. Eli smiled as she swayed, her hips rocking gently to the beat.

"Don't just stand there," one of the men seated at the bar said to him. "You better get over there before I do."

As soon as she was in his arms, Eli's entire body grew hot, and every nerve immediately stood at attention. She melted against him as they swayed in the small room, not caring that all eyes were on them. She looked up at him with eyes that seemed to sparkle in the dim light. He moved his hands from her hips around her bare waist so that he was holding her snuggly against him. She moved closer, her breasts pressing against him, her hips molded to his. He was so hard he ached.

\* \* \*

This was yet another mistake; she thought when she went into his arms. At his slightest touch, her body ignited. He was stiff and throbbing against her stomach. She could feel him straining against the zipper of his jeans. She moved closer, crushing herself to him, loving the feel of him, the smell of him. She rested her head on his shoulder, her lips brushing the skin of his neck. She ran her hand down his chest, reveling in the feel of hard muscle beneath the softness of his sweater. Slowly, she moved her hand down, pausing at his hip. She intended to stop there, but her hand seemed to have a mind of its own because its journey continued until it settled into his back pocket.

"The music's stopped," she whispered as they swayed.

"I know." His voice was a croak that surprised him. "I don't want to let you go just yet," he mumbled.  She looked up at him, her lips parted, her lids low, and all he wanted to do was kiss her. Every muscle in his body tensed as they stopped swaying and just stood there, locked together. As he lowered his head to kiss her, the blaring sound of static filled the place, followed by a collective groan.

"What happened to the TV?" Someone bellowed from the bar.  Eli averted his gaze, and the basketball game that had been on before snapped back into focus.

Slowly, she stepped out of his embrace. "I need to use the powder room. Order me another beer." She turned and disappeared down a dark hallway that led to the restrooms. Exhaling, Eli reclaimed his seat at the bar. The bartender brought two new beers, and a shot she slipped to Eli.

"I didn't order this," Eli said, holding up the shot glass full of tequila.

"No," the ruddy-faced woman laughed. "But after that belly rubbing you did with that one, I'd say you need a cold shower. Since you can't get a shower, I figure a shot would do you just as good." Everyone within earshot laughed. Eli held up his glass in a toast of agreement and swallowed it down. When she emerged from the restroom, Eli paid the tab, and they left.

"Goodnight." The bartender called after them, "Be good or be good at it." There was a chorus of laughter as they walked onto the sidewalk.

"What was that about?" She asked as they headed back towards Canal Street.

"Nothing," Eli said, but he was smiling from ear to ear.

"I'm still curious, Doc." As they crossed Canal and headed to Poydras street, Eli said, "how did someone like you end up being best friends with a rock star? You don't seem like the glam and glitz kind of girl."

"What kind of girl do you think I am?" She teased.

"Well, just from tonight, I'd say you are pretty damn terrific." She smiled and looked down at her feet.

"The Nicky I knew was about as far removed from a rock star as one could get. He was a character, but he didn't seem to crave the spotlight so much. I remember the first time I heard him sing. We were hanging out near Jackson Square, and there was a group, some up and coming band that was supposed to be the second coming of Nirvana or something, was playing a local club. The lead singer was god awful and Nicky, being Nicky, started to mock him. Finally, the singer had enough and told Nicky that he was welcome to come up and sing if he thought he could do better, and he did. At first, he just joked around, then when the band began playing The Beatles, "Hey Jude," it was like someone had thrown cold water over the crowd. They were hypnotized. He was beautiful. By the time he came off stage, he was famous. The Internet made him a star. He went viral overnight. By the time he got a record deal, he was already a worldwide sensation. He was a superstar, except when he was with me. With me, he was always the same old Nicky. We would sit on the sofa for hours watching old movies and television shows. He loved the *Twilight Zone* and *Night Gallery*. He was goofy and silly. He wore ducky pajamas and played Band Hero and Super Mario Bros with me. He still slept over when I needed a friend. He would fly me to wherever he was when he felt lonely. He was like a brother; he *was* my brother."

She spoke of her friend with such love and affection that Eli found himself a little jealous. Nicky had known her in a way that no one else had; they shared a past. And he would always hold a special place in her heart. How special and how deeply that went, he wasn't sure. But he was convinced that at one point, they had been more than just good friends.

"Why is it, Detective Cain, I feel so connected to you? It's like I've known you forever like I've – been with you. " She asked, her voice low, her eyes searching his face for some hint of the missing piece that linked them. He reached up, and without thinking, brushed stray curls from her forehead. Her skin felt like velvet, and he was overcome with an undeniable urge to kiss her. It was wrong, he knew, but he felt as if he had to do it, that if he didn't, he would regret it. He held her face in his hands and moved closer. Her body was suddenly on fire in anticipation.

"Probably for the same reason I can't seem to get you out of my head." He whispered, his lips brushing hers as he spoke. The sudden seductive tone of his voice made her swallow hard and lean into him. Her lids lowered, and she held her breath waiting, this is what she wanted. She was waiting for this. This was – a mistake. She took an abrupt step back, breaking their unexpectedly intimate contact.

"I have to go." She backed away slowly, taking the jacket off and handing it to him. "It was nice running into you, Detective." She smiled and started to unravel the iPod she held in her hands, slipping the buds back into her ears, then turned and jogged away. He stood staring at her disappearing form in confusion. *"I will have you, Doctor Kent."* He thought, *"Eventually."* He smiled to himself, shoving his hands deep into the pockets of his jacket. It still smelled of her, lavender.

* * *

She didn't stop running until she was in the elevator to her penthouse apartment. Once inside the metal box, she put her hands on her knees and exhaled. Angrily, she punched the wall and groaned at the fist-sized dent she'd made in the metal. What was she doing? Why had she done that? She had nearly let him kiss her. She'd wanted him to kiss her. She groaned, clutching the place on her stomach where he'd pressed into her, and her body burned. When the doors to the elevator opened, she spilled into her apartment and made a beeline for the shower. She needed to get Detective Cain off this case and out of her life, for his good.

She'd known it was stupid from the moment she'd laced those damn running shoes and headed out of her apartment. She never ran at night and never in shorts on the Riverfront in November. Jonas would kill her if he'd known she'd risked herself like that for a man. A man who had no idea who or what she was, but she couldn't help herself. She'd been compelled to do it and didn't understand why. She belonged to another. Absently, she stroked the nape of her neck, touching the damp curls there, and sighed. She had no business wanting Elijah Cain, none at all.

Groaning, she stepped into the shower, blasting her already hot skin with icy water. "Stupid." She mumbled. When Jonas found out what she was doing, or worse, her brother Remy, she'd never hear the end of it.

# CHAPTER FOUR

Two days after the doctor and detective had run into each other on the riverfront, Nicky Sky's casket was buried with great fanfare and without a body at St. Louis Cemetery #1. It was a jazz funeral that closed most of Canal Street for the better part of the afternoon. The entire Kent family was in attendance, though they all remained hidden behind the darkly tinted windows of a limousine. The few shots that the paparazzi could get of the infamously mysterious Kent clan entering and exiting the sedan were blurry at best. Photos of blurred images in dark clothes and sunglasses graced tabloids and gossip rags, with questions of their connection to the fallen idol. For an entire weekend, television specials and documentaries chronicled the meteoric rise and ultimate demise of rock superstar Nicky Sky.

❋ ❋ ❋

"What do you mean it's closed?" Riley asked their chief, who looked haggard and bogged down. Chief Briggs was not the type of man to let these things go, but Eli had the distinct impression that the order came from higher up. Someone powerful and possibly with a lot of money, someone, Eli suspected, with the last name Kent.

"The case is closed. That's the end of it. You stay away from Doctor Kent, no more questions, no more voodoo, or whatever it is you do." He waved a hand in Eli's general direction. "You have a backlog of cases, and your job is to catch murderers. Get to work," Chief Briggs told them. Briggs was a solid man, a cop from a family of cops. No nonsense and entirely by the book. Eli stared at him for a while before rising, leaving the tiny wood-paneled office, pulling Riley with him as he went.

"Sure, Chief." He said and closed the door.

"But-" Riley began to protest, and Eli silenced him. He, unlike Riley, knew enough not to ask questions.

Once they were outside of the office, Eli spun Riley to face him.

"Let it go. There is something about this whole thing that isn't right." He mumbled. "Someone has gotten the Chief to kill this case." Riley moved closer, his eyes searching Eli's.

"Did you get something?" He discreetly tapped his temple, aware that others in the squad room were giving the two curious glances but continued with business as usual. Eli was already thought of as an oddity. This hushed conversation was just the norm for them.

"I couldn't get anything. He blocked it, or he doesn't know, but the call came from high up, someone with money and power." Someone, he thought, named Jonas Kent.

"Well," Riley said, slapping him on the back. "Now, you have an actual reason to call Doctor Kent." Eli flinched slightly, taken aback. It was as if Riley had read his mind. "It's written all over your face." Riley assured.

\* \* \*

For the first time in years, she was intrigued by a man. She couldn't get the mysterious Detective Cain off her mind as she drove to her father's house on the North shore. Jonas Kent had a sprawling compound in a deeply wooded area in Mandeville. As she crossed Lake Pontchartrain, her mind wandered back to him and the current he'd sent through her. Familiar warmth began to spread between her thighs as she thought of his breath warm and sweet against her lips. The smell of him lingered on her well after she'd returned his jacket that night.

It seemed to soak into her pores, her hair. It infiltrated her senses for the remainder of the night. Even after her shower, that scent had lingered.

He was a strikingly handsome man. No, he was more than attractive; he was beautiful. She had never thought she would use those words when describing a man, but Elijah Cain was just beautiful.

He had intelligent, curious eyes and a funny crooked half-smile that melted her. And the dimples, damn those dimples. She groaned. What was wrong with her? Getting involved with Detective Elijah Cain would be the worst possible thing she could do.

The fact that he could see her thoughts as clearly as she saw his had been a surprise, but not a shock. Perhaps it was the spark of recognition she had seen flash across his face when he saw her or the fact that he'd dreamt of her. What had he called her when he spoke to his partner, "Angel?" She smiled to herself and pulled onto the wooded dirt road that led to her father's massive estate.

"What am I doing?" She mumbled, shaking images of him from her mind. She couldn't be doing this now. Something was going on with Nicky, her best friend, his body had gone missing, and she was fantasizing about sex with a stranger. She had to meet with Jonas tonight. Their monthly family dinner had turned into a complete and utter pain in the ass, but Jonas would know what to do about the Nicky thing. And where to look. He loved Nicky just as much as she had; she remembered as she revved the Range Rover's engine.

As she came closer to the house, the woods fell away to reveal a tree-lined road that led to the massive three-story structure that was Villa de Kent. It was an old plantation house from the 1700s that Jonas had renovated. The original columns remained, freshly painted a blinding white. The windows on all three floors ran from floor to ceiling and were bracketed by shutters painted blood red. Stone steps rolled out in a semi-circle from the veranda, which encircled the entire first floor and had ornate wrought iron railings and fencing. The second story had a mimicking balcony, and the third floor housed a widow's watch that she could never remember anyone using. Not that they would see anything but trees and the grounds surrounding the estate. As she got closer, she saw that the house was lit up like a Christmas tree. It was as if every light in the place was burning.

Jonas had added his generator station since there were no existing power lines out this far. It had cost a pretty penny and some ingenuity, but the house was almost entirely self-sufficient. Maybe a mile before the house, a large brick wall circled the actual compound, with its guard post.

She pulled her car to the gate and waved. The guard on duty tonight, Julius, waved and smiled.

"Evening Doctor Kent," he shouted from his booth as the massive wrought iron gates monogrammed with a giant calligraphy *K* swung inward. She drove onto the gravel driveway, passing an empty helicopter landing pad, before pulling to the semi-circle before the veranda steps. Jonas hadn't arrived from the airport yet, she assumed. Climbing out, she didn't bother taking her keys from the car. Who would possibly steal it way out here? Besides, Jonas's guards were armed, and all had itchy trigger fingers. She sprinted up the stone steps to the blood-red double doors of the home. From the decorative fan-shaped window above the doors, she spotted the enormous crystal chandelier that hung in the foyer; it was lit, throwing a pale golden light across the driveway, but the outside lights weren't on yet. Thinking this was odd, she turned and looked at the collection of cars in the driveway.

Her white-on-white Range Rover was parked directly in front of the steps to the front door. A road ran along the house's side that led to the 10-car garage in the back, but it was dark and blocked off by Jonas's black town car. The chauffeur, Philip, was sitting in the driver's seat, waiting patiently with a book in hand. Off to the side was a guest parking area. There was a black on black BMW-that would be her brother Gaston's and a shiny red sports car with the unmistakable Mercedes emblem gleaming silver in the fading light. That would be her sister Lisette's. The Ducati wedged between the two, with the serpent green paint and the snakeskin painted helmet on the seat that was the bone of contention. Remy was here. She stared at it for a while, nearly missing the ringing of the phone in her pocket.

Briar.

"He knows," he was saying as soon as she swiped to answer. "Jonas knows about Nicky. So does the Collective. I've been told to – I've been told to remove the problem." Her stomach dropped, and she felt her legs get weak.

"Briar..."

"Sorry, Sarge. He's been marked as a problem, and you know how the Collective feels about problems. I am sorry, love. If it makes you feel any better, his maker is also marked."

"The Collective needs to know that I do not approve of this decision," she snapped.

"I will make sure they are made aware of that, but I'm pretty sure you know how this goes." She did, and she hated it.

"Thanks for the call, Briar." She disconnected and paced the veranda for a moment, chewing her thumbnail. Who, she wondered, had informed the Collective? Who would do such a thing? Her eyes landed on the gleaming green of the motorcycle ensconced in the driveway.

"Son of a *bitch*!" She mumbled before storming into the house. Whenever there was trouble, there was Remy. She marched across the marble foyer into the sitting room. Most of the house had recently been redecorated in muted tones of gold, bronze, and beige. The sitting room was one of the few rooms with the original cedar walls and hardwood floors. Gaston sat on the oxblood leather sofa reading the newspaper when she stormed in. He was relaxed, even with Remy lurking around the house. In his usual preppy attire: khakis, white oxford shirt, and powder blue cashmere sweater. Gaston and

Lisette were Jonas's biological children with his first wife. They had accepted her coming to live with them, had even welcomed her. Remy, his only child with his second wife, was a different circumstance altogether.

When she entered, Gaston folded his paper and looked at her, immediately rising to his feet at her agitated state. Like Jonas, Gaston was tall and dark with wavy jet-black hair that he brushed back away from his face. Jonas, who had started life on the northern coast of Africa before migrating north to Italy, then France, had a distinct look. He had dark eyes and olive skin, and a robust Romanesque profile. He was handsome, and even though he was of slim build, it was all muscle. Gaston was a thicker, darker, more muscular version of his father. He clucked and shook his head the way he did whenever she was in a state.

"CeCe, calm down," he purred, taking her into his arms. She rested her head on Gaston's solid shoulder and exhaled. He smelled of soap and gentle cologne, and his light sweater felt soft and warm against her cool cheek. He tilted her face up to look into her eyes, holding her gaze before lowering his mouth to hers. The kiss was light and gentle at first and then deepened as his arms tightened around her, pinning her arms to her side. She struggled and pushed away, but he was too strong. He lifted her off the floor, her feet kicking out, arms pinned to her sides as she struggled. He slipped his tongue past her teeth into her mouth as she worked harder, angry tears streaming down her cheeks. Finally, she drew up her knee, catching him in the crotch. He released her, doubling over in agony, then he began to laugh a maniacal laugh, and if she had not been sure before, she was now.

"Fucking asshole!" She screamed, wiping her hand angrily across her mouth. "You fucking-" She charged at him and was lifted into the air again, this time from behind. "Whoa, CeCe." Gaston's voice came from behind her. The *real* Gaston.

"What in the world- CeCe, what-" Lisette came racing into the room, apparently from her office. She was still wearing her reading glasses. She only wore those for vanity reasons. They all knew Lisette had the vision of a hawk. Where Gaston was dark, Lisette was light. She was tall, as were all of Jonas's children, biological or otherwise, but that was where the similarities ended. She was slender but not skinny in a sleeveless black leather dress, exposing the appropriate amount of leg. Her hair was a beautiful shade of honey blond that hung in loose curls to her shoulders, her skin the color of toast, and her eyes deep and soulful brown, her features distinctly Creole. Lisette was the second born but the most ambitious and newly engaged. Gaston was the oldest, the heir apparent.

When Gaston finally released her, the Gaston impostor stopped laughing. He held still for a moment, the bones in his face shifting visibly beneath his skin. Even his clothes changed from the pale blue cashmere sweater and khakis the real Gaston wore to his uniform of a black t-shirt and skinny jeans.

It only took a moment before he was back to his true self, he was the same height and basic build as his brother Gaston, so it had been easy to fool her. She stared daggers at him as his face spread into a wide grin. Remy Kent was even lovelier than Gaston. He had the classic Moorish features of the Kent men, dark hair, olive skin, but his eyes were big and deep tobacco brown. Where Gaston was chiseled, Remy had a rather delicate prettiness to him. He was tall and lithe, not skinny, but slim. Remy was also cocky and brash, and being the youngest of the Kent children, he was the most adventurous. He harbored deep feelings for her that ran beyond familial, and his reaction to those feelings was to be a significant pain in her ass.

"You slimy little-" She couldn't finish her thoughts, so she rained curses on him in Mandarin Chinese.

"Remy cut that shit out," Lisette said in her no-nonsense manner. "Don't we have enough to worry about with Nicky running around the city like a fucking tourist?" She mumbled. He stood staring at her, a satisfied smirk on his lips.

"Wait. What? So, it's true?" He asked, suddenly serious.

"Like you didn't know. Did you tell the Collective?" CeCe blasted. "They marked him, Remy."

"Someone spotted him hanging around in the Quarter, getting a tattoo on Rampart Street. Waste of money." Lisette turned to leave the room but paused and came back to stand before CeCe. She took her glasses off to study CeCe's face.

"What do you know, baby sister?" She asked.

"The cops came to talk to me. They asked a few questions about Nicky. I answered, and they left. That's it." She said this matter of factly and met Lisette's gaze evenly.

"No, that's not it," Remy said, the smile finally falling from his lips completely. He moved closer and sniffed her, his eyes searching hers. "She sent Briar out," he declared.

"As for the detective- she has a thing for the detective?" He gripped her chin, his fingers digging into her cheeks. "Does whittle sister have a crush?" His tone was light, but his eyes had shifted, his pupils elongating into something animal, and his teeth, those damned teeth. "That's enough, Remy," Gaston just about growled from behind her.

"Jealous, big brother? Someone else is making her cream her panties other than big strong Gaston?"

"Stop it, Remy." Lisette put a hand on his shoulder. Ignoring her, he moved closer to CeCe.

"Just the thought of him makes you go all wet-" He reached down with his free hand to cup her crotch, and she'd had enough. She pushed him away with such force that he slid backward across the room. He dug in with his heels so hard that he stripped a layer of varnish from the hardwood floor, finally coming to a stop twenty feet away, at the opposite end of the room.

He had to put his hand down to keep himself from falling backward onto his butt. He looked at her, a glint of something like pride in his eyes and bared his teeth, those brilliant silver-tipped fangs, his eyes a serpentine yellow, and he made a sound that was no more than a hiss.

*"That'sss it sssissster,"* he taunted as she crouched in a practiced fighting stance.

"Remy, that is enough!" Jonas Kent's voice boomed from the foyer, and the entire house vibrated. The chandeliers throughout the first floor quivered as his footfalls echoed in the suddenly silent house. They remained still as he entered the room. Jonas Kent was a monster of a man. He stood six foot two and weighed just under two hundred pounds, all of it muscle. His stance was a Roman general, and the demeanor of an emperor, when he entered a room, his presence was felt.

Jonas still had hair the color of coal, save the silver starting at his temples. He was flanked on either side by armed bodyguards, both in dark tailored suits. Jonas himself wore a dark suit with a vibrant blood red tie, his signature color. He entered the room and took them all in. Remy and Gaston, with their teeth bared, Lisette was looking exasperated and CeCe, with fire in her eyes. Remy had calmed himself but still stood ready for another verbal assault on his precious sister.

"Retract those teeth. We are not animals." Jonas spoke clearly and crisply, with a slight French accent. Remy looked away from him, unable to control his anger. "Why do you constantly antagonize your sister?"

"She is not my blood," Remy spat.

"The problem is that you are all too aware of that fact. Come," Jonas exhaled sharply, motioning for them to follow. "Let's eat. I am starved."

As they exited the room, Jonas stopped Remy and gave him a warning stare. "She may not be your blood, Remy, but she trusts you. You, of all people, know what she has survived. You were there, Remy. Be careful with her. Don't do anything to break that trust again. She forgave you once. I'm not sure she would be able to do it again." Remy watched her as she passed and nodded. He was ashamed and angry because he did know. He'd seen with his own eyes what they were doing to her.

"You can't make her love you again, son. Don't push. Let her come to you. If she comes at all," Jonas said and patted him on the shoulder.

* * *

The Kent dining room was sprawling and just as elegant as the rest of the house. There was a rather sizeable Victorian era cherry wood table that was polished to within an inch of its life. The walls were covered with red wallpaper threaded through with gold vines; the chairs were high backed and delicate with red silk padding. CeCe took her seat next to Lisette, and Remy slid in across from her, his usual seat beside Gaston. Jonas, of course, sat at the head of the table.

As the butler, Frederick, served dinner, they chatted about the trivialities of their everyday work. Gaston, a lawyer, had just made partner. He was renovating a house on St. Charles Avenue, and the wiring had finally, after many months, been completed. Remy was in town only for a few days. He was a photographer, and in-between his bedding of models, he worked as a photojournalist and traveled to war zones worldwide.

Lisette was the editor of her magazine, '*Haute,*' which was based in New York. She spent three weeks a month in a Manhattan apartment with her soon-to-be-husband Giovanni. As they chatted about wedding plans and guests, flowers, and decorating tips, Jonas remained mostly quiet, savoring the flavor of his dinner, Kobe beef, extremely rare, and his favorite, special brand of red wine. Often, he glanced at CeCe, worry creasing his lineless face as he studied her profile. As the wedding chatter faded, Jonas cleared his throat and wiped his mouth with his napkin.

"I know you know about Nicky." He spoke to CeCe, and the entire room went still. "I also know that Briar has been asked to contain the problem."

She lowered her eyes to her plate and stared at the half-eaten steak. "Is there something you need to tell me?" She looked up at him and shook her head.

"You already know that I sent Briar to look for him." She stared at him in confusion.

"And his Maker?"

Again, she shook her head. "I don't know who his maker is. I thought the Collective kept a tight rein on that. I've also let it be known that I disapprove of the Collective's decision," she mumbled.

Jonas nodded and continued to eat. "What did the police say? They have spoken to you?"

"Yes, but…" She looked at him in confusion. "I had a strange reaction to one of the detectives. Detective Cain and I have some sort of connection."

"How?"

"He's a telepath. And something else. Something I haven't been exposed to before. We have the same eyes, and he has had dreams of me. For some time, I think. We seem to have a link. We- when we're together- it's like you can feel the electricity in the air."

"Is it a familial link?" Jonas folded his hands on the table and leaned back in his chair, contemplating this.

"No." She looked down at her hands. "Not familial." She couldn't stop the smile that pulled at the corners of her mouth; Just the thought of his hard-muscled body covering her caused goose flesh to rise on her skin.

"And you reacted physically? To the touch?" Jonas leaned closer, staring at her so intently that she flushed under his scrutiny. She looked up at Jonas, then the others at the table. They all seemed to be leaning forward in anticipation.

"I reacted physically to his thoughts. He was across the room, but the reaction was so strong, father. If he touched me- I don't know what would have happened. I have never been around someone-" She shook her head at a loss for words but couldn't stop the smile from spreading across her lips.

"What kind of physical reaction?" Lisette asked under her breath. CeCe looked at her with a smirk and lifted her brow.

Realization dawned on Lisette in an instant, and her eyes widened. "Really? How- much- did you react?" She mumbled.

"Too much to discuss here," CeCe mumbled back, and Lisette stifled a smirk.

"Well, I guess I need to meet this detective," Jonas proclaimed after an extended silence. The men in the room squirmed uncomfortably. This was not the kind of discussion a girl wanted to have with her father in the room. No matter how low she and Lisette had spoken, she knew that they had caught every word, every nuance of the private conversation. They all averted their gazes as she looked at them, all except Remy, who stared daggers at her.

"Does the Collective know who made Nicky?" CeCe asked, changing the subject.

"No. That is why Briar is on the case. As you know, he's the best tracker we have," Jonas said, and she nodded her agreement and sat back in her chair, distractedly chewing her bottom lip.

"This was done by a rogue. Whoever it was, did a sloppy job. It was not neat or refined. It was dirty." She shivered at the thought of his prone body in that bathroom.

"Dirty?" Remy leaned forward. His interest had been piqued, but he was way off.

"Not sexy dirty, messy dirty," she corrected, and Remy sat back in his seat, pretending to be disinterested. "Like they were not exactly sure what to do. He had bites everywhere, and his skull was fractured. He had a broken ankle, and there was a blood trail from the living room to the bathroom. I mean, that was done by something else. It wasn't one of us."

"Sounds like a Lycan attack," Gaston spoke but never looked up from his meal.

"No, there were no missing pieces." CeCe cut into her steak, relishing the taste of nearly raw meat filling her senses. A single drop of blood dripped from her fork to stain the antique linen tablecloth. Frederick made a soft clucking noise at the stain but never moved from his station.

"He was bitten, not fed upon," she corrected. "And too much blood for one of us or even The Originals." She shook her head. "This was really- something quite different. If I didn't know better, I would say a fledgling did this, but a fledgling wouldn't have left that much blood."

"Then what else could it be?" Gaston looked at Jonas for an answer. Their father sat at the head of the table pondering this, his brow furrowed in concern. Slowly and deliberately, Jonas rose, dropping his napkin on the remains of his dinner as he did. "I need to make a phone call. CeCe, can you get me pictures of the scene?"

"Of course, father. I have copies at my apartment. I can have them here in the morning." She also rose. She could have easily emailed them to him, but she'd learned a long time ago that those who knew where to look and what to look for could find them, and the last thing they needed was more attention. They all rose, preparing to go into the sitting room for coffee and dessert while Jonas made his calls.

"I also want to meet your Detective Cain," Jonas called to her as he left the room.

"He's not *MY* detective," CeCe corrected.

"He is now." Lisette gave her a knowing smile as she left the room.

* * *

She was still sitting behind the wheel of her car when Remy emerged from the house sometime later. As she watched him, she felt her cheeks flushed. They had flirted and teased each other for the better part of thirty years, but tonight when he kissed her, she had wanted him, if only as a substitute. It was unnerving.

As she'd kissed Remy, she imagined it was Elijah Cain, with those deep turquoise eyes and penetrating gaze. She imagined that he held her, his body burning heat against her own. Sighing, she watched Remy stride across the veranda. He was confident and unembarrassed about his unabashed sexuality about his want and need for her. It was a part of their nature, she assumed. But there was something about Remy; he had more of an edge, an underlying danger that sent flashing warning signs off in her mind. Perhaps it was because he had more demon in his blood than human. Maybe it was because of his shifting nature, which made him more animal than a man, that made her wary of him. Perhaps, it was because until a few years ago, aside from Nicky, he had been her closest friend. No matter what it was, she didn't love him the way he wanted her to, and she truly regretted that sometimes. She sighed and began banging her head on the padded steering wheel.

Remy paused on the steps, watching her for a moment, his dark hair ruffled in the cold air of the mid-November night. She had a long drive ahead of her, and it was well after eleven, but she was not the slightest bit tired. Those big dark eyes were focused on her when she looked up, considering her options. She could go home, read a book, do some work, keep her mind occupied until she dozed off or she'd lay awake thinking about Remy's hands and Eli's eyes and mouth, the way he laughed and the way his voice poured over her like hot chocolate. She could simply bed Remy and get it over with, or track down the detective, which was a much more thrilling but entirely out of character option. Finally, she smiled, her fingers going to the button to roll down the passenger side window.

He walked towards her, zipping his leather jacket and shoving his hands deep into the pockets. He poked his head into the warmth, a curious smile on his lips.

"Wanna go to Jinxie's?" She asked, and his smile spread into a full laugh.

"Hell yeah. I'll follow you." He sprinted over to his bike as she revved her engine.

She pulled off so fast that her rear tires kicked up gravel. As she waited for the gates to swing open wide enough to allow safe passage, Remy raced past her, his front wheel rising as he wheelied out into the darkness. Remy was a pain in the ass, she thought, but damn if he wasn't fun

* * *

She sat, focusing on the colorful fish in the tank that sat atop the bookcase opposite her. She'd spent too much time at Jinxie's with Remy the night before. What a disaster that had been.

The entire time, she'd had to fend off his increasingly aggressive advances, until finally, she'd gone home, alone and angry, Detective Elijah Cain on her mind. He'd invaded her dreams last night, leaving her tired and disagreeable today. She was even more ill-tempered because she'd had to come into the lab to check Xander's progress with the lab mice. They had a paper to complete for a medical journal, and she had to keep him on track. She knew that when she wasn't around, he spent most of his time making out with Bianca in her office. She didn't even make out in her office, not that she had much of an opportunity for that. Not lately, anyway.

"Are you listening to me?" Xander was waving a hand in front of her face. She blinked and came crashing back to reality. "What?" She snapped, embarrassed by the thoughts running through her mind but also angry to be taken out of them.

"I was saying that the messenger is downstairs. Something about a package-" She nodded distractedly and told Xander to bring him up. She took the photos from the folder she'd stored in her bag and flipped through them. The colors were so vivid. Her heart ached to see her friend lying on the cool white marble of his bathroom floor, a halo of blood surrounding his head. His eyes were open, vacant, devoid of the vitality she had known. He was still, his mouth pulled in a grotesque smile and tiny puncture wounds all over his body. If the coroner had examined him, they would have indeed suspected he was an IV drug user or some sort of sexual sadist, but she knew better. Nicky was the healthiest, most vanilla person she'd known. He'd never been a fast-food junkie; his drink of choice was chocolate milk. He'd drink occasionally but had no tolerance for it and had never made it a habit. He didn't smoke cigarettes, and his biggest vice had always been sexy blonds, brunettes, and the occasional redhead. His platinum blond hair, perfectly pore-less skin, and big blue eyes made him look angelic, making him the perfect rock star in the media age. Staring at the pictures of his death made her remember how full of life he was. Wiping a stray tear from her cheek, she placed the photos in an envelope before putting them in a cardboard photo envelope and sealing it. She was scribbling Jonas's address when the courier entered wearing her pristine blue and white uniform. She smiled but said nothing as she was given instructions on delivery.

"I need these in Jonas Kent's hands no later than two this afternoon. He's expecting them." She gave her a fifty-dollar tip and sent her on her way.

Unable to concentrate, she decided that she would go out for coffee and then work from home. She was too distracted to get anything done anyway. She rose to get her jacket, glancing at herself in the mirror, hanging on the back of her office door. She looked okay, she supposed, in her slim dark jeans, long-sleeved black and grey striped V-neck sweater, which exposed just enough cleavage. Her hair was pulled into a loose side ponytail, and a pair of bright pink low top Converse sneakers on her feet. She slipped on a pink blazer and newsboy cap before charging out the door.

She waved at Bianca as she exited the building. Bianca, of the tottering heels, heavy perfume, and bright red lipstick, sat behind the reception desk, chatting on the phone and spinning in her seat. "Where are you going, Doc?" She called after her.

"Home," she mumbled and was out the door. She knew that Bianca would be in the lab before she was out of the parking lot.

\* \* \*

Her favorite coffee shop, The Monkee Bean, was uptown on Magazine Street. She had to drive past her apartment to get to it, but they had the best lattes and the biggest chocolate chip cookies she'd ever seen. They always calmed her down and helped her focus. She opened the door and smelled the robust aroma of freshly brewed coffee and the sweetness of the pastries. As she waited for her turn in line, she felt something strange, electricity in the air and the smell of something familiar as she placed her order. Instinctively, she scanned the room as the girl behind the counter prepared her order. He was here.

For a moment, she thought she'd imagined him, but there he was sitting near a window, looking delicious in a dark blue t-shirt, a gray hoodie with a spiraling navy design running up one arm and bursting into an eagle across his chest. He wore dark denim jeans that wrapped around his muscular thighs and white sneakers. He was reading the sports section of the paper, sipping a cappuccino. When she received and paid for her coffee and cookie, she walked over, making sure he was alone before she approached.

"Are you stalking me, Doctor Kent?" He asked as she approached, his eyes still on the paper. She took off her hat and tossed it on the table, a sly grin on her lips.

"I'm not interrupting anything, am I? I don't want to impose." He shook his head, folding the paper and putting it aside.

"Not at all. Please." He motioned for her to take the seat across from him. She sat and suddenly became nervous.

"So," she started, "I guess the whole missing body case has been closed," she said in a nervous rush.

"Yeah, I guess the higher-ups thought it would look bad to have the police force lose a body. Either that or some big muckity-muck used his pull to avoid the media frenzy. You wouldn't know about that, would you?" He looked at her intently, and she found it hard to concentrate on anything other than his steady gaze on her face. He was watching her every move as if he half expected her to disappear in a puff of smoke.

"I'm surprised to see you here. I come here a lot. I would have remembered seeing you." She offered him a piece of her cookie, he politely declined.

"It's my first time here." He admitted. "It's my day off. Riley and his boyfriend invited a bunch of us over for brunch. I just didn't feel like heading home yet."

"Boyfriend?" She raised an eyebrow. It was rare to come across a man like Elijah Cain, handsome, smart, overtly male, and obviously enlightened.

"Yeah, Adam. He's a uniformed patrolman. He's a nice guy who makes a terrific Belgian waffle. He's a step up from some of Riley's other boyfriends." She nodded, a slow smile forming on her lips, and looked down at her cookie.

"I'm not gay," he said before the question arose.

"Oh, there was never a question." She met his gaze, her cheeks flushing hotly. His phone buzzed to life, and he rolled his eyes but didn't answer.

"Problem?" She asked, taking a sip of her drink, her eyes on him.

"Just someone I would rather not talk to right now," he sighed.

"Ahh, Ms. Deadwood, I presume," she deduced, and he chuckled.

"Yes. She's been calling me non-stop. I tried to let her down easy, but she's persistent and doesn't seem to understand subtlety."

"She understands. You're just a hard man to forget." She met his eyes, and he paused, his cup halfway to his lips. Silently, he placed the cup back on the table, his eyes smoldered, and she could feel the room warm as the electricity in the air rose. The lights dimmed slightly and flickered. The other patrons glanced up, and a few groaned, but no one paid a great deal of attention to the change.

"Really?" He asked, a twinkle in his eyes. In this light, they seemed more of an aquamarine than turquoise. He leaned back in his seat, openly observing her. She waved a hand at him.

"Please," she snorted, trying to rein in the growing warmth of her body. "You know you're gorgeous," she said, her voice low. "Just look around the room. The women are eating you up." He glanced around the room and found that a few women and a couple of men were openly ogling him. Slightly embarrassed, he shook it off.

"Once Ms. Deadwood got a taste, albeit a tiny taste, she realized that you are something special."

"What about you?" He absently reached for her hand; his thumb stroked the delicate skin of her inner wrist, and her mouth went dry. She looked down, loving the feel of his thumb against her skin. Just a few years ago, she would have pulled away. She had always been sensitive to anyone holding her like this, touching the delicate skin of her wrists. With Eli, it was okay, even arousing. His voice deepened, and he leaned closer, his eyes darkening to a deep navy.

"Would you like a taste?" Her cheeks grew hot, and she crossed her ankles, squeezing her thighs closed as a new heat began to grow. He gave her a wicked smile, and in one swift movement, he pulled her chair closer until her thighs were trapped between his legs, holding her still just in case she'd planned on running again. His smile widened, and those dimples made an appearance. Damn those dimples.

"Are you flirting with me, Detective?" She finally managed once she found her voice. She'd meant for it to sound light and fun. Instead, it came out low and throaty. She couldn't help but focus on his lips; they were full and soft, tilted up in the most delicious smile. She wanted to nip his bottom lip with her teeth.

"Well, I'm trying my damnedest." Her stomach fluttered at

his intimate tone. "How am I doing?" He had her hands again, his fingers stroking her palms so he could pull her closer still. The feel of his skin against hers made her pulse jump. She glanced down briefly and noticed that he was hard, his bulge straining painfully against the zipper of his jeans. She wanted to slide her hands into the waistband of his jeans and touch him, stroke his stiff shaft until he moaned. At the thought, her pulse raced, and he chuckled.

"I'd say we're moving in the right direction," he whispered, shocking her back into the here and now. She avoided staring directly into his eyes but studied him for a moment.

"That's a neat little trick. How long have you been a telepath?" She asked, her voice low.

"How long have you?" He retorted. "I've never come across someone I could read like you. Like we share-"

"A connection," she finished, and he nodded. "What else can you do?" She asked eagerly.

"You're not freaked out?" He sat back a bit thunderstruck. Only a select few had been comfortable with his abilities, and only Riley had ever asked exactly what they were. She shook her head.

"Not in the least. I'm smart enough to know that there are things in this world that defy rational explanation. They just are. I'm a scientist, Detective. We still don't know the full capacity of the human brain." She sipped her latte, hoping he didn't notice her shaking hand, and waited for him to speak. He smiled and told her of what he could do, of the precognition, his ability to recall other people's memories, the immunity to illness, and his strength. She sat transfixed.

"It comes and goes. Sometimes I can control it. Other times it just slips in and out. If I concentrate, I can read anyone. Sometimes, it's just a whisper or humming at the back of my head. At times it's as clear as if I thought or said it myself. I can't always read you, though, not like I have to. I know what you're thinking." She nodded and looked down at their linked fingers. When had that happened, she wondered. She licked the foam from her lips, and he watched intently. She looked at him, again wishing that she could leave, but there was something about this man that held her in her seat.

"I want to kiss you so bad right now, it hurts." When he spoke, it was like a growl, a low guttural vibration that seemed to come from his chest. The statement startled her and sent a warm, fluid rush through her at the same time. He took her hand and guided it high on his thigh until it rested on the hard bulge at his zipper. Slowly, he moved his hands up her arms and shoulder until they held her face and brushed his lips against hers. The room seemed to be filled with a rush of cold air, and his kiss moved deeper, his tongue sliding into her warm, waiting mouth. She tasted faintly of coffee and vanilla and pure sweetness. She let one hand move up to settle on his chest. His muscles tensed at her touch, and she leaned closer, restraining herself from climbing onto his lap. When he moved away, she kept her eyes closed, exhaling. Her eyes opened slowly, and she felt her bones turn to liquid under his smoldering gaze. Her lips felt kiss swollen, and she wanted him to do it again.

"That was a mistake." He touched his forehead to hers. "Now, all I can think about is kissing you all over. I need to know if you're just as sweet everywhere." He whispered.

Her heart did a little giddy-up, and she had to look away.

"*Je pourrais vous ai juste laissé.*" She echoed his low tone but had somehow lapsed into French. He laughed and shook his head.

"I understood that. Would you let me?" He said, and she blushed.

"Sorry, I grew up in a small town in France, *Roquebrune-Cap Martin,* and tend to fall into French without thinking."

Standing silently beside their table, a waitress, all of seventeen years old, smiled brightly as she placed a large piece of chocolate cake and two forks between the two of them.

"This is from the lady at the counter." They turned to follow the waitress's gaze. Bianca stood at the counter, a cup of coffee in her hand. She nodded her greeting and gave them the thumbs up before leaving, waving as she passed the window.

"Well, we'll have to thank her," he said, his eyes still on her lips. "So, this small town in France, Oaken Brune- Cap-" She laughed at his butchered pronunciation.

"*Roquebrune-Cap Martin*, it's right outside of Monaco. But I haven't been back in like forever. Jonas is from *Reims*, so French is commonly spoken at family dinners." She smiled sheepishly, nervously chewing her bottom lip, and picked up her fork, digging in to keep from speaking for a moment. She needed the butterflies in her stomach to calm down and the shaking in her knees to stop. He was staring at her mouth so intently, the heat from his gaze made her blood race through her veins, and her bones feel like liquid.

"Unless you want me to throw you across the table and do highly inappropriate things to you in front of all of these people, I suggest you not do that." Her brow furrowed in confusion. "Do what?"

"Bite your lip like that. It has to be the sexiest thing I've ever seen." His voice was so low it made her shiver. There was something dangerous about him, something dark that lay just beneath the surface.

"Nervous habit," She mumbled. She stared at him for a long time before she spoke again. "You want to get out of here? Maybe get some dinner?" She asked, and he nodded.

"I have the perfect place," he said with a teasing smile.

# CHAPTER FIVE

She followed Eli's black SUV across the bridge in her own Range Rover, the entire time telling herself that it was a mistake, that Jonas would kill her if he found out. This man was a complication that she didn't need in her life. Yet, here she was, pulling her car onto the street in front of a charming navy house with crisp white trim. She eased out of her car to stare at the manicured lawn surrounded by a beautiful black wrought iron fence. Tall Grecian pillars were lining the front porch and white Jamaican shutters at each window. He beckoned for her to join him on the porch. She smiled as she passed two white rockers perched on the porch, a small wooden table between them.

He held the door open, and she eased into the small foyer. The entire place smelled of Eli, she thought. She stared at the narrow staircase that led to the second floor and peered briefly into the living room. It was cozy with two overstuffed dark brown leather chairs that bookended a tall mahogany bookcase. A leather sofa faced a beautiful brick fireplace with a television mounted above the mantle. The hardwood floors were covered with thick rugs in rich earth tones. It felt warm and masculine and smelled of wood and crisp linen.

"Come on." He took her hand, sending a jolt of electricity through her, and lead her down the narrow hallway to the kitchen. She looked around the brightly decorated room before taking a seat at a pub table near a bay window that overlooked his patio and small backyard. The back yard was as neatly kept as the front, with a barbecue pit, lounge chairs, and a hammock hidden beneath two oak trees at the far end of the yard.

"Eli, it's so cute," she gushed. He glanced at her briefly as he surveyed the items in the refrigerator.

"Thanks, I think. So, what would you like?" He asked.

"What do you have?" She asked.

"I can make you whatever you want. I have steak, fish, pasta. What are you in the mood for?"

"I would kill for a pizza with pepperoni, sausage, and Canadian bacon and a nice cold beer." He closed the fridge and picked up the phone.

"Thin crust or deep dish?" He dialed quickly, placing two ice-cold beers on the marble island in the middle of the room as he spoke into the phone. She came to stand beside him, leaning against cool marble, her legs crossed lazily at the ankles as she twisted the top off her beer. She had just taken a sip when he stood in front of her, with his legs akimbo. The hard muscles of his thighs trapping her legs, his hands on the counter on either side of her. She took a sip of the beer, forcing it past the lump in her throat, as the feel of him pressed against her set her ablaze.

"Pizza should be here in about thirty minutes," he said, gently taking the bottle from her numb fingers, setting it on the counter. She bit her lip, waiting as he took the hat from her head so that he could look at her face without obstruction.

"What can we do for thirty whole minutes?" She asked. Eli kissed her, and the warmth low in her center erupted into a full-fledged burn. She leaned into him, her hands on the waist of his jeans; she pulled him closer, pressing her hips into him. There was a soft guttural noise that came from one of them; she wasn't sure which at that moment because he deepened the kiss, his tongue moving in to taste her. She gasped in surprise when he lifted her onto the counter, his mouth on her neck.

Under the soft cotton of his t-shirt to the hot hard skin beneath, her hands moved from his waist. He pressed into her, grinding his hips into her, and this time she knew the moan had come from her. He cupped her breast, his thumb worrying her hardened nipple through the layers of clothing, before slipping underneath. He nipped at her neck, his tongue tracing intricate little designs in her skin, and she held him tighter. He reached for the clasp of her bra, releasing it and freeing her breasts. When his hardened palm touched her bare skin, grazing her swollen puckered nipple, a shiver of excitement went through her.

He was so gentle, she thought. No one had ever been this gentle with her. They had wanted her, she supposed, but they had never kissed her the way he was kissing her, and that made her want him even more. The others had never made promises; they had never even *really* kissed her. No one had caressed her until she melted or even cared if she wanted them. Mostly they just forced themselves inside of her, grunting when they were done, leaving her covered in their smells.

*"You would never hurt me, would you, Elijah?"* She thought her breath soft and hot against his ear as he nuzzled her neck. He pulled away as if he'd been slapped and stared at her. She looked so beautiful, her lips parted and kiss swollen, her eyes hooded, and her breath was coming harsh and ragged.

"What's wrong?" She asked, suddenly self-conscious.

"Who hurt you, Doc?" He stroked her cheek with his thumb and watched as her eyes faded from vibrant turquoise to deep indigo. She shook her head and eased away from him.

"Don't do that," she whispered, sliding from the counter, refastening the clasp of her bra, and recapturing her beer.

"Don't go into my head like that." She turned her back to him. A look of pure pain briefly crossed her face. He felt something strange pulling in his stomach, and he wanted to just hold onto her.

"Doc-" He reached for her, and she slipped away, moving to the opposite side of the island.

"I shouldn't have come here," she said, looking for her hat. "I should go." She headed for the hallway, and he blocked her escape.

"No, don't leave. At least wait until the pizza gets here." She kept her eyes averted, and he squatted in front of her so that he could see her eyes.

"Don't make me beg, Doc. I promise I won't do it again. It just happens sometimes, and I can't help it. Please. I'll be good. Scouts honor." He held up his fingers in the Boy Scout salute, and she smiled.

"Were you ever a boy scout?" She asked, and he straightened.

"No. But I promise anyway. I'll even keep my hands to myself." To prove his point, he shoved his fists into his pockets, and she granted him a full smile.

"Okay, but just for the pizza," she mumbled, grabbing the beers and heading into the living room.

"Just for the pizza," he agreed and followed her.

* * *

The living room held a chill, so he started a fire in the fireplace and turned on some music, but his hands went right back into his pockets as soon as he was done. She slipped off her jacket and hat, her feet curled beneath her as she sat on the sofa, and he is one of the chairs. He made sure he kept his distance, and the conversation was stilted and halting. The tension was finally broken when the pizza arrived. She laughed out loud when the pizza delivery guy was asked to reach into Eli's back pocket for his wallet.

"Hey bro, I don't need a tip that bad," the thin teenaged delivery boy had said before backing away. She had done the honors, gladly. She would have given any excuse to touch him again.

"Okay, you can stop," she relented, and relief washed over him.

"Thank God. I was trying to figure out how I was going to eat like this," he teased.

It only took a moment, but they fell back into easy conversation, the earlier awkwardness forgotten. He spoke of his police work, becoming a homicide detective two years ago. He and Riley worked on major cases, including missing persons. She told of her research in nanotechnology, and he was surprised to discover he understood her jargon quite well. They spoke of books and movies, her favorite being mysteries and thrillers, even the occasional horror story. She had a love of modern art and sad songs. She slept with socks on and often left books in odd places. She discovered that Eli was also an avid reader and spent most of his time listening to music, rarely watched television, and spent most of his weekends working or running errands for Grace. He didn't quite understand art but appreciated beauty.

They talked and flirted until the sun started to fade, and the sky turned a deep shade of navy. He asked about London and Japan, and she asked him about why he'd remained single.

"Just never found the right person." He shrugged. She stared at him for a long time, looking for some fault in him, some imperfection. The only thing she could find was that perhaps he was a little too odd for the average woman, and he was very reserved, almost cold upon first impression. His intensity was terrifying, the way he looked directly at the person he was speaking to, and that whole mind-reading thing was a bit unsettling. But beneath the cool and calm, he was warm and impulsive; he kept that side of himself in check.

"You need to loosen up, Eli," she said as she sipped her second beer, her bare feet resting comfortably in his lap. He sat back, faking indignation.

"I have plenty of fun," he assured her.

"Really?" She folded her arms across her chest.

"I'm having fun right now. Whenever I'm with you, I have a good time." He stared at her for a long time, his hands kneading the soles of her feet.

"I wish you would talk to me, Doc," he said. "You can trust me. I mean, can I at least get your first name?" She bit her lip and looked at him through her lashes.

"I like when you call me, Doc," she demurred.

"Well, Doc, talk to me. Who hurt you?" He asked again, his tone low and steady. She looked at him for a moment and exhaled.

"I didn't have the best childhood. Things weren't always good for me," she mumbled.

"Have you been- were you?" He choked on the words, knowing the answer without her saying a word. She looked at her hands and remained silent. He pulled her forward until she was sitting on his lap and stroked her cheek.

"Look at me, Doc." She slowly lifted her eyes until they met his. "I will never hurt you."

She gave him a sad smile and cupped his face, brushing his lips gently with hers. The feel of her mouth on his made him hot, and he returned the kiss. With agility that she didn't know he possessed, he removed the band from her hair, letting it fall like a silken curtain. His hand moved down to cup her breast, and she pressed into him. Slowly, one hand moved up her thigh, his tongue playing with hers, she smiled against his lips. He looked at her curiously.

"What?" He asked.

"You promised you would keep your hands to yourself. You, Detective Cain, are a horrible boy scout." Sighing dramatically, he held his hands up over his head.

"You're right." He leaned back against the sofa and stared at the ceiling. He was so hard it hurt, but a promise was a promise. When she straddled him, he could feel her heat through her jeans and groaned. She brushed against him, her thighs tightening around him, her breast crushed against his chest. She linked her fingers with his, bringing his hands down to cup her butt as she writhed against him, her mouth warm and soft on his neck. He swallowed hard and looked at her through narrowed eyes. "What are you doing? Not that I'm complaining."

"Well," she said, her mouth close to his, "I never promised anything." She teased before slipping her tongue into his mouth. She tasted of pizza and beer and a warm sweetness that was all her. She ground her hips into him, her hands under his shirt, her nails leaving trails of heat on his bare skin, and he could feel his body tighten and strain against his jeans in response.

"You are making it so hard for me to be good," he mumbled. She smirked and then reached under her shirt, fumbling for a minute. He watched as she slipped a pale pink lace bra from one sleeve and tossed it aside. She took one of his hands, placing it on her breast; he could feel her hardened nipple through the thin material of her shirt. She sighed and leaned into his touch, her teeth raking her bottom lip.

"You play dirty," he mumbled and rolled her onto her back, where she rested against the cool leather of the sofa, his mouth on her throat. He moved down her body, pushing her shirt up, exposing the taut skin of her stomach. He lifted it further, exposing her breasts. He stared for a moment before taking one taut nipple into his mouth, sucking and licking until she arched into him, soft sighs of pleasure escaping her with every stroke of his warm tongue. His fingers worked on the snap of her jeans; when he'd managed to undo the button, he took his time pulling the zipper down so slowly it was agonizing. Finally, his hand moved past the denim and flimsy piece of lace; she called panties to cup her, and she pressed into his hand. She was wet and warm, and he wanted to sink himself into her. She pulled his face up to hers, wrapped her arms around his neck, and kissed him longer and harder than he had ever been kissed before; she took his breath away, her body molded against his, her long denim-clad legs tightening around his hips. She opened her mouth to speak, and his phone buzzed, jumping to life on the coffee table. He glanced at the screen and cursed.

"Shit, shit." He sat back on his haunches and answered, his breath ragged and shallow. "Somebody better be on fucking fire," he barked.

"Jesus," Riley gasped. "No. I-"

He hung up and turned to her. She was already sitting up, looking at her watch, wincing. It was well after seven. She and Eli had been together for almost eight hours. Outside, the sky had darkened. The only light was from the fire that cast an amber glow over her exposed skin.

"I should get going." She gathered her things, slipping her sneakers back on. Eli stood, running a hand over his face in frustration.

"I'll walk you out." He groaned, putting his shoes on so that he could walk her to her car, his body still stiff and aching. He held up her bra, watching her breasts move as she slipped on her jacket. Her nipples stood out in stark relief against her shirt. He licked his lips and shook his head.

"Keep it," she said, a mischievous glint in her eyes.

"I'm going to kill Riley," he grumbled as he followed her outside into the chilly night air.

* * *

They walked in silence, their fingers linked. She unlocked the car door and slipped her things into the back seat. He watched her, his gaze intense. She closed the SUV's back door and turned to face him, half leaning against the driver's door.

"Can I call you sometime?" She took his buzzing cell phone from his hand, noted the call flashing across the readout with a curious lift of her brow. She was tempted to answer to see who was calling and why. She was hoping it wasn't the woman he'd been on a date with the other night because she wanted to kill her. Sighing, she shook her head. What was she doing? She was having murderous thoughts about some unknown woman who held no interest for Eli. Pushing those thoughts to the back of her mind, she punched in her number under the name CeCe.

"CeCe? You don't look like a CeCe to me," he mumbled, but

at least he had a name, something other than Doc.

"Really? So, what would you call me?" Her smile faltered as she looked up at him. He was suddenly standing so close that she had to take a step back. His proximity made her anxious, and without thinking, she bit her lip.

"You're doing it again," he growled, his face hovering over hers, one hand holding her hip, the other at the nape of her neck. He pressed her against the car, holding her firmly to him, his mouth gliding over hers, and she felt her skin grow hot. He started at her cheek and then slowly moved over until his lips were on hers, his tongue exploring the ever-ready sweetness of her mouth. She moaned involuntarily. Her arms snaked around his waist to pull him even closer. She shifted her hip, pressing herself into him. Large warm hands pressed against her back as he backed her into the side of the car, cold metal against hot skin. She was on fire.

Damn it, how did he manage to keep doing this to her. She had never been like this with anyone else.

It took an exceptional effort for him to pull away, but he did. When he did manage to take a step back, she'd been thoroughly kissed. Her body tingled from her scalp to the soles of her feet. She felt herself sway slightly before her eyes drifted open. She stared at him with heavy-lidded eyes, her lips slightly parted.

"Sweeter and sweeter every time," he whispered. Reluctantly backing away from her, he adjusted her hat and stroked her cheek. She climbed into the car on shaky legs and waved as she pulled away from the curb. She watched Eli grow smaller and smaller in the rear-view mirror, her knuckles grasping the steering wheel so tightly that they had turned white.

* * *

*"Oh, mon bon seigneur,"* she thought. *"This is a problem."* How could she keep her distance from a man who drew her

like a magnet? This situation had just gotten a lot more complicated. You can't keep a man at arms distance when he kissed like that. A sexy smile curled at the corners of her mouth as she remembered his touch and his words. The ring of her cell jolted her back to the here and now. Jonas was calling.

"Yes, Father," She tried to clear her throat and sound normal, but she knew she didn't. She had just been thoroughly kissed. You can't sound normal after that.

"Are you alright?" He asked, his voice filled with concern.

"Fine, I'm fine. I'm driving. I assume you got the pictures." He had, and he found them as disturbing as she had. This was saying a lot. What was bothersome to him were the bite marks. Jonas was shocked by the blood loss and the violence.

"Even Fae aren't this vicious. So much blood, so messy. I think you were correct in your assumption, CeCe. This is something different, something demonic," he said. "Something I have never seen before. I need to know what happened in that bathroom. Do whatever is necessary to find out."

"Well, there is one possible option," she mumbled.

"Utilize it. Nicky's time is running out. You need to find him before Briar does. And even though he is trying his best to stall, the Collective won't wait much longer before calling out another locater. One who does not care who you are or what Nicky means to you."

* * *

CeCe mulled over his statement long after she'd hung up. She nervously chewed her bottom lip as she parked her car and marched through the lobby of her apartment building. She knew a way to find out what happened. She knew who could help. The question was, would he be willing to do that for her. She could always make him do it; she had her ways. But then he did seem to be immune to her in that way. The problem wasn't whether he would do it; the question was how long she could resist her attraction to him.

"Oh hell, CeCe, just ask him," she mumbled to herself. Just the thought of calling him so soon sent a nervous tingle through her. The taste of him was still on her lips as she entered her apartment. Dropping her bag onto the nearest sofa, she froze and sniffed the air, her eyes narrowing in expectation. Backing into the entry hall, she deftly opened the closet and pulled out a fencing foil, carefully removing the protective guard that ran from the tip to the base of the shaft. Kicking off her shoes, she padded through the apartment, the foil at the ready. There shouldn't be anyone in here; she had a doorman and security. Damn it.

He jumped from the loft, landing in a predatory crouch in front of her, his hair standing on end. She swung at him, just missing his ear. He hissed at her, fangs bared and charged. He was fast, almost undetectable, as he rocketed across the room. She was faster, swinging out with experienced ease, slicing his cheek, and he backed off when thick dark blood poured from the wound.

"Shit, CeCe. That stings!" He yelled, even though the wound was already healing.

"You scared the shit out of me. You have no idea how easily I could take your head off. What the fuck are you doing here?" She asked, giving him a push before returning the foil to an umbrella stand and running her hands through her hair.

"Don't smile. Do you know how pissed I am with you right now? How did you get in? The entire Collective is looking for you. Briar is looking for you." She said Briar's name with emphasis, and his eyes grew wide.

"You said that I was always welcome. I guess it held over. Why would Briar and the Collective be looking for me?" He asked, lazily stretching as if she hadn't just dropped a bomb on him.

"Briar is looking for you because I asked him to. That was before the Collective decided that you needed to be contained. Why are you here, Nicky? The vampire rock star thing getting old?" She spat, going to the kitchen for a bottle of water.

"Contained?" He asked. "What does that mean, like put me in some safe house? Do I get to go live in the Kent fortress? Or do they shepherd me off to some exotic location for safekeeping?"

"No, it doesn't." She stared at him with sadness in her eyes, and his face softened a little.

"I just wanted to see my best friend. I wanted to let you know that I was okay. Didn't you miss me?" He hopped on the countertop, smiling broadly. Gone was his natural tan. His skin was pale and powdery; his deep blue eye seemed watered down, almost pastel. He looked hollow, a faded version of the superstar he once was. He was wasting away. It was evident that Nicky did not have the fangs to be one of the undead.

"Of course, I missed you, but you're in so much trouble. Nicky, what have you done? Who did this to you?" She asked, exhausted, and saddened by his appearance. She took his face in her hands and pressed her forehead to his, tears streaming down her face.

"It wasn't my choice, CeCe. I thought after it happened that I would make the best of it. I just can't do it, C." He pulled away and went over to the window.

"What do you mean it wasn't your choice?" CeCe barked. "It's part of the covenant."

"I don't know what it was or who it was. It changed from this groupie-"

"I have told you about bringing groupies back to your apartment and hotel rooms. You never listened to me, and now you've been killed." She slapped his arm. "Was she *Fae*? Was she *Lycan*?" She sat crossed-legged on the sofa, her eyes on the back of his head.

Nicky stood at the window, in dark jeans and a black t-shirt that seemed to hang off him. His hair looked almost white against the moonlight. There was nothing worse than watching a vampire starve himself. He would eventually die, and it would not be pretty or painless.

"Here," She went to her refrigerator and took out a bottle of red wine. She uncorked it and poured some into a glass beer mug, and placed it into the microwave for a few minutes before handing it to him.

"Drink this. You need to eat." She insisted and watched as he finished the entire thing. Once he handed her the mug, she repeated the process and prodded him into finishing the entire bottle. "Now tell me what happened."

He returned to his place at the window, staring down at the street below.

"She-it-was something I have never seen before. Older. It wasn't completely vampire, or lycan, or a Fae for that matter, some sort of shifter, I think. It was able to change- to make herself into something- horrible. I remember being bitten. I don't remember dying. I remember waking up in that coffin and that I couldn't breathe, not that it matters anymore. I remember someone else being in the room at the funeral home. I couldn't see, but I could feel someone. I thought it was you for a minute, but then I realized it was a man. It was like he was there, but not there." He turned around to face her; his eyes were luminescent with tears.

"It wants me to come to it. It wants me to be a part of some sort of nest or commune. It kept telling me that I was special, rare in a world of ordinary. And that there would be more; that I was beautiful. It wasn't there when I woke, I thought that your sire would be there when you wake, but I was alone. Except for the man, but I knew he was just watching from somewhere else, some other time. Anyway, I left the funeral home looking for- I don't know what. It took me a while before I realized that I was dead. It took a stoned fan on Royal Street to tell me. '*Dude*,' he said, 'you're *dead. Wicked.*' " He mimicked and shook his head. "I looked for my maker, but she's –it's not normal. Not even for you guys, it's bizarre. I can feel it, and I can hear it, but we have no home. I have no home. I have no clan, no family – I'm lost."

"That is unusual. Your maker should have been there, Nicky. It's part of the covenant. Sires are responsible for their brood. They teach you how to hunt, how to survive. You become family." He was kneeling before her in the blink of an eye, his head on her lap.

"You are my family. If I wanted to be changed, I would have come to you or Remy. I would have chosen to be a Kent. I didn't want to be this way. I just don't know what else to do. Sunlight doesn't work. It hurts, doesn't kill." She stroked his hair and thought for a moment and shook her head.

"You don't want to die, Nicky," she whispered.

"I don't want to live like this either." She loved Nicky, even in his present state, but she couldn't hide him here. He would have to be somewhere safe, somewhere without so many windows. Nervously, she chewed her bottom lip as her mind worked overtime.

"Well, as much as I love you, you can't stay here." She sighed after a long while. She went to the telephone. "There's no protection for you here. That just isn't going to work. We need someplace with a dark room so that you can sleep."

"Because of your cop? You reek of him, by the way." Remy's voice came from the elevator that acted as her front door.

"What the hell- How'd you get in here?" She screamed in frustration. "What's the point of having a freakin' doorman if anyone can just waltz into my apartment?"

"I have my ways." He smirked, his fangs bared, his eyes completely black.

"You're dating a cop?" Nicky asked, still lying in a heap on the sofa.

"Not dating. She's planning on fucking him, though. That is if she hasn't already. Isn't that right, Little Sis?" Remy stroked her cheek, and she slapped his hand away, fire lighting her eyes.

"Don't start with me right now, Remy. I need you to take care of Nicky. Keep him safe. Keep him out of sight. Take him to Mandeville, he'll be safe there, and I'll let the Collective know that he's been taken care of. I need to get a handle on his maker. " In one swift movement, she'd hoisted Nicky into the air by his collar, his feet dangling like those of a marionette, and shoved him towards Remy. "We will find out what this thing is that it changed you, Nick. Remy, don't come into my apartment again without buzzing in first." She walked past them to press the call button for the elevator.

"Or what?" Remy was at her side in an instant, in that same moment, the tips of his fangs brushing seductively at her throat. She gave him a hard shove and spun on her heel, lifting her foil from the umbrella stand and held it at his crotch. She moved the sword upward in one swift movement, then back down, slicing the buttons from his shirt, grazing his skin beneath. He inhaled as the air hit him.

"Never forget that I'm older, faster, and stronger than you. And I can gut you like a fish." She gave his crotch a tap with the tip of the sword and winked at him. "Keep him safe, Remy." She was suddenly serious, and Remy gave her a quick nod.

"Who keeps a fucking sword? I mean, really?" Nicky asked Remy as the elevator doors slid closed.

*  *  *

He'd watched her car until it was just a dot in the distance before he looked at the buzzing phone in his hand. "I swear you have the worse timing in the world. What is so damned important?" He snapped.

"Jesus, E. Who pissed in your cereal? I've just been calling to ask if you wanted to come over for dinner." Eli deflated, all his anger and frustration seeping out of him. "I didn't – interrupt anything, did I?"

"You did. Now CeCe's gone, thanks for that." He headed back into the house, staring at the discarded hairband on the floor, and smiled. The fire was down to embers, and the remnants of their dinner, an empty pizza box and drained beer bottles, sat idly on the coffee table.

"Who the hell is CeCe?" Riley snorted. "Another woman du jour Grace ambushed you with?"

"Doctor Kent." There was a long silence followed by a hoot of laughter.

"No fucking way." Riley laughed.

"Yes. We ran into each other at the coffee shop and decided to eat dinner together. She's such a cool chick, Riley. The more I'm around her, the more I like her." He held the thin, delicate lace of her bra and sighed. This fragile material was a physical representation of the CeCe Kent he had seen today, soft, pretty, and easy to break. There was so much to her; he still didn't know, but he wanted to know all about her. He smiled, putting it up to his nose, he inhaled. It smelled of lavender and vanilla and her.

"Are you-sniffing? Oh, E, are you crying? "

"No, I'm not crying. She left something, and it smells good." Guiltily, he shoved the bra in-between the sofa cushions. Riley was silent for a split second and then started to laugh.

"Oh my God, Elijah Cain, are you sniffing her panties."

"No," Eli spat indignantly.

"You are, aren't you, you big perv. You're sniffing Doctor Kent's underwear."

"I'm not sniffing her panties." He argued, and Riley laughed even harder.

"Oh man, Eli-"

"It's a bra. And don't call me a perv," Eli mumbled. Riley laughed even harder still until it was a loud snorting guffaw.

"I'm hanging up now." He grumbled, and Riley attempted to stifle his mirth.

"Okay, Okay. I'm sorry." He held his laughter for as long as he could, which was about thirty seconds before he started again. Rolling his eyes, Eli blew out a big puff of air.

"Good-bye, Riley."

❋ ❋ ❋

*The click heels on the obsidian floors echoed in her head as she rushed towards the raised voices at the end of the hall. When she burst into the room, they all looked at her in confused irritation. The Dark sisters, three women, two men, looked at her in mild confusion before continuing their usual nonsensical, unending debate, which now bordered on laughable.*

*"I have news," she gushed, her eyes alight with excitement, her smile turning her pretty face into something feral and hungry. They ignored her and continued to talk at each other until their voices melded into one loud disorganized bellow. Irritated, she stomped her foot and slammed a hand on the dark wooden table in the center of the room. Those seated looked at her with a start, those standing slowly quieted, all eyes focused on her.*

*"Now that I have your attention," she said, straightening the dark suit jacket she wore. "I have news that may help our cause." She said, her eyes on the woman at the head of the table. She was pale with snow-white hair and an ethereal smile, her delicate fingers laced together on the table as she waited.*

*"It seems that we have a Ghost." She squealed, and there was a gasp.*

*"What type of ghost?" The woman at the head of the table asked, her eyes narrowed suspiciously.*

*"Not sure, but he's big. Whatever he is, he's powerful and ancient. And he's very into our precious Doctor Kent. If I'm right, I believe that he may be our way in. He's been bound, though, but if you're ever around him, you can feel the power just beneath the surface. And get this, his eyes-just like hers. They change color like hers. That has to mean something."*

*"And he doesn't have allegiance to the Collective?" The woman asked, leaning forward, a new sparkle in her eyes. As if she'd struck gold, she smiled.*

*"No, my Queen. He is unclassified. He can be turned without*

repercussion. *If he's who I think he is, we can take down the Collective and the Council."*

*The Dark Queen sat back with a smile, "Come sit next to me and tell me everything you know."*

# CHAPTER SIX

Eli was startled when his phone rang that night. He was in the first-floor study he'd converted into a gym when his cell phone sang to life. He picked up the phone, breathless and sweaty.

"Yeah," he breathed.

"Detective Cain, am I interrupting you?" She asked, her voice low and sultry. He smiled, his voice lowered to a seductive baritone.

"No, I was just working out, Doctor Kent. It seems I had some tension I needed to release. What can I do for you?" He could feel himself smiling like an idiot.

"I know that this is weird, and you could say no if you want, but I was wondering if you could help me out? I need your services. I can pay you."

"Pay me? What *services* are you requiring?" He teased, unable to stop his widening grin. He wiped the sweat from his brow and listened as she explained. She started to speak, then paused, then started again. Suddenly it burst from her in a rush, the photos, and Jonas's private investigation into Nicky's death, her feeling that something was very, very wrong, and his unique talent.

"I'll understand if you don't want to do this. I know you could get into trouble, but this is bothering us. I haven't told anyone what you could do, but we're sure it wasn't an accident or a suicide. We just need to know for sure. I need to know." She was finally silent, and Eli imagined that she was anxiously biting her bottom lip, waiting for his response. He only mulled it over for a moment before he spoke.

"Let me call Riley, and we'll meet you at Nicky's apartment

in thirty minutes," he said. "Don't worry. We'll help you."

*"What harm could it do?"* He thought as he ended the call. Besides, he'd get to see her again, and that was always a plus. He sprinted up the stairs to shower, speed dialing Riley as he went.

"I need a favor." He said when Riley picked up.

* * *

Nicky Sky had lived in the penthouse apartment of an exclusive and expensive building in the center of Downtown New Orleans that overlooked the Mississippi River. Eli and Riley found Doctor Kent sitting in the lobby, waiting nervously. She was in a yellow velour tracksuit, a sheer white t-shirt beneath the jacket, and white Nike's, her hair in intricate braids down her back. If he didn't know better, he would have mistaken her for a teenager. She nervously wiped her palms on her thighs as she stood to greet them.

"I'm so glad you could come. I know you didn't have to, but it just bothers-" Eli held up his hand to stop her, nodding his head slightly, and she immediately fell silent. Riley watched their interaction with something close to awe. They didn't speak but simply fell into step together and headed towards the elevators. The doorman watched them for a moment pressed the button for the penthouse, his arms folded across his barrel-like chest.

"I'm sorry, but no one is allowed in the penthouse. Not until they clear out the rock star's stuff. Too many fans have tried to sneak in," he said in his most authoritative tone. He was a large man, with dark eyes and what Eli supposed was a permanent scowl.

"Of course, Stan," CeCe spoke in the sweetest tone she could muster. "But honestly, do I look like a fan? Do you remember me, don't you, Stan? I'm Doctor Kent. Nicky was my best friend."

"Sorry, Doc. No one gets in. Not even you." He shrugged helplessly. "Rules."

She touched his hand, her eyes locked with his, and she smiled.

"I understand. But you will let me in, of course. My friends and I need to get up there, and you will let us up. You want to let us in, don't you, Stan?" His eyes got heavy, and he stared at her sleepily, his head bobbing up and down slowly.

"Thank you, Stan. I appreciate it," she purred. "Now you go and make sure no one bothers us."

Without another word, the burly doorman stepped aside and went to stand at the lobby entrance. He didn't budge as she pushed the call button and waited as the elevator doors slid open. Eli and Riley shared a puzzled look as they stepped into the waiting elevator with her.

\* \* \*

"*Holy hell*," Riley mumbled. "Okay, the gay rumors were definitely wrong. No gay man worth his salt would live in this-designer hell." Garish was an understatement when it came to Nicky's style. The apartment was a study in overkill. They entered the foyer and were greeted with beige marble from floor to ceiling. The chandelier, which hung low enough for Eli and CeCe to duck as they entered, was a god-awful combination of brassy gold with bronze monkeys dangling from it holding crystal bananas.

The main hallway was an assortment of Greek statues in various stages of undress and a fountain that protruded so far away from the wall that they had to walk single file to get around it.

The living room was covered in a white shag rug that resembled fake fur; there was a faded bloodstain in the middle of it as if someone had tried halfheartedly to clean it, and none of the furniture seemed to match. There was a Victorian sofa in deep green and an art deco dining room in black and white, his kitchen was a study in stainless steel, and his bedroom was gothic chic. Statues from Greece, Japan, Africa, and South America dotted the landscape, none fitting into the overall theme of the rooms they housed. He had two grand pianos in the dining room, one white with silver trim, one black with gold trim. In his music room, which had once been a bedroom, vintage guitars lined up in Plexiglas cases, all on display and some autographed. He collected vintage posters from The Who, The Beatles, Jimi Hendrix, and Woodstock.

"He was eclectic," Eli mumbled. CeCe smiled lovingly at the collection of oddly placed furnishings, running her fingers over a marble bust.

"He was lazy and rich. His decorator was an art student with a tight ass and big boobs, and he let her do whatever she wanted because he thought she was cute. The only rooms in this place that are one hundred percent Nicky were this one and his studio." She pointed to a room they hadn't seen; a suit of Samurai armor blocked it from view.

They walked through the apartment, and Riley became fascinated by Nicky's pictures with music legends, The Rolling Stones, Stevie Wonder, Madonna, Eddie Vedder, Prince, Lou Reed, Michael Jackson, and Elvis Costello all smiling at the new rock god. There were pictures of Nicky partying with Beyonce and Jay- Z, Lady GaGa, Kanye West, Chris Martin, and Gwyneth Paltrow and The Black-Eyed Peas. He turned to point out a photo of Nicky Sky with Bono and Green Day at the Superdome when he noticed Eli staring at the blood-stained rug, his thumbs rubbing at his itching fingertips.

CeCe stood nearby, biting her bottom lip, her hands clenching and unclenching. She watched Eli curiously before moving closer to Riley, who stood frozen, his eyes glued to Eli's back.

"What's happening?" She whispered anxiously.

"He's there. Just watch him; make sure he doesn't hit his head. When he goes down, he goes down hard. Try not to touch him. I think it brings him out of it," he mumbled and moved to stand closer to Eli.

\* \* \*

As Eli stared curiously at the faded bloodstain on the rug, the chill in his bones started, and the air left his lungs. The room went hazy, and the days moved backward at breakneck speed. He felt people moving around him, in reverse, coming in and out of view until finally, everything came to a bone-jarring halt. Eli felt a little winded as if he'd been running, his heart racing. The room came into razor-sharp focus in shades of black, white, and gray.

Nicky Sky rolled onto his side, from his place on the rug, just inside the open door leading to the balcony. He sat up, looking around the room groggily. He was in a white t-shirt and snug-fitting jeans, debris from a raucous party surrounding him. Outside, the midnight sky was split in two by the sharp crack of lightning. He rose slowly, touched a swollen red mark on his neck, and flinched. He turned to walk out of the room, his back covered in bright red, his hair sticking to it in thick clumps. The smell of the place made Eli nauseous. The thick scent of blood and bile made his stomach turn. Nicky peeled the shirt off and entered his bedroom; Eli inched behind him. There was a woman sprawled across the bed, naked and immobile, her long blond hair hanging past her shoulders, covering her face.

Eli blinked and found himself in the bathroom as Nicky stripped and entered the shower, his head down, eyes closed, and water soaking his head. Slowly he reached up, and his eyes widened in surprise at the dried blood on the back of his hand. He looked at both hands, his face contorting as he opened his mouth to scream in horror. He looked at his feet as the bright red pooled and went down the drain. Stumbling out of the shower, he noticed the bloody footprints that led to the shower and screamed a silent scream of terror. Wet and naked, he jettisoned from the shower, slipping on the uncovered white marble, his ankle snapping, twisting at the most awkward angle possible. Eli winced in pain for him. Nicky's pretty face twisted in anguish; he was yelling something, something Eli couldn't hear, but Eli mumbled "*Brittney*" out loud.

Something behind him moved, and Eli spun to see the blond get up, her face hidden as she contorted, and her bones moving beneath her flawless skin. It made his skin crawl to see it break down, moving crablike towards the bathroom door. It moved quickly, scampering from one side of the room to the other, the entire time, its features contorting, reshaping, the skin-crawling as if a million centipedes were writhing just beneath the surface.

"Oh, God." Eli groaned, tears filling his eyes as he watched the thing approach.

Nicky was pulling himself up, tears in his big blue eyes; he seemed paralyzed with fear as the thing moved closer to the room. It passed through Eli, and he felt sick loneliness, pain, and pure rage riling in the creature. It paused for a moment, and Eli was sure if he felt his presence the same way Nicky had at the funeral home, but it continued to move toward Nicky.

It touched his cheek, its mouth close to his neck, then it was biting him, a dozen needle-like teeth tearing the flesh at Nicky's throat. He went down hard, his head slamming against the floor, his body rigid as it drank from him. Blood coursed from his neck in great tributaries, pooling on the floor beneath him. He began to cough bubbles of blood as he choked, his body shaking violently, but he didn't fight. The little monster bit him all over, in some sort of frenzy; it seemed almost sexual as it rubbed its naked body over Nicky's prone form, smearing blood across pale skin. It was vulgar in a sick, visceral way. Eli heaved, tears filling his eyes, but he didn't move.

Finally, the thing stopped when Nicky lay utterly still, a gaping wound at his throat, his body covered in tiny holes. It crouched on his chest, a curious look on its face. It touched

Nicky's mouth, and he immediately began to vomit, his body purging itself of everything. It watched this with something like fascination before turning Nicky's face, pulling his jaw open. It leaned closer, so close that they were nearly kissing, and vomited something vile and dark red into Nicky's mouth. He coughed. His body seemed to vibrate, fighting against it, but the thing held a clawed hand over his mouth. He convulsed, unable to breathe or lift his limbs. He was paralyzed, Eli realized, not yet dead but very near. Then suddenly, he was still. The thing stood slowly, watching him with a look of appreciation and wonder, and then it walked out of the room, passing through Eli as it did, and the room went black.

❄ ❄ ❄

"Detective Cain." He was on his knees, CeCe kneeling in front of him, holding his face in her hands.

"Eli." It took a moment before he could speak or focus. He was having trouble breathing for some reason.

"Take your time. Breathe, slow deep breaths," she said, and he realized she was cradling his head against her chest. She smelled of honeysuckle, lavender, and vanilla. Her tone was soothing as he regained his ability to breathe.

He stood slowly, his legs shaking.

"I need to get the fuck out of here." Riley draped one of Eli's arms around his shoulder, and CeCe took the other. Together they helped him out of the apartment and to the elevator where he slumped against the wall, his eyes closed as he tried to forget that awful little - elf? Fairy? Hobbit? What the hell was it?

He didn't speak until they were in the lobby, and he had gained some semblance of his composure. As they crossed the lobby at an advanced clip, the doorman waved absently, telling them to have a good night, his face blank, eyes vacant.

"Thank You." CeCe brushed his cheek with the tips of her

fingers. The doorman blinked and yawned as if he were waking from a dream. He watched the three of them curiously but said nothing.

Eli stared at her as they continued to the parking garage. When Riley jogged ahead of them to the car, Eli grabbed her arm, pulling her aside.

"I don't know what kind of shit you're getting me into, but I think I just saw your friend killed by a vampire elf," he whispered angrily. She looked at him strangely.

"What?" She was stunned. His grip on her arm was like banded steel. His eyes flashed bright blue for a moment, and she felt her pulse race.

"I have no idea what you're talking about." She spoke in a hushed whisper. "What did you see?" He looked up to see Riley staring at them and let her go.

"What I saw was some fucked up shit," he grumbled and walked away, his head pounding. Riley continued to walk, staying ahead of Eli and CeCe, not wanting to intrude on whatever was going on between them. She trotted after Eli, her shoes making no noise as she approached.

"What happened? Was it an accident? Did he kill himself? What happened?" She stood in front of him, blocking his path. Eli moved left, and she moved with him blocking his progress.

"Talk to me." She placed her hands on his chest, right above his heart, and looked into his eyes. He stared back, his jaw clenched, and the garage became an inferno in seconds. She was in his head, reliving the memory as if she'd been there, tears streaming from her eyes as energy pulsed beneath her fingers. The heat was unbearable; the fluorescent bulbs began to explode over their heads in rapid succession.

Riley ducked and covered his head as sparks and glass showered over him. The heat reached such an intense level that windows in the cars parked nearby begin to crack, car alarms sang to life until they reached a deafening chaotic cacophony. Riley moved out of the garage in an attempt to avoid being burned by the falling sparks and looked up to see headlights and lights exploding throughout the four-story parking garage. There were surprised shouts and yelling as the building lit up like the fourth of July.

"What the fuck-" Riley mumbled.

CeCe began to shake, her body racked with uncontrollable sobs, but she was unable to stop. She couldn't tear her eyes from Eli's. Her face contorted in misery as the demon elf came to the forefront, massacring her friend. She made a noise that was somewhere between a sob and a scream, her knees giving out, and she finally released Eli's gaze as she sank to the ground. He took a shaky step back; his head throbbed to the point of blindness. He closed his eyes and knelt before her.

"What did you do to me?" He asked.

"I'm sorry," she choked, slowly rising to her feet. She moved sluggishly, her legs weak, and her vision blurred. She started wandering, her legs unstable; her head felt as if it would explode from the pain then she felt herself falling before she blacked out.

❋ ❋ ❋

*He was cold. This place was cold and still, the only sound the gentle brushing of the wind against the linen curtains that surrounded the silken pillows upon which he rested his aching body. The room smelled of exotic spices, and he could hear the crackle of a fire somewhere, but the warmth never reached him. He rolled onto his side in a ball, trying to preserve his body heat, when someone entered the room.*

*He opened his eyes and sat up startled, a rush of terror and panic overwhelming him. He absently clutched his chest and heard the jingle of bells. Looking down, he saw that he had bracelets around his delicate wrists, bracelets with dozens of tiny golden bells that sang with every movement of hands that weren't his. He was confused for a moment, staring at the delicate fingers, and noted that the bracelets also had a small loop made into them, circles that looked as if something was supposed to be laced or hooked into them. He stared at the places where the metal had been worn down, the shine dulled from multiple uses, and frowned. These were slave bracelets, he thought. He was a slave.*

*A shadow moved beyond the curtain, a hand slowly moving up to part the thin material. He swallowed hard and waited as a man came forward, his face stern but familiar. He smiled, but it didn't reach his midnight eyes, and a new chill went down his spine. He hated this man, not just hate; he wanted him to die a painful and humiliating death. The man wore a long besht, a robe with a stiff collar embroidered in gold, his hair was thick and curly, and his face, which once had been handsome, was set in a determined scowl as he stared into the darkness.*

*"Calie, come to me." He spoke in a deep, authoritative tone, in an ancient form of Arabic, yet he understood it clearly. Before he knew what he was doing, Eli felt himself rising from the bed. No, he thought, this wasn't his dream. This was someone else's dream. No, not a dream, he realized when his feet touched the cold stone floor.*

*This was a memory. This was HER memory. Somehow, Eli had fallen into Doc's memories.*

*He felt himself moving around to where the man stood waiting, his eyes on the bells that jingled at his ankles with each cautious step. She came to stand before the man, her eyes on his feet, which were covered by gold slippers that twinkled in the dim firelight. She felt the warmth of the fire here, warming skin that had been covered in gooseflesh. She was only a few inches shorter than this man, but he was built like a wall. She, on the other hand, was slim, malnourished, and sick. The man looked past her to a table laden with untouched food.*

*"Why do you not eat? Is the lamb not to your liking?" He asked, his tone laced with concern.*

*"It is fine," she mumbled. He went to the table, leaning over and inhaling, before turning to look at her. She avoided his gaze, knowing he smelled what she had dozens of times since she'd come here. They had put horse dung in her food again. It was the servants, the ones he'd trusted to care for his most precious plaything,*

*and yet again, they had failed.*

*He called to his guard, who entered without looking upon the woman standing at the foot of the bed. They never looked at her. They were not allowed to lay eyes on her. Those who had dared to look upon the face of the King's obsession had paid with their lives. As would the servant responsible for her care. She used to feel bad for those poor souls, but now she felt nothing. Their misery was over; her suffering would never end as long as this man lived.*

*The guard received his order and left as quickly and as quietly as he'd come, his eyes never even drifting in her direction.*

*"Have you been washed in preparation for the service of your king?" He asked, a smile playing across his lips. He touched her hair, letting the dark silken strands slip through his fingers. One hand moved down the front of the silken crimson robe she wore. Stepping closer, he released the tie and pushed it off her shoulders, watching it fall to the floor. He tugged at the gold chain around her waist, pulling her forward so he could inhale the perfume of her skin.*

*"Yes," she whispered in a tired husky voice. He leaned forward, his lips brushing hers, and Eli could feel her revulsion and the subsequent relent as she succumbed to the kiss. It would only be worse if she fought him. He pulled her closer, crushing her to him as he sank his fingers into her hair. She remained limp in his arms, even as his swollen cock pressed into her. She cringed but remained still, compliant as he ran his hands over her body.*

*"I would give you the world if only you loved me. I would make you my queen," he said, his brow furrowed in pained desperation. "Tell me that you are mine, that I have your heart, my sweet little goddess," he begged. He stroked her cheek, but she remained silent. She didn't have to say anything, it didn't matter what she said, and he would never let her go.*

*He grasped her face, his fingers biting into the tender flesh of her cheeks as he forced her to look at him.*

*"Say you love me. You want me, do you not?" She stared at him and forced her mouth to move through the pain.*

*"Yes, I love you. I want you, my king," she said, her tone flat.*

*He released her face, his hand moving to cup the soft curls at her apex roughly. He forced a finger inside of her, the pain sharp and unyielding as he sought a real answer to his question. She bit the inside of her cheek to keep from screaming out.*

*"Your body does not lie as easily as your mouth." He bit. He forced her back, grasping her wrists and holding them over her head. Eli could feel the bracelets cutting into her already raw wrists as the small hoops were fitted on hooks secured to posts at the foot of her bed. She didn't make a sound when he did the same to her ankles, pulling her body until she was spread eagle and exposed. Her body was taut, pulled, and stretched until only her toes grazed the cool floor. She had become familiar to this humiliation; she had become accustomed to much more in the time she been here.*

*"I see I must prove to you again that you are mine and mine alone," he mumbled. She said nothing when the "king" dropped his robes, exposing a soldier's toned, muscled body. He was already hard, his eyes dark and sinister as he approached. Roughly, he grasped one full soft breast in one hand just before forcing himself inside of her. The pain was abrupt, intense, and she could not help the whimper that escaped her as he began to thrust into her body. He continued to push into her with a ferocity that would leave her weak and bleeding when he was done. She refused to scream as he tortured her already sore and tired body. Instead, she bore the agony in silence, unable to stop the tears that flowed freely from her eyes as she prayed for death to claim her.*

❊ ❊ ❊

Eli woke as pain ripped through the pit of his stomach. He was panting and drenched in sweat, his heart aching. He rose from the guest bed slowly, his body hurting all over, and stumbled down the hall to his bedroom. The cool wood of the floors felt good on his aching feet, and the warmth from the heater took the sweaty chill from his bare chest, but his head still throbbed from the fireworks earlier that night. Only now, his chest hurt with an ache he had never experienced before.

Pushing the door open, he stared at her, tossing in her fitful sleep. He and Riley had gotten her to his house and put her into his bed. Riley had undressed her, but now Eli stood looking at her in her pale-yellow bra and panties if that's what you wanted to call them. She'd kicked the covers off, her body kissed by moonlight. Easing into the room, he tiptoed to the bed and covered her, and brushed a stray curl from her face. She looked so vulnerable and peaceful, her brow slightly furrowed, her lips pursed in an angry scowl.

He stroked her cheek, and she flinched, then relaxed into his touch. His heart ached at the thought of what he'd just experienced. She'd been raped. That was why she was so closed off. She had been hurt and damaged, and the nightmare had been a prolonged experience from the way she spoke. He took a deep breath and shook it off.

As surreal as the dream had been, it had also been vivid and detailed. He'd felt the bracelets cutting into her wrists and ankles, the pain as the self-proclaimed king had forced himself into her. The dream had been like an Arabian fairytale gone bloody.

"What did they do to you, Doc?"

He sat on the edge of the bed; he intended to lie beside her until he saw the silver chain glinting around her neck. He touched it, pulling it from the covers to look at the pendant that dangled between his fingers, and shook his head.

"Okay," he thought, "Now, you really have some explaining to do."

❊ ❊ ❊

She awoke with a start; the sun was beaming down on her in the wrong direction. She sat up, disoriented, and looked around her unfamiliar surroundings. The room was large and decidedly masculine. The floors were a polished hardwood stained black, the walls a pale shade of slate, trimmed in bright white. She looked at the dark mahogany furniture, a dresser with silver pulls, a black leather chair in the corner, and the dark wood and leather headboard. The wall pictures were all black and white landscapes, all with the same black wooden frames. A flat-screen television was mounted on the wall above a fireplace facing the bed and was housed in the wall that shared a new white door. She was beneath a fluffy down comforter in the prettiest shade of teal blue she'd ever seen. Lifting the covers, she realized that someone had undressed her; she wore only her bra and panties. Lying back against the pillows, she closed her eyes and tried to block out the memories of the night before. She needed to talk to Jonas; they had a rogue on their hands.

"How do you feel?" She opened one eye and looked at Eli, leaning in the doorway that led to what she assumed to be the bathroom, wearing a towel tucked tightly around his waist, another draped around his shoulders, and nothing else. Water beaded on his bare skin, curling the soft, springy hair on his chest. He smiled at her, showing those perfect white teeth and those damned dimples. There was a snag in her chest, and warmth growing much lower. She crossed her legs tightly and closed her eyes.

"Like little men are exploding, blasting caps behind my eyes. Where am I?" She mumbled, chancing another look at him. He was broad-shouldered, she had known that, but his skin was flawless. Thoughts of running her tongue from his neck to his navel seemed to invade her mind. She wanted to touch the muscles of his stomach; if there were such a thing as an eight pack, she would say he had it. He was moving now. She watched through her lashes as he came closer to the bed, sitting on the edge, the towel falling slightly open. With effort, she averted her gaze, and he adjusted to make sure he didn't flash her.

"My house, my bed. You went down quickly last night. Riley caught you right before you hit the ground."

"Did you-did we-sleep-"

"I slept in another room." He answered with more than a little regret in his voice.

"Did you—undress me?" He nodded slowly.

"I was a perfect gentleman. It was not easy."

*"Oh, my Lord,"* She mumbled, closed her eyes, and pulled the comforter over her head. He laughed, a low sexy chuckle, and she squeezed her eyes shut.

"I'm teasing. Riley undressed you. I'll get you some aspirin and something to drink. Tea? Coffee? There are some things we need to discuss."

"Coffee would be great," came her muffled reply. He laughed again, and she felt the mattress give as he rose and moved away from the bed.  There was an extended silence, and she peeked over the edge of the covers to see Eli in the bathroom. He'd closed the door only slightly, and the angle of the mirror gave her a view of his perfect ass as he slipped on his boxer briefs and a pair of well-worn and faded blue jeans. Shaking her head, she pulled the covers back over her face as he exited the room to pad downstairs barefoot.

Once he was out of the room, she dashed into the bathroom, and using a towel and toothpaste as a makeshift toothbrush, she brushed her teeth, scrubbed her face until it shone fresh and clean, then hurriedly undid the frayed braids from her hair, giving it a good combing through with her fingers. She looked at herself in the mirror, giving her armpits a sniff and adjusting her boobs, before catapulting herself back into the bed, under the covers, and feigned a pounding headache.

Eli had a cup of coffee and a bottle of aspirin in his hands when he came back. The aroma of fresh hot coffee and cream filled the room, and she inhaled deeply, smiling in anticipation. He sat gingerly on the bed, handing her the cup. She sipped slowly as he opened the aspirin bottle, shaking two into her hand. He'd remembered how she took her coffee, she realized.

"Three sugars, two creams," he mumbled with a shy smile.

It always struck her that a man so beautiful and straightforward could also be sweet and shy.

"Are we going to talk about it, or are you going to keep lying to me?" He asked. His voice was light, but she knew he was serious. "There is more to this story than you're letting on. There is more to you, right?"

"I'm not lying to you." She swallowed the pills, her eyes on him as she sipped her coffee. When she felt the heat in the room rise, she looked down into the mug, suddenly fascinated by the swirling brown liquid. He placed his fingers under her chin and forced her to look at him.

"Explain this." He held up a long thin silver chain, on the end of which hung a unique pendant with a heart with tribal wings sprouting from the sides. She looked down at herself and realized that he must have removed it when he'd undressed her.

"It's something I've had for a while," she said, reaching for it. He pulled back, holding it out of her reach.

"Ok." He nodded. "Then explain this." He held the pendent next to his chest, watching the expression on her face transitioned from confusion to realization to astonishment. She leaned forward and ran her fingertips over the dark mark just above his heart. She hadn't seen it before, but they matched.

"A birthmark?" She asked incredulously. He nodded but remained silent, watching her for any indication that she could tell him more. She bit her lip, and then in a quick movement, tossed the covers back. She moved closer, turning her back to him, and lifted her hair. Just below her hairline at the nape of her neck, was an identical mark. He ran his fingers over the mark, and a chill went down her spine. He ran his hands over her bare shoulders; his lips touched her skin, warm and soft, moving slowly up to her neck. She sighed and let her backrest against his chest. When he cupped her breasts, she decided that letting Eli Cain kiss her while she was half-naked in his bed was not the best idea. She eased out of his arms and shook her head.

"Honestly, I have no idea what's going on. All I know is that Thing killed my best friend in the world for whatever reason." She turned back to face him, covering herself with the comforter.

"But he's not really dead, is he?" Instead of answering, she sipped her coffee. But did she need to answer; they both knew that the French Quarter's sightings were real. She knew more than that, but she wouldn't allow him into that part of her head. She took the necklace from him and slipped it over her head. He stared as it rested perfectly between her breasts. "You know what this mark means don't you?"

"I should really get going. I promised Jonas that I would supervise the staff for tomorrow's Thanksgiving dinner. I have some things to do before I drive across the lake in the morning-" She tossed the covers back without thinking and stood before him in pale yellow lace that left very little to the imagination. He'd honestly forgotten that Thanksgiving was the next day. Looking at her at that moment, all six feet of glowing caramel skin and dark wavy hair, he'd forgotten his name. He couldn't think of anything except that amazing ass of hers only a foot from his face. He wanted to bite it, he thought. He reached out and ran a hand over the waistband of the scrap of lace she considered underwear, and her breath caught. He smiled and licked his lips; the blood rushed from his head to another more alert body part. His mouth went dry, and his throat felt as if it sealed shut.

"We aren't done." Eli cleared his throat and tried to look away as she unfolded the thin white t-shirt she'd worn beneath the soft yellow velour tracksuit jacket.

"I believe we are. I asked you to help, and you did; I'll tell Jonas what you saw, and he'll look into it. You can get back to your life. You can forget about me." He frowned as she tried to influence him the way she'd influenced the doorman the night before. Only it wasn't working. She was pushing, trying to erase her from his memory, only he pushed back. Startled, she backed off.

She turned her back to him again. His eyes roamed freely over her muscular thighs and calves. She was flawless. Something about the smooth line of her spinal column made him want to run his tongue from the nape of her neck down to the crack of her wonderfully round ass. He wanted her more than he'd ever wanted another woman in his life. It caused an ache in the pit of his stomach and a throbbing much lower; quite frankly, he burned for her.

"Have you ever done that before? Shared someone's memories?" He asked, his voice strained and heavy.

"No." She answered quickly, her voice sounding shrill to her ears. She flinched and cursed herself. He rose slowly, coming to stand behind her, his hands on her shoulders.

"Have you ever shared an attraction or bond to anyone as strong as ours?" He was closer, his body so close that she wanted to move back to solidify their connection.

"No." This time she managed a more level tone, much to her relief. Every nerve in her body felt as if someone had taken a torch to them.

"Have you ever wanted anyone as much as you want me?" She closed her eyes and tried to calm her racing heart.

"Just stop, okay? You're making this too hard, and it shouldn't be this hard to leave. Let it go, Elijah. Let me go. I'm not what you think I am." Her voice, barely a whisper, quivered. Her hands shook nervously, and she balled the t-shirt in her hands.

"Do you know that ever since I met you, I can't think straight? All I think about is you- kissing you, touching you. And I have a feeling it's the same for you, isn't it?" He smelled of mahogany teakwood and soap, his breath minty with a hint of coffee brushed her cheek. He took her earlobe into his mouth, nipping at it with his teeth, and she moaned. Slowly, he ran a finger down her spine and her breath caught in her chest, her knees buckled for the intense need for him.

"Yes. But-"

"And you're just going to walk away from that?" It took

all her resolve not to turn to him; she knew that once she faced him, looked into his eyes, she would be gone.

"I have to. Whatever is going on is some, and I quote, *really fucked up* shit. I think it's best if your involvement is minimal. I don't know what's happening, but I feel that this will be bad. I've already gotten you too involved in this." She couldn't seem to figure out how to put on her shirt. She couldn't think. He'd buried his hands in her hair, pulling her back against him as he nibbled her neck. She took a deep breath and focused on getting dressed, which became a moot point as he rubbed his rock-hard shaft into the small of her back. The touch of him, stiff and throbbing against her, set her skin ablaze.

"You think I'm going to let you get away from me?" She attempted to snort indignantly and shook her head. Then, with his hands on her waist, he turned her to face him and kissed her. Her breath left her as his tongue began its study of her mouth; he held her still, one hand at the nape of her neck, the other holding her against his growing erection. The hand he'd placed on the small of her back moved past the band of her panties, cupping the tender flesh of her perfectly rounded ass, holding her hard against him.

She dropped her shirt to the floor, her fingers moving through the frayed belt loops of his worn jeans, pulling him closer. This was so stupid and wrong, but she wanted to feel his skin against hers. The temperature in the room, which had been warm and inviting, suddenly dropped to near freezing. He lifted her, sitting her on the dresser, her back against the mirror, her legs wrapped around his waist. He moaned as her heat touched his stomach. They paid no attention to the neatly organized cologne bottles and a lamp that crashed to the floor, filling the room with conflicting fragrances. She groaned as he moved the lacy panties aside and touched her. His fingers teased her before he slipped one deep inside, stroking her until her body wound itself into a tight coil of pleasure that roiled from the center of her and spread. She had never felt this before, never been so close to such a pure euphoric pleasure. Her body twisted as he slipped another finger inside of the soft wet center of her. Her legs trembled, and she made a deep animal noise. Her body shaking, she pressed against him, her hips rolling against the feel of his hand, and she exploded.

Eli kissed her on the cheek; she clung to him until the last spasm of pleasure wracked her. She could feel him smiling against her cheek. She wrapped her arms around his neck, pulling him closer, her mouth moving hungrily over his, her tongue tasting him. She took his hand in hers moving it down to the soft curls at her center.

"I don't want you to stop." She tugged at his bottom lip with her teeth. He slowly slipped a finger deep inside of her again, and she moaned.

"Mmm," she sighed, nuzzling his ear. "Good boy." She panted.

His mouth left a trail of fire down the hollow of her throat, his fingers moving until she gasped. As his tongue gently teased the pulse point throbbing in her neck, he was overwhelmed by the need to bite her. He wanted to drink her in, taste the warm dark fluid pumping through her veins. He wanted to feel her life surging into him. The need was so strong that he opened his mouth, his teeth digging into her skin.

She moaned, and he was snapped back to reality. When he finally released her bra's clasp and revealed her breast, her nipples puckered in expectation. He took one into his mouth, his teeth grazing the tight nub until she whimpered. Her hands moved over his muscled back, down past the waistband of his frayed jeans, pushing them as far down as they would go before, she undid his fly. Slipping her hand inside, as she stroked, he seemed to grow harder, his body vibrating in her hand. When he let an involuntary moan escape, she chuckled. Eli lifted his head from her breast and looked into her eyes; she had the most deliciously devious smile on her lips. He arched a brow as he removed the scraps of lace. She lifted her hips and helped him, lifting one leg as he slipped them off. He moved closer still, his mouth moving between the valley of her breasts, his hands on her hips. He pulled her toward him, pushing her thighs open wider. He looked at the soft, moist curls at the juncture of her thighs before opening her like a flower. When his mouth touched her, she inhaled sharply, her body melting around him. How, she wondered, did she ever believe this was a mistake?

He pulled her even closer; she thrust her hips up to meet every delicious stroke of his tongue. She ran her hands over the soft curls at the back of his head, then sank her nails into his neck. He deepened his kiss, his tongue torturing her, bringing with it wave after wave of unbearable euphoria, and she could feel herself being pushed over the edge. His teeth grazed the sensitive, already stimulated skin at her core, and she felt herself tumbling into blinding bliss. She groaned, mumbled something decidedly sexy and nasty in French before her back arched and her legs tightened around him. She made a deep guttural noise. It was almost primal as she came hard and long, her thighs shaking around his shoulders.

He waited until her tremors subsided, then he began again. When his lips touched her again, she groaned, her fingers clutching the edge of the dresser in surprised rapture.

"Oh," she moaned softly. He held her thighs, his tongue teasing her until she felt as if she were on fire, unable to control her own body, her muscles jerked; her legs trembled as she cried out. He wasted no time bringing her to the brink again, and she whimpered from the sheer exhausting pleasure of it. He gently grazed the tender flesh of her inner thigh with his teeth, and her body convulsed involuntarily. Her back thudded against the mirror above the dresser, sending the photos on the wall to the floor with a resounding crash.

"I was right," he mumbled, his mouth still against her thigh, "Just as sweet everywhere. I want you so much."

"Eli." She couldn't believe the tone of her pleading voice as she rocked against him. She wanted him more; it felt as if her body was on fire. She lifted his head, bringing his mouth up to hers, and kissed him with a need that bordered on desperation. She wanted him inside of her; she wanted to feel his thickness filling her.

*"Faire l'amour me, Élie."* She whispered breathlessly.

He understood it as clearly as if she'd spoken English. *"Make love to me, Elijah."* She'd said, and he just about melted. He stood between her hot thighs, the bulk of him straining against his jeans, and he watched her hands slip the frayed denim jeans and cotton of his undershorts down over his hips. She was kissing his chest, his neck, her teeth grazing the skin at his jawline. His eyes drifted shut when her hand moved down to release him from the constraints of his jeans.

"Eli, you okay? I-" Riley paused in the doorway for only a second, his gun was drawn, before blushing and turning his back to them. "Oh, my God. I thought- Oh my God." Riley gasped and started to giggle like a little kid.   Eli moved quickly; lifting her, he hurriedly deposited her on the bed, shielding her from Riley's prying eyes, and began pulling up his pants.

"Damn it, Riley, get out!" Eli barked.

"Sorry, sorry. Eli, when you get a minute, you have a guest. Another- guest." Riley couldn't conceal the smile from his voice as he half stumbled half ran from the room. They remained frozen as they listened to him clumsily descend the stairs. CeCe started to giggle under her breath, hiding her face behind her hands.

"Shit, he has the worst timing in the world." Eli cursed under his breath. "I'll get rid of them, you-" He hastily buttoned his jeans and tugged on a faded sweatshirt. "Don't move." To punctuate his statement, he leaned over and kissed her thoroughly. She wrapped her arms around his neck, drawing him down onto the bed, wanting to feel the weight of him on her.  Eli closed his eyes and exhaled, fighting the urge to climb on top of her. With a great deal of effort, he drew himself out of her grasp.

"Stay just like that," he growled. She leaned on her elbows, her lids hooded, and her gloriously naked body was shimmering in the early morning sunlight. She began chewing her bottom lip, and he made a low annoyed growling noise before leaving the room.

\* \* \*

Hannah Freeman stood at the bottom of the stairs and was just about to take a step up when he came bounding down.

"Good Morning, Eli. I'm sorry- I knocked. Your friend was nice enough to let me in. I hope I'm not interrupting anything. We heard a noise, and well, your friend told me to wait here." She had the brightest smile plastered on her face, and Eli knew immediately that he should have waited a few minutes before coming down to greet her. He glared at Riley, who leaned against the wall with a bright knowing smile on his lips. Hannah's eyes drifted over him in genuine appreciation, and he had no recourse but to let her stare at his evident erection.

"Good morning, Hannah. Surprised to see you here. To what do I owe this honor?" She completely missed his sarcasm. Before she could spew the well-prepared speech she'd planned about her family inviting him and Grace to their home for Thanksgiving dinner, Riley spoke up.

"Hey, Eli, aren't you going to introduce us? All of us?" He looked at Hannah, then that devious glint returned to his eye. "Riley Quinn, this is Hannah Freeman. Hannah, this is my partner and friend Riley." Riley nodded to her, taking in her lime green twin set, perfectly coiffed ponytail, and tight jeans. She wore four-inch stilettos and enough lip gloss to glaze a ham. She looked strictly country club soccer mom to him, not at all Eli's type. She gave Riley a brief once over, a smile plastered on her face.

"Pleased to meet you, Riley." She spoke through the smile, and Riley became instantly uneasy.

"Nice to meet you, Hannah. Would you like some coffee?

What about Doc? Think she wants coffee?" Riley asked, his eyes on Hannah. He rocked back and forth on his heels, like a child, his hands clasped together at his chin. "No worries, I'll go see for myself." Riley excused himself and headed up the stairs at lightning speed, glancing back at Hannah a few times before shaking his head.

"You have company?" Hannah's smile seemed strained as she tried to hide her curious disappointment.

"Yes, a friend. She had a little accident last night. I let her stay until she felt better, so right now isn't a good time. Thanks for stopping by. I'll call you later," he explained as he steered her towards the door. She stalled, moving quickly from his grip.

"Sure, but I came to invite you to Thanksgiving dinner. I know that Grace and Boogie are your only family in town, and I was hoping you would join us. Daddy would be so happy to meet you face to face. I talk about you so often; he's beginning to think I made you up."

"That's great; I'll try to make it. Text me the specifics, okay." Again, he pointed her towards the door. Again, she avoided his grasp and spun to face him, her back nearly against the door as she spoke.

"If I didn't know better, Eli, I'd think you were trying to get rid of me." She laughed nervously, a harsh, high-pitched sound that reminded Eli of a cat in heat. Her laugh faltered as she looked at the figure descending the stairs; her face froze in slowly seething anger. He *was* trying to get rid of her, she realized, and now she knew why. Eli turned to see what had caught Hannah's attention.

His heart began to beat a little faster at the sight of her, and he inhaled deeply, her scent filling the room. CeCe was coming down the stairs, zipping her jacket, her dark hair hanging loosely around her shoulders. She looked radiant. She glowed, her skin dewy, her lips still kiss swollen. She looked like a woman who'd just made love. Hannah's smile faltered as she realized why Eli been hurrying her out of his home. And why he'd come down the stairs half dressed with a major hard-on.

CeCe looked up, her smile falling as her eyes rested on Hannah, her expression tightening. She tilted her head, her eyes narrowing as she stared at the woman at the bottom of the stairs. She slowed her pace, her hands on the zipper of her jacket. Then she smirked a little and continued her slow, almost deliberate descent.

"You have a guest, so Riley will take me to my car," she said. The expression on her face was something Eli had never seen before. Her nose twitched slightly, and he smiled. She was jealous, and for some juvenile reason, he found great satisfaction in that knowledge. CeCe stood before him, her back to Eli as she extended her hand and a sugary sweet smile to the other woman.

"Hi, I'm Doctor C. Keegan Kent." She gave Hannah's hand a polite shake.

"Hannah Freeman." The other woman smiled just as sweetly, her voice dripping sugar.

"Nice to meet you, Hannah. I was just leaving," she turned to look at Eli. "I- thanks for your help," she mumbled and took a step back. He snaked an arm around her waist, pulling her to him, his lips brushing hers.

"I told you not to move," he teased.

"I have to go, Eli." Her face grew hot at the feel of his body going hard the moment he crushed her breast to his rock-hard chest.

"No." The word came out in a loud bark, "I'll take you. We weren't finished-"

"I think we are," she mumbled, her cheeks growing hot. Eli's gaze on her face was openly wanton. She avoided his eyes, but the hairs on the back of her neck stood on end as he stroked her back.

"Not even close," he mumbled, his erection pushing harder against her stomach.

# CHAPTER SEVEN

**B**efore she could protest, the front door opened, pushing Hannah forward until she nearly collided into the back of CeCe. She gasped as a form filled the doorway, blocking the sunlight and casting a wide, deep shadow across them. He was so tall that he had to bend over to enter the foyer and so broad he had to angle himself sideways to get through the door. He wore black jeans with chains looped through the belt loops, heavy dark biker boots, and a dark leather jacket over a thick black sweatshirt, the hood of which hid his face. His monstrous hands were encased in black leather fingerless biker's gloves. As he entered, CeCe shook her head and exhaled.

"Briar," she said without needing to turn around and look at him.

Briar stepped fully into the room, closed the door behind him, and removed his hood. He was a massive man, with the face of an angel. Eli knew that, like CeCe, this man was much older than he appeared.

His eyes were bright, crisp, emerald green, his skin as smooth and pale as marble with a smattering of light freckles. He had a straight nose and even white teeth except for the curiously sharp canines, and when he smiled, his eyes lit up. There was two days' worth of stubble growing on his chin, giving him a slightly roguish look. He looked like, in all honesty, a Celtic God. He had short spiky auburn hair and two long thin braids the hung past his shoulder. His eyes scanned the room, coming to land on CeCe, and sighed.

"I've been looking everywhere for you, Sarge." His heavy Irish brogue was slightly musical and held a tinge of laughter.

"How did you find me?" She asked, turning to face him, a worried expression crossed her face. He smiled even wider.

"Well, it's my job, isn't it? To find people."

She nodded her agreement. That was Briar's job. Sighing in exasperation, she rephrased the question.

"What are you doing here?" Briar looked at the other people in the room, all standing slack-jawed at his appearance, then looked at CeCe and said something in a language Eli had never heard before. He glanced at Eli, then at CeCe, who nodded. Her response was in the same unfamiliar language, and when the giant began to protest, she held up a hand and repeated her request. Briar looked at the others, the smile fading from his eyes as he nodded curtly, bowed at the waist.

"As you wish," he said in English, turned on his heel, and walked out, just as quietly as he had arrived.

They stood in stunned silence for a moment as CeCe watched Briar leave. She turned to look at the three standing together. Hannah, who had eased closer to Eli, had a terrifying grip on his arm. CeCe thought that the entire terrified damsel act was just the excuse Hannah needed to get closer to Eli. As she stared at them, Hannah gave her a sly smile and molded her body against Eli, who stood like a block of stone, his jaw clenched. He narrowed his eyes and stared at her suspiciously, and she looked down at her feet. Riley stood on the stairs, slack-jawed. No one spoke, or blinked for that matter, for a full minute.

"What the fuck was that?" Riley asked, breaking the awkward silence. CeCe sighed heavily.

"That was Briar," she said, avoiding the questioning gaze of Eli.

Riley raced down the stairs, threw the front door open just in time to see Briar mount a monster of a Harley. He looked like something out of a nightmare, all gleaming black metal, and polished chrome, his head encased in a helmet designed to look like a flaming skull with a long red Mohawk. He glanced at Riley and winked before lowering the visor then tore off down the street.

"What the fuck is a Briar?" He spun CeCe around to face him, his face beaming with excitement. "And where do I go to get one?"

* * *

They rode in silence. Eli wasn't sure how to broach the subject of what happened the night before or that morning. The giant who'd come into his house and spoken to her in what was that language? He sighed heavily and pulled to a stop at a red light. She sat beside him; her face turned away from him, her shoulders slumped.

After the shock of Briar's visit and the interruption of Riley and Hannah Freeman, Eli had insisted that he bring her to her car.

"Don't move," he'd said to CeCe through clenched teeth. "You have got a lot to explain."

She hadn't said anything, only stood silently waiting. Hannah had been ushered out of the house by Riley immediately. He'd made a point of letting her know that Eli, no matter how nice, was not interested in her. CeCe, who stood shaken, was surprised when Riley engulfed her in a bear hug.

"Whatever is going on, just know, he cares about you," he'd whispered in her ear. "So do I."

She didn't know why she was crying. That was a lie. She was falling in love with Eli, and she had no idea what to do about it. If he knew who she was, what she was, he would run screaming. She couldn't stop the sudden flow of tears as she clung to Riley for a moment, enjoying the comfort of his embrace. It had been so long since she'd been hugged without some sort of sexual connotation. She snuggled closer, feeling safe, and cared for in Riley's arms. After a moment, he held her at arm's length and smiled at her.

"Okay, you even cry pretty. How is that fair?" He teased,

wiping away her tears. As Eli approached, Riley backed away and disappeared into the kitchen.

"I'll see you when you get back, E," he called to Eli.

Eli stared at the back of her head and then slowly reached for her hand, lacing his fingers with hers. She turned to face him, sliding closer to him in the bucket seat of the SUV. She rested her head on his shoulder. He was thinking about what to ask first, how to ask without sounding like an ass. He wanted to know who Briar was to her and just how he knew where to find her. He wanted to know if she had any idea what had happened between them the night before and what the hell was the language. She spoke to the mountain she called Briar, and why had he called her Sarge? He wondered.

"I don't know what that was last night. Briar works for Jonas. He has a talent for locating people and things. Anything. He calls me Sarge because he says I was a drill sergeant in a former life. And it was Gaelic," she said and felt him jump in his seat.

"I forgot you could do that," he mumbled. She sat up and looked at him, studying his profile. For a moment, he couldn't tell what she was thinking; her thoughts were jumbled and confusing; nothing was coming across clearly.

He pulled the car into the parking garage where she'd left her car the night before. There were still traces of their last visit. Several vehicles were getting new windshields and windows; a few had scorch marks from the bursting lights' sparks. The light fixtures were all replaced, and glass was cleaned from the floors by rather disgruntled looking workers. Eli parked near her car and turned off the engine before turning to look at her.

She was staring out of the window in deep thought. Again, he reached for her hand, drawing her closer to him, kissing her until she melted against him. When he released her, she rested her head on his chest, her hand over his thundering heartbeat.

"What is your earliest memory, Eli?" She whispered.

The question was entirely out of the blue, and he looked at

her curiously before answering.

"I don't know. I suppose junior high school-" He was silent for a while, as he realized that he didn't remember anything before junior high school. Not birthday parties, or playing in the yard, riding bikes with his friends, little league, nothing; there was a void where his childhood should be. It was as if his life didn't start until he was in his early teens.

"Don't you find that to be a little strange? Most people can remember as far back as three or four years of age. I can remember as far back as my second birthday. Why can't you?" He couldn't answer. He hadn't thought about it. He hadn't realized that there was a gap, no one had brought it to his attention before, but his past was a huge question mark.

"Have you ever met someone who seems to know you but you can't remember them? Someone you went to high school with or says you look like someone they know? Or have you been somewhere and felt as if you'd been there before?"

"That happens to everyone," he grumbled.

"But it happens to you more than most, I'll bet." He didn't answer, but he had to admit that she was right. It happened to him at least three times a week, but he'd thought nothing of it until now. "I also bet women come on to you like crazy. You can't go anywhere without women flirting with you and throwing themselves at you, right?" She asked, her finger tracing intricate designs across his chest.

"I'm sure you get even more attention than I do." He kissed the top of her head.

"I have boobs, Eli. Even if I didn't have ahead, I would get attention just because of that." He chuckled, the deep rumbling in his chest making her tingle. He had the best laugh, she thought, deep and hardy, wholly male. They were silent for a while, snuggled together in the front seat of his SUV. She didn't want to move; she had the horrible feeling that if she moved, she might never see him again. But wasn't that what she wanted?

"What do you know about the supernatural?" Outside, the

sky had become overcast and gloomy, fitting her suddenly sullen mood. The rain was in the air, which meant Thanksgiving Day would probably be a damp, depressing affair.

"Like ghosts and goblins?"

"Like that thing that attacked Nicky." And like you, she thought. She chewed her bottom lip, her face sorrowful as if she were dreading the words coming out of her mouth. When Eli didn't respond, she pulled away from him and got out of the car, slowly sliding off her seat and closing the door with a resounding slam. Before she made her way around the back of the car, Eli was standing beside his closed door, his hands in his pockets. He looked incredible standing there, watching her with something close to bewilderment. That *aw-shucks* look he was giving her was melting her resolve. She walked quickly past him, hoping to avoid a confrontation. That was nearly impossible because their cars were parked so closely together. He grabbed her arm, pausing her progress.

"I've disrupted your life enough. We can say goodbye right now. I'm pretty sure your *girlfriend* will be relieved." She said the word girlfriend as if it were a vulgar term. And she felt as if she were going to cry, which made no sense to her. She shouldn't be crying over this man; she'd only known him for a few very bizarre days.

"Girlfriend?" He was utterly at a loss. Then it slowly dawned on him. "You mean Hannah? Hannah's not my girlfriend. I wouldn't even call her my friend."

"Really? Because she was throwing off a solid *back up bitch* vibe," she said.

He shook his head and started laughing.

"How cute, you're jealous," he said and continued to laugh while she fumed.

"I don't get jealous." She growled and folded her arms across her chest. He laughed even harder.

"Stop it." She stomped her foot like a spoiled child and could feel her face getting hot. "I'm not jealous," she yelled.

They both knew that was a lie, her eyes were narrow slits

of dull blue-grey, and her lips were pinched so tightly that they were nonexistent. Eli stepped closer, and she took a step back, angry at herself for being jealous of a woman who was simply talking to Eli. It's not like he was hers or anything. But they had shared something, something electric and sexual. He had planned on making love to her that very morning. He'd kissed her until she was breathless, and when he'd touched her- the thought of it made her body react in a way that frustrated her. He was hers; she was startled by her thoughts. When had he become her anything?

"Hannah is not my girlfriend. I don't even know how she found out where I live. Believe me; she doesn't even register on my radar." He stopped laughing, his hand moving to stroke her cheek.

"All I see is you." He leaned closer, his mouth next to hers. She looked at him, her head tilted as she studied his expression.

"Just-forget it. Forget me. Okay? " *'Before things get too deep,'* she thought. *'Before I fall completely in love with you.'* She chewed her lip nervously, and he seemed to dissolve, his face softening.

"I know that you're already wet just thinking about me." He was kissing her before she realized what was happening. Her back pressed against the passenger door of her car, his hands in her hair. She felt him pressing against her stomach, and the fire began again. His hands moved down her torso, under the thin material of her t-shirt, until he was caressing her breasts. She moaned into his mouth, her hands pressed against his chest.

"No, not okay. I can't forget you." He said matter-of-factly. His next kiss seemed to drain all the fight out of her, and she yielded, her arms circling his waist as she swiveled her hips against him. He whimpered softly, his hands moving down to hold her hips hard against him. He wanted her, right there hidden between the two parked cars. Or so they thought. A car rolled past, the driver honking his horn.

"Get a room!" He shouted before speeding out of the parking lot.

"I've got to go," she whispered and slipped out of his arms and into her car.

"We're far from over, Doc." He said, and she stared at him for a moment before starting her car. He was right, of course.

"Celeste," she said, a smile playing at the corners of her mouth. "My name is Celeste."

\* \* \*

"Thank God." Bianca accosted ceCe as she entered the lobby of her apartment building. The tiny blond hugged her so tightly that she could hardly breathe. For such a little thing, Bianca was surprisingly strong. When she released her, she gave her a quick once over. "Where have you been? Your father has been looking for you. You didn't answer your phone, and he had Xander and me and some walking mountain named Brian looking for you all night." She looked for Xander, who was nowhere to be found.

"Briar," she corrected, "found me. Where's Xander?"

"He went home. You know he has an aversion to the sun and people, the world in general, really." Bianca mumbled. "Where have you been? Why didn't you answer your phone?'

As she thought about it now, CeCe realized that she'd left her purse locked in her car when they'd gone up to Nicky's apartment. It would have never occurred to Riley or Eli to get her purse before they left. She dug into the bottom of the bag and found her phone, no bars indicating that her battery was dead.

"I stayed at a friend's house, and my phone is dead," she mumbled. "I'll call as soon as I get upstairs. I didn't mean to worry you." She was tired and in need of a cold shower. The effects of Eli's last kiss still disorienting her.

"Was this *friend* a certain sexy ass detective I saw you

cuddled up with at the coffee shop yesterday?" To her amazement, CeCe blushed. "I will take that as a yes. Since you don't seem any worse for wear, I will leave you alone. Have a happy holiday weekend, Doc. See you Monday," she called, sashaying out of the lobby, the smell of her costly perfume lingering in the lobby. The day doorman watched her backside with open interest as she left on those teetering heels and tight jeans, her blond ponytail swinging with her sway.

*  *  *

As the elevator doors opened into her foyer, CeCe tossed her purse on a table and kicked off her shoes as she made her way through the living room. The message light on her telephone flashed bright red, alerting her to the number of calls she'd missed.

"You know, I'm having trouble understanding why I pay so much for a secured building when anyone can just wander in off of the street," she said, turning to look at her father sitting on the sofa. He was flipping through one of her architecture magazines in the dimly lit room. The curtains were still drawn from the night before, and he hadn't bothered to open them. Instead, he sat in the dark, waiting. She was surprised to find that he was completely alone, with no bodyguards to be seen.

"Where have you been?" He didn't look up as he spoke.

"I was with Detective Cain." She sighed and stripped her jacket off. Rubbing her tired eyes, she walked over and kissed Jonas's cheek. "He's something special, Father." She sat crossed-legged on the sofa next to him.

"Talk to me." Slowly he closed the magazine and took her hands, and listened as she poured out everything that had happened in Nicky's apartment. The bites, the needle-like teeth, the way it changed, and how she had pulled all of it from Eli's memory. She told everything right up to her waking up in his bed and Eli giving her aspirin and bringing her home.

"He's not just a telepath or empath, Father. He's something unique. When we are together, and we focus on each other, we change atmospheres. We can make a room hotter or colder, and the electricity-we can shift nature. I feel so connected to him like I'm supposed to be with him. He is so gentle with me, and he cares for me, not just what I mean or who I am. He cares for –me. And Father, he has the mark. Could it be him? Could he be the *one*?" Jonas patted her hand and grimaced. There was something that he wanted to say, she thought, but he was holding back. He knew something; she realized—something about Eli.

"What do you know that you aren't telling me?" She asked, and Jonas shook his head.

"I don't know anything. I suspect that you may be right about your detective." When she didn't correct him, insisting that he wasn't *her* detective, Jonas's brow rose. "There is something *you* aren't telling *me*, my dear. He took *care* of you. I would like to meet him. Will you be inviting him to Thanksgiving Dinner?" He asked, slowly rising, hiding a sly smirk. She eyed Jonas and shook her finger at him.

"Oh no," she said with a smile. "I'm not getting caught in that trap. I bring Eli to dinner, and then he'll be before the Collective. Nope. She was not happening, Jonas Kent. " He laughed, and she stood to hug him.

"Okay. I understand. Briar said that you were fine, but I wanted to see for myself. Call me, overprotective." He kissed her on the forehead.

" I will see you at the house. I have some things to take care of in the city. Lisette and Giovanni should be there when you get there. We have a lot of important people coming in for dinner tomorrow. Everything must be correct. Yes?" She nodded.

"*Oui*," She kissed his cheek and walked him to the elevator. Once he left, she slipped into a hot bath, her mind still on Eli, his hot kisses, talented hands, and good Lord that mouth.

"Lord help me," she mumbled before sinking beneath the

bubbles.

* * *

Riley sat at Eli's small kitchen table sipping his coffee and looking at his watch when Eli strolled in an hour later, a smile on his face.

"Finally," he breathed, throwing his hands in the air. "Are you going to tell me what's going on?" He was yelling at Eli before he could close the back door, sliding a cup of coffee over to him.

"Grace called, invited you and Adam over for Thanksgiving dinner." Eli sipped his coffee, watching as Riley's face turned bright red.

"That's not what I'm talking about. I'm talking about why you left a very naked, extremely hot, and willing woman lying in your bed. "

"Oh, I don't know, maybe because my partner came in right before we-"Eli smirked.

"Came?" Riley teased. Eli couldn't help but laugh, a deep throaty chuckle, as he sipped his coffee. "I wouldn't necessarily go that far. But you did interrupt the grand finale. What are you doing here, anyway?"

"I was coming to check on you two. Last night was pretty intense. When I got here, Ms. Freeman was tiptoeing into your back door, so I followed. I asked her what she was doing here, and while she stammered for an answer, I heard a crash and moaning. I knew it was Doc, but I thought she was –hurt." He grinned and shook his head.

"Celeste. Her name is Celeste." Riley arched a brow at the dreamy, almost bewildered way in which he spoke her name. It was as if the mere mention of her name put him in a trance. Eli cleared his throat and sheepishly looked down into his coffee cup.

"There is something about her when she's not around. All

I do is think about her. She gets me. All of my weird shit, she doesn't seem to mind. She has some weird shit of her own, but I can be my freaky self around her. I mean the thing last night with the lights, the Mack truck who came looking for her this morning, the locator who works for her father."

"Briar," Riley said dreamily. Eli mimicked Riley's arched brow with an additional smirk.

"Anyway, that language they spoke, she said it was Gaelic. Who the hell speaks Gaelic? There is something all wrong with her. But when I'm with her, it just seems right." Riley was duly impressed. He stared into his cup, not sure how to broach the next subject. "There's more I haven't told you." He exhaled sharply and looked at Riley, who waited patiently. He explained the matching birthmarks, her necklace, and her attempts to push into his mind to remove herself from his memories. She had tried and tried, but he was stronger than she was and had pushed her away. When he succeeded, she had been shocked. He also had to admit something else to Riley, something he had barely admitted to himself.

"Riley, she speaks French and-when she was talking to Briar- I understood it. I understood all of it. She told him that she was fine and that she would call him later. I had no idea what the language was, but I clearly understood it. All of it."

\* \* \*

The sun was setting as she pulled her car into the garage at the back of the house. As the large metal door slid silently closed behind her, she turned off the ignition and slipped from behind the wheel of the Range Rover, her sunglasses still in place from the long drive. As she slammed her car door closed, she paused for only a second before spinning on her heel, blocking the blow that came from behind. His arm went through the driver's side window of her car, shattering it, and she was furious.

"Son of a bitch," She yelled, dipping left as her assailant came at her again, swinging a hard right that was aimed at her jaw. She ducked, and he missed her cheek by mere inches, his fist plowing through the wall at her back. Staying low, she landed a right jab to his side, then an elbow to his back as he tried to pull his hand free. He hit the floor with a thud. He bounced to his feet, wiping blood from his lips, a look of pure hatred in his midnight dark eyes.

"What is your problem?" She yelled as he charged again. Once upon a time, she had enjoyed the rough play with her adopted brother. They had spent years ambushing each other, but lately, his rough play had become all-out assaults. They both knew he had no chance of winning a fight with her, no matter how hard he tried. What he was doing was pissing her off.

He came at her again, swinging wild blow after blow, each of which she blocked with ease. She swept her leg out and took his feet from beneath him. He fell back and sprang back to his feet. He smirked before running at her, screaming like a lunatic.

"Will you cut it out?" She screamed before landing a quick uppercut to his jaw. He stumbled backward, fangs drawn as he ran at her. Launching himself into the air, she took an incredible leap back, landing on the hood of Gaston's shiny black BWM, looking down, realizing the heels of her boots were going to scratch the paint, and cursed. Gaston was going to be pissed.

Remy laughed and continued to charge her. Fully angered now, she sprang, sailing through the air, her knees catching his shoulders, taking them both to the hard cement floor, her knees pinning him to the ground, her hands at his throat. He coughed a laugh, and her grip tightened.

"What is your fucking problem?" She screamed.

"I was just making sure you hadn't lost your edge. I don't want you going soft." She let him up and shook her head. "What's that supposed to mean?" She walked away, looking at the damage she'd done to Gaston's car and the damage Remy had inflicted on hers.

"It means," he straightened his clothes, "That I wanted to make sure that you hadn't gone soft since you're fucking the cop. You know, the way you did when you were with the vamp." She froze for a moment before looking over her shoulder at him. He was smiling a nasty little smile, his arms folded across his chest as he watched her. She turned to face him, mimicking his posture.

"Is that your oh so clever way of asking if I have had sex with Eli?" He hooted with laughter.

"So, it's Eli now? Wow, Eli. Nice. Well," He pushed himself away from her car, leaving massive dents where his hands had pressed into the metal, and started walking towards her. "Briar did find you at Eli's house this morning; after, of course, he found your car abandoned in the parking garage at Nicky's apartment building, not to mention the fact that you had been incommunicado all-night last night. We know you spent the night with him."

"So, you assume I had sex with him?" She asked. He was standing so close; his breath was warm on her face and tinged with alcohol. His dark eyes flashed a bright yellow as anger flared his nostrils.

"I can smell him on you." He lifted a lock of her hair and inhaled. "You aren't supposed to be with him, CeCe. The Collective said-" She pushed him away.

"Fuck the Collective. Since when do you care about them? The Collective says a lot about things they don't understand." She mumbled and rubbed her forehead. He put his arms around her and held her close,          "He doesn't know what you are," he growled through clenched teeth. "He doesn't understand."

"He doesn't understand. But he will. " She whispered before turning to walk away.

* * *

She was staring at her reflection in the vanity mirror, a frown creasing her brow. She didn't look any different, but she felt as if she did. She leaned closer and stared at her lips, her eyes, her breasts. She had been made love to that morning, and she felt as if she should look different. She stood and let her robe hang from her shoulders, staring at her underwear-clad body. She absently touched the pendant that hung between her breasts. Shouldn't she be glowing? She wondered.

"You are glowing." She started at the sound of Lisette's voice. Pulling her robe on, she blushed.

"I didn't hear you come in." She mumbled.

"I suppose you hadn't. I've been knocking on your door for five minutes." Lisette sat on the edge of her bed. Her once flowing honey-blond hair had been chopped into a boyish pixie cut. She wore a blood-red leather dress that emphasized her cleavage and hugged her curves. One thing about Lisette, she was the walking talking epitome of a sexual predator.

"Let me guess you have Detective Sexy on the brain. Bianca called and filled me in on the hot chocolate you've been hanging around with." CeCe could feel her cheeks burning.

"You did it, didn't you?" Lisette clasped her hands together in excitement. Celeste's entire body felt warm under her sister's scrutiny.

"No, we didn't." She turned away, walking into her closet, Lisette hot on her heels. Celeste's closet was as large as a small bedroom, lined with gowns and furs that she rarely wore. One wall alone housed rows and rows of shoes and boots, all arranged by style and color. Her shirts were hung on a high bar, also arranged by color. Her pants and dresses were organized from long to short. There was an island in the center of the room, every side sporting at least a dozen drawers that housed her jewelry, t-shirts, and lingerie. She skirted around the island through a door on the other side of the closet into the massive marbled bathroom, Lisette still in pursuit.

"Well, what *exactly* did you do? Take a deep breath and start from the beginning, and don't leave anything out." Lisette was on the edge of her seat as she waited, her hands on her cheeks as she listened.

* * *

As usual, during the holiday season, the Kent house was full. Even though Thanksgiving wasn't until the next day, Jonas had invited several of his cohorts to spend the long weekend at the manor. Not quite a black-tie affair, but they were expected to dress for dinner. Tonight, she had chosen a hunter green silk wrap dress that moved with her curves. She wore simple gold Christian Louboutin heels and a thin gold chain at her throat, accenting the deep green nicely. The long silver chain lay flat beneath her dress, nestled between her breasts as it always did. Her hair was pulled away from her face in an elaborate braid that hung over one shoulder, showing off simple gold hoop earrings.

Celeste came down the massive staircase just in time to see Remy escort a rather statuesque blond across the foyer into the dining room. She smirked as he glanced up at her and gave a sly wink. That was Remy, she thought, so quick to find solace in another's bed. It didn't matter really who's bed, as long as the body was warm and willing. Over the years, he'd come home with a plethora of unusual bed partners. It had become a sort of game to see who he would bring home. As she reached the landing, she paused and held out her hand. Gaston came to stand next to her and reached into his pocket. Exasperated, he placed a crisp one-hundred-dollar bill into her palm, and she laughed. There was a long-standing bet between the siblings about who Remy would bring to any given event. Gaston had bet this time; his guest would be a male lust demon. Celeste had upped the ante by saying, human female.

"You know," she'd said, "just to try to piss me off." She knew Remy and his motivations better than either of his biological siblings ever would.

"I don't think it's fair that you can read minds. How do I know you didn't cheat?" She looked at her older brother in his crisp navy-blue blazer and bright red tie, his hair still glistening from his shower. Her eyes were wide and innocent, her mouth a perfect O.

"You mean you don't trust me?" She asked.

"Hell no." He laughed and placed her hand in the crook of his elbow. He escorted her into the dining room, both chuckling as they took their seats.

❋ ❋ ❋

Dinner with Jonas's associates was an arduous task for her; she was antsy and disjointed the entire night. Her mind kept replaying the two previous days, thoughts of the clawed murderer of her friend, her new ability to share Eli's power, and Eli's hot, hungry mouth on her skin. That was what bothered her the most, his warm eager tongue teasing her in places that she hadn't been touched in years. She exhaled sharply, steadying herself. It was going to be a long night, she thought. Gaston stared at her, and she gave him a rather sad smile before turning to her meal. Her eyes met Lisette's knowing eyes across the table; they shared a smile before CeCe focused on her meal.

The seventy-five guests sat at the grand dining table as they were served several courses of everything from gumbo to duck à l'orange, sweet potato pie to Crème brûlée. Many of the faces were business acquaintances of Jonas's. But there were random guests, like Gaston's law partner, an odd little man with owl-like eyes and dreamy quality. There was also Gaston's assistant, Stacey, who was obviously in love with him. Lisette and her rather swarthy fiancée Giovanni sat with their heads together most of the day. And of course, there was Remy, who sat across from her with his model du jour. A rather large German woman with white-blond hair and eyes the color of ice. On more than one occasion during the meal, she caught this Nordic goddess of a woman staring at her with open hostility.

"What's with Brunhilda?" Gaston whispered in her ear during course five or six.

"Don't know, don't care," CeCe mumbled. Remy sipped his wine and stared at her, a self-satisfied smirk on his arrogant face.

"So, where's your cop, CeCe? Didn't deem him proper for a family gathering?" Remy snarled.

"Unlike you, who will drag any of your random conquests to family functions? What's this one called?" She motioned towards the blond.

"One warm body is as good as any other. This is Ingrid. She is a very good friend. Tasty, right Gaston?" His tone was lewd, and she nearly tossed a dinner roll at him, but Gaston grabbed her wrist and gave Remy a flash of his teeth. His eyes turned completely black, without a hint of white, and he growled, a sound so low and threatening that she shivered. She had never seen Gaston so angry, and his grip on her wrist became painful.

"Remy, stop it," Jonas spoke in a voice that only the four of them could hear, the other guests had no idea what had just happened, and it was best to keep it that way. The last thing they needed at dinner was a confrontation. But it took Gaston longer to regain himself.

"Gaston," CeCe touched his cheek, and he looked at her with those onyx eyes.

"Don't you smell it?" He whispered and nodded towards Ingrid.

Then it became apparent as to why he couldn't stop. She could smell it all right, warm and sweet and so mouthwateringly delicious. She leaned forward, looking at the faces of those around the table, and realized that most of them had transformed: animal-like eyes and bared teeth. Some involuntarily, some hungrily, all wanting a taste. They could smell her blood. Ingrid was on her period. Remy had done this on purpose; Ingrid wasn't his bed partner du jour. Poor clueless

Ingrid was dessert. She would be shared and used until they had gotten their fill, then glamoured into near oblivion.

*"Like a lamb to the slaughter,"* she thought. Little did she know just how true that was.

# CHAPTER EIGHT

Frustrated by the way the others had pounced after dinner, CeCe went to her room, a bottle of wine tucked under her arm. The one thing she hated about these things was the sacrificial lambs brought in to satiate the masses. The poor souls were brought in and fed upon, then glamoured to the point of stupidity before being released. It sickened her after witnessing it over the years, the ferocity with which they attacked. The poor deluded sacrifices would leave weak and confused if they left at all. On more than one occasion, they had become overzealous in their feedings, and the poor human would die. She had never participated, not needing blood to live, she didn't crave it the way they did, but she had witnessed it. That had been more than enough.

She had finally managed to doze off once her nerves had calmed, not realizing that she was not alone as she slept. She was laying perfectly still in a blissful sleep when it entered, filling the room, which smelled of burning wood, fresh linens, and her bath oils, with the stench of rotting flesh and animal. It was at the foot of the bed, crouching and looking at her with animal-like eyes, its vast black wings wrapped around it like a cloak. It had long, narrow fingers, shaped like talons dangling between its legs as it watched her sleep with curious fascination. She rolled onto her side, moaning softly in the throes of an alcohol-induced dream. Slowly, it crept across the bed, so lightly she didn't feel its approach, but its smell grew more potent as it moved closer, and she wrinkled her nose as the scent assaulted her. It stared at her in wonder, gently using a finger to push the hair out of her face, its feline eyes blinking slowly as it burned her features into its memory. It marveled at the smell of her hair, the softness of her caramel-colored skin, the high cheekbones, and achingly beautiful face.

"Lovely," it whispered. "You are much lovelier than the other one. Much prettier, much shinier," it hissed, its breath hot and putrid near her ear.

"The other is pretty as well." Its voice invaded her dreams, and she was bombarded by images of Eli bloody and choking, a gaping wound at his throat, his eyes staring heavenward.

"The perfect pretty." It whispered. Eli's body twitched, and he tried in vain to hold his hands over the pouring blood. He was choking to death, and she could hear screams. Somewhere far off, she could hear the screams of a hysterical woman. Then she saw her own hands covered in blood, his blood. He looked at her with pleading eyes and tried to speak; only nothing would come, only more blood. He reached for her, and she fell to her knees as the life poured out of him. The screaming never stopped. It only got louder and turned into sobs of agony. As the last light of life flashed in his eyes, Celeste realized the screaming woman was her.

Shocked by the icy cold of its touch as it ran a human finger across her bare shoulder, CeCe sat up, suddenly wide awake, and flipped on the light to find nothing there. The smell of fetid meat and animal remained, as well as a definite chill on her skin, but no demon. She looked around the room, checking to make sure what she saw was just a figment of her very vivid imagination, a bad dream. The doors that led to the balcony were securely closed and locked, the fire dying in the fireplace. She stoked it, adding another log to the hearth before climbing back into bed. She lay with her eyes closed, awake, waiting for it to come back. Thankfully, it didn't, not to her, anyway.

* * *

*It was hungry, but it couldn't eat the woman. No, not yet. She was full of alcohol, and that made the taste unbearable. It stood on the balcony outside of CeCe's bedroom, looking down at the party-goers gathered on the patio below. There was light and music and laughter coming from the French doors that led to what it supposed was a sitting or living room. It jumped up and perched on the wrought iron railing and leaned forward, sniffing the air. It hissed at the stench of demons and supernatural beings that floated on the late November air. The combined scents of those gathered below were nauseating. Standing to leave, balancing on the thin rail, it stood preparing to take flight to find better hunting grounds when a sweet smell wafted down from the third floor. It was warm and young and -Human.*

*It soared upwards, landing with surprising grace and agility on the third-floor balcony. The smell was more pungent here, almost cloying. It stretched out a hand, and the window slid silently open. Slowly and stealthily, it slipped in and with lightning speed came to stand at the foot of the bed at the center of the wonderfully delicious aroma. On the bed, naked and sleeping, was a woman. She was long and lean with alabaster skin that looked as if it had never been touched by sunlight. Her hair was pale silver in the moon-light and fanned out against the deep burgundy duvet. Her face was round and cherubic almost, like a child's, completely innocent in sleep. But her body was far from childlike. She had round full breasts and a bottom and thighs tight enough to bounce a coin off. It moved closer and inhaled deeply. It was a shame to spoil such beauty, it thought, but she would be delicious.*

\* \* \*

Eli found himself thinking of CeCe again that night. The smell of her lingered on his sheets and pillows. He had picked up the photos, cleaned the broken glass from the cologne bottles and the lamp, but she was still here. He couldn't close his eyes without thinking of her soft and yielding, waiting for him. Whenever he closed his eyes, he imagined her lean naked body surrounded by the deep teal of his comforter. He pictured those heavily lidded eyes and kiss swollen lips, and his body reacted. He rolled onto his stomach, burying his face into his pillow, which only made it worse. It smelled of her. Even with the lingering scents of his destroyed cologne bottles, her scent seemed to dominate the room. Giving up, he jumped from the bed and made his way to his make-shift gym.

Once he'd worked himself to exhaustion, he surrendered and headed back to his Celeste scented bed. He dozed off with the slight feeling that he was being watched. He reached out to pick up any nearby thoughts; he got his neighbor who was wishing she hadn't eaten that third piece of pie; she had acid reflux that was killing her. A man walking his dog wished it would hurry up and pee so that he could get back to his movie. It was the same man who always let his dog go in Eli's yard; he could feel the guilt rolling off him. There were random thoughts from his surrounding neighbors, most regarding too much food or drink or shopping in the morning, or starting a diet, and then there was something else.

An animal. He'd never picked up an animal, but this one thought that it was hungry. Ravaged, starving for some fresh meat. Preferably alive, something to hunt. Then it was thinking of him, watching him, sleeping and wondered what he would taste like. That thought was quickly dismissed in favor of him joining them, becoming its kin.

He was half asleep when he realized that it wasn't an animal, exactly. It was something more than that, but not exactly human either, and it was getting closer. He rolled over, not wanting it to realize that he was awake; slowly, Eli reached beneath his pillow, his hand on the handle of his gun, and he waited. After only a minute, he caught a glimpse of something darting past his bedroom window. It was large and dark, moving extremely fast, like a blur in the night air. That couldn't be right, he was on the second floor, and there was no way anyone could be up there. He slipped from between the sheets and peered out of the window, just as a cat landed on the steps of his front porch below. It was a peculiar shade of purple-gray and had large silver eyes. It looked at him and hissed, then sprinted away. Eli was utterly baffled, realizing that he knew that cat. Its mind was a scattered mess, but it had distinctly human thoughts, murderous thoughts about him. Not murderous, more possessive, jealous. As it melted into the shadows, he watched it began to shift into a more human form easily and then disappear around a corner. A nervous chill went through him. *"Don't go out there."* He told himself. *"It's gone. No harm, no foul. It's all good. Go to sleep. You're in the middle of a dream, so go to sleep, Eli. Leave that thing right where it is. Leave it alone."*

He didn't.

He'd put on his shoes and jacket and went after it. His gun was tucked securely in its shoulder holster. When he rounded the corner, he found the street empty, aside from a lone person, heading towards the levee in the ferry landing direction. As quickly and as quietly as he could manage, he followed.

It wore a hoodie, black, and baggy jeans. With its head down and a determined stride, he couldn't decipher sex or race. It was either a teenage boy or a small woman, he thought. It was young; he decided because it was quick and agile. It paused for a moment and lifted its face to the sky, sniffing, and he could see the faint outline of a pixyish face in the moonlight. It slipped into the trees at the base of the levee near the river, moving like a lynx into the darkness, making no sound, ruffling no leaves. He stood back and waited, watching, his chest suddenly tight with fear.

A young woman came jogging around the corner, a large brown dog trotting beside her. She had earbuds in her ears and an mp3 player strapped to her arm. Her reddish-brown hair swung behind her as she bounced along the levee. In the early twenties, she was young and smiling at the large goofy brown mutt of a dog with his floppy ears and tongue hanging happily out of its mouth. She felt safe with him as a protector, he realized, and continued her nightly jog, feeling light and carefree. Dread crept into the pit of his stomach, and his body was covered in a cold sweat. He was running, as fast as his legs would carry him, adrenaline pushing him to move even faster, his heart hammering in his chest, but he was still too far away to stop it. He waved his hands in warning, yelling for her to move, to run away; she only glanced at him, slowly removing the buds from her ears, her face twisted in confusion as she tried to decipher his warning, her eyes locked on the shining barrel of his gun. The dog barked excitedly, bouncing back and forth when the dark form swooped down, and the dog was gone. The sound of pained yelping echoed in the still of the night. She screamed in shock, and Eli continued to yell, quickly, closing the distance between them.

When she finally thought to run, it was too late. Its talons swiped at her face moving in a blur of dark feathers and blood, opening hideous gashes in her beautifully pristine skin, her jaw hanging askew, her scream lost in a gurgle of blood. She dropped to her knees, and it knocked her to the ground, its mouth buried in her jugular, making greedy slurping noises, like a baby suckling its mother's breast. The smell of burning flesh and the creature's animal stench filled his senses. Eli lifted his gun and fired, hitting it in the shoulders and back, with no effect. The bullet holes seemed to shrink as soon as they appeared. No blood spilled from the wounds, only the mushroomed bullets. It seemed to shake off the shots as nothing more than an annoyance, too preoccupied with its meal to be concerned. Eli continued to fire, unloading his weapon into its back. It only hissed at the distraction. With an unfathomable strength and speed, it lifted the woman's limp body and launched itself upward, soaring like a rocket into the void of darkness. With shaky hands, he holstered his gun, scanned the sky with his eyes and mind for any hint of the creature. There was nothing, just him breathing heavily, puffs of white billowing from him. His heart thudded against his ribs, the smell of blood, the creature, and death wafting in the night air.

* * *

Celeste awoke to complete chaos. There was screaming coming from the third floor and the sound of pounding feet in the hallway outside of her room. She sprang from the bed and threw her bedroom door open as Remy raced past.

"What is going on?" She yelled, racing to catch up with him as he bounded up the stairs two at a time.

"Someone killed Ingrid." He mumbled. It took a moment before it dawned on her that Ingrid was the Nordic blond who had been Remy's date and subsequent dessert.

"What?" She paused for a moment, only to have someone, one of Jonas's guests, bump into her on his way up.

Instead of running up with the rest of the mob, Celeste closed her eyes and concentrated. She quickly faded from the steps and manifested in the guest bedroom where Ingrid's body lay broken and bloody. She moved through the crowd, pushing past the men that encircled the bed. Jonas, Remy, and Gaston stood bedside, staring in confusion at the remains of the once radiant beauty. They were dumbfounded at the state of her wounds. She lay on top of the covers, pieces of her flesh torn away in chunks; there were millions of tiny holes all over her body, oozing with something black and yellow. The smell was horrific. Those who had found her so delicious the night before were turning up their noses in disgust.

"I have never seen anything like it." Gaston was saying as she moved closer. "What could have done this?" Lisette gasped as she buried her face in Giovanni's neck. He was the only one in the room who seemed pleased by what he saw. He thought it was beautiful, the mangled death of this woman, smiling the way one might smile at a work of art. CeCe felt her stomach churn. Pulling her eyes away from Giovanni's smirking face, she touched Jonas's arm.

"It was here- the thing that killed Nicky," she said. "Last night, I thought it was a dream." Jonas placed his hands on her shoulders and looked into her eyes.

"What are you saying, Celeste?" She took a deep breath.

"It was in my room last night. It could have been me." He pulled her into his arms, clutching her, his eyes on the poor dead girl.

"It could've been me," she whispered.

* * *

Eli banged on his desk in frustration. He hadn't been able to go back to sleep after witnessing the jogger's murder. Nor had he been able to report the incident to anyone. What would he say? Who would he tell, other than Riley, of course? Instead, he'd spent the remainder of the night scrolling through site after site on demons, fairies, and vampires. He'd even looked into the possibility that the damn thing was a chupacabra. When the words on the screen had begun began to dance around in front of his eyes, he called Riley for help.

Right now, what he needed, he thought, was a cup of coffee and a hot shower. He sat back, rubbing his eyes with the heels of his hands as the scent of freshly brewed coffee wafted into the small study. He stopped rubbing his eyes, his body still as he listened. He could hear the tell-tale beeping and steam release of the machine two rooms away. Someone had started his coffee maker. Standing slowly, he reached into the desk drawer for the .22 Glock he'd bought for Grace some time ago. He'd gotten it after a series of burglaries had plagued some of the homes in the Quarter. Grace, being Grace, had balked at the idea.

"No, Eli. I do not want a weapon in my house. Besides," she'd said with a wave of her hand, "I have Boogie. That's almost like having a pit-bull."

So now it lived in the bottom drawer of his desk. Stealthily, he removed the safety before moving cautiously down the hallway. Once he got to the archway that led into the kitchen, he hugged the wall before quickly scanning the room. Then he paused and listened for movement; there was none. He instinctively sniffed the air, but all he could smell was coffee. Closing his eyes, he reached out with his mind for another thought pattern. There wasn't any. He was alone.

He moved into the kitchen and found it-empty, yet the coffee maker beeped and chugged along, all on its own. He stood staring at it in confusion when he heard the familiar click of Riley's key in the back door. He walked in whistling, looking fresh and well-rested.

"Good morning, E." He chirped, but Eli didn't respond. Riley moved closer and followed Eli's line of vision to the coffee pot taking note of the gun against his thigh.

"What are we looking at?" He asked.

"Coffee maker."

"I can see that. Why are we staring at the coffee maker?" Riley clarified.

"It's making coffee," he mumbled. Riley stared at Eli's profile in confusion. It had finally happened, he thought. Eli had blown a fuse. Shaking his head, Eli looked at Riley and sighed.

"I haven't blown a fuse. I'm saying that it started working on its own. I didn't turn it on." Riley stared at the pot as well. It was not one of those new electronic marvels that could be programmed. No, this was old-fashioned, pour the water in and push-button, no-frills manual coffee makers that they had stopped making in the early 1990s.

"Are you going to shoot it?" He asked.

"Don't know yet," Eli answered, honestly. He inhaled the intoxicating aroma and sighed before snapping the safety back into place.

"I guess that's a no." Riley shrugged before tossing the black leather backpack he had slung over his shoulder onto the table. "So, what happened? You turned it on and forgot?" Riley asked.

"No." Eli put the gun on the table and rubbed his tired eyes. "I was in my office thinking that I needed a cup of coffee and a hot shower-" They both froze at the sound of running water coming from upstairs.

"Son of a bitch." Eli grabbed the gun and sprinted up the stairs, Riley hot on his heels. They burst into the master bathroom; guns were drawn to find this room, also empty. The shower was running, steam already fogging the mirror as they scanned the room. Silently, Eli signaled Riley, who nodded before moving into the bedroom to search. They searched each room, every closet, and every nook and cranny someone could hide and found - nothing.

Riley holstered his gun and stared at Eli, who slumped on his bed, the Glock in his hands.

"What the hell is happening?" Eli mumbled. "Riley, could you turn off the shower-" Before the words were out, the water in the bathroom immediately stopped. Riley physically jumped about a foot in the air and then looked at Eli, his large blue eyes wide with sudden acknowledgment.

"E, I think that you're doing this," Riley said.

Eli shook his head. "No-"

"You said you were in your office *thinking* you needed coffee and a shower. The coffee maker started, right?"

He nodded. "But that doesn't-" Riley shook his head in protest.

"Think about it, Eli. No one is in this house. You would know if someone else was in here. You already know that you have some weird shit with you, so why would it be such a stretch?"

"There is no way I'm doing this. I'll prove it." He stood and faced Riley. "I need a nice hot shower." He annunciated every word, a smirk tugging at the corners of his mouth. The smirk fell, and Riley lifted an eyebrow when the shower started, steam billowing from the open bathroom door.

"You were saying?" Riley folded his arms across his chest. Eli shook his head before heading into the bathroom.

"Don't make me shoot you, Riley."

* * *

Celeste sat alone before the dais in the center of the room. Behind her, the gallery where proceedings could be witnessed remained silent and still, cloaked in darkness and very empty. She looked down at her hands, which were sitting in her lap as she patiently waited for the inquisition. The room was dimly lit and draped in deep burgundy curtains. Behind the dais hung a large circular mosaic in bronze, silver, and gold and ancient symbols reminiscent of the zodiac representing each species of the Collective. She sighed heavily as her eyes drifted over the dimly lit members of the Collective as they spoke to each other in hushed tones. Here her powers were muted, and she couldn't hear a word

The one thing she hated about the chamber was that it was protected; no magic could be used here. Even the Collective's powers were limited to flashing in and out. There had been a serious protection spell cast on this place centuries ago, so strong in fact that the only way in was to be teleported in by a standing Collective member or one of their Sentries, like Briar, or a member of The Grey, the Collective's Security. She yawned and exhaled loudly, folding her arms across her chest and tapping her foot. Jonas shot a warning glance at her, which she ignored. He was always warning her about something she either did or said here, but those warnings never really fazed her. They wouldn't do anything to her. There had only been one person ever physically expelled from the Collective that had been Remy, former Commander of the Grey. That had been Lilith's doing; Lilith, the High Regent of the Collective, the highest-ranking member. She was also a vindictive bitch who had some sort of vendetta against the Kent's.

"We cannot find this creature in any of our histories, Celeste," Lilith spoke to her, and Celeste found herself sitting up a little straighter in her seat. As she spoke, Celeste couldn't hide her disdain. Lilith was small, willowy with long fiery auburn hair that hung to her waist in a thick loose braid. Her skin was so pale; it was translucent from living all these centuries without the kiss of sunlight, even though she could venture into the sun, unlike others. Her eyes were bright, almost white-rimmed deep red, which compelled complete honesty from most investigating them. Celeste was not affected by that at all. She was immune to most, if not all, magic. She paid attention because nothing Lilith said was ever what she meant.

"I have never seen anything like it myself," Celeste answered in as few words as possible.

"And how did you happen to see this-creature?" The deep gruff voice of Julian seemed to fill the room. Celeste turned her eyes toward him, and her calm quickly evaporated. Julian was tall, with olive skin, dark wavy hair, and the face of a silent movie idol. He was devilishly handsome with a thin scar that ran across his right cheek, giving him a slightly dangerous look. Unlike the smooth serenity that was all Lilith, Julian was pure raw sexual energy. He always looked at Celeste as if he would just as soon kill her as he would fuck her. He was also a sneaky, underhanded bastard who seemed to be obsessed with her every move.

When she turned to him, he smirked, showing off silvery-white fangs. His amber eyes danced in the dim light. He had always been more wolf than man, she thought, always a predator. At one time, there had been talk of her possibly becoming his mate. She thanked God every day that he had mated with another Lycan, a wickedly vicious bitch with the ever-appropriate moniker of Deva, or D-Evil as Lisette often referred to her.

She could tell by his smirk that he already knew the answer to that question. Her eyes narrowed as she stared at him but did not answer. If she said anything about Eli, the Collective would want to bring him in, and Julian knew that. How

THE FIRST TO FALL

he knew was the question. He had spies everywhere; she just couldn't always tell if they were his, Lilith's, or the Dark Fae.

"Celeste." The sound of Lilith brought her back. "Answer the question."

She scanned the Collective from end to end. On the far left sat Silver Wolf, A Navajo skinwalker, whose youthful appearance belied her age, which Celeste estimated had to be near four hundred years old. Her symbol on the crest was the Owl. She was seated on the opposite end of Julian's dais, as Lycans and skinwalkers often clashed. She had heard rumblings that Julian and Silver had been lovers once upon a time and that she was responsible for Julian's scar.

Next to her was Karim. Beautiful and silent with thick dark hair, deep tawny skin, and eyes that were such a cool pale green that they reminded her of ice. She had spent hours running her fingers through his thick dark hair and kissing his pillow-soft lips. Though his expression never changed, she could see the shadow cross his face. He knew what it meant if Elijah was what she thought he was. It would devastate him, and that would crush her heart. But if it was true, if Eli was what she thought, she had no choice. She gave him a nearly imperceptible nod, and he lowered his gaze briefly. When he lifted his icy green eyes to her, he gave her a reassuring wink, and Celeste made a face. She was granted a smile from him, something he did not do very often, but it was as if the heavens had opened when he did. No matter what, Karim would always be special to her. His symbol on the crest was that of a crescent moon, an obvious choice.

Next was Jonas, a Dhampir, a human-vampire hybrid; their symbol was the chimera, the beast of two natures. The only human on the dais was Sophia Redwine, a White Witch. Sophia sat in silence, her eyes on the knitting needles in her lap, the constant click-click-click of the needles the only sound in the room. Though she seemed preoccupied and feeble, Sophia was sharp and aware of everything going on around her. Her symbol was a simple starburst.

Asmodeus or Adrian represented the demon contingent as he now preferred, one of the seven princes of Hell. Known as The Prince of Lechery, he was a lust demon and all that implied. He was an exceptionally beautiful Asian man with perfectly chiseled features, dark brown eyes, and thick dark hair in his human form. He was one of the oldest members of the Collective; being more than twelve thousand years old, he was by far the most laid back with a surfer style and frat-boy demeanor. His symbol, for obvious reasons, was that of a crown.

The Fae were represented by Javier, who was so beautiful in the natural state that he had to fend off women constantly, which explained why he rarely ventured out among humans. Though the preternatural were drawn to him, humans nearly riot when he is nearby. Of all the Collective members, he made her the most uncomfortable. Javier, or the Bastard, was petty and vain and conniving in many ways, most of the Fae. They were tricksters by nature, which was why their symbol had always been a man with two faces. He sat with his cheek resting on one hand while the other juggled two spheres of bright green and gold light. He yawned dramatically but said nothing, as his hooded eyes settled on her.

Lilith lifted one delicate brow, and Celeste noted that her symbol, the wreath of laurel, hung just above her head on the crest, almost like a crown. Celeste sighed but refused to answer.

"Is there a reason you aren't speaking?" Silver asked, her tone more concerned than curious. Julian leaned forward, his elbows on his knees, chin resting gingerly on his fists.

"Yes, Celeste, is there a reason?" He lifted his eyebrows in quick succession, and she cursed his very being. "Is there something you're hiding from us? Something you don't wish to tell the Collective?" Javier sat up a little straighter in his gilded chair, his bright eyes dancing with delight.

"Is there something, CeCe?" He pried, his voice deep and rich, dripped with his heavy aristocratic accent.

Helplessly, she looked at Jonas, who closed his eyes and gave her a quick nod. She had to talk. It was evident that Julian would tell-all, and the Collective would drag Eli in here if she didn't. That was what she was trying to avoid. Damn it. She hated him. Mentally, she cursed the bloody cur and plastered a smile on her face.

"I'm not hiding anything," she growled through clenched teeth.

Julian sat back with a satisfied smile and crossed his legs at the ankle.

"Well then, love, tell us all about your Detective."

# CHAPTER NINE

Riley was sitting at the kitchen table with his laptop open, volume upon volume of mythology and occult books on the kitchen table before him as Eli entered refreshed from his shower. He strolled in wearing khaki cargo pants and a white button-down shirt, his feet bare.

"Find anything?" He sighed, peering over Riley's shoulder to stare at the computer screen.

"I have found out that there is some weird shit in the world. But I think I've found something worth a gander." He reached past the laptop to an old ratty leather-bound tome with pages so worn that the words were barely visible.

"You remember the other night when we went to Nicky's apartment, and Celeste did that –thing to the door-man?" Eli nodded as he poured himself a cup of coffee.

"Vaguely," he mumbled. Riley rolled his eyes and plowed on.

"It's called glamour. It's used by witches, mostly to change their appearances or disguise them for whatever reason. It's a form of hypnosis." Eli shrugged.

"Well, she didn't use it to disguise herself. I doubt if she's a witch." He snorted.

"Anyway, it's also used by, get this –Vampires and-" He just about squealed, and Eli shook his head.

"Celeste is not a vampire," Eli grumbled, and Riley threw up a hand of protest.

"Dhampir." Riley finished excitedly.

"What?"

"Dhampir. They are some sort of vampire-human hybrid. I

haven't found much on them, but what I have found is pretty interesting. It seems that they have a lot of the same abilities as vampires, but they can walk in the daylight, and they can reproduce-sexually. It says here that vampires and Dhampir use glamour to influence victims to allow them to feed, to do their bidding, and to illicit sexual favor in some."

"I don't think she uses it to illicit sexual favor," he mumbled to himself as he took the book from Riley and scanned the page.

"She's not a Dhampir. Or a vampire or a witch or a succubus or any other fairy tale monster you can think of, Riley. She's probably like me, a little odd, somewhat psychic. And very, very smart. That's all."

"A *little* odd?" Riley snorted. Ignoring him, Eli pressed on.

"You were supposed to be looking for that- thing I saw." Riley took the book and shoved it into his bag, and sighed heavily.

"I bookmarked some things on the computer," Eli stood and watched as Riley clicked through renderings of demons and mythical creatures. A few images reminded Eli of the beast, but none were a proper match. Once they had exhausted all of those, he poured through the stacks of books that lined the counter. It was late afternoon before they had finally given up the ghost.

"It's like a combination of things, but I don't see anything even close," Eli grumbled in exasperation. "Now what?" Riley rubbed his tired eyes, yawned, and closed the last book when Eli's telephone sprang to life. With his own weary eyes burning, he reached blindly for the cordless. Before he could say anything, Grace had already begun to talk.

"Where are you? Everyone's here, and we're starting dinner service in exactly forty-five minutes. You better hustle your ass if you want crabs in your gumbo or stuffed bell pepper." The line went dead.

"Now, we go eat," he said, stretching his tired back. "Before we miss the gumbo."

＊ ＊ ＊

Celeste leaned back in her seat and closed her eyes; her legs stretched out casually before her. "What do you already know?" She asked Julian.

"We know that Briar found you at the Detective's home in the wee hours of the morn." Julian mimicked Briar's Irish brogue. She rolled her eyes, fucking Briar, she should have known. Before he'd become an investigator for the Collective, Briar had been part of Julian's pack and blood brother. The bond between them was eternal.

"The *Detective* is Elijah Cain. He and his partner were assigned to investigate Nicky's disappearance from the funeral home. I was questioned because I was Nicky's physician of record. He has some pre and post cognitive abilities as well as being an empath and a telepath."

"That doesn't explain you being at his house, now does it?" Javier teased, and she shot him a warning glance. She could throttle the two of them. She'd always questioned seating the two biggest troublemakers together on that dais, but who was she to challenge the mighty High Regent.

"As you know, Jonas asked that I identify who or what had embraced Nicky without the Collective's knowledge. From the photos provided by my contact in the forensics office, I could tell that this was something – unusual. It's not a vampire-like we first suspected, but it's not anything I can place either. Knowing that Detective Cain has post-cognitive ability, I asked him to help me do a walk through at the crime scene. I didn't understand just how powerful he was at the time. I didn't understand that he doesn't just sense or see what happened before, he has the unique ability to go back to another time in a given location, and it's some sort of astral projection. We had some encounters before where we shared an electric attraction, I guess, is the term. We failed to realize that when someone like me has any contact with someone like him when his emotions are so close to the surface, we can share memories. The sheer force of his emotions, pain, and terror was so intense that it caused an electrical surge, knocking out transformers and nearly setting a parking garage on fire. It was too much for me, and I blacked out. Detective Cain and his partner took me to his home to recover."

They shared looks of confusion and wariness, all except Adrian, Julian, and a titillated Javier. They just smiled. "Something else happened, didn't it?" Adrian asked. She cursed under her breath, leave it to a lust demon to pick up on what she was trying to hide.

"No." She hadn't even finished the word before Adrian stood before her. He'd flashed out of his seat to stand before her studying her. Slowly, he circled her chair, then reached out and grasped her chin, turning her head from left to right, inspecting her profile, before staring long and hard into her bright turquoise eyes. She tried to pull away, but his grasp tightened. He leaned closer, his nose nearly touching hers as he stared into her unblinking eyes. When her bright blue eyes flashed silver briefly, he smiled triumphantly and released her.

"My, my, my." He tisked and waved a finger at her before going back to his seat. "Technically, she hasn't had sex with him," he announced, and CeCe felt her face grow hot from embarrassment. "But if she's seeing him again, that technicality will become nonexistent. Our little princess has finally found a mate."

Julian leaned back with a self-satisfied smirk on his contemptuous lips, his arms folded across his chest.

"So, you chose a human." Sophia cleared her throat at Julian's sardonic tone. "Pardon Sophia, a mortal, to be your mate. You have had your choice of anyone in the Collective. You could have had kings, gods, *me,* and you choose a mere man. What a disappointment you are, Celeste. What do you have to say for yourself, *Tanrıça?*" Julian used his native Turkish tongue to taunt her with the title she abhorred, *Goddess*.

She met his stare. Her eyes faded from vibrant turquoise to gunmetal as she leveled him with a gaze.

"He is not what you think he is," she said in a low steady tone. "He's not merely a man."

Adrian clapped his hands together in excitement. "Now we're getting somewhere."

He laughed, and Celeste looked at him out of the corner of her eye, her lips curling into a knowing smile. Adrian knew. He was a demon, after all. He knew things the others didn't.

The click-click-click of Sophia's knitting needles stopped abruptly as she focused on Celeste over her glasses.

"He isn't, is he?" Her voice was soft but powerful. She removed the glasses, which were merely for show as Sophia had perfect vision, and smiled. "He's the one you've been waiting centuries for, isn't he dear?" Celeste again felt the warmth grow across her cheeks, and her eyes faded from grey to soft aqua. The one thing that always gave her away was her damn eyes; their color always reacted to her emotions, just like Elijah's.

"Yes, he is. He bears the mark," she said softly. "He bears the mark of the Nephilim."

There was a collective gasp, then a flurry of questions bombarding her. She nearly fell backward out of her seat when they surrounded her. Lilith, Julian, and Sophia were the only ones to keep their seats as the room's noise and energy level rose. Questions were being lobbed at a rapid-fire pace, and she couldn't think, let alone decipher who was asking what. Jonas stood with his back to her, keeping the others from toppling her over as they advanced.

"Quiet!" Lilith bellowed, and, in a blink, everyone had resumed their seats and stoic postures. All except Julian, who was still suspiciously eyeing her, he was leaning forward, his elbows on his knees as he watched her. She returned his stare, her eyes narrowing, the grey again overtaking the vibrant blue, and he was suddenly pinned to the back of his chair. His face twisted in agony, and she could feel the evil little smile curling her lips. She squeezed tighter, her eyes becoming slits as she focused her energy on squeezing the life from Julian. His eyes bulged, and his skin turned a fascinating shade of deep burgundy as he struggled for air. He clawed at the invisible hand that grasped his throat in a vice as he struggled in vain against her, her eyes locked with his as he silently plead for his life. That was what she wanted. She wanted him to beg to remember that she was the most powerful being in this place.

"*Caelestis*," she blinked at the sound of her actual name, breaking the connection. Julian slumped in his seat, inhaling sharp, ragged breaths, his hand massaging his throat. Her powers had broken through the protection spell, not wholly, but enough to sting. She looked sheepishly at Lilith and gave a halfhearted apology. "If he truly is Nephilim, with the abilities you claim he has, why haven't we been aware of him?"

"Because he's not aware. Someone has bound him, a few things are coming through, but he isn't fully aware of all he can do, what he's capable of. I have tried to break through, but his mind is veiled in some pretty potent magic."

"Do you think that you can share his memories again, to act as a sort of conduit for the rest of us?" Silver asked, her eyes alight with growing excitement. They all were excited; Celeste could feel it coming from them in great waves. A Nephilim that neither the Collective nor Dark Fae knew of, with his abilities, had so many implications that they were becoming unhinged. They were quietly waiting for an answer. She could feel the anticipation and anxiety filling the room. It was stifling. "Can we meet him? See for ourselves? Maybe we can break through the bond?" Silver asked.

"I don't know. I mean, whoever bound him must have had a very good reason, right? We don't even know what kind of magic is holding him. Couldn't it get dangerous?" This was precisely what she didn't want to happen. She wanted to keep Eli out of this; he had been protected from the Collective for a reason. "He knows nothing of this world; he knows nothing of what I am. He may just be a lower level Oneiroi or another type of dream walker," she demurred.

"We will send Briar. He is familiar with the detective, correct?" Lilith's question was rhetorical. She knew the answer to that question; obviously, they all had known that Briar had located her at Eli's the previous morning. Closing her eyes, she shook her head. "Then he will bring him to us."

She was prepared to protest when she heard the clatter coming from the back of the room. She stood and spun on her heels, prepared for whatever was coming for her, only to find Briar manifesting, knocking over chairs, his face bloodied and bruised. He took a drunken step forward then collapsed to his knees in the center of the dimly lit room. He flashed quickly from man to wolf, then back again. She could hear Silver calling someone unseen for assistance as he looked up at her with a sad crooked smile.

"Sorry, love, it took him. The little bugger took Nicky. I had him, but it took him. Stronger than it looks." He mumbled and coughed. Blood splattered across the front of her shirt and jeans.

"Put up a hell of a fight, though." He fell, his head hitting the polished grey concrete with a dull thud. As he lay, his shirt rose, exposing the white flesh of his toned stomach. A large chunk had been bitten away by dozens of needle-like teeth, exposing the muscle beneath. Mixed in the blood and gore, something thick and black slithered across the wound, tightening as the air touched its oily skin. The smell that emanated from him was of sulfur, rotted flesh, and pure canine. She recognized that foul stench as soon as it assaulted her nostrils. It had lingered in her bedroom the night before and had permeated the guest room in which poor Ingrid had lain dead. She knelt beside him, cradling his head in her lap as Lilith summoned for more help.

"Nicky, he was different, love. Something was different. He's-changed." He coughed, and blood sprayed from his mouth, spattering her cheek.

"I think I'm hurt, Sarge." He smiled, exposing blood coated

teeth, and closed his eyes. She could feel Jonas pulling her away from the injured Lycan as Silver and Julian knelt beside him, each touched him, eyes closed in concentration, and then the three were gone. The tears that she'd refused to let fall streamed down her cheeks in rivulets. Not just for the injured Briar, but also the missing Nicky.

"*What is happening?*" She asked herself.

"It's going after Eli." She half choked. "I have to help him." She turned to look at Jonas and Lilith. The sheen of tears made her eyes glow in the darkness. "I have to talk to him, Jonas. I'll get him to help just-just send me to him." Jonas kissed her forehead, and then she was gone.

Once she was gone, Jonas and Lilith shared a concerned look. "She's getting stronger," Lilith sighed.

"Should we be worried, Jonas?" Sophia asked.

He looked at the remaining members of the Collective before rubbing his eyes and sighing heavily. For the first time in many years, he felt all of his 800 years. He'd managed to keep her safe for all of these centuries, and he knew, eventually, that he would have to let her go. He'd hoped that day would never come. Yet, here it was. She was getting too strong; she could break through the magic that was centuries old and more powerful than all of them. Lilith touched his arm with concern and obvious affection, and he eased away from the contact. It was as if her touch burned him. There was bad blood between Lilith and the entire Kent clan. She had removed Remy as Commander of the Grey, excommunicating him from the Collective. She had used others to obtain her position as High Regent. Her predecessor had died in the most suspect fashion. Murdered, many said, by Lilith herself. Lilith, who'd coveted the position in the Collective and Jonas's heart. But even now, years after Arbor Kent's death, she only had the Collective. She would never have Jonas's respect or his love.

"Yes," he seemed to deflate at the word and shook his head. "We should all be very worried." He exhaled before turning to leave the room.

* * *

Grace loved the holidays. She loved them so much that by Thanksgiving Day, she had the whole place decorated for Christmas. She had Boogie prepare a buffet of all the things she loved. There were the traditional trappings of Thanksgiving, turkey and stuffing, green beans and mashed potatoes, and cranberry sauce. But there were also the classic New Orleans Thanksgiving staples, baked ham, seafood gumbo, oyster stuffing, candied yams, and of course, bell peppers stuffed with Gulf shrimp and crab meat, which were Eli's favorite. Pumpkin, pecan, sweet potato pies, and bread pudding with rum sauce lined the buffet table as neighbors, family, and friends helped themselves. Some of Grace's more famous musical neighbors came in and played for guests who danced and drank and had a rip-roaring time. Ever the gracious host, she insisted that even the homeless kids who hung out around Jackson Square, the gutter punks and runaways, got their fill on this night. Boogie had always protested letting street trash into the house.

"One of these days, they are going to knock you over the head and rob you blind old woman," Boogie had blustered on more than one occasion. But she always made sure they left with doggie bags, clean new clothes, and fresh blankets. She would deny it, but she had a softer heart than Grace.

When Eli and Riley had entered, Grace, who had been in an in-depth conversation with the laughing red-faced mayor, turned a beaming smile on them.

"There you are." She came over and gave them each a hung and loud smacking kisses on their cheeks. She held Riley at arm's length, "Where's Adam? I expected to see him here." Riley smiled just as brightly, but Eli noticed that it didn't quite reach his eyes.

"He went home for a holiday. He'll be back on Monday."

That explained it. Adam was born and raised by devout evangelical Christian parents in a small town outside of Lake Charles called, Brimstone. And that was all there was to say on that subject.

"Get something to eat before it's all gone. Eli, Boogie saved you two peppers. She put them in the kitchen." She smiled brightly and kissed Eli again.

"I need another drink; my glow is starting to fade. Enjoy." She twirled away, and Eli couldn't help but smile. Riley watched Grace with quiet awe. At her age, she still moved like a woman at least thirty years younger.

"What is it about your grandmother that makes her so wonderful?" he asked.

"Probably the liquor," Boogie mumbled as she came to stand beside them. Riley turned and kissed her cheek.

"Hey Boogie," Eli kissed her forehead and gave her a bear hug lifting her off the ground. She pushed fruitlessly at his shoulders, squirming in a feeble attempt to getaway. He put her back on the floor and laughed as she playfully slapped at him.

"Why do you do that?" she asked.

"You act like you hate this, but I know you don't. I've seen you sneaking food to the homeless kids in Jackson Square."

She gave him a narrow-eyed stare and smiled. "I saved you some peppers and gumbo in the kitchen. Make sure you get it before you leave." She patted his arm as she walked away. Eli smiled after her. His Boogie, to know her was to love her.

* * *

The night was warm enough for the patio doors to be open, and guests spilled out into the crisp November air. Eli had greeted old friends he hadn't seen in years; he danced and drank and shared small talk. For once, he was completely relaxed. That was until he heard that nails on chalkboard laughter that raised the hairs on the back of his neck.

"Elijah, there you are. I have been looking everywhere for you." He turned and came face to face with Hannah Freeman. She was in a nude dress with a black lace overlay that clung to her slight frame. The deep v of the neckline showed an obscene amount of cleavage that had been lotioned until it shone. Her thick hair hung in loose sexy curls around her narrow face, and her make-up was done to perfection. Behind her stood a rather stiff man in a dark grey suit and bright red tie, and a suspicious look on his face. Next to him, a woman who was simply an older version of Hannah. The parents, he thought, and he managed a tight smile.

"Hannah," He leaned over and gave her the obligatory kiss on the cheek in greeting. She smelled of some sweet flowery perfume that tickled his nose, overpowering his senses. He stifled a sneeze as he held out his hand. "These must be your parents? Mr. and Mrs. Freeman, so nice to meet you." Hannah smiled brightly and looped her arm through his protectively, pressing her breasts into his side. "Daddy, Mama, this is Elijah. Elijah, these are my parents Lowell and Ana Freeman." She looked at him as if he were a prized pig, her eyes large and dewy.

Lowell Freeman took Eli's hand and gave it a brusque shake, nodding his head in acknowledgment but said nothing. Lowell openly sized Eli up, while Ana just about gushed.

"I didn't know Grace had such a handsome grandson. Hannah has spoken so highly of you. It's a pleasure." Eli nodded and searched the room for Grace. "She tells us you're an officer with the New Orleans Police department. Do you wear a uniform? I always thought a man in a nice uniform was so dashing." He smiled weakly.

"No, ma'am, I'm a detective. I wear plain clothes."

Lowell cleared his throat. "Ever shot a man?" He looked at Lowell curiously. "I have." Lowell blustered, and Ana slapped his arm.

"Lowell, you have not cut that out. He's trying to scare you off. Be nice to Hannah's young man." He gave a tight laugh and searched the room for rescue. When had he become Hannah's anything, he wondered? Riley stood near the bar on the patio with Boogie. They both raised their glasses in a toast as they laughed.

He made a mental note to pay the two of them back for this very soon.

* * *

Celeste manifested on the sidewalk underneath a balcony on the corner of Ursulines and Burgundy. She stood for a moment, waiting for nausea and dizziness to subside before she mentally searched for him. There was always that jarring, almost seasick feeling after being transported in and out of the Collective's chamber. Mostly because it wasn't her power used; instead, it was like being propelled through space in a gyroscope. She took a deep breath, closed her eyes, and listened. He was nearby and in some sort of distress. She could hear the music and laughter coming from behind a high stone fence covered in delicate ivy, making her way down the block. Eli was behind that wall. She could feel the tension in his body and an overwhelming need for rescue. Yet the desperation wasn't due to any imminent danger; it was something else. Moving closer, she felt her curiosity piqued by the strange emotion roiling through Eli. There was a definite need for help but no panic or pain, just the need for someone to get him away.

She found herself pushing through the crowd milled around the heavy wooden double doors that stood open in greeting to all. She stood on the threshold, peering inside, and smiled. She eased further into the foyer and found the place teeming with people, from the well to do to street people milled around with heaping plates of food. The music bounced off the walls, and laughter seemed to emanate from everywhere. The room was dressed for Christmas in shades of white, blue, and silver. The whole place smelled delicious, like Christmas and Thanksgiving and home. Near the open patio doors was an enormous tree flocked to look as if it had been caught in a gently falling snow, and then she saw him.

Eli stood head and shoulders above the crowd. He was clean-shaven and wearing a blue-grey sweater and dark denim jeans. He looked delicious, and she wanted to take a bite out of him. She had an overwhelming urge to go and wrap herself around him. Just the thought of his mouth and hands on her caused gooseflesh to rise on her skin. Damn it, if he weren't the sexiest thing she'd ever seen—the things she would do to him.

Giving herself a mental shake, she studied him a little closer. Something wasn't right. He was smiling tightly, his eyes darting to the bar where Riley and a redhead stood smiling and laughing at him. When she noted Hannah Freeman was gripping Eli's arm, he made sure he stayed put as they spoke with an older couple. Celeste had to admit; Hannah looked beautiful. She'd stepped up her game since their last meeting, and she was more than sure this little bitch was in heat and had Eli's scent. She could feel the immediate fury rising in her, and she wanted Hannah's blood and a fair bit of her hair, too.

Celeste felt the devious smile start as she moved into the living room, passing a mirror as she exited the empty foyer. She paused and looked down at herself. She was wearing jeans and a white tee that had been splattered with blood and grime from Briar. Her hair was a tangled mess piled high on her head, her blood splattered, and tear-streaked face was a mess. She smelled of blood and sweat and animal.

"Oh, this will not do," she mumbled. She looked around before slinking into a shadowy alcove to change. One good thing about being who she was, instant wardrobe changes were always possible. She closed her eyes and snapped her fingers. There was a quick flash, like that of a camera, and she was done. She went back to peer in the mirror and smiled at what she saw.

"Okay bitch, let's play," she mumbled and adjusted her breasts before turning on her heel. She was gunning for Hannah Freeman, and in this man trap of a dress, she was loaded for bear.

* * *

Eli was mouthing what he would do to Riley, who stood laughing at the bar when a scent caught his attention. It was warm vanilla and light flowery lavender with just a hint of honey. From the corner of his eye, he glimpsed a glint of gold, moving through the crowd. Turning his head, he saw her, and his mouth went dry, and his body hot immediately.

Her hair hung over one shoulder in long dark cascading waves of black silk. Her eyes seemed to capture his with laser-like precision. She wore a short gold dress that dipped dangerously low in front, exposing her bare golden skin from neck to cleavage, and clung to the toned muscles of her upper thighs. She was tucking something into a small clutch she held in her perfectly manicured hand but looking at him coyly through long dark lashes. His eyes moved over her long, lean legs and gold stilettos. He could still feel those legs wrapped around his waist as she pressed her warmth against him. Every nerve in his body came to life at the thought of her.

As she approached, the crowd backed away, giving her a wide berth. Heads swiveled as if on pivots as she sashayed through, her eyes never straying from his face. She bit her bottom lip, and his body ignited. What was wrong with him? He had never craved a woman the way he craved Celeste. He had always been regimented and in complete control of his carnal urges. Except with her, something about her made him lose all semblance of control. It was as if she had cast a spell on him, and he was helpless against it.

In unison, the Freemans turned to see what had captured Eli's attention, and the stoic façade of Lowell Freeman evaporated. He stared at the Amazon stalking toward him, sucking in his gut instinctively. Ana's smile faltered for a moment as Eli slipped his arm from Hannah's death grip and walked toward her, his intent clear. He closed the space between them in two steps and took her into his arms, his mouth covering hers in a kiss that made her knees buckle. She clung to him to keep from falling, her fist balling into his sweater as she held onto him for dear life. His mouth was hot and hungry and tasted of champagne. Eli had her face, his hands buried in her hair as he thoroughly kissed her. She felt that kiss down to her toenails. When he finally released her, she looked at him through her lashes.

"I take it you're happy to see me." She breathed.

"You have no idea. What are you doing here? How'd you find me?" He asked, stepping back to hold her at arms distance, taking her in with genuine appreciation.

"I have many, many talents, Detective Cain," she whispered, resting her head on his cashmere covered chest. She exhaled sharply and shook her head, trying to break the spell he had on her.

"We need to talk," she was saying, as Riley, Boogie, and Grace moved closer to the Freemans watching with amused interest.

Riley could just about feel the steam coming out of Hannah's ears as she stared. Ana and Lowell simply watched in confusion.

"That her?" Grace asked in a mock whisper. Riley smiled broadly.

"Oh yeah, the one and only. Didn't I tell you; they look like they were made for each other?"

Boogie sidled up to Hannah, a mischievous glint in her eyes as she said, "Looks like you're shit out of luck, girlie. You can't compete with that. It's like putting a Shetland pony next to a thoroughbred. You're cute and all, but you ain't gonna win this race." Boogie laughed and gave Hannah's shoulder a conciliatory pat, which Hannah slapped away the way one might shoo away a fly.

Determined, Hannah sauntered over once again, possessively looping her arm through Eli's.

"You remember Hannah," Eli tilted his head towards Hannah, his eyes still on Celeste. She inclined her head to Hannah, who stood tight-lipped. "And these are her parents."

Polite as ever, Ana Freeman rushed forward to shake Celeste's hand, a radiant smile on her face, yet there was a look of profound befuddlement in her eyes. On the other hand, Lowell Freeman had a look of pure unadulterated envy in his lustful eyes as he glared at Celeste. He edged Hannah aside, dislodging her from Eli's hip, to get a closer look at Celeste. He lowered his voice to a nearly comical baritone and held her hand a little too long, staring a little too blatantly.

Riley cleared his throat and broke the contact between the two when he saw Celeste try and fail to slip her hand out of Lowell Freeman's grasp politely. He smiled brightly and gave her a tight squeeze, "How are you doing, Doc?" He asked. A fleeting look of concern darkened his features.

"I'm fine, Riley. Thanks."

"CeCe, this is my grandmother Grace Babineaux." Celeste extended her hand, which Grace ignored and embraced the woman. Then her body went stiff. She pulled back; her smile faltered but never dropped. She looked into Celeste's eyes, and her breath caught in her chest.

"It is so nice to meet you, *Caelestis*." Her voice cracked slightly as she stared at Celeste, whose eyes widened in surprise at the use of her given name. Grace swallowed hard but never took her eyes from the younger woman. She nervously stepped back, bumping Boogie as she looked at Celeste with something very close to awe.

"What did you call her?" Eli asked.

"What?" Grace looked at him, a bit distracted and confused. Celeste extended her hand to Boogie. "You must be Boogie," she said. Boogie took her hand in both of hers and nodded.

"So, you're the one, huh?" She asked, giving Celeste an appreciative once over.

"The one?" Celeste asked. Boogie tilted her head toward Hannah, who stood with her mouth in a tight little line.

"The one leading Eli around by the short hairs and putting the twist in that one's panties. You've got his nose wide open. Not that I can blame him, I mean, look at you. When you walked in, every Johnson in the room stood at attention."

"Boogie!" Eli snapped, but it was too late. She'd already said it. Celeste stifled a snicker as his temperature rose a few degrees. Boogie always had a way of embarrassing him, but then that was Boogie. She had no filter, and whatever she thought always managed to slip from her lips. Celeste kissed him on the neck before Boogie grabbed her right arm, and Riley took her left.

"Ignore him, come on. We'll show you around. Riley and I will give you the grand tour." Before Eli could protest, they had whisked her away. She turned too looked back at him with a knowing smile as he watched her. She could feel the heat of his gaze as he took note of the back of her dress; better yet, the lack thereof. The dress dipped low in front, exposing perfect caramel cleavage, but the back was nonexistent, giving him an eyeful of toned bareback down to the small of her back. He made a noise close to a high-pitched squeak and closed his eyes.

"Goddamn." Lowell Freeman whispered and slapped Eli on the back, suddenly in a more cheerful mood. "You lucky motherfucker."

"Lowell!" Ana snapped, her plastic smile finally dropping.

"Daddy!" Hannah barked in unison. Lowell looked at the two of them with little remorse.

"Do you *see* her?" He asked the two women with a slight degree of indignation. "Sorry, sweetie," Lowell kissed Hannah's forehead and held her close in a conciliatory hug, giving Eli the thumbs-up behind her back. Eli followed Lowell's gaze as she was introduced to guests at the party. Her eyes drifted over to Elijah every once in a while, a smile on her berry-colored lips. She narrowed her eyes before she turned away, and he saw a fleeting shadow crossed her face. There was something wrong, something she wanted to tell him but wasn't sure. She was hiding something. He stared for a while longer, grabbing a glass of champagne that was being passed on a tray by the few servers that hustled through the crowd. *"Why was she here,"* he thought. And how did she know where to find him? He'd always known she was hiding something, but what?

Everything in him screamed Run! Stop! Danger! But he ignored the warnings. He was falling for her, and he couldn't stop himself. How could he control something more natural than breathing? Sure, she was evasive, closed off, and secretive. She was from one of the wealthiest families in the world. That was just par for the course, he supposed, self-preservation.

He'd seen Grace shut down when people got to close, now that he thought about it. Celeste and Grace had that in common, among other things. They were both shielded with a tightly held group of close friends and family. They were strong-willed, beautiful, effervescent women. They attracted people like bees to honey, but they kept the world at arm's length. Hell, Celeste was the sexiest, funniest, smartest, loveliest woman he'd ever met, and she had never been made love to, not really. How was that possible? Better yet, how had she never been truly, completely in love? How could someone look at her and hurt her, use her? How had she remained so much of an innocent, well, not entirely innocent? She did melt when he kissed her, her body growing hot and wet at his slightest touch. She was uninhibited and seductive and playful, yet she was still pure. He sipped his drink and watched her being moved through the crowd by her over-enthusiastic escorts.

"Curiousier and curiousier," he mumbled.

Grace stood beside Eli so quietly that he'd forgotten she was there. He turned to her, lifting a brow.

"Okay, what is it?' He asked, and Grace visibly jumped at

the sound of his voice, then laughed, giving Eli's arm a playful punch.

"She's lovely, Elijah. Just lovely." She tucked her arm into his and walked him out into the cold night air and soft jazz played by her neighbors' makeshift band. Lovely was a term that Grace reserved for people and things she did not particularly care for. Had something about Celeste shaken her? He'd seen it when they'd embraced. Something had happened, and Grace had momentarily stiffened. And she had called her something, what was it she'd said?

"What did you call her? *Caelestis*?" Grace paused only for a moment.

"I think I must have slurred my words. And it's tacky for you to bring up how tipsy I am." She paused and turned to look up at him. "I think she is stunning. She's very-tall." He shook his head and was about to speak when Grace placed her hands on his face and looked into his eyes. There seemed to be serenity about Grace that always made him feel safe and that everything would be fine. She smiled and kissed him on the cheek. "She makes you happy, *Cheri*, then I am happy."

He smiled and held onto her wrist and sighed. "I do like her, but-"

"But what?" She held his eyes, waiting.

"There's something *wrong* about her." He hadn't wanted to say it out loud, but there it was. There was something strange and wonderful and very wrong about her. Grace laughed, giving his head a shake before releasing him.

"Some say the same about you, Elijah. But you're wrong in the right-est way possible if that makes any sense."

"No, it doesn't." He laughed and kissed the top of Grace's head. "But I get what you mean." He sighed.

"Good. Come buy me a drink." Once again, she said, looping her arm through Eli's, guiding him over to the open bar.

\* \* \*

Celeste stood next to where the Zydeco band played a slow fais do-do, rocking to the beat, a glass of champagne in her hand. She closed her eyes and inhaled the sweet smell of the night-blooming jasmine from Grace's garden and let her mind wander. She tensed slightly when she felt the approach of someone from behind. "By the twitching in my thumbs," Celeste mumbled, "something wicked this way comes." With a satisfied smile, she turned to see Hannah standing with her arms folded across her chest, a tight smile on her overly glossed lips.

"You think you're hot shit, don't you?" she asked in a low, angry tone.

"Pardon?" Celeste widened her eyes and feigned innocence. Hannah dropped her arms, her hands balling into fists, and narrowed her eyes.

"So that you know, you've met your match. I will not step aside for you or anyone else. Eli -"

"Is just not that into you?" Celeste finished. "You don't know what you're getting yourself into, Hannah." Hannah shook her head.

"Maybe you don't know what you're getting into." Hannah countered. "This little kitty has claws and teeth. And I don't fight fair." Celeste tilted her head and studied the other woman. There was something that caught Celeste's attention, a hint of something unnatural in the flash of the girl's eyes. She took a step closer and sniffed the air around Hannah, then smiled. Hannah stepped back.

"What are you doing?" she stammered, her eyes wide. Celeste smirked and folded her arms across her chest.

"You may have claws, but you huff and puff just like a little-wolf." Hannah's eyes narrowed as she stared at Celeste. Her deep brown eyes flashed briefly, glowing bright amber. The scent she'd smelled that was hidden beneath the sickeningly sweet perfume was all lycan. So, it hadn't been Briar who'd given her up. It had been little, Ms. Freeman.

"So, you're Julian's little pet? Or are you part of Deva's clan?

You're an outstanding actress. You even had me fooled, pup, but your game is done." Hannah's face tightened. She opened her mouth to speak when Eli approached and took Celeste's hand.

"Dance with me, CeCe." She smiled at Eli, but her eyes remained on Hannah. He turned his back as he coaxed her to the small dance floor. Celeste hesitated and smiled briefly at the other woman exposing glistening white fangs and flashing eyes sparked with blue fire.

"*Be careful where you tread, little pup. There be hunters in these woods,*" Celeste whispered into her ear as she brushed past

* * *

"What was that about?" he asked, drawing her into his arms as the band switched from Zydeco to "*At Last*" by Etta James.

"Girl talk," she mumbled, melting into him. He looked down at her.

"You're lying," he said.

"Yep," she agreed, draping her arms around his neck, her head resting on his shoulder. She closed her eyes and listened to his heartbeat, indulgencing in the feel of him against her, his hand on the small of her bareback, pressing her hips tightly against his rock-hard body, and her skin warmed. He was assaulted by her scent and made a soft happy sound.

"I love the way you smell. I haven't washed my sheets because I can still smell you when I go to sleep," he confessed. "And what is it about you that makes me admit these things to you?" The feel of her body pressed against him made him harder than he'd ever been. She moved closer, her hips moving against the bulge in his pants. The feel of the rough material against his already vibrating groin made him growl deep in his chest. His reaction to her was always visceral, and he knew just from being that close to her that she was wet for him. Leaning over, he nipped at her neck, just above the vein that pulsated there. He could smell her blood pumping just beneath the surface, her skin grew hot to his, and her scent seemed stronger, and the smell of lavender seemed to envelop him. Again, he found himself longing to sink his teeth into her tender flesh and drink from her long and deep. Instead, he kissed the skin just below her ear.

"Eli, we really need to talk." She looked up into his eyes, and the world seemed to disappear. All she saw was him. He was looking at her with smoldering heavy-lidded eyes, and she felt her body go weak. She was lost; all she could think of was kissing him, of kissing every naked inch of his body. He leaned closer, his lips moving over hers with such a fierce need, she couldn't breathe or think. All she could do was tighten her arms around his neck to pull him closer. She nipped his lips with her teeth before pulling away.

"Are you finally ready to let me in on the big secret?" He teased, and she looked down.

"There is so much you don't know." Her voice was nearly a whisper.

"About you?" He placed a finger under her chin and forced her to look at him. She gently pulled his face down to her so that her lips could touch his again. This kiss was soft and tender, but her need for him was still strong, but she needed to tell him before it went any further.

"About everything. Take me home, Detective." She breathed against his lips.

\* \* \*

Grace stood close to Boogie as they watched the two of them dance, their bodies so close not even air seemed to get between them. Boogie sighed.

"I think he's found the one, Gracie," she whispered. Grace looked at Boogie with a sad smile and tear-filled eyes.

"I think you're right, Boog. And I think we're all in big trouble."

# CHAPTER TEN

I t had only taken a couple of minutes for Eli to get his car. She snuggled closer to him in the front seat, their fingers intertwined.

"So where are we going, Doc?" His voice was low and thick and sexy; his entire body was humming in anticipation. She sighed, her head resting on his shoulder, the fingers of her free hand moving slowly up his thigh.

"I live on the top floor of the Cotton Mill." She whispered, her tongue darting out to tease his earlobe. The Cotton Mill was a former warehouse transformed into luxury condos about four blocks from the riverfront, high-end, and exclusive. She gently nibbled his ear, her lips leaving hot little kisses on his neck, and he hit the gas, making a beeline for the place.

As he swung the car onto North Peters Street and headed towards her building, her cell phone came to life.

"Damn it," she grumbled as she punched the speaker button, wanting to continue her exploration of his thigh, and continue moving her lips down his throat.

"Where are you?" Lisette just about yelled in her ear. Eli's brow lifted at her sister's rather abrupt tone.

"On my way to my condo. Why?" She mumbled, taking Eli's earlobe between her teeth.

"Are you eating?" Lisette barked. "What are you doing?"

"What do you want?" She bit back.

"Is someone with you? You sound funny." Lisette persisted.

"I swear to God, Lissy, I'm going to hang up if you don't get to the damn point," she growled, her hand resting on Eli's crotch. He made a deep guttural noise, and she smiled deviously.

"Remy is at Jinxie's drunk off his ass and picking a fight with Julian Onder. I need you to get to him before he starts a war. I'm not going to get there in time." Celeste rolled her eyes.

"Why can't Gaston go? He lives right on St. Charles." She sat up, pulling her hand from Eli's in frustration.

"Jonas sent Gaston to Prague for some asinine reason or other. He's landing as it were, now. Could you please get Remy? This could be trouble CeCe. You know how stupid he gets, and Julian is just looking for a reason to tear into Remy's ass."

"He does have that effect on people," she mumbled. "Fine, I will get him before he gets himself killed." She grumbled and disconnected. She looked at Eli, frustration, and anger building up in her. "So where is this Jinxie's?" He asked, waiting for directions.

"You don't mind?"

"Oh, I mind, not as much as my dick right about now. The sooner we get-Remy is it? That's your younger brother, right? The sooner we get him squared away, the sooner I get to be alone with you. No more interruptions." She kissed his cheek. Their little talk was going to have to wait a little longer. Not that she was all that eager to say anything. What she wanted was to be wrapped in his arms in a blissful cloud for as long as possible. She could postpone the inevitable, just for a little longer.

"I owe you," she whispered, a warmth growing in her chest. Something soft, something she had never felt before with a man.

"And I plan to collect," he mumbled before putting his foot down hard on the gas pedal again.

* * *

Instead of heading towards her apartment on Annunciation Street, he turned onto St. Charles Avenue and headed to State Street. Exhaling, he focused on the road putting his most base need for her at bay, for the time being anyway.

"*All good things*," he told himself as he tried not to stare at her long silken legs in the dim lighting cast into the interior by the streetlights outside. She shivered as they drove, the dress not providing much warmth. Leaning forward to adjust the heat, the draping at the top of the dress shifted, and Eli caught a glimpse of her breasts. They were full, perfectly rounded, her nipples erect, like caramel kisses. His hands itched to touch her, to take her into his mouth. A tiny groan escaped him involuntarily.

"Too hot? Want me to turn it down?" She asked as a flare of warmth blasted the interior.

"Yes, but it has nothing to do with the heater." He saw her smirk, and he was sure that she was biting her lip the way she did, but she didn't say anything.

Thinking they were heading to some night club; he was naturally surprised when he recognized the brick wall that encircled what had at one time been a psychiatric facility and at one point had been a military hospital. They stopped at the gate where two rather large guards were posted before the intricately designed golden gates.

They approached the car on either side, both so large that they nearly had to kneel to look into the windows. Eli rolled down the windows as they moved closer when he realized that they were twins. Both huge with thick dark hair and tobacco brown eyes. He had never seen eyes like that on a person before; they reminded him of a canine's eyes.

"Good evening," the one on Eli's side of the car spoke with a thick Southern drawl. Their thoughts were distinct, sort of wild, and haphazard.

She leaned forward into the light and smiled before saying something in Russian. The two smiled and returned her greeting. The thick Southern drawl was replaced with perfect Russian. The way they spoke to her, with such fluidity in ease, there was no doubt that it was their native tongue.

"Eli, these are the Kulivichek twins. Ivan," the one on Eli's side of the car inclined his head. "And Vlad." The twin near Celeste lifted a hand in greeting.

"Your brother is in there. I guess that's why you're here." Vlad said.

"Have fun. Call us if you need help." Ivan gave them a knowing wink before he motioned to someone inside the little guard booth and the gates swung open. As they drove through, a third man, just as big, but with blond hair, waved at them. "Have fun, Ms. CeCe." He called in the same Southern twang.

"Come here often?" Eli teased.

As they roared up the driveway, the place looked nothing like Eli's vague memories. The land had housed a full hospital, recreation facility, a separate office building, and cottages on the outer perimeter. They were no longer there; instead, the land had been converted into a palatial wonderland. The house sat up high on a man-made hill, a white English Country manor, with vines of ivy and roses creeping up the sides. The surrounding land was all meticulous gardens of flowers and fruit trees. The greenery seemed to be neon, filling the night air with an eerie glow. It was as if they'd driven into a greenhouse or a Thomas Kinkade painting. The air was heavy with flowery perfume and something else, something mystical.

The street wound towards the house, and her heart began to thud in her chest. Remy was in there. So was Julian, and this night could go one of two ways. His surroundings would have too entranced him to be concerned about what he was seeing, or he would run screaming into the night, never to be seen again.

Eli guided the car to the circular driveway at the front of the house, where valets, all young men, all with angelic faces, parked vehicles. They were all bright-eyed and smiling, none seemed to be over the age of 15 years, and all had bright rosy cheeks. Cherubic was the word that came to mind. As they got out, one of the young men touched his arm, and a sudden feeling of calm overcame him.

"What is this place?" he asked numbly. Celeste took his hand; her smile looked a bit strained and nervous, her palms sweating as they crossed the threshold into what could be a disaster of monumental proportions. She stole sidelong glances at Eli, his eyes wide with wonder as she led him into her world. This would be her litmus test. There had only been one other person she'd allowed to venture into this part of her world. Well, one human person, and that had ended in catastrophe. If he could deal with the crazy surreal world that she lived in, he would surely be able to handle the truth of who and what she was. At least, that was what she was hoping.

"It's Jinxie's," she said, watching as his eyes became alight with excitement.

* * *

Inside the house, Eli wasn't sure what to make of the place. The floors were polished black marble, the walls slate, and even though the outside was blindingly white, the inside was dark greys, black, and red. It reminded him of a bordello.

He followed Celeste into the great room, which was packed with the oddest collection of people Eli had ever seen. They were young for the most part, many of them stunning, but there were a few who seemed to hum with vibrant color and others who appeared to have a matte, almost dustiness, to their skin. Then there were the large ones, like those at the gates, maybe eight or nine of them, male and female. Women and men were running around dressed as fairies with large elaborate wings, their faces painted in glitter and all, their topless bodies painted with leaves and flowers. They flitted through the garden and danced in cages, strategically placed throughout the entire first floor. As the fairies floated around the room, they left a trail of fine gold and silver glitter on everything.

"Freakin' pixie dust, don't inhale it," Celeste mumbled, brushing the sprinkles from her dress, but it was too late. One of the female fairies touched his cheek, and Eli was overcome with a feeling of absolute joy and release.

Most of the waiters, shuffling through the crowd with trays of drinks and hors d'oeuvers, were dressed in togas and held stony expressions, bowing as they passed. Celeste grabbed two glasses of wine, handing one to Eli before they moved further into the room. He felt his face spread into a wide, almost maniacal smile, and for the life of him, he didn't know why. There was a scream somewhere in the back of the house, followed by a loud laugh, then a splash. Someone, a woman he thought, had been thrown into a pool. The music was loud and undulating. People moved, swaying wherever they stood, some in various stages of undress and others either wholly unaware or merely unconcerned. Celeste watched Eli closely, his eyes a cobalt blue, dancing drunkenly. Smiling, she relaxed, but only a little.

"What *is* this place?" He asked again, but before she could answer, there was a scream of delight coming from the entryway of the great room. No one looked at all surprised or even looked at the petite woman with dark hair.

She was only about five feet in heels, but she seemed to fill the room with her presence. Her eyes were large, sharply slanted upward, and overpowered her small face. She wore a bright green 1950's style cocktail dress; her skin's paleness was in deep contrast to the bright red of her lips, the darkness of her hair, and the vivid grass green of her eyes. She looked to be in her mid-twenties and giggled like a pre-teen. Her hair was a short cap of dark Betty Boop like curls that came down just long enough to cover her ears' tops.

As she approached, Eli felt his joy rise. He was downright giddy. There was a bright light of joy around her, radiating in waves to those around her. His own eyes began to glow bright turquoise in response, and he smiled down at her goofily.

"CeCe, so glad to see you." She held a martini, almost the exact shade of green as her eyes, in her right hand, hugging Celeste with her left arm. She had a deep southern drawl, a bright smile, and he assumed that this was their hostess. She looked at Eli approvingly, her eyes roaming his body from head to toe.

"My, aren't you a big one?" She said breathlessly. "Are you big everywhere?" He tilted his head to the side, his hands going inexplicably to the button of his jeans.

"Well, let's find out," he teased. She stood waiting expectantly. Celeste put a staying hand on him, shaking her head when he looked at her curiously.

"Detective Elijah Cain, this is my good friend Jinxie Monroe. Jinxie, Eli Cain." He took her outstretched hand and gave it a brisk shake.

"It's a pleasure," he said, finding himself wondering what was happening to him; he felt so free, so completely relaxed. She held onto his hand tightly, surprisingly strong for someone her size.

"It certainly could be." She gave him a wink and picked up a glass of something pale pink as a waiter hustled by.

"Welcome to my home." Jinxie handed him the drink, and he obligingly took it. "CeCe, I think the party you are looking for is occupied somewhere on the third floor. Ya'll have fun now, hear." She gave him another wink before sashaying away. Eli had the rim of the glass to his lips when Celeste took it from him.

"You don't want to drink that. It's Jinxie's special nectar. You'll wake up three days from now naked in a ditch somewhere in Plaquemines Parish." She downed the entire glass before taking his hand and leading him into the room. For the most part, he just observed the evening, standing beside her and watching as she laughed and talked, her eyes coming to rest on him every once in a while. Everyone seemed to hold her in some sort of reverence, like their own personal celebrity. He also found it odd that they all bowed to her, like royalty.

Once in a while, he would feel a stray hand caressing him, his chest, and his butt. Once, someone reached for his crotch, only to have their wrist grabbed by Celeste. He had found himself more than once touching others. He was randomly stroking the flame-red hair of a woman in a white dress. She smiled and leaned into him before Celeste came and dragged him away.

"Oh, CeCe doesn't share her toys?" The woman pouted, and if he hadn't known any better, he would have sworn that Celeste had hissed at the woman. There was a silence, and then the offending young woman bowed her head apologetically before leaving the room in a hurry. She sat him on a sofa nearby to keep an eye on him and continued her conversation with a large male and dusty-looking woman.

As he watched her, he felt someone watching him. He sought out his watcher, his eyes falling on a youngish man in either his late twenties or early thirties. He was tall, muscular, but not bulky. As men go, he was pretty with dark unruly hair, and eyes so large they shimmered. His skin was dark, a deep tan but seemed to have an undercurrent of light or something just beneath the surface. He wore a red shirt with intricate black designs running diagonally across the bottom and black leather pants. He stared holes through Eli. Eli smiled goofily at him.

As he turned away, he came face to face with another man, large with dark hair and skin and eyes the color of an autumn sunset. He stared at Eli and growled low and deep in his throat.

"Watch yourself, *pislik*," he mumbled through clenched teeth. Eli stared at him and smiled.

"Don't call me an asshole, *pislik*," Eli growled back, suddenly aware that he spoke Turkish. The other man stepped closer; his eyes sparkled with fire. Eli smiled. His blue eyes alight by the prospect of a fight. He hadn't fought for as long as he could remember. He needed a good fight.

"You must want me to rip a hole in your hide, boy." Eli

grinned stupidly.

"Oh, you think this is funny?" The fist that was intended for Eli's face was stopped when Celeste grabbed the man's wrist. He growled again as she dropped the hand and gave him a look of warning.

"I see you've met Elijah. Eli, this is Julian. I see you've moved onto another man in my life to pick a fight with. I knew you were obsessed with me, but really." Julian laughed, and she smiled, folding her arms across her chest.

"Don't flatter yourself, CeCe." He growled. "I just don't like the trash that you seem to drag around." She snorted.

"Really? Is that why you're here trying to start a fight with Remy? Honestly, Julian, don't we have enough to worry about right now? I don't need you, two idiots, trying to start a turf war while we're in the middle of-" She glanced at Eli, who had wandered away from them. She spotted him walking up the stairs. Sighing, she turned back to Julian. "In the middle of this mess." He smirked and took a long hard appraising look at her, and ran his tongue over one of his rather large incisors.

"I must admit, you are looking mighty foxy." Julian ran a hand over his mouth, his eyes traveling up and down her body. She snorted again.

"Foxy? How 1975. I want you to cool it with Remy. Please, Julian, I've got bigger fish to fry tonight. The last thing I need is to be a referee. Help me out here." Julian's bravado faded at the desperation in her tone. He glanced at the stairs as Eli disappeared down the hallway.

"That detective, you're right about him. Something is binding him, but it's so close to the surface you can smell it. If he is what you say he is, we will have bigger problems than this creature and whether or not I take a bite out of Remy's narrow ass." She smiled weakly and patted Julian on the arm as he walked past her.

"Yes, I know."

The fact of the matter was, if he were what she thought, this would go beyond the Collective. This would go straight to the Council of the Gods. Exhaling, she continued her search for her errant brother to drag him home and put him to bed.

Eli wandered around the labyrinth of rooms upstairs. He'd discovered what he assumed to be an orgy. There was a mass of bodies writhing around, all oiled up and moaning, like a pile of snakes knotted together. Another room held a trio where one man was being tied up, and two small Asian women took turns throwing bologna at him. Each time a slice slapped against his bare skin, the man would moan in ecstasy. This, Eli discovered, was a pleasure he would never understand. There were more exotic forms of sexual release going on in other rooms of the house. He found the party attendees to be a rather bizarre and artistic bunch, colorfully dressed, rainbow-maned people, with dancing eyes. Sure, he received a few curious glances but never more than that as they practiced their diversions. Jinxie's place was like Bourbon Street on Halloween, and he found himself very at home in this place. None of this seemed odd or out of place to him; it seemed, for lack of a better term, familiar.

As he made his way back down into the great room, he could hear raised voices and breaking glass. Pushing his way through the crowd, he could listen to Celeste and a man yelling at each other. She stood with her hands on her hips, tapping her foot in frustration as Eli's silent stalker and Julian grappled in the center of the floor. Celeste stepped in between them without a word and held her hands up. She looked at Julian, who angrily swiped at the blood trickling from his lip. He lunged, and she shook her head, staying him with a silent pleading look. Julian seethed, his eyes drifting over to Eli, who stood watching before he bowed his head, turned, and stormed out of the room. Celeste grasped the other man by the arm and ushered him to the side of the room as the party continued. The man stumbled drunkenly, and Eli smirked. One thing about being a cop in New Orleans, you could spot a drunk a mile away, and this guy was past drunk. He was completely wasted.

Jinxie appeared out of nowhere beside Eli, now in a lemon yellow 1950's style tea-length party dress with a full skirt and matching pumps, standing next to him shaking her head. "Poor, Remy. That boy has been in love with her for as long as I've known him. He just can't get past the fact that she's his sister. And Julian- well, we all want a piece of Julian." She said matter of factly.

"That's her brother?" he asked, watching as the two had a heated disagreement on the opposite side of the room. He was gesturing wildly, and she simply managed to look annoyed, her arms folded across her chest as he continued his manic rant. Celeste was unflinching in her steeliness, and she said something that made Remy step back an inch; he looked as if she'd struck him.

"Don't get me wrong. It's not as deliciously incestuous as it sounds." Jinxie continued. "CeCe was nearly an adult when Jonas and Arbor adopted her. Remy is only a year or so older than her. It's not like he's known her since she was a baby. To him, she came into his family as is. There was even talk that Jonas wanted her specifically for Remy. To marry, be his woman or whatever the hell it is you people do now." Jinxie explained. She scooped one of those pale pink drinks from a passing tray and handed it to him. He downed it without even tasting it. "I believe that you fuck who you fuck until you get bored, and then you move on. So maybe they should fuck and get it over with. But they will never do that. She is the *Caelestis*, after all. She is special." Eli nodded dumbly, his eyes on the heated exchange. There was that name again. He looked at Jinxie, clearly intending to ask her what exactly *Caelestis* was when Remy's voice seemed to echo through the entire house.

"Him? Him?" Remy was saying, waving his hand in their direction. Celeste stood taller, her back straight as she poked Remy in the chest with a finger. She was saying something in a foreign language, from what Eli could catch from his vantage point. Her mind was like a steel trap, her body rigid with anger and frustration. Remy had done something, something she found disgusting and mean spirited. He opened his mouth to say something, but she uttered one phrase, and Remy shrank, devastated.

Bored with their fight, Jinxie turned to Eli, studying him openly. "What are you?" She asked. He shrugged numbly. "You're not one of the Fae, though you're pretty enough. I don't get *Fae* from you. And even though you're big enough, I don't get anything animal from you-so. That's not it. You are not a child of Eve?" He looked at her in confusion.

"I am a child of Pauline Babineaux Cain." He muttered drunkenly.

"Babineaux? You're Gracie's boy." She slapped his arm as if it all made perfect sense. "Of course. I knew you looked familiar; the eyes are a dead giveaway. I should have seen it, but your auras kind of funny. It's all muted. That's what's throwing me off."

"You know Grace?" he asked, his eyes still on Celeste and Remy.

"Honey, I know everyone. I've been haunting this city for centuries." Once again, she handed him one of the pale pink drinks. This time he actually tasted the nectar. It tasted fruit, and he was sure some sort of alcohol, yet he couldn't place it.

"That's good," he muttered, and she quickly handed him another, her hand coming to rest on Eli's ass. He paid no attention, even when her tiny hand began moving in a slow circular motion. "And what are you?" he teased. She pulled her hair back to expose delicately pointed ears.

"Pixie, of course." She gave his arm a teasing slap. He touched one of her ears; his eyes were wide with wonder.

"Sweet," he whispered.

He glanced back towards Celeste and Remy. He was closer now, running his hands up and down her arms, speaking to her in low tones, his head nuzzling her shoulder. He leaned in t kiss her but was greeted with a resounding slap across his face. Remy grabbed her by the arms and gave her a hard shake. Eli was at her side in the blink of an eye, his hand wrapped around

Remy's neck as he lifted him off the ground. He never had in his life felt as much rage as he did at that very moment, and it took all his willpower not to tear Remy's head off. There was a hushed gasp in the room as Remy struggled. Eli looked up into Remy's startled eyes. His own turquoise eyes sparked to life as his fury grew. He couldn't hear anything except a strange high-pitched squeal in his head as he focused on hurting this man. He pinned Remy to the wall with such force it splintered.

"Don't you ever touch her like that again," Eli growled? Remy's eyes grew wide with terror as Eli slammed him into the wall. "I will destroy you," he spat. His eyes seemed to glow neon, and Celeste felt her heart in her throat.

"Let me go, you crazy bastard." Remy tried to pry Eli's fingers from his throat, but they just tightened, his nails digging into the tender skin until he drew blood. Celeste watched in terror as her brother struggled. Knowing how strong he was, he should have easily broken Eli's grip. She touched Eli's arm, which felt like solid granite and drew his attention to her.

"Eli, let him go." Celeste's voice was the only sound that seemed to break through the haze of fury, and he slowly let Remy down. When he released him, Remy, who was suddenly very sober, huddled in a corner trying to catch his breath, his hand rubbing his bruised and battered neck.

"Who the fuck is this guy?" He croaked and looked up at Eli, who towered over him.

"This is my *detective*." Celeste stared at Eli with wide, fascinated eyes. His skin had taken on a deep ebony hue; his eyes illuminated, and when he smiled, her heart stopped. Those perfectly even white teeth and that damn sexy dimple of his were only emphasized by the long white incisors that glinted in the light.

Jinxie sashayed over, handing Eli another of those A sweet-tasting pink drinks. "I like a good brawl as much as the next pixie, but y'all are killing my buzz." She smiled slyly as Eli downed the drink and stared at the glass in satisfaction.

"How many of those has he had?" CeCe barked.

"Three, four, twelve. Who knows?" Jinxie teased, and Celeste leveled her with a gaze that would have withered a charging bull.

"Don't toy with me, pixie. How many?" Jinxie shrugged.

"Ten at least." Celeste sighed and looked from a drunken Eli to a somewhat sobering Remy. Neither of them would be easy to get into the car, and she was not dressed to carry them. Closing her eyes and counting to ten, she took a deep breath before turning back to Jinxie.

"I need to get these two home, and since you were so helpful in getting them in their current states, you're going to help me." Jinxie looked completely stunned but didn't dare to oppose Celeste in her current state, or she'd be the next one pinned to the wall.

Getting them into the car was made ten times easier by the Kulivichek twins, who hauled the men into the back of Eli's SUV as if they were mere children. Celeste slid behind the wheel, her frustration ebbing as the pixie dust and cherubs that flitted around Jinxie's garden lightened her mood. Eli looked over at Remy as he was buckled into his seat.

"You're Doc's brother?" he asked. Remy nodded.

"And you are the chosen one," Remy snarled. Eli stared at him in confusion. He knew that something about this entire night was wrong; something was off about all of these people. But he couldn't get his mind to move past the overwhelming feeling of ecstasy. He felt lightheaded and fuzzy but sound like he was floating on a pink cloud. He frowned. Yes, something was wrong, but he couldn't figure out why for his life.

"Am I drunk?" he asked Remy.

"Lil bit," Remy agreed. "But doesn't it feel good?" Eli sighed and closed his eyes. He had to admit, it did.

* * *

"Do you need us to follow you?" one of the twins asked Celeste in Russian.

"No thanks, Ivan. I think I've got it now." She glanced at Jinxie, who had eased into the passenger's seat, her large eyes downcast, and her large pointed ears hanging low. The thing about pixies is that they were more or less errant children. They weren't generally mean spirited or even hurtful in any way. They were basic in their need for mischief; it's what kept them young and fed their magic, what kept them alive. Laughter, pleasure, and joy surrounded them wherever they went and fed them. It was why no one was ever sad in Jinxie's garden. Anger seemed to melt away once you inhaled the wafting floral scents that hung around the outside of the house like a shroud.

Also, like errant children, they did pout and sulk when reprimanded. Celeste looked over at Jinxie, who'd changed once again to blue jeans and a bright pink V-neck sweater. She looked even more childlike as her feet dangled off of the edge of the front seat of the monster SUV. Celeste had never realized just how small she was until they were seated beside each other in the car. Her heart softening, she sighed.

"I'm sorry I yelled at you," she conceded, and Jinxie's ears flicked just an inch. "I tell you what. You can stay and play with Remy at the St Charles house."

She just about lit up the interior of the car as her ears perked up, and she smiled brilliantly at her. "Just don't-break anything," she warned, and Jinxie nodded. She spun around in her seat to look back at Remy, who was smiling drunkenly at her.

"Well, alright," he hooted. The last time she had allowed Jinx a little *"playtime "*with Remy, he'd ended up with a broken collarbone.

"So, what are we going to play, Suga?" She asked excitedly, her eyes dancing with mischief.

"Whatever you want, Jinxie." Remy laughed. "Whatever you want."

Eli was vaguely aware of his surroundings as they moved through the city. He was mildly amused that the St. Charles house, as it was referred to, was a mansion, a massive thing with wrought iron gates and a circular driveway. He was conscious of someone hauling Remy out and tossing him over their shoulder like a sack of potatoes, someone large in a dark suit. He also remembered that same someone moving him from the back seat to the front, and he could feel Celeste beside him. He could smell her, lavender and vanilla and all Celeste. He felt Jinxie kiss his cheek as the same someone snapped the buckle on his seat belt and turned to see Celeste driving his car.

✻ ✻ ✻

Once they were moving again, he was all too aware of her and her alone. In the confined space of the car interior, she filled his senses. He could smell her scent wafting in the air, intoxicating him. Her caramel skin beneath his fingertips felt as soft and smooth as satin and seemed to glow in the moonlight. He traced intricate swirls across her bare thigh and kissed her neck. His hand dipped into the loose cowl neck of her dress to cup one full breast, his thumb teasing her tightened nipple.

"Eli," she gasped, trying to focus on the road. They weren't that far from her apartment, but the traffic at Lee Circle was always kind of tricky. He pushed the material aside, exposing her, and she squealed in shock.

"Eli, people can see in here. You're going to get us arrested." She gently pushed him away with one hand.

"Well, I suggest you hurry up." When he lowered his head and took a tightened nipple into his mouth, her eyes drifted closed from the feel of his hot mouth on her skin. The blaring of car horns shook her back to reality as she swerved into the next lane.

"Eli, I'm driving," she moaned, pushing him away again. He

raised his lips to brush her cheek, his mouth next to her ear.

"I have never wanted a woman as much as I want you," he mumbled before he put his tongue in her ear. The sensation was a shock of pleasure, and she felt her eyes drifting closed. Again, horns blared, and tires screeched as she shot through a red light avoiding a collision by inches.

"Shit, Eli," she growled and pushed him away. "You're going to get us killed," she mumbled.

"You're the one driving," he teased, and she shot him an evil glare. "Okay, Okay." He sat back in his seat, his hand still resting on her bare thigh. "I'll be good."

When the car finally came to a bone-shattering stop, the seat belt tightened across his chest, snapping Eli to his seat. She exhaled and turned off the motor before looking at him, her anger melting away at the intense way he was looking at her. He was looking at her like he was going to eat her alive.

"Okay," she breathed, "Okay. We're here." On shaky legs, she climbed from the Lexus SUV cab to stand in front, waiting. He eased out of his seat, and slowly made his way to her, his hands on either side of her, pushing her back against the warm metal hood of the SUV. Leaning over, he kissed her slowly, softly, his tongue moving into her mouth to taste her. When he released her, he stepped aside so that she could stalk toward the elevator; Eli followed silently, his hands on her hips. Her every nerve was on fire from his touch, along with the added adrenaline of nearly killing them both in a fiery crash. If it weren't for the surveillance cameras, she would have mounted him in the garage. He followed her past the public elevators to a door that appeared to be the closet entrance. She placed her thumb on a hidden pad, and the door slid open to reveal an elevator large enough for perhaps two average-sized people. For the two of them, it was a close fit.

From the moment the door slid closed, he seemed to fill the space, looming over her, blocking the light from the single fixture. She took a step back and felt the cool metal of the wall against her bare back. He reached for her, his hand slipping into the silken waves of her hair, his mouth moving slowly over hers. The kiss took her breath away, and she pressed herself hard against him, her hands balling into a fist against his chest.

"You're going to ruin my sweater," he smiled against her lips. He took her wrists and held them high above her head with one hand. The other hand cupped her breast, his thumb torturing her nipple as his mouth took hers. When he moved the material aside, and the air touched her bared skin, her breasts tightened, her nipples became rock hard pebbles begging for his touch. She chewed her lip as he lowered his head so slowly, taking one hardened nub into his mouth. She sucked in sharply as the immediate rush of pleasure assaulted her.

"You are so beautiful," he mumbled as his teeth grazed the tender flesh. It was as if every nerve in her body converged in that one spot.

"I want you so much, Doc." His voice was so low and thick. She had to open her eyes to make sure it was him. He was looking down at her with those bright blue eyes; his entire body, tense and stiff, pressed into her.

* * *

The elevator pinged, and the door slid open. But instead of a lobby, they exited into a posh living room of a penthouse condo. She reluctantly backed away from him and led him in, dropping her purse on a nearby table as she did. She took his hand and backed into the living room, the elevator door closing behind him.

Eli stared around the open space of exposed brick walls with a long dark marble island that separated the kitchen from the living area. The room was open with plush sofas in vibrant jewel tones, rugs covered the marble floors, and every wall seemed to house artwork from several cultures. In the center of the room, there were two marble pillars, and against the far wall a staircase. She had a wall with kabuki masks flanking a suit of Samurai armor. There was a Middle Eastern tapestry hung on a wall and a freakishly pointed metal art piece jutting from the wall near the kitchen area. It was ten feet tall and had metal peaks all crested with sharp pointed tips that stood four feet away from the heavily wooded base. One stumble, and one could easily be skewered. From the Japanese weaponry on the walls to the stacks of books on the floor, he could see her in every aspect of the room. Taking his hand, she led him up a narrow glass and metal staircase to her bedroom.

The room was not at all what he expected. Downstairs was a jewel-toned study in eclectic modern style, the kitchen a stainless steel and sterling silver hodgepodge of clean, simple lines. Even the rather terrifying artwork had a simplistically modern feel. Looking at that open space downstairs had given him a very distinct sense for the well-traveled multi-faceted Doctor C. Keegan Kent.

The bedroom was all Celeste. The first thing he noticed was that the room was bathed in moonlight from the skylight over the bed. It was a large room with warm gold walls and light-colored hardwood floors. Near one of the large floor-to-ceiling windows was a sitting area with a small white love seat and a little dark wood table. He smiled at the stack of books piled up on the floor. The walls were covered in abstract artwork in deep reds and purples. He briefly took note of a dresser near an open door that led into a bathroom and dressing area. The thing that he zeroed in on, besides the gorgeous woman in front of him, of course, was the bed. It was a romantic king-sized bed that dominated the room with delicate metal scrollwork and concrete wood posts adorning the headboard. The comforter and pillows were a warm and inviting deep purple matching the drapes at the windows that bookended the bed.

She turned to him, her breathing harsh and shallow, those ever-expressive eyes, glowing a deep dark blue with dancing silver flecks. The soft gold of the dress against her moon kissed skin made her look unearthly, ethereal. Eli pulled her close, running his hands through her thick blue-black hair, his lips brushing her forehead. She pulled his mouth down to hers, one hand moving under his sweater's soft cashmere to the hard muscle beneath. She pulled away long enough to pull it up over his head and tossed it away. She paused, staring at the bright blue t-shirt he wore underneath with the Superman S emblazoned across the chest in red and yellow. Lifting a curious brow, she stared up at him in amusement.

"Riley's idea of a joke. He buys me one every Christmas." Sheepishly, he pulled it over his head and tossed it to the floor. His sheepish grin melted away, and he looked at her with apparent want, and her skin grew hot. He ran a hand over his mouth and took a determined step towards her, his hand on the nape of her neck. His mouth moved over hers, a hand on her lower back, pressing her hips against him. He was straining against his jeans, his body on fire for her, his mouth moving down her neck, his hands on her breast. He pushed the soft gold material aside and took one breast into his mouth, and she arched into him, rising on tiptoe to allow him easier access to her aching body. His mouth was hot, and she leaned forward, raking her nails over his smooth back.

As he teased her with his tongue, his hands moved under the hem of her skirt, up muscled thighs to the soft skin of her naked rear end. He smiled, lifting his face to hers. "It was bothering me all night," he whispered against her lips.

"What?" she asked.

"Trying to figure out what kind of a scrap of lace you considered panties were under this dress."

"Disappointed?"

"Not at all." He smiled against her lips, his hand moving to cup the soft, moist curls at her center, his fingers teasing her. She pressed against his hand, her body moving against him slowly. He slipped a finger inside of her, stroking slowly in smooth movements until she was moaning into his mouth.

"Make love to me," she whispered, and he stopped for a moment, his entire body coiled tight. His breathing was strained and labored against her ear.

"Are you sure?" he asked. The last thing he wanted to do was to rush this, to make her regret trusting him. And in his current state, he wasn't sure he would be as gentle as she needed. If he had his way, he would have been her first, her last, her only. He knew that once he made love to Doctor Celeste Keegan Kent, he would never be able to leave her. He touched her cheek, rubbing her kiss swollen berry-stained lips with his thumb.

She kicked off her shoes and took a step back, sliding the clingy gold dress from her shoulders and down her hips until it lay in a gold pool around her feet. She kicked it aside and stood under the skylight, the moonlight playing across her skin. From the glowing caramel skin, blue-black hair, and vivid turquoise eyes to the full breasts and runners' legs, she had the classic hourglass figure and soft curves of a pin-up. She watched as a muscle worked in his jaw, as he took her in, his eyes glowing in the darkness. He wanted to say something, but honestly, his throat had gone dry at the sight of her. She stood waiting, and when she nervously bit her bottom lip, he was finally able to breathe again.

"You could have left the shoes on." He teased, closing the space between them dipping his head to take possession of her mouth. He held her against him, and the feel of her soft naked body against his sent a new surge of electricity through him, and his cock strained against the constraints of his jeans in protest.

She kissed him, her tongue playing with his, tasting him while her nails raked across his nipples. The unexpected sensation made him suck in the air. She looked up at him, her eyes wide with concern. She was doing something wrong, she thought. She had never really been an active participant in this part of sex. For her, sex and pain went hand and hand. She looked up at him, her face a mix of emotion.

"Did I do something wrong?" She asked breathlessly, and

his heart ached. For a woman with such confidence, she seemed so unsure, so sweet and innocent. To see her like this, so vulnerable, with those large blue eyes and angelic face staring up at him, he wanted her even more. He kissed the tip of her nose.

"No, baby, you're doing everything right," he lifted her hand and kissed her knuckles, each little kiss, sending a wave of warmth through her. She bit her lip, a twinkle of something devious in her eyes as she began lowering her hand until it rested at the waist of his pants. Slowly, she unfastened them and pulled the zipper down. She moved with such deliberate slowness that he nearly cursed. He did curse when her hand-dipped lower., her mouth hovered just inches from his neck as she stroked him slowly . He could feel her breath tickle his skin when she nipped him with her teeth.

"Am I doing this right?" she asked in a low, sweetly innocent voice. He swallowed hard as she continued his voice thick as he forced it through his tightening throat.

"Yes," was all he could manage. She pushed his jeans lower, freeing him, as she continued her steady caress, his shaft becoming slick from his wetness. To add to the torture, she kissed his chest, slowly, moving her mouth down the length of him. The feel of her soft full lips just below his navel made his breath catch.

"Shit," he cursed under his breath as his body reacted by tensing. He was so hard now he was in pain. He felt as if his skin were on fire. She cupped his balls, and everything in him tightened. He was going to come right there in her hands. He put one hand on her shoulder and pulled away, his breathing labored.

"Damn, you're about to make me finish before we even start," he mumbled. "And we can't have that."

He moved to lift her, and she backed away shyly. Celeste had never been tiny or delicate, nor was she fat, but she was over six feet of solid muscle. Even though Eli was a big man, she knew that carrying her was not an easy task, not by a long shot. Determined, he cupped her under the buttocks and lifted her against him.

"Eli, I'm too heavy-" she began to protest, and he stopped her with a kiss.

"No, you aren't." He lifted her as quickly as if she were a rag doll. She wrapped herself around him, her moist warmth pressing against him, and the muscle in his abdomen twitched in anticipation. She dipped her hips lower until the wet slickness of her rubbed deliciously against his shaft. He moaned as she began a new stroke, using that deep warm slick center of herself instead of her hand. He could feel that hardened nub at the center of her moving against him, feel her getting wetter, her breathing coming harder as she moved slower, each stroke of her body accompanied by a whimper. She put her head on his shoulder and moaned, her body glistening with a sheen of sweat as her orgasm overtook her. She held him tighter, her body pulsating against him, and his balls tightened even more. She was so hot, so sexy, and he wanted her so much he could cry from the agony of it. It took a Herculean effort for him not to thrust into her. But he couldn't. That would hurt her, and he never wanted to cause her an ounce of pain.

He held her, even though his knees were getting weak as she came, her legs tightening around him. "Fuck," he cursed before dropping her onto the bed. She still had her legs clasped around his waist as they tumbled onto the softest down comforter he had ever laid upon. Not wanting to crush her with his weight, he rose to his hands and knees, his pants awkwardly low on his thighs, confining his movements. He rolled to one side and kicked off one timberland boot then the other. "You're going to make me come before I'm even inside of you," he growled. She looked up at him with wide innocent eyes.

"Really?" She breathed, licking her lips, and he shook his head, a chuckle rumbling his chest. She was playing with him; she was doing it on purpose. She knew exactly what she was doing to him. And she liked it. She gave him the sexiest half-smile he had ever seen and purred seductively.

"You are evil." He growled as she moved against him. She was perfection, long toned legs, the flat musculature of her stomach, the full high breasts that begged for his touch. Lowering his head, he took one breast into his mouth, his tongue continuing the delicious torture his hands had begun. She moaned and pulled him up so that her mouth was against his and pushed his pants down with her feet.

He backed away, standing so that he could quickly free himself from the remainder of his clothing as she watched. She'd seen him partially naked before, but this was altogether different. She looked him up and down, taking in every single wonderful inch of him. He moved with the quiet grace and agility of a predator, like a cat. Every inch of him seemed to tense, every muscle in him rippled with a ferocious power that lay just beneath the surface. He looked at her with a hunger that made her mouth go dry. This was not a man to be trifled with, not at all. Looking at him made her wonder just what he had done for someone to bind him so completely. If he were this powerful and seductive with his abilities under lock and key, what was he like when he was unfettered? Her eyes moved over him, from the set of his powerful angular jaw to the wide span of the muscled chest, to a narrow waist and hips. The strength of his thighs was evident in every deliberate step he took closer to the bed. Her eyes fell to the part of him she had avoided looking at but had toyed with so much in the past few minutes. Under her gaze, his shaft seemed to grow harder and thicker. She found it difficult to swallow or breathe as he came closer still. She wanted him, and she could see just how badly he wanted her.

"*Oh man,*" was all she could manage before he was on top of her, his mouth on her again.

"You are perfect," he whispered. "You're so beautiful. I want to make love to you until the sun comes up." He moved slowly, deliberately, down her body lowering his mouth to the warm apex of her, his tongue toying with her until she arched into him, a sound of guttural pleasure escaping her.

Even though the room was decidedly chilly, her body beaded with sweat. She felt as if her skin were on fire. Every touch, every flick of his beautiful tongue, brought her closer and closer to the edge. When she began to descend into that abyss of pleasure again, her body shaking from the power of her orgasm, he moved and quickly slipped inside of her. She gasped in rapturous surprise at the feel of him hot and hard inside of her. Her orgasm continued, and her body seemed to vibrate from the sheer joy of it how he'd managed to be so gentle amazed her, the sheer strength and size of a man whose touch made her writhe in ecstasy. She wrapped her legs around his waist, drawing him closer. Her body tightened around him. His ragged breath was harsh in her ear as he held himself in check.

"Eli," she whimpered, her nails digging into his back. He held her hips still and tried to collect himself. She ran her hand over his head; the feel of her fingers moving through his low-cut curls seemed to drive him over the edge. He wanted to move, to push deeper into her, but he held steady, waiting. She began to move slowly, her body writhing against his until he could no longer breathe.

"Slow down, baby. I don't want to hurt you." He kissed her softly, and she could taste the sweat beading on his top lip.

"I'm a big girl. I can take it," she whispered before catching his earlobe between her teeth. She smiled slyly and shifted her hips once more taking, him deeper into her. She was so warm and welcoming, her body tightening around him as if she were meant for only him. Placing her hands on his hips, she pulled him into her to the hilt. He moaned, his resolve melting; he joined her, his body moving with hers, causing delicious friction until soft moans escaped her. Her arms and legs tightened around him as she moved with a new ferocity. He buried his face in her neck, his mouth on her bare skin, nearing his breaking point.

He moved back to sit on his haunches, gathering her into his arms, until she sat astride him. She sucked in sharply as she settled onto him, her chest rising and falling as he held her to him. He looked into her eyes as he rocked her slowly against him. Running one hand down the center of her until he found that heat at her center and gently stroked, she grasped his shoulders as her body went into sensory overload. Every muscle, every nerve, every molecule of her sang with unimaginable joy. Before she could stop herself, she felt the teeth, those fucking teeth. She'd been able to hide them before, in his bedroom, by clenching her lips shut and hiding her face. But now, he would see what she was, and he would leave. Tears began streaming down her cheeks as his tongue teased one breast, then the other.

"Am I hurting you?" He breathed near her ear, holding on to the last threads of restraint, his eyes glowing in the darkness, his skin hot under her touch. She groaned as he shifted slightly, filling her. "Are you- Is this-?" He panted.

"No, you aren't hurting me. No." She held his face in her hands and kissed him deeply, her tongue playfully teasing his. She nipped his bottom lip hard enough to draw blood, but he didn't seem to feel it. "No, don't stop. It's just- don't stop." She whispered as she moved over him with a new zeal and he lost all semblance of control. He moved in and out of her in smooth, fluid motions. She could feel him stretch and grow inside of her, and it was a pleasure she'd never experienced before. Her body moved with him as if they were born to fit together. She matched him thrust for thrust, her body slick and smooth, her nails digging into his back and shoulders. She cooed words of encouragement that made him hotter than he'd ever been before.

"You're so wet, so warm. I want you so much. So much," he breathed against her throat.

"Oh God," she choked, and he quickened his pace, his body moving roughly, his mouth covering hers, his tongue deep in her mouth. She tasted the nectar on his tongue, the strength of him inside of her; every sense seemed to be on fire and filled with him. They were one, moving in unison. He was buried so deeply inside of her, he couldn't tell where he ended, and she began.

She tasted the skin of his collarbone; finally, her teeth dug in, he tasted of something she had never experienced before. There was sweetness, purity, something old, ancient, and compelling in him, and she was gone. Her hips moved in slow pulsating circles, her body melting around him as the warm ache she'd felt before seemed to fill her entire body and multiply as she cursed him and his ancestors in French. She clung to him as her body was overcome with the most intense pleasure she had ever experienced. She came hard; her body shuddered violently, as wave after wave of sheer ecstasy rolled over her. She made a noise that she couldn't believe was coming from her. It was a deep guttural, almost primal growl as she dissolved into unfathomable ecstasy.

His voice was a ragged raspy curse whispered into her hair. He held her head in place, his fingers in her hair, he rode his wave of joy, his mouth on her neck. He had a sudden urge to bite her. The feel of her mouth on him, those teeth in his skin, as she sucked, he lost complete control of himself, and he buried his face in the curve of her neck and grunted something incoherent. He wanted to stay just where he was. He wanted to live with her body connected to his at all times.

She stared at him in amazement as his body transformed into something darkly beautiful. His skin was the color of onyx and shone like polished marble. She watched as deep blue tribal symbols etched themselves into his upper arms as if drawn by an unseen hand. They moved fluidly from his shoulders down his arms until they circled his wrists. She stared in awe as they flamed vibrant neon blue that matched his glowing eyes, which had lost all human semblance. They were large and bright with no pupil, no whites, just an endless cerulean sea that bore into her. He was even more beautiful, and it brought tears to her eyes. She touched the birthmark on his chest that now shone a pure white. Again, she felt her body slipping into throes of ecstasy, her thoughts clouding, somewhere far off; she thought she heard Eli follow her into the pink cloud of bliss that surrounded her.

He held her, his breathing rough and his heart racing. They lay in a sweat-soaked heap, Eli on top her of his body twitched now and then from the aftershock before he lay utterly still. She closed her eyes, loving the feel of his weight on her, and waited until his skin and eyes returned to something closer to human. She exhaled, her pulse racing as she realized what she had done. He was the one they had been searching for, the myth, the fallen one, and she had just signed his death warrant.

*"Son of a bitch!"* she thought. She had just fucked them both.

*   *   *

Finally, he rolled onto his side, collecting her in his arms as their breathing returned to normal. She moved in his arms so that she faced him, resting her head on his shoulder. She looked at him with a tight smile. His eyes still glowed brightly in the darkness of the room, but the fangs were gone. So were the blue etchings and onyx skin. After a few minutes, her eyes drifted closed, so she didn't feel him getting up. He went into the bathroom. When she felt the soft warmth of a towel between her thighs, she flinched slightly. Opening her eyes, she looked down to find Eli cleaning her. The heat of the towel felt beautiful on her skin; he was so gentle, carefully touching her. No one had ever cared about after; she had always been made to clean herself if at all, and here he was taking the time for her. She made a little noise of embarrassment, and he looked up at her, concerned.

"Was I too rough?" he asked. She touched his lips with the tips of her fingers and gave him a small satisfied smile. He held them to his mouth, kissing each fingertip softly.

"No, it was perfect," she whispered.

He returned to the bathroom; she could hear the water running and a curse as he knocked something over and found herself smiling. It felt good with him here, even if he was destroying her bathroom. After a minute, he returned, coming to lie beside her, pulling the covers up around them. Immediately she rolled toward him, resting her head in the crook of his arm. She dropped a kiss on his bare chest.

"I guess your tongue isn't the only talented body part you have, Detective."

He tilted his head to one side, staring at her curiously before kissing the tip of her nose. There was something different about her, he thought, something special, but he couldn't remember what it was. He should, but he seemed to be immersed in a pink fog. There was something that he should be aware of about her, something wrong, but he'd forgotten what it was.

He held her tighter, kissing the top of her head, his hands on the curve at the small of her back. She lay there stroking the soft, springy hair on his chest, her eyes closed. Finally, she exhaled, her body feeling scrumptiously boneless, and the teeth retracted. She stretched against him, and he playfully ran his fingers up and down her thigh until she felt him, hard against her lower stomach. Her whole body tingled at his touch. She sat up, gently coaxing him to lie on his back.

"What are you doing?" He chuckled.

"The sun isn't up yet. I'd say you still have a few hours. Do you want to- again?" She straddled his hips, her eyes on his face. He cupped her ass, holding her as he positioned himself beneath her.

"For future reference, you never have to ask that question again." He chuckled.

❊ ❊ ❊

*He hovered above the skylight, looking down as Celeste lay in* the tangle of Eli's arms. He moved lower, setting down lightly on the roof. She seemed so happy, so contented. It had been a long time since he'd seen her that happy. Nicky walked around the perimeter of the skylight, his hands deep in the pockets of his pants. They would be looking for him soon, the creature and the others. So, would the Collective and the Dark Fae. He was changing, he knew. That was why he'd left the safe house Briar had put him in. He didn't want to risk that he would transform into something-worse. Worse than the bloodsucker he thought he'd become once he'd awaken from that casket. More than the walking dead.

He could hear the whispers from the others in his head, calling to him. Getting for him to do things he never wanted to do, be what he never wanted to be. As he watched his friend now, his very best friend, he could feel himself becoming angrier. It wasn't his anger; it was their anger. They were speaking to him, calling him to kill her.

"Destroy the Caelestis before it is too late for us," they called. "Before he becomes who he was." Nicky pulled his hands from his pockets and stared at the sharp bird-like talons that had taken shape. His skin was a slick yellow-green, and he was sprouting a dusting of baby-fine black and yellow feathers. What was he becoming? He wondered. What sort of monster had he been turned into? What was left of his shining platinum hair was greasy and lay flat against his head. His once vibrant eyes were sunken into dark hollows in his skull. He was not the beautiful Nicky Sky that the world had known. He wasn't even the romantic tortured vampire he believed he'd become upon his awakening. No, he thought as he rose slowly into the depths of the night sky, he had become an abomination, just like the others, and he needed to leave before he did something that could never be undone.

# CHAPTER ELEVEN

She had just dozed off when the insistent buzz of her intercom began. Moaning, she rolled out of bed and searched the room for something to wear. She blindly grabbed his Superman t-shirt, pulled it over her head, and stumbling over one of Eli's shoes, made her way downstairs to the intercom.

"What?!" She yelled.

"Open the fucking door!" Remy bellowed at her. Rolling her eyes, she looked at the wall clock mounted over her stove.

"Remy, it's two in the morning. I thought you were playing with Jinxie."

"We're done playing. Open the fucking door," he yelled.

"No. Go home." She hit the do not disturb button on her intercom and returned to bed. As she snuggled in closer, Eli wrapped his arms around her, kissing the corner of her mouth. He groaned and sat up.

"What are you wearing?" he asked sleepily. "You should be naked, woman." She giggled as he ran his hands under the shirt, lifting it over her head. He sat with his back against the headboard, looking down at her. "The sun isn't up yet," he mumbled. She climbed astride him, her knees resting snugly on either side of his hips. He kissed her, his hands caressing the full roundness of her butt.

"You have the best ass," he mumbled against her lips. She laughed.

"Is that all?"

"Not at all. Your breasts are perfection." He placed his hands over her exposed breasts. "But this," he kissed her collarbone. "This is my favorite spot." He ran a string of tiny kisses from one shoulder to the other. His mouth was against her neck, teasing and tasting her; she sighed and felt his lips curve into a smile. She leaned against him; when the door was thrown open so hard, it bounced against the wall. At the same instant, the lights came on. Eli rolled, tossing Celeste onto the bed before he stood.

She gasped and covered herself as they turned to see Remy standing in the doorway, his face twisting with rage and disgust.

"Celeste, what the fuck!" He bellowed, and she could see his yellow eyes glowing.

"Boy, you better have a damn good reason-" Eli started, his eyes so pale blue that they were nearly as white as his growing fangs. The stare he centered on Remy was glacial and deadly. Celeste felt the chill in the room as a feeling of dread filled her.

"Remy, I told you to go home. What the hell are you doing?" Celeste had pulled on her robe and was stalking over to Remy, whose eyes were as wide and round as saucers.

"CeCe, Really. Come on! Are you actually fucking this guy? What the fuck are you thinking?" he yelled. Eli took a step; Celeste sprinted across the bed to get between them, placing a firm hand on Eli's chest. She could feel the heat radiating from him, and his skin was changing from a soft chocolate brown to a mottled black. The etched mark on his chest blazed a bright crimson as his anger rose.

"Holy fuck," Remy gasped, and Celeste dropped her hand, backing away from Eli for a second. The sight of him in mid-transformation startled her. He had gotten bigger somehow, not just taller but broader and bulkier. His shiny black skin was streaked through with bright blue scrollwork; he practically glowed. This was not good, not at all.

"Shit. Wait here," she barked at Eli, who sat heavily on the bed, his eyes narrowed as he stared Remy down. Celeste pushed Remy out of the room, down the stairs, and into the living room.

* * *

"That is who you give it up to? Jesus Ce, his dick looks like a fucking toddler arm." He stumbled down the stairs, his eyes back to their usual brown, wide with shock.

"Will you shut up? He can hear you," she whispered to him, continuing to push him across the room into the kitchen.

"Holy shit, is he-damn it! Why doesn't the Collective know about him?" He blathered.

"Because *he* doesn't know what he is. He has some sort of binding on him. There are momentary bleeds, but for the most part, he doesn't know. Didn't you see his eyes? Your pixie fuck buddy gave him that damned nectar. I'll be lucky if it doesn't fry his brain." She ran a hand through her tangled hair. "And they do know. I'm supposed to bring him in. I just have to figure out how." She chewed her thumbnail.

"So, you plan to fuck him into submission?" Remy screeched.

"No, don't be vulgar. You know me better than that. The sex thing just- happened."

"An unclassified and untrained Nephilim hybrid, and you're fucking him. Are you suicidal? If the Collective or the Council doesn't punish you, then the dark fucking Fae will. Do you know what they would do with an unclassified? You don't even know what he is. And you're fucking him. After all these years, you couldn't keep it in your pants until you got him to the Collective? My God, CeCe." He stomped his foot like a spoiled child whose favorite toy had been taken away.

"No, they won't punish me. I'm of Nyx. They can't touch me. And he wouldn't either. He would never hurt me, no matter what state he's in. I think he's part of the Oneiroi, a dream walker or something of that nature." She rubbed her tired eyes and exhaled. "And I kept it in my pants for centuries, which is more than I can say for you," she mumbled.

"But you don't know where he came from. He could be one of the *Apepos* or a *Rabisu* demon. We don't even know what pantheon he's from Ce," he whined, and she had to agree, but she felt no malevolence from him.

"I think he is pre-pantheon. Whatever he is, he's still Nephilim." She sighed. "I haven't seen anything that would make me think that he was anything but good."

"Really, because what I just saw scared the shit outta me. His cock alone is enough to give me nightmares." He shivered, "And you opt for that monster over me?" Exhaling, she faced her brother.

"He's no more of a monster than you or me." Remy lifted his eyebrows and gave her a *"duh,"* expression. Exasperated by him, she shook her head. "We are not monsters. We're – gifted." That elicited a snort of derision.

"Yeah right. I guess you forgot the villagers chasing you along the French countryside with torches and pitchforks. They weren't yelling *'Kill the gifted,'* Celeste." He grunted before hopping over the back of the sofa to land with a muted thud. He snorted again before propping his motorcycle booted feet on her rather expensive coffee table and folded his hands behind his head as he stared at her. His relaxed pose incensed her even more. Angrily, she kicked his feet off of her table and stood over him.

"Remy, what are you doing here? The Kent men have no concept of privacy." She mumbled. He was silent for a moment, studying her closely. He was standing before her within seconds, his eyes searching hers.

"You have actual feelings for him, don't you? You slept with him because you- Celeste, do you love him?" His voice was so low that it was nearly a whisper.

"What?" She barked out a choking laugh but averted her eyes.

"I said, do you love him?" She could see the pain in his eyes, and she ached for him. She folded her arms across her chest and shrugged. "Answer the question, CeCe. Do you love him?"

He said each word deliberately. She bit her lip and looked down at her bare feet. "It's either yes or no. It's not that diffi-cult a question."

"You know that we don't deal with love. We don't fall in love, isn't that the Collective's stand on it. Love and emotion equal death." She turned away from him, not wanting him to see what he'd done as tears dampened her eyes. Remy had al-ways been able to bring her to emotional extremes; there was never a happy medium with him.

"Ce, other than Nicky, I think I know you better than any-one else in this world. I know when you are just playing with someone, and you have done that plenty, even with me. But this man- this thing has you all turned around, doing things you would never do. You actually had sex with him, Ce. That's something you have managed to go years without doing. So, there is something there. Right? Right?"

"Why are you here again?" She kept her back to him, not wanting him to see the panic that rose in her as she realized that, yes, there was something there. Something she was not accustomed to feeling. It made her nauseous and excited and terrified at the same time. But it wasn't as simple as love. This wasn't at all what she needed right now. She wiped the tears away and inhaled.

"Please, Celeste- Because if you do, I will go to the wall for you against the red-headed menace," She smirked at his affec-tionate name for Lilith, "but if he is just a plaything, just some passing lust, I say let him go." Remy came up behind her and wrapped his arms around her waist. She leaned against him, her head resting on his shoulder, and for the first time in many years, she felt no lust from him. There was no sexual under-tone to the embrace, no shifting of the hips or tell-tale pres-sure in the small of her back. She turned to face him, Remy was only a breath taller than her, but right now, he looked and felt the part of her big brother and best friend. "I can see it in you, and believe it or not. I only want the best for you. I want you to be happy, and I know that it's part of your make-up to feel deeply, unlike the rest of us. But – I saw the mark. This is going to be a problem, especially since he doesn't know what he is. It can be very dangerous, *coeur tendre*."

He was such a sweet, such a good-looking man. She touched his cheek and smiled at the pet name that only he called her, *tender heart*. It went against everything she was, everything known about her to everyone other than Remy and Nicky, and now, of course, Eli.

To the Collective and all others within their world, she was known as *Vitiosa Forma, Vicious Beauty*. According to them, she was a heartless machine and not meant to love. It would have been so much easier if she had chosen Remy, to care for him as he cared for her. She wished she could love him. She hoped that it were as simple as that. There would be no passion, but she would be safe, and she would be cherished, protected, and most of all, she would be left alone. Remy would love her and make her happy. He would make sure they never harmed or harassed her again.

If not for Eli, she would have thought that enough. But Lilith's vendetta against Remy would never allow it. If the Council had its way, she would be already linked to a Collective member, most likely Julian or Karim.

Karim, she thought how she loved that man. He would always hold a special place in her heart. And she knew that he would do absolutely anything for her, but their timing had never been right. They had missed their chance because he wasn't the One. Absently, she rubbed the mark at the nape of her neck and sighed.

The One, the great and magical FallenOne who would rule her destiny. That had been the Collective's master plan all along, control of the ultimate power, and she was the key. She guessed she'd just thrown a six-foot-eight-inch wrench into that plan. If Eli was a problem, the Council might not allow it.

Sighing heavily, tears still threatening, she gave Remy a cheerless smile. "Have you heard anything about Briar?" she asked, rubbing her forehead.

"He was in pretty bad shape, but they say he's doing better. Already giving them shit about his dinner. *'A man needs meat.'*" He did a perfect imitation of Briar's thick rolling brogue. "You know Briar; you can't keep him down for long." He smiled, but it didn't reach his eyes. He always seemed haunted when he spoke of Briar, the once-great love of his life. She wondered if they would ever work that out, but she dared not ask. Not like he'd answer anyway. Remy glanced nervously back at the closed bedroom door; his face creased with worry.

"Why are you here?" she repeated, and Remy looked at her sheepishly. He was there, he'd finally confessed because he and Jinxie's playtime had involved chocolate syrup, strawberries, and clogged hot tub jets, which had flooded Gaston's bedroom, ruining the carpet in the master suite. The water had then seeped into the floor, ultimately cracking the ceiling of the dining room, smashing the antique chandelier that had been original to the house, destroying Gaston's dining table, which had once been in the Palace at Versailles. Gaston had come home early, and Jinxie being Jinxie, disappeared. Remy had found himself on her doorstep.

"I was actually coming to crash in the guest room when I heard moaning. I thought you were hurt. I didn't expect to find you playing reverse cowgirl with the cop with your hair full of fuck knots." She absently touched her tangled hair.

"You can't tell the difference between someone in pain and someone so obviously not?" she mumbled. He smirked and lifted a brow.

"They sound eerily similar."

"Guest room." She pointed to a door beneath the stairs as she turned and headed up the stairs. "You have been spending too much time with Jinxie. Spend more time with humans, Remy. You're starting to scare me." She could hear him laughing as she closed her bedroom door behind her.

❖ ❖ ❖

It was still dark when he woke again; the moon was high and bright in the night sky. Feeling more relaxed than he had in years, he moved closer to Celeste, kissing her bare shoulder before snuggling in closer to her. He inhaled sharply and caught a trace of the stench of a rotting animal. He sat up slowly, his eyes scanning the darkness of the bedroom. Something was in here, something small and moving through the room. He saw a shadow from the corner of his eyes and turned to find discarded clothing piled on the chair in the corner. The smell faded, and he thought that perhaps, he was letting his imagination get the better of him. He settled back down when something large and dark cast a shadow from the skylight, blocking out the glow of the moon that had just illuminated the room in pale shades of silver. Now there was something up there, watching. When he turned to look up, he saw nothing but the moon staring back at him.

*"Get a grip, man,"* he whispered to himself.

Sighing, he turned to look at Celeste, who slept peacefully and unmoving beside him. He snuggled close, smelling her natural scent, slightly sweaty but sweet, like vanilla and, as always, lavender. She lay on her side, her back to his chest, and it amazed him how perfectly they fit together. He stared at her for a while, gently brushing the hair from her face, and realized that she was cold. He touched her cheek and found it to be ice cold, and she wasn't breathing. Terror ripped through him as he gave her a shake, his hand landing in something wet and sticky, the scent that filled his nostrils metallic and surprisingly enticing.

Blood.

His heart banged frantically in his chest; he turned on the bedside lamp and found that he was lying in a pool of blood. Her face was ashen from blood loss. A scream bubbled up in his throat as he rolled her onto her back. Her throat was torn open viciously. Something black and sticky oozed from the wound coating his hand and forearm, biting into him, burning into his flesh, leaving the skin broken and yellowed. Her head lolled sickeningly to one side, her once vibrant eyes stared at him but seeing nothing, her lips an unnatural shade of purple.

*"You've lost another detective."* Nicky Sky spoke from the foot of the bed; his pale skin seemed to glow in the moonlight, his eyes a vivid blue. Shaking his head slowly, he smiled, exposing frighteningly pointed teeth coated with thick dark viscera that dripped on ashen skin. Right before Eli's eyes, he began to flake away like dust in a strong breeze.

Eli pulled Celeste's limp and lifeless body into his arms and began to scream, a guttural hollow sound that seemed to come from some unknown source deep in his soul.

\* \* \*

"Eli. Eli, Elijah." He was being shaken hard by surprisingly strong hands; the lights came on, and his eyes snapped open. Celeste was still leaning across him, her eyes worried. He sat up with a start, grabbing her by the shoulders, and turned her head left then right, inspecting her neck.

"It's okay. It was just a dream. Baby, it's just a dream." She stroked his cheek, her face anxious with concern. He stared at her for a moment, his hands on her flawless neck before pulling her into his arms.

"You're okay. You're okay," Eli whispered over and over as he stroked her hair. She pulled away, looking into his panic-stricken and terrified eyes.

"I'm fine," she assured, kissing him softly on the lips as if to prove her point. He held her for a while longer, waiting for his heart to stop racing and exhaled.

"Are you going to tell me what that was about?" They'd settled back under the covers, her head on his pillow.

"Just a nightmare. I'm sorry if I scared you." He breathed, his arm thrown over his eyes. She rolled over to face him.

"About?" she asked.

He peered at her from beneath his arm and sighed, then

draped his arms around her naked body and shared her warmth, his lips on her bare shoulder.

"Did I scare you?" he asked quietly. She nodded sleepily. "Sorry."

"You never have to apologize to me for anything about you. Never." She kissed the hollow of his throat and draped one long smooth leg across his hips. She wanted him again, just once more before the dream was over. She wanted to live with the memory of this night forever. "Never." She repeated softly, snuggling closer until she lay with her warmth cradled against his newly awakened body. She let her hand move lower, running her finger across the soft tangle of hair just below his navel. He sucked in from the shock of pleasure and chuckled. "Sweetie, you are something else," he whispered.

"You have no idea," she agreed.

* * *

It was just after sunrise before Celeste managed to wiggle out of Eli's arms long enough to use the bathroom. Her bathroom was awash of pinks and whites, with neatly hung monogrammed towels coordinating with the fluffy pale pink rugs. There was a glass-encased sauna shower, with beautiful Italian marble walls and floors. The toilet was a little room just behind the shower with its door for privacy.

Her bathtub was a white cast iron claw-footed slipper tub that had been custom fitted with massage jets and was large enough to hold at least two people. It faced a long high window that overlooked the downtown skyline.

Filling the tub with hot water and her favorite bubble bath, she slipped her sex sore body in, turning on the massage jets, and relaxed into the steaming warmth. Who knew sex could make every muscle in your body ache and sing at the same time, she thought? As the bubbles tickled her toes, she had an overwhelming feeling of dread. Eli would be awake soon, and he would remember all of the things he'd done and seen. He'd remember, and if he responded badly, that could be bad for everyone. Really bad. Apocalyptic.

She'd known what he was for sure when they'd arrived at Jinxie's. It was obvious he wasn't normal; he was special, even by their standards. Even Remy, in his drunken rage, had known what he was. After a moment, that's all it had taken. A moment and Remy had known, so had Julian. For Lilith, it would only take an instant. And knowing that bitch, she'd use him then discard him when she was done. It's what she'd done to Remy, and she would do it to Eli without batting a pretty little eye. Sighing, she closed her eyes and slipped beneath the surface of the water. When she came up, wiping the water from her eyes, he was standing there, naked and smiling.

"Good morning," he sunk into the tub at the opposite end, sending water sloshing over the sides.

She studied him as he pulled one of her feet to his chest in the depths of the warm soapy water. She watched as the glow from his eyes finally faded. That meant he was completely sober. That meant they were going to have to talk soon, and that was something she was dreading.

"How are you feeling?" she asked cautiously. She didn't want him to freak out on her suddenly. "Tired, but in a good way, alive, hungover, a pounding headache, and very satisfied. I also had a bizarre dream. I dreamt that your friend Jinxie told me she was a pixie and that your brother and I nearly came to blows. " As he spoke, he began to knead the arches of her feet. She laughed lightly, trying to make it sound effortless. Eli lifted an eyebrow but continued to knead the sole of her foot slowly.

"Funny, huh?" he mumbled, his eyes on her face, watching for any hint of change in her demeanor. She swallowed hard; he knew something. She could see it in his eyes.

"It seemed so real."

She shrugged, placing both of her feet high on his chest. "Well, you had a lot to drink last night. I, on the other hand, was too exhausted to dream. That is, of course when I was allowed sleep." She let one-foot sink beneath the water, toying with him. He moaned softly, going hard almost immediately.

"You, Elijah Cain, are something to behold. Your stamina is incredible," she whispered.

"What's the deal with you and Remy?" The question was so sudden that her brow shot up in surprise.

"Right to it, huh? Okay, well, we're really close in age, flirted since I came to live with Jonas, he was my first friend, my best friend until Nicky; there was an attraction, though one-sided. We've never gone on one date, made out a little but that's about it."

"I would say there's more to it than that." Eli's strong fingers kneaded the soles of her feet, and he was making it hard to concentrate.

"A long time ago, he wanted more, but since he broke up with the love of his life, he's been...different. But no matter what, he wants me to be happy, I suppose." She sank lower into the water.

"And what do you want?" His voice was low and expectant. She looked into his eyes and sat up a little straighter.

"You." It was a straightforward comment, no pretense or playfulness, and he appreciated that. He continued his massage of her feet, a satisfied smile on his face.

"You don't hold, back do you?"

"No. If I don't tell you what I want, how will you know?" A smirk teased the corners of her mouth as she watched him contemplate her statement with amusement.

"I've never shared a bath with someone," he said finally, sounding a little amazed.

"Really? I doubt that. I see you having women doing whatever you want them to. All you have to do is flash that little dimple, and the panties come off. "

"Nope. That is not my style. Just because someone is willing doesn't make them attractive. And how could I ever want anyone else as long as you're in my world? You've corrupted me, Doc." He kissed her big toe, and a shiver went through her. All it took was a touch to bring her blood to a boil.

"That was my plan all along." She lifted her brow in quick succession, twirling an invisible mustache, and he laughed.

"You are diabolical." He teased, and she playfully splashed water at him.

"You don't know the half of it." As she spoke, his cell phone chimed to life from somewhere on the bedroom floor, possibly underneath a pile of discarded clothing. She lifted a curious brow but said nothing. She could remember that phone ringing off and on most of the morning and Eli's total oblivion to it. She wasn't even sure he knew where it was or if she even cared, for that matter.

"I know where it is and who's calling." He mumbled at that particular moment. The most crucial thing in his world was the muscled curve of her calf.

"Hannah Freeman. Man, she's got your scent- like a dog after a bone. I bet you have women throwing themselves at you left and right. Are you sleeping with her too? Have your cake and eat me too?" He laughed at her bawdy remark and shook his head.

"Not my style. My last relationship lasted three years. She was a great girl, but she was needy, and we had nothing in common. She said I was too black and white and that I saw no grey. She also said I had no passion and that I was too closed off and never really let loose. Grace hated her."

"Why do you call her Grace?"

"Because- she's just always been, Grace. She doesn't look or act like a grandmother. And she would kill me if I called her Nana or Granny. She's a true old New Orleans broad, you know." he shrugged. "I think you two will like each other once you get to know each other."

"Why do you say that?"

"You're a lot alike. Strong, smart, graceful, funny –beautiful-but I find you much, much sexier." His voice took on a strange tone, one she couldn't identify.

"Are you close to her?"

"Yeah, she's the only family I have; her and Boogie, and Riley, of course. We have a standing lunch date once a week. And at least every other week, she tries to set me up with someone just like the girl she hated; socialite types, who spend their time planning charity events and bridal showers, boring pretty girls who pose well for pictures. Ironic, isn't it?"

Celeste thought about that for a moment, then shook her head.

"Not really, Eli. Even though she didn't like your ex, she figured that's your type. So that's where she's starting. She wants you to be happy. She wants you to have love in your life. That's what parents want for their children."

He'd never actually thought of it that way. Oh, he knew Grace loved him and wanted him to be happy, but she had no idea what he wanted in a woman until last night. Hell, until a few days ago, he hadn't known. When she put it in those terms, it made sense that Grace would do what she did; she had no other point of reference. He kissed the sole of her left foot, and it tingled up her thigh. "Well, I have you, so that won't be an issue anymore, now will it?"

"Elijah Cain, are you falling in love with me?" she fanned herself and fluttered her eyelashes, a coy smile teasing her lips. She was teasing, but his face was suddenly serious. He was staring at her, silent and solemn, and she thought that perhaps she had said something wrong. What he felt for her was pure primal lust, not love. Love was not allowed. She was supposed to choose a mate who would best suit her and the Collective. She was to marry for position and political reasons, never for love, not that he'd proposed marriage. For a second, she felt an odd twinge of some unrecognizable emotion twisting in the pit of her stomach.

"I didn't-" she stammered nervously, not wanting to burst the bubble that surrounded them. Not just yet, anyway. It would come to an end soon enough, but not just yet. She hadn't had him long enough yet. Her growing dread ebbed when she looked at him. He smiled and ran his hands up her calf to her muscled thigh, his eyes on her face.

"I think I may be." Her heart skipped a beat at his words, and her breath caught in her throat. "There is something about you. I feel like I've known you my entire life; like we're supposed to be, somehow. A whole world opened up for me when I met you. From the minute I met you, all of the puzzle pieces of my life fell into place, with you right in the middle of it."

There was a great big piece of the puzzle he wasn't seeing, she thought, and she didn't want to have to tell him what it was. Damn it, if only she hadn't been called before the Collective, she could have kept him hidden. She could have kept him her secret. But now that they knew, she would have to bring him in. If she didn't, they would send one of the others, one who wouldn't care in what condition he was brought in. They made their money whether the capture was dead or alive.

Nervously, she chewed her bottom lip, something he found increasingly sexy, and he told her so. "It makes me want to bite you." She didn't say anything. Something was bothering her, something she still had hidden from him. He probed her mind and again came up empty; there was a veil over her mind. She had a funny way of doing that. She could close herself off completely from him. She locked her entire life away behind a wall.

"You do that a lot don't you?" he asked. She looked at him, confusion flickering in her eyes. "You close yourself off from people. You know you never mention any friends other than Nicky. Only your family. And you moved to the city, over an hour away from them. You lock yourself up in this high-tech penthouse at night and go to a locked away lab to work. You don't even have pictures of your family on the walls. I've been with you for hours, and your telephone hasn't rung once. You are incredible, smart, beautiful, loving, funny-what, are you hiding from? It's like you're of this world, but not in it. You keep yourself outside of it. Why do you lock yourself away from the world, Doc?"

"What do you want from me, Eli?" she asked quietly, sinking lower in the tub. A smile lifted one corner of his mouth as he moved through the tepid water, splashing some over the sides as he came face to face with her. He hovered, between her thighs, his damp skin against hers, and she saw that dimple. She rose to meet him, her tongue darting out to lick that little dimple, her dimple.

"Everything. I want everything from you," Eli whispered, his teeth nipping at her earlobe. She held her breath and closed her eyes, wanting so much to give herself entirely over to him. She wanted to give him everything, but she couldn't. Not yet. If the Collective had their way, she would never be able to give him more than these few blissful hours. They were going to take him away from her; she knew that from the moment she'd spoken of him in their chamber. They were going to take him from her, just as they'd taken away everything else. She couldn't tell him that she was alone because of what she was, what she could do. If she had been bound, blind to the world as he was, then and only then could she have him. But that would never be. They would never allow it. If she were to go against them, they would make sure she never saw him or the light of day again. Or even worse, they would simply kill him. She sniffed as tears threatened, and he pulled back so that he could look at her. He sat back and studied her face, worry creasing his handsome face.

"Baby, what's wrong?" He'd never wanted to hurt her, and somehow, he had. "I'm sorry. I didn't mean to upset you."

She shook her head and wiped her tears away, putting on a brave smile. "It's not you. I'm sorry."

"I would never, ever hurt you," he whispered and leaned back against the opposite end of the tub, pulling her to sit astride him. She held his face in her hands, and looking down into his eyes, she could see that he meant that. She could also see that his eyes had darkened to a midnight blue she had never seen before, and her breath caught.

"How much of last night do you remember?" she asked, her eyes scanning his face. Panic was rising; her heart thudded against her ribs as she waited for him to say something. He thought for a moment, his thoughts still hidden in a pink fluffy fog. He shrugged absently.

"I remember you." His hands, which were on her waist, slowly moved up, his palms spanning her back as he pulled her closer. "I remember this." He leaned forward, licking droplets of water from her chest. He kissed the valley between her perfect and ample breast, his hands moving down her hips. Playfully, she slipped out of his grasp.

"Don't start with me, Elijah Cain. I'm sore and stiff." She stepped out of the bath, wrapped herself in a fluffy pale pink towel, and headed into the bedroom.

"I'm getting pretty stiff myself. I get so hard just looking at you that it hurts," he groaned. She glanced at him over her shoulder with the most devilish glint in her eye.

"Poor baby. Want me to kiss it and make it better?" She cooed, letting the towel droop enough for him to get the full view of her naked ass as she walked away.

Eli was on her within seconds, tossing her over his shoulder and dropping her soundly on the bed. She screamed and giggled as he looked down at her. There was gentleness behind his eyes and, as always, something else. She stroked his stubbly and scratchy cheek, his smile so bright it reached his eyes. He was such a beautiful man, she thought. She was suddenly serious as she kissed him softly.

*"I want you to always remember us like this,"* she thought. *"Always like this."*

* * *

He watched her sleep. Her hair fanned out over his chest like a silken scarf. Her face was relaxed and free from makeup. She looked angelic. Her long, lithe body was tangled in the covers. One leg tossed over him, the long caramel expanse of her back exposed. She slept with her hands tucked under her cheek, the way a child might when she pretends to be asleep. He smiled and ran a hand over the lean muscled back, leaning over to kiss her shoulder. She shifted slightly, her mouth falling open, and she began to snore. It wasn't a light snore; it was like a lumberjack's loud and droning. Amused, he leaned over and pinched her nose, wondering if that would ebb the noise. She bucked and slapped his hand away but didn't wake. She mumbled something incoherent; leaning over, he kissed her cheek before he slipped out of bed and slipped his jeans on before padding downstairs. If he couldn't satisfy that hunger, he should definitely satisfy another.

* * *

Remy was sitting on one of the fluffy deep purple sofas in the living room when he walked down the stairs. He glanced at Eli as he entered the room, then turned his attention back to the show he was watching and the bowl of cereal he was eating. Eli watched with amusement as Internet video clips flashed across the screen, and a tall thin man made sarcastic comments about the performers' mental abilities.

"You still here?" Remy asked around a mouth full of cereal as Eli made his way into the open kitchen.

"Apparently," Eli mumbled and began searching for something to eat. Celeste seemed to live on a steady diet of soda, red wine, and fruit. The stainless-steel fridge was full of fresh fruit and some suspect vegetables. The top two shelves held dozens of bottles of red wine and a book of poetry. Smiling to himself, Eli placed the book on the counter. He'd seen several half-read books scattered around the apartment in the strangest locations. It was as if she got distracted and just left her books wherever she was, but they all had been carefully marked so she could pick up where she left off when she finally found the book again. Shaking his head, he rummaged around in the freezer until he found breakfast sausages. He removed them and searched the cabinets until he unearthed the pancakes' ingredients, several more books, and a cordless phone.

"Well, by all means, just feel free to make yourself at home," Remy grumbled. Eli ignored him as he continued his preparations for breakfast.

"I don't like you." Remy sat at the black marble island that separated the kitchen from the open living area. He looked like a teenager with his tight black jeans and an oversized t-shirt. His hair was matted from sleep, his feet bare, and he moved as quickly and quietly as a predatory animal. As he sat on the leather bar stool, the chains that dangled from his jeans rattled against the wooden drawers beneath the tabletop.

"The feeling is mutual," Eli snarled back at him. Remy snorted and continued to eat from a monstrous bowl of what looked like mushy Fruit Loops. He watched as Eli easily cracked eggs into a bowl and began mixing batter.

"You wanna know why I don't like you?" he asked.

"Not really," Eli said with a blindingly bright smile. Remy gave a dry laugh and shook his head. "You know I'm going to have to kick your ass for screwing my sister," Remy said.

"You want some pancakes first?" Eli asked as he poured the first circles of batter onto the heated griddle. At the same time, the smell of sizzling breakfast sausages filled the apartment, and Remy's mouth watered. Shrugging, he pushed the bowl of mushy cereal aside and sighed.

"Yeah."

* * *

They sat across from each other at the island; Remy stared at Eli while forking a mouthful of pancake. He'd already eaten one monstrous stack and was working on his second. Eli shook his head, wondering how someone who ate the way

Remy did manage to stay so slim. The man should weigh a ton. Eli narrowed his eyes as he studied the younger man. Like Celeste, there was something otherworldly about him, something unnatural but not like her. His otherworldliness was unique to him.

Remy returned his stare and smiled.

"There are things about her you don't know," Remy mumbled through a mouth full of pancake.

"I'm sure there are," he agreed and continued to eat. Remy studied the other man and continued to devour the food that lay before them. Eli was larger than Remy, bulkier, with a pleasant enough demeanor. He was also stronger than anyone Remy had ever come into contact with before. He had to be a part demon, that he knew. He could smell that on him. Something about Eli made Remy nervous, and though he hated to admit it, he was a little afraid of him. It wasn't just the size of the man or the aura of power and ferocity that surrounded him. No, he'd been around men like him his entire life. He'd even taken down a few, that wasn't it. It was the unflinching way Eli looked him straight in the eye. It was probably an asset as a cop, but in day to day life, it was unnerving and somewhat intimidating. Elijah Cain exuded pure, undiluted danger.

"She's not like other women. She doesn't really do relationships," Remy said through a mouthful of sausages.

"We'll see." Eli effortlessly flipped a pancake into the air, catching it in the pan.

"She can be as mean as a viper; she'll attack if she feels threatened." Remy pulled the neck of his ratty t-shirt to the side, exposing a long-jagged scar that ran from his shoulder to his armpit. If Eli didn't know any better, he would have thought Remy's arm had been nearly severed. "See this, CeCe did this the first time I tried to kiss her."

Eli lifted a brow that made Remy smirk in satisfaction. There was a devious glint in his eyes. "Come on, man, you know we aren't blood. She's adopted, and she's – well, you know. She kind of draws you in with those eyes and that smile. But when Jonas first found her, she had been treated – like an animal, worse. She was damn near feral. She was so thin, so broken-" Remy shook his head, and Eli got a clear image of Celeste. She was covered in filth, her eyes hollow and haunted, and her feet bare. She lay on the floor, barely alive and covered in blood, her clothing ripped, her body broken. She was dying, crying for help in a voice that was barely audible from lack of use.

"Who did that to her? Who could hurt her like that?" Eli whispered, a pain growing in the pit of his stomach. He could feel the heat rise, his skin prickling in sudden, irrational rage. Remy paused mid-bite to look at him.

"I forgot you could do that," Remy mumbled at the spark of blue fire in Eli's eyes. That fire immediately went out, as Eli met Remy's suspicious gaze. Shaking off his anger, he snorted.

"It's something she'll have to tell you. And she'll tell you about it when she's ready. Don't push; you push, and she pushes back. Sometimes she'll push you completely out of her life." He stared into his plate; Eli could feel the pain coming from Remy in waves. It didn't take a telepath to see that something had broken between the two of them, something Remy had tried to repair. The wound had been restored, but some sort of scar remained, a barrier that had taken Celeste away from him, something from which he could never, ever recover.

"What did you push her about?" Eli asked. Remy shrugged, a sad smile curving his syrup covered lips.

"What I did? As you've probably noticed, Celeste has trust issues."

It was Eli's turn to give a derisive snort. "Oh, I've noticed."

"Well, she has good reason. Her life, her family, her birth family are a bunch of fucknuts. Every one of them, lunatics. Her mother, sister, aunts - all bat shit fucking bonkers. Her father was never around when she needed him, the classic fairytale nightmare of a life complete with a murderous mother and sister."

"Murderous?" Eli echoed.

"Yep. Murderous. Like I said, bat shit fucking bonkers. But Celeste lucked up with her grandmother, who, though not able to raise her herself, made sure she was safe and protected until she wasn't. And when she wasn't, things happened to her. People used-hurt her." He trailed off, lost in memory.

"Until you found her." Eli's voice was low and heavy, the tightness in his chest, making it hard to breathe as he walked through Remy's memories.

Remy let out a shaky breath but kept his head down, not wanting Eli to see the tears, the sadness in his eyes. "Her grandmother arranged for that as well. She made Jonas promise to find her and care for her and keep her safe. And he has. We all have, for the most part. You can't help but want to protect her. To love her." He shoved a fork full of pancakes into his mouth.

"So, you carried her from the-dungeon, was it?" Remy gave Eli a goofy pancake laden grin.

"You could make millions with that little trick," Remy said.

"Sorry. It comes and goes sometimes. You have a very odd thought pattern." Eli mumbled as he stared at Remy. His thought pattern wasn't like an average human; it wasn't clouded like Celeste's either. It was scattered and random, distracting, almost like an animal.

"Yeah well, I fall on my head a lot." Remy laughed it off. "Do you do that to Celeste? Because it would really piss her off. She's used to people falling at her feet and doing what she wants. She's *special*. You have no idea how irritating it is to be attracted to someone who's fucking perfect," Remy said, giving Eli a once over and shook his head. He openly admired Eli's bare chest sprinkled with soft dark hair, his chiseled face, and ass. Remy had to admit that Eli was gorgeous. He moved with a decidedly sexy swagger that he hadn't really noticed before, but now watching, it kind of hypnotized him. That deep chocolate skin rippled over rock hard abs and toned biceps. Remy's eyes wandered down the expanse of the bare chest to the jeans that hung dangerously low on slim hips. His own body reacted to the man in a way he hadn't expected. Remy stared at Eli's mouth, that devilishly sexy smirk and a hint of a dimple that sometimes appeared when he spoke. When he finally decided to speak, his voice was low and thick.

"Of course, you don't, because you're fucking perfect. You are beautiful and sexy as hell. Can't say that I would kick you out of bed either." His eyes darkened as he absently licked his lips. Eli stared at him and lifted a brow in question.

"Does that work often?" He asked.

"What?" Remy gave him a practiced angelic smile.

"The flirting. I mean, is this your way of trying to scare me away? Of course, by being a cop, I have to be homophobic, right? Since your veiled threats didn't work, you move into seduction mode? Is that it? I'm supposed to be terrified by your coming on to me?"

Remy laughed and shrugged. "It was worth a try. Am I making you uncomfortable, Detective?"

Eli leaned forward, his palms flat on the marble countertop as he looked into Remy's eyes.

"Believe it or not, your being gay doesn't bother me. What does bother me is the fact that you would get in the way of the possible happiness of someone you claim to love."

"I don't see it that way. I see it as protecting her." Remy met Eli's gaze and spoke in a low, measured tone. "I have picked up the pieces after men have used her. She looks tough, but she's not. If you hurt her-it will destroy her, man. She has never- she's never given herself over to someone. Not like she has with you. If you're just in it for sex, it's going to break her. If that happens, I'm going to have to break you."

Eli stared at Remy for a long time before exhaling and running a hand over his face.

"I won't hurt her."

"I pray to God that's true. I would really hate to have to fuck up your issue," Remy grumbled.

# CHAPTER TWELVE

He was so tired that he saw double as he poured through the Occult and Mythology section of the library and had come up empty. Now he was working his way through Demonology and Urban Myths. When the picture first crossed the screen, he had to blink, thinking his eyes were playing tricks on him. After all, he had been at this since early that morning after a paltry three hours of sleep. After searching for Eli and Celeste, he'd left Gracie's house, who'd mysteriously disappeared without a trace. They had missed the stomping temper tantrum Hannah had treated them to when another party-goer had told her that Eli had left hours ago, "with the chick in the gold dress. They tore outta here about an hour ago. Not that I blame him."

Hannah had a meltdown of spectacular proportions. He'd never in his life seen someone actually seethe with anger. Hannah had seethed and blustered and cried, her face puffy and red with fury. She had been a terror to behold until her father had to sedate her practically. It was a beautiful disaster, and he and Boogie had relished every second of it.

After a quick nap, he was back at work. Some administrator from Tulane University had been at the party telling him all about the special Occult section in the library, and he'd come in as soon as the doors opened. Flashing his badge and his smile, he'd been allowed into the special collections. Now, close to noon, he'd gone over everything he could think of, looking for that little monster Eli had described. Something about the entire case was starting to nag at him. Not just the case but Celeste herself. After watching her last night, watching her interaction with Grace and Hannah, there was something about her that was just wrong. Instead, he'd found this. He stared at the 15$^{th}$ Century artist rendering that had been discovered in the South of France nearly one hundred years ago. He rubbed his eyes and enlarged the picture, and the breath left him.

"No fucking way," he breathed.

The drawing was a perfect rendering, so much so that he couldn't take his eyes off of it. He looked closer before zooming out to read the story that accompanied the photo before clicking the print button. "*Caelestis filia Nemesis et Anhur*," he read and repeatedly mumbled. He'd clicked on so many images and stories that he was sure they would either eject him from the library or charge him for all of the paper and ink he was using.

"*Caelestis*," He'd heard that name before; he'd heard it from Grace just last night. Shaking his head, he plugged the name into a search engine and was amazed at the number of articles that popped up, thousands of sightings and stories going back as far as the 5th Century. The one image that felt as if he'd been gut checked was a marble statue that had been uncovered in 1745 and was dated back to about 900B.C. as far as anyone could tell. It was one of the oldest artworks ever discovered in such pristine condition. What made this particular sculpture noteworthy was its being a statue of a presumed Egyptian that had been sculpted from Greek marble and unearthed with Amazonian artwork near Turkey. The woman was tall, standing in a warrior's pose with a quiver of arrows thrown over one shoulder and a bow in her hand. She wore the draped garb of the Greeks and the distinctive armor of the Amazons, but the necklace and cuffs at her wrists were truly Egyptian, as was her bone straight hair and facial features. She looked like a mighty and formidable warrior, one that he wouldn't want to meet in a dark alley. Even in stone, she looked decidedly dangerous. What made a chill run down his spine was the accuracy, the perfect beauty of the likeness. He read and re-read the caption and exhaled. "*Caelestis filia Nemesis et*

*Anhur, Dea regina Amazonum,"* which had been translated into English as *Caelestis, daughter of Nemesis and Anhur, Amazonian Queen, Primordial Goddess of Justice."* Riley stared slacked jawed at the perfectly preserved sculpted face of Celeste.

\* \* \*

The soft drone of a melody was what brought her out of the most delicious sleep she'd had in forever. As she came awake, she realized that it wasn't music; it was a ringtone. As she blindly felt around the nightstand, she found an iPhone and pressed it on.

"Hmmm." She moaned as she focused on the bedside clock. It was just after eleven in the morning, but the room seemed surprisingly dark. Rolling over, she groaned as her tired muscles protested. She noted the drawn curtains and the shade that had been drawn over the skylight. Eli had figured out her remote system for her skylight.

"Where have you been? I have been calling you for hours," a hysterical, high pitched man yelled into her ear. She frowned, reaching for Eli, who was no longer in bed. "Are you listening to me?" the man squeaked.

"Who is this?" she asked, her voice still heavy from sleep. The man was so silent for so long that, if it weren't for his breathing, she'd thought he'd hung up.

"Well?" she asked, sitting up and stretching. The smell of something delicious was wafting in through the open bedroom door, and she could hear voices droning from the kitchen. She sat up, rubbing the remnants of sleep from her eyes. "Hello?" she asked. "You still there?"

"This is Detective Riley Quinn. Who the hell is this?" he came back with a sharp, authoritative tone that she was sure he used as an intimidation tactic; she knew him too well to be intimidated. She smiled as she noticed her pink covered phone resting beside the bedside clock.

"Oh, hi, Riley. I must have picked up Eli's phone by mistake. This is Celeste. Let me get him." She yawned and rolled out of bed. As soon as her feet hit the floor, she was dressed in Eli's discarded Supermen t-shirt. She glanced at herself in the mirror before giving her head a shake. Her hair smoothed into place, and the sleep creases disappeared from her cheek. She looked and smelled as fresh as a morning daisy as she padded downstairs in her bare feet.

He turned to look at her as she descended the stairs, and her heart began to flutter. The man was just so damn sexy. He was barefoot, his jeans hanging precariously on narrow hips as he flipped pancakes with practiced ease. She looked at Remy, who gave her a pancake-laced smile as she approached.

"It's Riley." She handed the phone to Eli as she stared at her brother curiously.

"So, you're okay with this now? After your temper tantrum last night, now you two are buddies?" She shook her head; Remy gave Eli a lascivious leer.

"What can I say," Remy laughed, his tone low and seductive. "He kind of grew on me."

Eli winked at her, sliding a steaming plate of pancakes, sausages, and fresh fruit over to her before speaking into the phone. Riley's voice was high and loud in his ear, yelling incoherently. "Well, good morning to you too, Riley." He sat on the stool beside her, kissing her forehead, his hand resting on her thigh.

"Where have you been? I have been calling you since last night. You left me at Grace's without a word. I had to let Boogie drive me home, and you know Boogie drives like a damned lunatic on meth. I'm lucky I made it home in one piece. Grace has been looking for you everywhere. I went by your house this morning and found that damned Hannah Freeman lurking around again. But now I see you were shacking up with the Doc." Moving away, Eli turned his back to Remy and Celeste, who were too deep in conversation and stacks of pancakes to pay attention, and he exhaled.

"Is that why you called, Riley?" He turned to look at her. She was listening to Remy tell a rather animated tale, laughter lighting her eyes.

"No. I did some more searching for that-thing you saw, and I found something that you need to see. It's about Doc. I think you're right, E. There is something very different about her." She absently licked syrup from a strawberry that had migrated too closely to her pancakes. The way her tongue darted out and licked the sticky sweet tip of the berry, her lips wrapping around it as she sucked, his body reacted. His mouth went dry and his throat tight. When she bit into it, the juice ran down her fingers and dripped onto her chin. She made yummy noises as she licked her fingers and smiled demurely before returning her attention to her brother.

"Yes, there is. There is something very different about her," Eli agreed.

"Eli, are you listening to me?!" He started at the sound of Riley's voice reverberating in his ear.

"What? Yes, you need to see me. Give me a couple of hours-"

"I'm Uptown right now. We can meet at Ricky's on St. Charles in an hour." He disconnected before Eli could reply, which was just fine by him. He had other things on his mind. He strolled to Celeste, a hungry look in his eye.

"Can I have a taste?" he asked. Before she could react, he'd kissed her.

Remy, who stood near the sink, made a low groaning noise.

"Can I have a taste, too?" he teased. Eli lifted a brow. "Are you talking to Celeste or me?"

"I'm open to either actually." He leaned lazily against the counter, his arms folded across his chest, his slim legs crossed at the ankle. Celeste gave him a warning look, and he shrugged before strolling into the guest room.

"Oh well," he called as he left the room. "Maybe next time." He closed the door to the guest bedroom behind him.

"I guess you've figured out that Remy's sexuality is-"

"Ambiguous?" Eli finished, and she nodded, seductively licking syrup from her lips.

"That's a good way to put it," she agreed before her lips touched his again. "You still hungry?" he asked.

She dropped her fork and draped on the arm around his neck.

"Not for pancakes," she said.

* * *

"I don't have my usual nightmares when you're around," he said against her hair. She lay draped over him, her fingers tracing little circles in his chest hair. They hadn't managed to make it to the bedroom this time. They had made it to the deep purple sofa in front of the television. Now they lay tangled in each other's arms underneath a bright red chenille throw that barely covered them.

"How would you know- we've barely slept." she snorted. He yawned and held her closer.

"I saw it Wednesday night," he said, staring up at the ceiling. "It was outside of my bedroom window, turned into a cat." She stiffened but waited and listened as he told the story of the creature on the levee and the poor jogger who'd been carried off into the night sky. He'd watched the news and discovered her name was Amanda Seville, and she was a twenty-three-year-old nurse who lived alone. Her body was found by a fisherman on a riverbank near Grand Isle in the following morning's early morning hours.

"Did you file some sort of report?" She sat up, pulling his Superman t-shirt back on, and hugged herself.

"What was I supposed to say? I saw a vampire demon elf thing turn into a cat on my porch, then turn into a person, hide in some trees on a levee, and kill a jogger? I tried to stop it, but it flew away into the darkness, taking the woman with it into the night sky. Oh, and this was well after midnight. They would think I was drunk or crazy or both. Everyone in the department already thinks I'm some sort of psychic freak. This is strange even for me."

"It was at Jonas's house that night. It killed one of the guests. Remy's –friend. Before that, it was in *my* room. It was watching me sleep, Eli. It could have easily killed me. Why didn't it? " she said, chewing her thumbnail.

"It's watching us, Eli." She whispered more to herself than to him. Exhaling, she shook off the chill that went down her spine.

"I need something to drink," she muttered before heading to the kitchen. Eli slipped on his pants and watched as she grabbed a bottle of red wine from her fridge and pulled the cork out with her bare hands. She tossed the bottle back, some of the deep red running down her chin. When she finally took a breath and placed the bottle on the counter, he noticed the smell. It didn't have the fruity aroma of wine; it smelled metallic, like copper or-blood.

She wiped her chin with the back of her hand and looked at him. He could see the pulse in her neck speed up as she watched him move closer. "Doc, what's going on?" He asked, suddenly concerned. "You're scaring me."

"I came looking for you last night because there are some things I needed to tell you," she said, as a precursor to the speech she had prepared in her mind the night before. She moved closer, taking his hands into hers. Her hands seemed so small in his, so delicate and tiny. Her scent assaulted him, and he wanted to kiss her again.

"Eli, what do you remember about last night?" she asked, holding his hands in hers. She looked into his eyes and tried to see if he could read her memories as clearly as she read his, to see if he could break through the pink fog that clouded his memory. He struggled for a moment, pieces coming back vague memories that had no connection and seemed to be completely random.

"What you said about me, not being completely honest,

it's true. It's why I keep myself isolated. I'm not what you think I am."

"What do you mean?" he asked. She slipped her hands from his and ran a hand over her face. "I'm older than I look. My parents, my life-" She drifted off, not knowing how to continue but knowing that she had to. It needed to be said. Frustrated, she closed her eyes and clenched her fists.

"Doc, whatever it is can't be that bad." She opened her eyes and looked at him. He was searching her face for some hint of what she was trying to say.

"I care about you so much," she whispered. "I was born," she started again. "My family-" she paused again, her brow creased with the weight of her confession, and she exhaled.

"Just say it, Celeste," Remy said as he emerged from the guest bedroom. He wore blood-red leather pants so tight they looked as if they had been painted on. He pushed up the sleeves of the V-neck sweater in the same shade of red above his elbows, his eyes on them. He moved further into the room, his black boots making a soft thunking noise against the carpet. Eli looked at him closely, noting his eyes were so black that his pupils were indistinguishable. Funny, he thought, he'd have sworn Remy had brown eyes.

"Will you shut up?" she barked. "I thought you went home." She stood, suddenly nervous, and her eyes began to glow.

"Nah, I thought you might need a little back up," he said with a toothy grin showing off a pair of gleaming white fangs. Now that, Eli thought, was definitely something he would have remembered. "He seems the type to need a little-convincing," Remy teased.

"Okay, now you really need to tell me what's going on?" He took a nervous step back, dropping Celeste's hands. He would never believe her if she just told him. Telling wasn't enough. It never was.

She looked at Remy, who seemed to hold his breath as he waited. Dreading that she had to do this at all, tears dropped from her eyes, hitting the floor as she stood silent. Eli watched in silence as Celeste took a knife from the cutlery block on the island and sliced her forearm open, from wrist to elbow. He'd only had a second to register what had happened before he sprang into action.

"Jesus Christ!" He grabbed a dishtowel before hurrying back to her side. The blood poured out in a thick vivid river, pooling on the floor at her feet. He grabbed her arm, intending on putting pressure on the wound to stop the bleeding, as she stood unmoving. He looked at Remy, who seemed unfazed by what had just happened but watched him instead of his sister.

"Oh baby, what have you done?" he choked, "Why are you just standing there?" He barked at Remy, who folded his arms across his chest and watched. Eli's stomach churned in what he briefly thought to be hunger as the scent of her blood wafted up to him. The smell was sweet and warm, and he was tempted to lick her, an impulse that had gotten stronger each time he was with her, an impulse that he quickly ignored.

She didn't have to look at him to see the shock on his face when the blood was wiped away. Beneath the soaked towel, her skin was perfectly intact. There was no hint of a cut or even a scratch. Stunned silent, Eli put his fingers under her chin and forced her to look at him. He let out a high-pitched startled scream and took a nervous step back, stumbling on the rug, his eyes never leaving her.

Her eyes were full neon cobalt, void of any hint of white; her teeth were fully extended, long sparkling white with very pointed tips.

"Holy-What are you?" he asked softly, backing away. "Are you a vampire? No, I've seen you in daylight-unless that's just a myth-what are you?" he repeated, sitting heavily on the nearest sofa. He thought he was dreaming or still drunk from the night before because there was no way this was really happening. "Or am I losing my mind?" His eyes never left the two of them. His blood ran cold,+
and gooseflesh rose on his bare skin. This couldn't be happen-

ing; he just couldn't be seeing what he was seeing.

"You aren't losing your mind," she assured, glancing at Remy, who stood watching for any signs of trouble. Eli looked from Remy to Celeste then back again.

"Are you going to kill me?" he asked, and Remy snorted.

"As if we could," Remy murmured.

Celeste shot him a look, and Remy instantly fell silent, his face solemn. Eli watched her as she retracted the teeth and her eyes faded back to some semblance of a human. "And no, I'm not a vampire. "

"Oh, she's much more than that." A deep, heavily accented male voice came from the elevator as the doors silently slid open.

"Gaston," she breathed as he entered the room.

He was slightly taller and wider than Remy, but the resemblance was incredible. They shared the same thick wavy hair, his cut shorter and neater than Remy's slightly spiked Mohawk, but their skin was the same deep tawny shade of golden brown, and they shared those deep brown eyes. He wore khakis and a button front, pale green oxford shirt rolled at the wrists. He looked like an older, more sedate version of his brother. He had none of the bold cockiness that seemed to surround Remy, yet he still held the same aura of danger and mystery. He looked at Eli and smiled, tilting his head in curiosity,

"And so are you, isn't he, CeCe? My God, isn't he extraordinary? One might even say he was –beautiful." He moved closer to Eli, running a casual hand over the man's bare arm, his eyes coming to rest on the mark on Eli's chest. When Eli flinched and rose to his full height, Gaston narrowed his eyes and sneered.

Possessing none of Remy's soft prettiness, Gaston was rugged and chiseled, sophisticated, and held himself with an air of superiority and entitlement. He inhaled deeply, his eyes closed as he became intoxicated by the smell of Celeste's freshly drawn blood. He opened his eyes, revealing that they had become a liquid black that shimmered in the light. His fangs were long and pristine as if he'd never used them, and razor-sharp. His eyes lingered on Eli for a long time, taking him in with something like lust but not quite. No, not lust, Eli realized. It was awe.

"Remy, have you had the pleasure?" He spoke in a calm deep voice, his eyes never straying from Eli.

"No, not yet," Remy rocked back on his heels. The mocking smile, as well as the fangs, had returned. For some reason, the fangs seemed to fit Remy more than they did his brother. Perhaps it was his demeanor or his threateningly jovial persona. No matter what, right now, he trusted Remy a hell of a lot more than he trusted Gaston. Gaston studied Celeste and then turned his attention back to Eli. His brow creased in the study, then rose in surprise.

"You've given yourself to him. Then this is your Detective Cain." He sneered, his eyes flashing. Many thoughts played across his face, but nothing seemed to be appropriate to address. He glanced at Eli again appreciatively and took note of Celeste's tear-stained face.

"He is a good physical match for you. You have made your choice; I hope he proves to be worthy of you. For his sake, at least. We will leave you then. Remy-" Remy was visibly disappointed but did not protest. Gaston rose purposefully, kissed his sister's cheek, and headed toward the exit, Remy trailing along obediently, and for once, silent. Before the elevator doors closed, Remy looked back at Eli.

"Whatever you do, Detective, don't piss her off. She's pretty, but she is Death. She would kill you without a second thought." The doors closed, shutting out Gaston's maniacal chuckle.

❋ ❋ ❋

The silence in the room was palpable as they were left

alone. Eli stood away from her, his mouth open as he stared at Celeste. His Celeste was- he shook his head. He didn't know what she was. "What's more than a vampire?" he finally asked. She suddenly found it difficult to put it into words. She closed her eyes and exhaled.

"It's complicated." she sighed. That was the understatement of the century, Eli thought.

"Did you infect me? Is that why you're telling me this now? Am I going to turn into – what are you?" he asked suddenly, rubbing the bite marks on his shoulder. He was stunned numb. His mind refused to work clearly but shot to several conclusions at once, his foggy memories from the night before coming back in a chaotic, incoherent rush. "You drugged me into forgetting." he accused.

"No. I- didn't. It wasn't a drug exactly- and I warned you not to drink it. I can't infect you or influence you. I have no power over you. None. Your will is your own. That's the thing that makes you my perfect match. Eli, look at me. You felt it when we met. There is something that draws us together." She spoke slowly, hoping he would understand what she was alluding to. He shook his head in confusion and threw his hands up.

"Okay, look, I'm trying really hard not to freak the fuck out, so just tell me. What are you? Are you in some sort of cult? What are those people called- Harps? Those people who wear costumes and pretend to be fairies? Or Magicians? Is this some sort of illusion like David Blaine? Or that mind freak clown?" He stood and started walking towards her.

"You mean Live Action Role Players, and no, we aren't LARPS- this is real." She rubbed her temple with her fingers and exhaled. Now it was her turn to pace.

"Okay, Okay. I can do this. If he freaks, he just freaks." She stopped pacing and looked at him, her eyes narrowed. "You were raised Catholic, right?" He nodded. "Okay, then you have heard of the Nephilim." Again, he nodded, this time slowly.

"We-" she pointed to him then back to herself, "Actually-

You- are the Nephilim. That's what the mark means." She indicated his chest. He stared at her for a moment, then snorted disbelievingly.

"Angels don't have fangs." He said, eyeing her suspiciously. This woman was crazy, he thought. "*Absolutely bat shit bonkers,*" as Remy had eloquently put it.

"I'm not crazy. Just- I'm not Nephilim at all. What I am- doesn't technically exist." She spoke in a rush, and Eli stared at her for a long time, unblinking. She twisted her fingers and chewed her lip nervously as she waited for him to react. He sat down slowly, his eyes on her. She was beautiful and seemed so small and delicate standing there in his bright blue Superman t-shirt that hung just to her thighs. She ran a hand over her hair and waited.

"You're fucking insane," he finally said with a choking laugh. "And you've brought me into your psychosis."

"I am not insane. Neither are you." She exhaled and shook her head, kneeling before him; she took his hands into hers.

"All of this business with your friend Nicky- did you do that to him?" he asked.

"No, of course not, you saw what did that. I had nothing to do with Nicky's change."

"Is Remy a Nephilim?" he asked

"No. Remy is a different sort of crossbreed. Remy is a Dhampiric shapeshifter."

"Jonas?" he pressed. She exhaled and stood, rubbing her brow.

"Jonas is a Dhampir, a daywalker, human Vampire hybrid. "

"So, this entire time, this whole murder mystery missing body shit was just a trick to get to me? I knew you knew more than you'd let on. So, this was some kind of game for you. You and your family pull in some dumb ass off the street and play with their heads- for what?"

"Of course not, Eli. I don't play games, especially not with you. I have never lied to you. I care about you. Nothing between us is manufactured; it's all real. I'm real."

"All the bites, during sex, you were infecting me or feeding on me-" he rambled. She was trying to grasp his train of thought, but he was scattered, confused, and agitated. All she could do was wait and answer his questions as calmly as she could. He hadn't left yet, she told herself over and over again. He was still there; he was still listening, and that mattered more than anything else.

"No. It's a pleasure thing during sex. Like love bites, not too deep, and very little blood is taken. Didn't you like it? I mean, wasn't it enjoyable? I tried to make it as pleasurable as I could. I thought you liked it."

He shook his head, dismissing her question. It had been enjoyable; he couldn't deny that. Making love to Celeste had been the most amazing sexual experience he'd ever had, and even though rage and confusion were bubbling inside of him at that very moment, he still wanted her in the worse way. Looking at her, standing with her arms wrapped around herself protectively, she was barefoot and make-up free. She looked like a kid, a scared kid.

"Your brother said that you are more. What exactly does that mean?" he said the words carefully. He tracked her progress as she moved to the other side of the room. She closed her eyes and took a deep breath. Silently she lifted a remote and pushed a button. The curtains in the living room slid closed, blocking the rapidly fading daylight. She turned to look at him, and her glamour fell away, revealing bright blue eyes flecked with silver. Her hair seemed to shimmer a deeper, darker shade if that were possible. It was so black that it seemed to glow violet. Her skin even held a golden glow, as if she had a personal spotlight. He took a curious step forward, staring.

"I am the *Caelestis*, Goddess of Redemption and Justice, daughter of Nemesis the Greek Goddess of Vengeance and Anhur, Egyptian God of War, beloved granddaughter of the primordial Nyx, cursed by the Gods to sustain my immortality with the blood of others, and marked by the Fallen One as his true mate. I am the Queen of the Order and Keeper of the Nephilim, the guardians of justice and man. Just-just know that I've never done this for anyone outside of my family, Elijah. And not even all of them, only a few. That's how important you are to me, that I'm willing to do this." She pulled the t-shirt over her head and stood back.

"Just watch, okay? Don't be scared." She stood before him in naked perfection, and her body began to vibrate. After a minute, she rose a few inches into the air. She seemed to hum, a dull glow illuminating her silhouette.

"What the absolute fuck?" he whispered to himself and stumbled back a step. She opened her arms and opened her eyes, and her entire body burst into blindingly white light, filling the apartment with an overwhelming feeling of peace and an underlying current of danger. Her flowing jet hair began to rise around her face in waves of brilliant white shot through with silver. She wore a long white Grecian gown that came to her feet and draped over one shoulder, corseted by the gold armor of a warrior, beautiful ornate golden Egyptian cuffs were at her wrists and neck. A long golden spear appeared in her hand, a quiver of arrows and bow was on her back, and a gleaming sword strapped to her hip. She looked fierce, a living effigy of a mythical perfection. Tears came to Eli's eyes as he stared at her. An overwhelming feeling of serenity and worship filled him, and when she looked at him, the lights in the room buzzed and brightened until they began to explode. She was beautifully terrifying, he thought. She was a warrior queen.

He took a cautious step forward, drawn to her, unable to stop himself from going towards her, his hands reaching. He wanted to touch her, *taste her*. His final thought shook him to his core, and his knees went weak.

After a few seconds, the light faded, and she landed softly on the floor, her bare feet settling effortlessly on the floor, her human glamour flickering back in place. She stood naked again, her eyes vacant, her entire body trembled, and the glamour dropped , her body glowing subtly in the dim room. She looked as if she had a light on inside of her; she wobbled unsteadily for a moment and then collapsed onto the floor. He took an anxious step forward and then stopped as she held up her hand. He knelt in front of her, not sure what to do or say or even how to react. He didn't know how he felt, surprised, disgusted, and frightened. And somewhere deep down, he was relieved, which was the most surprising emotion of all. He didn't want to run. This, he knew, was something she needed to say and something he needed to hear.

"Don't. I'm fine. It just takes a lot of energy to do that. And I don't feed as much as I should," she barked, but she didn't move for a while. He gently touched her cheek and felt the tension in her body ease away.

"What exactly are you?" He asked again, softer. It still wasn't connecting in his already overworked mind. Was she a Faery? An angel? He was moving towards her, but only slightly. His conflicting emotions played across his face as he looked into her watery eyes. She looked so young and vulnerable sitting on the floor, her body limp from weakness.

"I am the *Caelestis et Nemesis et Anhur*. Granddaughter of the primordial Nyx, which means I am a Goddess, an immortal. I am very old, Eli, very, very old. In our world, we have rules and government- known as the Collective. I am above the Collective and a part of the law. I am Keeper of the Nephilim, but I am not one of them, not like you. As you said, I-*we* are of the world, but not in it." She repeated his words as she looked into his eyes, her hand on the mark of his chest. It took a moment for him to understand. She looked sympathetic and immediately lowered her gaze. "My mark was given; you were created with yours."

He felt as if he'd been doused with cold water and half laughed before he realized what she was saying. Eli slowly rose, backing away from her, running a hand over his mouth and chin. He half choked as he tried to swallow his throat suddenly dry. What she was saying couldn't be right. His head swam, and he took a dizzy step back. This couldn't be happening; he must still be drunk from the night before, he thought. Or he was drugged. That had to be it. Celeste had warned him off of the frothy pink concoction Jinxie had offered. Maybe it had been laced with some sort of psychedelic drug, and he was on an extended trip. He ran his hands over his face. A fine sheen of sweat had formed over his top lip, and his heart was racing wildly.

Her eyes were narrowed as she searched his face. Unable to think with her looking at him like that, he turned his back to her and threw the curtains open, looking at the darkening sky. It was going to rain soon; he could smell it in the air. The wind had picked up, and the trees below in the courtyard swayed slightly in the breeze. What she was saying couldn't be right. She didn't really mean what he thought she meant.

"Me? Are you trying to tell me that you think I'm whatever you are?" He turned to see her stand with great effort, wiping the blood away from her nose with the back of her hand. She shook her head and was instantly dressed in jeans and a dark blue argyle sweater. Her hair pulled away from her face in a long braid that hung down her back. He gapped at her in astonishment. On unsteady feet, she stumbled to the kitchen, her hands out in front of her as if she were preparing herself for a fall.

"Yes," she croaked. "To some degree. You are an immortal, one of the divine. I wasn't sure at first, but then when–I tasted you during our lovemaking, I saw your true form. I knew, without a doubt. It explains our link, our strong attraction. It's in our chemistry, in our blood. We were destined to cross paths, Elijah. The first time we met wasn't the first time we've met. You marked me. When you called me Angel that first day, I knew that you had known of me, on some level, months before we ever met face to face, am I right? Tell me, that first day, before I entered the room, you knew I was coming, didn't you? It was like you could smell me; you could feel me, right?"

She was right, of course. He had sensed her; he had felt her and knew deep down that he was on the verge of something. He'd dreamed of her, and when he saw her face to face for the first time that afternoon, he'd known that they would be together. He'd never wanted anyone more than he wanted her and had openly pursued her. Something he had never done before. But he wasn't like her. He couldn't be, he thought.

"Tasted me? I don't have fangs, Celeste. I don't drink blood- I don't light up like a fucking Christmas tree or levitate. My eyes don't glow –"

"Really? Because they glowed pretty brightly last night while we were making love. And how would you know, anyway? You can't remember a major part of your life, Eli. Don't you think that's a little weird that a huge chunk of your childhood and adolescence is missing? Do you remember your first kiss? How about your kindergarten teacher? So how can you know for sure?"

"How can you know at all?" He yelled.

"I know because I've never wanted anyone the way I want you. I never wanted to protect anyone like this before. I never wanted to tell you, but I had to. The Collective found out about you, and that is something I never, ever wanted to happen. Never." She reached for the wine bottled and downed the remainder before reaching for another one. He watched as some of it dripped from her chin, leaving a deep red stain on her skin. The smell filled his senses, and he realized why it didn't smell like the fruity aromatic wines he'd been accustomed to; it was because it wasn't wine. She was drinking bottled human blood.

The smell of it was appetizingly sweet and robust, and he found himself wanting to taste it, his mouthwatering at the prospect. He was also slightly aroused, and that raised his ire even more. Even though he wanted to, he couldn't take his eyes off of the deep red liquid dripping down her chin. More than anything, he wanted to lick it mingle the taste of the tangy metallic blood with her honeyed tongue.

"It's donated from family members. I have an entire pantheon of cousins, aunts, and uncles who make sure I'm well stocked. Would you like to taste it? I know you want to taste it. It's a hunger in you, deep down, buried somewhere. You want to taste it. You want to know what I taste like, don't you?"

She tilted her head and presented her neck to him. He could hear her heartbeat. The throbbing of her pulse seemed to echo in his head, drowning out all rational thought. He took a cautious step forward, his mouthwatering, as he focused on the growing thump-thump of her heart, the slight movement in her neck. The warm blood coursing through her veins smelled so sweet, he could just about taste it. For a moment, the urge was surprisingly overwhelming, and he became enraged, not only with her and what she was saying but with himself for even wanting it. His mouth watered at the smell, the taste of fresh warm blood flooding his mouth. Angrily, he narrowed his eyes before fury erupted.

"Of course not. This is fucking ridiculous. I know who I am. This is stupid. This is not real. I'm dreaming, or in a fog or high, and any minute I'm going to wake up." He screamed, unable to control his impulses. He turned away irately, to curb his sudden and astonishing craving. Heatedly he slipped the discarded Superman t-shirt on and began searching for his shoes. Her scent was on the shirt, and he cringed at the sudden want of her. He wanted to bury his face in her hair and inhale, but he needed to leave. He needed to get out of this place before he went as insane as she was.

"Could you stop yelling? My head is throbbing. And you are fully awake. Believe me, I understand that this is a lot of information, Eli, but it's the truth." She downed the second bottle, wiping her mouth with the back of her hand, her lips stained deep red.

"Okay," she exhaled, "think about it, Elijah. All of your abilities, all of the things that make you abnormal to normal human women, make you feel normal with me. We feed off of one another. Our abilities are so similar that we can even link them, make them stronger. And the sexual connection-we fit together so perfectly; we change temperatures when we make love. When I look at you- really look at you, into your eyes, the entire world stops. We were destined, Elijah."

"Is this, between us–real for you? Do you feel anything? Do you even have emotions, or is this just how you suck people in-so that you can feed?" He choked out the words. He'd turned on her so quickly that she took a step back, startled. The color was coming back to her cheeks, the rosy glow-giving her an appearance of strength.

"Yes. Of course, it is. Do you think I would have given myself to you if it weren't real? I have dreamed of you, too. I have waited centuries for you." She moved closer, reaching for his hand, and he backed away, taking a nervous step out of her grasp. She'd said centuries, he realized, and ran a hand over his mouth. Centuries. This woman, who looked no older than eighteen in her bare feet and fresh face, was older than most of the civilized world.

Centuries.

"This can't be real," he gasped.

"Everything between us is real, Eli. I have never lied to you. We belong together. I feel I have emotions, I hurt, I cry-I lo-"

"I can't be what you say I am, Doc. I can't. I'm not a-a blood-sucking fucking monster like you!"

❊ ❊ ❊

He regretted the words as soon as they were out of his mouth. He closed his eyes, feeling the pain of the emotional gut-punch he'd just leveled at her before looking at her. She looked as if he'd struck her across the face. Tears rimmed her translucent eyes.

"Wow," she whispered. Stunned, she stared at him as if she'd never seen him before. "A monster? You think I'm-a monster? I gave myself to you, body and soul, I was ready to give you my heart, and you think I'm a monster? You didn't think I was a monster last night when you were fucking me. No, then I was your beautiful, perfect Doc. You are the one with no emotions, Eli. You are the monster, not me. I may lock myself away, but it's to keep emotionally handicapped, self-righteous fucktards like you out." She started to walk away, but he grabbed her arm, and she pulled away.

"*Descendez de votre main de moi avant que je déchire Votre bras foutu au loin.*" She bit in French. Every word dripped with venomous disgust, and he understood that clearly. "Get your hand off of me before I rip your fucking arm off." She looked at him with unbridled anger and hatred, and he never wanted to see that look directed at him again. He withered under her steely gaze. For the first time, he saw the woman who had given Remy that hideous scar. He saw the chained girl hidden away in a dank dungeon. He saw the *Vitiosa forma*, the Vicious Beauty, and he hurt for her. She glared at him, pulling herself away, emotionally, and physically. He could feel her leaving him, and he felt something inside of him breaking. This was wrong; something was telling him that this was wrong. He couldn't go, there was so much more that needed explanation. He needed to be here, with her.

"Celeste, wait, I'm sorry. I didn't mean–"

His senses tingled as she moved away from him, her mind closed like a steel trap, blocking him, an angry heat emanating from her. She smelled of blood and lavender and sex; she smelled of him. He could smell something else, Remy, he supposed far off and faint. He was scared for a split second, but the emotion was fleeting, instead replaced with anger and regret.

"Doc, I didn't mean it that way. This is just - you can't expect–"

"Yes, you did, Eli! You meant it exactly that way! I knew getting you involved in my life was a stupid mistake. I told you to let me go. I told you to forget me, but you kept on. You just couldn't let go. You had to push. And now, now that this gets a little too well this time, I'm letting go for you. Just go, Eli. Bury your head in the fucking sand. We will deal with this on our own. Go keep pretending that you are normal, that you're human. Keep pretending that your world makes sense because I have bigger things to deal with right now."

"Celeste, this isn't ending, not like this. I still care-"

"Well, whoop-de-fucking-do! *Care* for a *monster* like me? You don't *care* for me; you want to continue fucking me. You don't call someone you care for a monster. You don't accuse someone of sleeping with you as some sort of sick game. I have lost so much waiting for you. I have lived my life looking for something that I knew might never happen. But then I found you and you- I opened my whole world-" Her eyes blazed violet, and her fangs drew out entirely. She trembled with rage and hurt, and tears stung her eyes as she spit out the words before turning away from him.

He moved closer, pulling her into his arms. Holding her back to his chest, his face buried in her hair, deeply inhaling the scent of fresh jasmine. He silently had her as she struggled against his bear hug. He couldn't think of anything to say that would make it better, so he kissed her hair, her neck, her tear-stained cheeks as she continued to fight him.

"You can't expect me just to accept this, Celeste. You can't throw this at me and expect me just to say OK. You have to know that I still-" *Love you.* The words were right there on the tip of his tongue. He loved her, crazy floating ball of light, human, Faery. He didn't care; he loved this lunatic of a woman. So why couldn't he say it? It was as if the words were locked in his throat.

"Get off." She finally broke from his steely grasp, moving across the room, not looking at him. Even though she was angry, she refused to hurt him, and he knew that she could. To hold that kind of power in check proved to him that she was more human than he was and that she still had some sort of feeling for him. She was a protector.

"Just get away from me. The Collective will be sending someone for you." She said, mounting the stairs that led to her bedroom.

"Doc, this is a lot to try to wrap my mind around. This is crazy-I mean-" He started to follow her up the stairs into her bedroom and stopped short at the sound of her voice.

"If I'm such a lunatic, why don't you ask your precious Grace how she knows Jinxie, Detective Cain? For that matter, ask her how she knew my name, my real name."  For the first time in his life, Elijah Cain's heart felt as if it were split in half, and the bottom dropped out of his stomach.

"Doc."

*"Congé juste avant que vous me fassiez la haine vous."* He froze his hand at his sides in defeat. It was barely a whisper, but he heard her clearly. The pain in her voice tore at him.  She didn't slam the bedroom door, only pushed it closed gently, not bothering to look at him anymore. The elevator chimed open behind him, and he turned to find his shoes, sweater, and jacket neatly folded on the table in the foyer.  As the door slid closed, her words echoed in his head.

# CHAPTER THIRTEEN

Eli climbed behind the wheel of his SUV, the keys dangling in the ignition, her words still stinging. The afternoon sky had turned as dark as his mood. Thunder rumbled somewhere in the distance. He stared at the street ahead, debating whether or not he should leave or should he go back up there and make her talk to him. *Don't push her*, Remy'd said, *she'll push you back.*

Finally, he turned the key as her final words came back to him, "*Leave,*" She'd said through clenched teeth, "*Before you make me hate you.*"

The car sparked to life immediately, and he tore off down the street, burning rubber as he went. As angry as he was, he couldn't help but know that what she said about him had to have some truth to it. He was different. That was a known fact. He had never been sick, not that he could remember anyway. He didn't have memories of childhood scrapes or pets or getting chickenpox or breaking a limb. He didn't remember summers in the country or trick or treating on Halloween, learning to drive. He didn't even remember his parents. He drove aimlessly for hours, with no idea of where to go. He couldn't be whatever she said he was, part angel. That was not possible. He would definitely have noticed if he'd had fangs, wouldn't he? As if to confirm, he looked at his teeth in the rearview mirror. His canines were a little sharper than normal, a little fang like-but no. He shook his head in disbelief.

He would have known, wouldn't he? Maybe she'd infected him, and he was starting to change. She'd turned him. But she'd said she hadn't, that she couldn't. Was that the truth? She hadn't lied to him, but she had kept a major secret. But a

THE FIRST TO FALL

secret wasn't a lie, now was it? And she was right; Jinxie had told him that she knew Grace, he did remember that. And Grace had called her *Caelestis* the night before. He'd clearly heard her. But Celeste had quickly changed the subject, covering for her. Why hadn't he remembered that?

Because he hadn't wanted to, that's why. All he could see was Celeste; all he could think about was getting her into bed. He had become a man possessed when it came to her. He'd let lots of things about her slide because he had wanted her more than he had ever wanted any other woman. He'd only seen what he'd wanted to see. Even Riley had admitted that something about her was wrong.

*  *  *

Finally, he came to a stop before the familiar white wooden fence that hid Grace's house from the world. He hit the buzzer frantically, leaning on it until Boogie's irritated voice came over the intercom.

"Hold your damn horses!" She screamed, and almost immediately, the gate swung open. His car came to a screeching halt behind Grace's never moving car. He slammed it into the park and ran across the yard bursting through the back door like a wild man.

Boogie was standing in the kitchen in gray flannel sweats, her hair standing on end, tapping her bedroom slippered foot in irritation.

"Boy, what in the world-" He brushed past her, his face set in determination.

"Where is she, Boogie? Grace!" He trudged through the house. "Grace!" He boomed, his voice causing the fine china and chandeliers to rattle. He knew that he was loud, but the volume of his voice had startled him, but he couldn't stop himself.

"Grace! Where are you?" Boogie trailed behind him, running to keep up with his long strides through the downstairs.

"She's on the patio. What is wrong with you?" He could hear the panic in Boogie's voice, but he couldn't stop to worry about her right now. He needed Grace. He paused at the French doors that led to the patio so abruptly that Boogie ran into him. Eli was as solid as a tree trunk, and Boogie bounced off of him, landing on her butt with a thud. He turned and closed the doors soundly, giving Boogie a warning look before he stalked toward his grandmother.

* * *

Grace didn't even look up as he rumbled toward her like a raging bull. She continued her gardening in a pale pink tracksuit and matching crocs. Even at this late hour, she was wearing a gold chain and bangle earrings. The afternoon rain had left the cobblestone patio slick, and he came to a sliding halt before her.

"You need to talk to me right fucking now!" he bellowed. Grace lifted a delicately arched eyebrow and noted his eyes, glowing bright turquoise in the moonlight, but she continued pulling weeds from one of her potted plants. She picked off a bud and held it to her nose, inhaling deeply.

"Night-blooming Jasmine," she said, after a moment, "known for its intense fragrance at night. Can you smell that? Doesn't it smell wonderful?"

"Grace, I didn't come here to talk about your motherfucking flowers. I have just seen some freaky shit, and I need answers right fucking now." He was near hysterics, pacing and gesturing wildly, his shoes slipping on the cobblestone tiles. In frustration, he took the boots off and tossed them across the patio.

"Watch your language," she bit, "that goddamn Pixie. I should have known she would open her mouth. There is nothing they like more than causing trouble." She exhaled, taking off her gardening gloves and tossed them on a table. "Sit."

"I'd rather stand," Eli murmured, pacing back and forth like a caged animal.

"Elijah Cain, I said *SIT!*" Her voice seemed to reverberate throughout the entire block. The windows of the house shook, and Boogie scampered away from her post, peering at them through the closed French doors. Unable to do anything else, he immediately dropped into a chair opposite her, staring with his mouth agape at his delicate grandmother. As if on cue, Boogie came out of the house with a bottle of bourbon and two glasses on a silver tray. She placed it on the table gingerly and left them alone, as quickly as her legs would carry her. She peered at them briefly before disappearing into the darkened house. Grace tossed her mane of silver hair.

"It's called *reboare vox*," she said when he stared at her. "The *rough* translation is thunder voice. What do you know?" She poured him a drink, which he took willingly.

"I know that I just spent hours in bed with a woman, a beautiful, sexy woman, who makes me feel alive and normal, with the softest skin, and eyes the color of the ocean who turns into a ball of white light and sprouts fangs when she's-"

"Let's just call it excited." Grace finished for him as she tossed back her shot. "You would too if you hadn't been bound. There has always been a little seepage, but I could see it beginning to unravel last night completely. She brings it out in you. I could tell just by the way you speak of her that she was special. She *is* extraordinary, Elijah. She's the *One*, your one and only." She studied him. He remained silent, his body tense in anticipation. He braced himself for what was to come. He knew that what she was about to say would confirm everything Celeste had told him, everything that deep down, he knew to be true.

"Okay, I guess we start at the beginning, the very beginning." She poured him another drink. "First things first, as you probably have figured, there are more than humans in this world. There are three roads of evolution. There are the

Children of Eve, which are pure human beings. There are the Children of *Lilith* or the Fae. Those are your preternatural humans, those with a touch of demon blood in them. You know, the Faeries, skinwalkers, vampires, shapeshifters, and that ilk. We-" she indicated the two of them, "are Children of Divinity, which means we come directly from the Gods. We are part of the Grigori, who, as you know from Bible Study, were angels who assisted the Archangels in the creation of Eden. Well, these angels found the daughters of Adam and Eve so beautiful that they lusted after them; some even took wives and created offspring, giants, known as Nephilim. Supposedly, this made God so angry that he cursed those Grigori who had betrayed Him, threw them out of Heaven, made them demons, or worse, mortal. God sent the Great Flood to cleanse the Earth of the wanton killing and destruction perpetrated by the Nephilim." Eli nodded. That was common knowledge. Anyone who'd spent as many years in the Church as he had would know this.

"For the most part, that is true. But the human world only knows a part of the story. By the time the Bible was written down, it had been decided that separating our worlds was the best and only option for their protection. Humans, I mean. Anyway, what you really need to know is that there is only one true God, above all. One, the creator of us all. Understand?" He nodded numbly.

"Why am I not drunk?" He asked, tossing back another shot of bourbon.

"That was part of your binding. We put a false memory of being wasted and sick, so you have always curbed your drinking. I mean, how would it look for a man to drink endlessly and have no effects from it?" She sighed. "I, on the other hand, can get completely shitfaced, whenever I damn well please."

He stared at the glass in his hand, poured another drink, and nodded. "Okay, one God," he prompted.

"Yes, well, there is a complete infrastructure of deities under him; God created every pantheon for a specific purpose;

mostly to monitor their bastardized versions of humans, demons, Fae, all of the others on the outside of humankind. The major issue with God and these deities came in with their selfish use of humans in their petty power struggles. The gods are like-" She struggled for an analogy. "Do you know Peter Pan?"

"Don't tell me he's a real person too!" Eli screeched, and Grace laughed.

"No. I mean the story; do you know the story? In it, Peter tells Wendy not to say there is no such thing as fairies because each time those words are spoken, a fairy dies. That same principle applies to the gods; only they don't die. They sort of fade and lose their abilities. The only thing that can kill them is the big guy." She pointed up, and Eli nodded.

"And the mythical *First to Fall*, the first angel, who came before all others, and who technically doesn't exist. Well, not as far as anyone can tell. There is no written history of him, no temples or artist's renderings. He was said to be the prototype for all humans having both human and angelic attributes. The Nephilim, those born of human women, possess that symbol on your chest. Those are descendants of the first, and since the First has no real classification, he was known as **The** Nephilim or the God Destroyer. It was foretold that he would find the most powerful goddess, she who crosses pantheons, and together they would be the savior or destruction of the world as we know it. He and he alone can guide the fate of the Caelestis, the most powerful goddess ever born," she said, taking another drink. "He is a myth among the preternatural; an all-powerful being, the first of his kind, created by God before all of the other deities and humans alike. The *First* is the boogeyman to non-humans. You better watch out, or the *Fallen* one will get you. But no one has ever really seen him or knows what he looks like. Not really. Of course, some say they've seen him, but there are people who say they've seen Big Foot too. That was just some nut in a hair suit, by the way. The Nephilim, you know from the Bible aren't exactly what they were reported to be. They were giants and part human, but the human part was never prominent. They are also sterile, punishment for the blending of the species, or maybe just a glitch in the genetics. They were killing machines, doing what they are ordered to do. But being mostly Divine, they had no concept of Grey areas. A sin is a sin, is a sin. All sins were punishable by death. *All sins.* You see the problem, right? The real problem came when the gods, petty little bitches they are, started pitting humans and preternaturals against each other. This led to chaos and debauchery, which in turn led to the Nephilim slaying entire cities. That led to the forming of the Council and the Collective, a monitor for the monitors as it was. Once they were put into place, the Nephilim were wrangled and locked away until a proper Commander was trained to make sure they didn't get out of hand; The Keeper of the Nephilim. All except the *First*, who was hidden behind a human face." She stroked his cheek, and he shook his head.

"Celeste mentioned the Collective-what is that?" He asked, and Grace exhaled and took two more drinks before she began.

"The Collective is more or less our government. They make sure human-preternatural interactions are limited. Every region has its own Collective with seven or eight members who handle issues within that region. We live well beyond the laws of man. A few hundred years ago, there was an uprising in the Northern European region. Some of the Dark Fae got the idea to take over Ireland. Think the United Nations or NATO of the underworld. Treaties were established, and laws were set. There are renegades, but the Collective, the judicial system, keeps order. The Nephilim, in that scenario, would be like the CIA. They both are governed by the Council of The Gods, which is governed by God. If there were a pyramid, I would be under the Council but above the Collective." She took another shot and waited for the next question.

"So, you are Nephilim?" He asked, and she smiled.

"Finally, the question I was waiting for. I am descended from the First. That's how I know that you aren't sterile." She opened her mouth, and her fangs appeared, like shining pearls against her beautiful café au lait skin. She retracted them just as easily and shook her head, her silver hair darkening to a rich shade of mahogany that hung to slender shoulders. Her face seemed to brighten as the illusion of age dropped to reveal a woman of no more than twenty, with dancing green-grey eyes. Eli stared at her, and his breath caught.

"Figured it out yet?" She asked, crossing her legs. While he wasn't drunk, she was definitely a little tipsy.

"You're not my grandmother, are you?" She shook her head and smiled, a dimple appearing in her right cheek, his dimple. You're my-"

"Daughter," she said slowly. "My mother was human, which slowed my aging process."

He abandoned the shot glass and took the bottle. With two massive gulps, he finished it before studying her. He could see himself in her, but he always had the same mouth and smile. He touched her face as if his touch would bring the old Grace back. It didn't. Her cheek was soft and warm and very real. She leaned into his touch and smiled. For a brief flash, he had the strong image of her as a child in his mind, soft brown cheeks pressed to his. He looked at her with warm, loving sky-blue eyes, tribal markings on his face, and an ornate collar around his neck as he stared at Grace, who was no more than four years old. He was sharing her memory of him, of her father and he could feel the love, no not love, the adoration, pour from her four-year-old body. Tears filled his eyes, and he blinked them away, wanting, no needing to look at her longer.

"My daughter," he whispered. As if to prove her point, she unzipped the track jacket and pulled the neck of her t-shirt sway to expose a small birthmark, his birthmark, on her collar bone—the mark of the *Fallen*.

"Just how old are you?" He asked, changing the subject quickly.

"I was born in 1452. A.D. We age, but we do it gracefully. When we reach puberty, our aging slows drastically."

"You're over five hundred years old? Then how old am I?" He asked, and she shrugged.

"I don't know. You have no real way of knowing. You were around before Jesus. I know that. Maybe twelve thousand? Maybe a million. No one knows. It's not like you're a tree, and we can cut you open and count the rings. You don't have an age, Eli. And you seem to have stayed the same age for eons. You have gone by many names. My mother knew you as Olorun, the supreme God. Others have called you by several names Chayyliel, Duma, but only a few know your true name. And she is one of the few." He nearly fell off of his chair.

"And your mother?"

"My mother was a Benin princess. She was seventeen when you married, nineteen when she died. Her name was Aunii. I'm part human and part angel, the true definition of Nephilim. But I'm not a guardian. You shielded me from that, kept my abilities hidden from gods and man. That's why I felt it important to protect you from yourself. When my mother died, she was pregnant with your second child, a boy. Before the Council was created, many preternaturals and humans alike were slaughtered on a global scale during the uprising. My mother was a casualty. I was spared because of my human appearance. You were hidden by some of the village elders, protected and worshiped as leader of the tribe. They avenged you and my mother and my unborn brother. It was a horrible time, Eli, just horrible. You blamed yourself because even though you loved Aunii, you knew that she was not your fate. She was not your destiny, but you swore to protect her, and you couldn't. The guilt made you insane. It made you very dangerous." She shook her head; she was well beyond tipsy and moving towards drunk.

"Why do I crave blood? Her blood." He nearly choked.

"Because that was how the first fed. There were no people, no animals, no fruit. So, you fed on each other. The blood of the divine is different, ambrosia. You need it to live. So, once a week, at our lunches, I would slip it into your food." She mumbled, sipping her drink. He stared at her in shock.

"Why don't I remember this? Why don't I remember being in junior high and high school? Why don't I remember my childhood? Why don't I remember centuries of my life?" She shifted uncomfortably under his gaze and took two rather large drinks before gathering herself to press on.

"You have no childhood memories because you were never a child. After my mother's murder, you were so enraged-I wanted to protect you, keep you safe. You were reckless, uncaring, and I was being pressured by the Collective and the Grey, the Collective police force, to keep you out of trouble. In your true form, you look nothing like the Nephilim. You are an entity unto yourself. They thought you were a demon. By the time they realized what you were, they wanted you dead. If you had been with the Caelestis then, you would have surely turned her against them. You would have destroyed all of them, and they were terrified. She was hidden, kept away from you, safeguarded so you wouldn't be able to locate her. A bounty was placed on you, several actually. No one knew your human face, they only knew you as the *Fallen*, so I had you bound so that you could live safely, as a human. I needed you to appear completely human because you were vulnerable in your state, but they would never suspect you. Unless, of course, they saw your mark, and not many know what it means. I had a white witch put a protection spell on you. I planted memories because it was the only thing I could think to do, bind you, and give you a new history every fifteen years or so."

"Were you ever going to stop?"

"I don't know." She shrugged.

"How am I supposed to know who I am?" He asked through clenched teeth, his eyes glowing in the moonlight. "You stole my life, Grace." She put her glass on the table, staring at him, shaking her head. The fury that rose in him was startling; he could feel his anger rise at the thought of years of his life gone. The time that he may not get back, the memories he'd lost.

"I saved your life," Grace said softly. "I gave up my own life to make sure that you were safe." She whispered.

Anger and hurt tore through him as he realized what she had done, what Grace had given up for him. She had lived her own life hidden from the world to protect him. She had never married, never had children, and never really lived because she loved him. Feeling something odd, Eli reached up and touched his teeth. He raced to the nearest mirror, which hung in the foyer, and looked at himself. His eyes blazed neon, and his teeth were long, sharp, pointed, and tinged metallic. He touched them, shocked to realize that they were attached.

It was as if someone had kicked him in the gut, and the realization of what he was hit him full in the face. He was not human. As he watched, the anger seeped from him, and the fangs retracted, the neon in his eyes faded. In that moment of clarity and self-realization, Elijah's entire world collapsed, and he went numb. He stumbled back to the living room where Grace stood, looking at the crackling fire Boogie had started. She didn't say anything as he sat heavily on the sofa, his eyes filled with tears.

"I never altered your personality, just your timeline, and hid a little part of who you are. You are still Elijah Cain. You just seemed so happy-so at ease with being normal. You had no connection to our world. I wanted to keep it that way as long as I could. Of course, I knew eventually I would have to tell you. I guess today is that day." Grace turned to approach him with another shot of bourbon in her hand. She handed it to him and patted him on the shoulder. "Come on. I have some things to show you."

It took him nearly an hour of sitting with Grace, looking at old photos of him through the decades, before it sunk into his head. He flipped through pictures of himself through the decades; Disco was not a good look on him. He was dumbfounded, but here was his proof. It was all laid out before him, his life, in pictures, a record of several lifetimes that he couldn't remember.

As they moved into the 1980s, the pictures turned to videotapes, then compact discs and digital recordings. Stunned, Eli witnessed his high school graduation in four different decades. He saw himself at proms and dances, Christmases and birthdays, parties with friends, college parties, and fraternity functions. He saw himself as a soldier and a sailor, a zoot suit-wearing hipster and a civil rights militant. He'd lived several lives and remembered none of them.

"Now you know," Grace said, "You may never remember any of your past. I apologize for that, but at the time, I thought I was doing what was best for you."

"You didn't think I would realize that I wasn't getting any older. What if I married a human woman and she started to age, and I didn't? Don't you think that would have sent up a red flag?" She shrugged.

"I would have dealt with it. I just wanted you to be safe and happy, and if I had to keep creating memories for you, I would. We live very long lives, Elijah. Very long lives and sometimes forgetting is the greatest gift possible."

"Celeste turned into a ball of blinding light. Can I do that?" He swallowed a shot. His eyes burned. He wanted to be drunk, to numb the ache in his heart and the pain in his head.

"No. You are the *Fallen*. She is *Caelestis,* the goddess. I could feel it the first time I embraced her." When he said nothing, she sighed heavily. "As the story goes, her mother is Nemesis, the Greek goddess of retribution. Her Greek grandmother is Nyx or Night. Her father may or may not be Ahnur, an Egyptian God of war. He was also known as the Slayer of Enemies. You put those together, and you have one of the most fearsome creatures ever born. She was hidden for years but supposedly raised by the Amazons, where she learned to fight. You met her sometime after that because she has your mark, meaning you claimed her. That's all we really know. There is not much more known of her life after that point. Some believed she was captured by the Greeks and tortured to death. Some believe she was finally tracked and killed by her mother, who found her existence to be a reminder of her rejection by Anhur, who cast her off after the child was born. There are stories of her as a slave in Persia and other stories of her spending centuries being tortured in Tartarus or some other dominion of hell. Some say she burned a Hell realm to ashes before disappearing for years. No one knows for sure what happened. She will not speak of it, but she is the stuff of legend. She is that mythical ghost, the female warrior's prototype, the precursor to Wonder Woman and Xena, Warrior princess. She is Justice, the great equalizer, Karma if you will. You see, my dear sweet father, as far as history is concerned, for all intents and purposes, Celeste Kent, the *Caelestis* does not exist."

She took another drink, and she waited as Eli sat numb and unmoving for a moment. His eyes watered as he grabbed the bottle of bourbon by the neck and drank. It burned and warmed him as it went down, and he liked it. But it wasn't numbing him the way he wanted to. It wasn't taking away the hurt and anger. After two more of her silent drinks, she looked at him.

"I think the binding is broken. Your abilities will be more pronounced as it fades. Now that you are becoming-yourself again, you can decide if you want to align yourself with the Collective or the Dark Fae or neither. But they will be coming now, all of them. Along with the binding, a cloaking talisman was put in place that is no longer viable, so they will be sending the locators to find you. All preternatural beings are monitored and tracked. I suppose you've noticed that we have a very pronounced sense of smell that will increase, your vision and hearing will also become more acute. Have you noticed if Celeste wears your clothing or sniffs you a lot? It's sort of a mating dance; she'll wear your scent to mark herself, to make it known that she is yours. Your understanding of all of this will come back in time."

"And what would these other *abilities* include?" He asked warily.

"Speed, strength, and a few other things...you're a real-life superhero. You can be mad at me all you like because I know you love me, but I suggest you talk to your Celeste. It was hard for her to let you into her world, and you slapped her down. No one rejects the *Caelestis*. She must care for you, or you would be dead, if not by her hand, then by her family. They are extremely protective of her. She showed you her soul, Elijah. That's got to count for something."

"She won't talk to me-"

Grace raised a hand to shush him. "Don't be stupid. Of course, she will. She loves you enough to tell you the truth. Now you have to love her enough to go after her. Please, don't be a dick," she said, and Eli grunted.

"Watch your mouth," He muttered but found that he was smiling at her. He looked at the pictures, casually flipping through when something struck him, a question he hadn't asked but was nagging him. Grace rose slowly, yawning before she kissed his cheek.

"Lock up when you leave. I'm going to bed," she sighed, giving his cheek a gentle pat. He grasped her fingers, holding her still.

"There's just one more thing," he said, and Grace lifted one the perfectly arched brow. "Why do we have the same eyes, the Doc and I?" He asked, and Grace smiled.

"I thought you understood. Elijah, you aren't *a* Nephilim. You are **the** *Nephilim*. You are justice and retribution, the first Angel, the divinity from which all other angels were born. You fell from the vast darkness that happened when heaven separated from the earth. You are the Destroyer of Gods, the Father of The Grigori, and the overseer of Eden. That's why I kept you hidden because of all those that came after you are terrified of what you can do, of who you are. You- like Celeste, technically, do not exist." She knelt before him, taking his hands into hers as she looked at him with those big eyes glistening with tears. "You are the alpha. Elijah, you are closer to God than the entire Council combined, a higher divinity than all others on earth or in the heavens. You're the boogeyman, the God Slayer, the *Keyser Söze* of the preternatural world. You *are* the First to Fall. You, Elijah Cain, are a *god,*" she whispered.

\* \* \*

Confused and angry, but with his questions answered, Eli made his way to his car. He was numb, his hands gripping the steering wheel as he stared straight ahead. Absently, he reached for his cell phone, which lay in the cup holder at his side, and dialed blindly. Riley picked up before the first ring was complete.

"What's wrong?" He asked, his voice threaded with worry and mock calm.

"I need to talk. Are you still at Ricky's?" He glanced in the rearview mirror at his teeth. With a little effort, he bared his fangs. Yup, they were really there. He shook his head, and they retracted. According to Grace, his knowledge of whom and what he was made the spell weak, soon it would fade all together, and he would remember everything. Maybe. That part had never been clear.

"I'm still here," Riley assured before hanging up the phone.

He hoped Riley was better at accepting this than he had been. He looked down at his cell phone, which he'd left on the passenger's seat after talking to Grace. He had twelve missed calls, all from Celeste. Twelve voice mails from her as well. He just wasn't sure he wanted to talk to her just yet, because what would he say?

He'd hurt her.

Unintentionally, but he'd made her cry when she was trying to tell him. She needed his help, and he'd known it. Grace had been right, she had cared enough to tell him the truth, and he would have to be brave enough to accept that he needed her in his life more than he needed to be human.

\* \* \*

She'd cried from the minute he'd left, throwing herself across her unmade bed and sobbed like a teenager who'd gotten her heartbroken. It still smelled of him and their lovemaking, which made her heartache even more. In a fit of anger, she'd stripped the linens from the bed and the clothes she'd worn the night before and set them ablaze in her bathtub. She watched as they burned to cinders before dousing the flames. It didn't make her feel any better.

Slowly, she'd moved into the shower, scrubbing her body until every hint of his smell was gone, which seemed to be a nearly impossible task. She could smell him all over her, in her hair, in her sweat; she could taste him on her lips. Sighing in defeat, she got out of the shower and dressed in jeans, a dark blue v neck sweater, leather high heeled boots before pulling her hair into a ponytail that rested between her shoulders.

Her head still hurt a little, and she was still a little woozy from transforming to her other-self. It had been such a long time since she'd done that. She didn't do it that often because it took so much out of her, and the only way to return to full strength was to drink blood. The bottled blood she kept had helped, but it was nothing like fresh human blood. In her days as an Amazon, it had been easy to come by; it was nothing to feed during their many battles. Or she would have slaves brought to her. There were even willing participants, ready to sacrifice their blood to the goddess. But now, it was a little more difficult for her.

She sat heavily on the bed, then lay back and closed her eyes. She'd called Eli, left a dozen messages all had gone unanswered. She redialed his number and waited. It went to voicemail. Angrily, she tossed her cell phone across the room where it hit the wall and shattered into pieces before the tears started again.

Why was she calling him? He should be calling her to beg forgiveness, she thought. She still wanted him, stupid but true. And she needed to get to him before the others did. The Collective would be expecting him. If she didn't show up with him soon, Lilith would send someone else, someone less gentle.

She threw an arm over her eyes and exhaled, trying to block out the world. She must have fallen asleep because she awoke with a start as thunder crashed nearby. Rolling onto her side, she looked at the clock. The digital green numbers flashed twelve thirty-three. Standing slowly, she stumbled into the bathroom, passing the pieces of her shattered cell phone on the floor. Her eyes were dry and itchy, and she believed swollen. This was different. She couldn't remember the last time she had cried like this. Not even when she'd been held prisoner had she shed tears. No, this was a new kind of pain. She didn't like it at all.

She switched on the bathroom light and stared at her face in the mirror, and groaned. Her entire face was puffy and swollen; her eyes rimmed bright red and dry. She looked horrible and tired. She'd turned on the faucet, splashing her face with cold water, when she heard something. Standing perfectly still, she turned the water off and listened.

The rain was pitter-pattering on the windows in a staccato melody, and the apartment was silent, but something was moving in her apartment. She couldn't hear it, but she knew it was there, moving slowly, quietly. Cautiously, she pulled an ornately carved Bō staff from her closet and stalked into the living room.

"Remy, if that's you, I'm going to kick your ass," she bellowed as she stood waiting. The room was still well lit. She'd forgotten to turn off the lights when she'd walked away from Eli, but it was empty.

"Nicky?" There was no response. She closed her eyes, sniffing the air, inhaling deeply. Not Remy, she thought. It was an animal, something old, ancient, very nasty, and slightly familiar. There was something buried or masked that she felt she should know but couldn't seem to wrap her mind around whom or what it was. Her heart began to race as she heard weird scraping as it moved above her.

"Celeste," its voice was low, disembodied, and held a heavy ancient accent. "You are one of us."    She searched the room waiting and watching, her senses on high alert. Her motto had always been strike first, strike hard, and make sure they stay down.  She moved further into the dimly lit space and noted a small rectangular window that was slightly ajar. Staring, she recalled Eli saying that when he'd seen the thing, it had changed into a cat. A cat would fit into the window with no problem.  It would also explain the animal smell. Moving slowly, she advanced into the darkness beneath the loft. Her ears pricked for sounds of movement, her eyes keen and aware of every shadow in the dark. It was here, and it was watching her.

"Okay, where are you fucker?" She asked in a sing-song voice and waited. Her eyes narrowed, waiting for the faintest hint of movement. Something to the right of her moved, and she turned to see it sitting on top of the bookshelf, just under the stairs. It was crouched low, its hands dangling between its scaly knees staring at her. Its silvery feline eyes focused on her, thin lips spreading into a wickedly delighted smile. The fingers were long and talon-like, with something thick and black at the tips.  It was nude and had small pert breasts and a penis that dangled from a dark thatch of hair between its legs. It also seemed larger than when it had attacked Nicky. Was it possible that this thing was growing?

"There you are, you vicious little bastard." It smelled feral, and it looked strangely excited as she stood in a well-practiced fighting stance, the Bō Staff at her ready. Celeste looked like a denim-clad warrior princess, and the little creature seemed to light up in excited glee. She took a moment to assess the situation before she smiled at it, waiting for the inevitable.

"Beautiful. So rare," It said. It continued to speak in a language Celeste hadn't heard in years, a dead language. Palaic, the language of the Hittites, she thought.

"Join us. You will be the center of our family. I will even

get the cop for you." It was standing in front of her in a second. Its speed was terrifying, but she managed not to flinch. When it moved to kiss her cheek, Celeste didn't react the way it believed she would. She didn't react the way Nicky had, falling to his knees and going weak. Instead, Celeste bared her fangs, her eyes sparked with something angry and dangerous; she was itching for a good fight. With a deceptively sweet smile, she gave it a seemingly gentle push, the heel of her hand connecting with the center of its chest. It flew across the room, a look of shock and pain on its face as it slid backward, away from the Amazonian beauty, and into the bookcase it had perched on just moments before. It dug its claws into the floor in a failed attempt to slow its momentum before it slammed into the bookcase, splintering it into pieces and being swallowed in a cascade of books.

As it recovered, Celeste smiled, her fangs and blazing blue eyes giving her face an added threatening element, and bounced from one foot to the other like a prizefighter preparing for a heavyweight bout.

"You picked the wrong night to fuck with me," she snarled, twirling the staff with practiced grace, coaxing it to come forward. Startled, it crouched low and sprang at her like a jungle cat, its nails digging into the wood floor; Celeste swung the staff with practiced ease and batted it back until it collided with the staircase. There was a loud cracking noise as it bounced off of the banister.

It fell awkwardly, not able to recover enough to right itself before landing on its back on a coffee table with a bone-cracking thud, and then sliding off onto the floor, one of its black raven wings crumbled.

Without hesitation, Celeste moved within inches of the demon, still in a crumpled pile on the floor. She kicked it in the ribs, her eyes manic as she stared at the fairy-like thing.

"What are you?" She murmured, leaning closer to look at the skin that was so thin it was nearly transparent. She was reminded of the flawless perfection of Lilith's skin, blue-white and smooth as a baby's. Its large slanted eyes and pointed ears were definitely Fae, and the wings. Black wings weren't always a sign of some sort of Dark Fae creature, but the smell was absolutely demonic. It reached up and grabbed her ankle, pulling her legs out from under her. She landed hard on her back, dazed for a moment, the staff rolling from her hands.

Quickly, she rolled onto her hands and knees and tried to rise to her feet as fast as she could. It grabbed her ankle again, and Celeste kicked it in the face with the thick stacked heel of her boot, then again in the forehead. It hissed, and thick dark blood poured from its nose. The third kick connected with its jaw, and she could see the way its face moved and corrected itself. She'd cracked its jawbone. She smiled with grim satisfaction as it released her, in obvious pain.

Celeste was on her feet when it jumped onto her back, its arm under her chin, cutting off her air supply. She was going to blackout soon. Feeling the room spinning, she did all she could think to do. Celeste launched herself backward, hitting the wall that held the nasty piece of artwork of metal points, barbed wire, and spikes. She dug her heels in and pressed back with all of her strength, her teeth clenched from the effort. It howled in pain and released her, falling to the floor. Celeste sprinted across the room, jumping across the back of one of the sofas, landing solidly on the coffee table, in search of the staff or her fencing foil or something; it was time to knock the fucker out. Instinctively, she turned to see where it was, seconds before it flew at her. She caught the full force of its weight in her chest and mid-section.

They barreled backward over a love seat, hitting the hardwood floor with a crash, knocking over a table, one of Celeste's favorite lamps shattering. She vaguely registered it as she and the demon grappled on the floor. It swiped at her face, its claws skimming her cheek. Celeste grabbed its flaccid penis and pulled fiercely.

"Never fight naked, bitch," she growled. It howled and swung out, missed its mark, and punched her hard in the breast; she heard and felt the crack of her ribs. The pain was so unexpected and vicious a strike that the wind was knocked out of her for a moment.

"Mother-fuck!" Celeste screamed, grabbing her aching chest, rolling onto her side. At that moment, it had her, straddling her chest, pinning her arms to the floor with its skinny scaly knees, and holding her head still. It hissed and began making a noise like it would be sick and began convulsing as it prepared to infect her with its thick, black-red poison. Its mouth was close to hers, and it seemed to weaken its grasp for a millisecond as she saw the nastiest lougie ever hacked upcoming from between the thin white lips. Celeste screamed and moved her head just as the gelatinous substance hit the wood floor with a stomach-churning splat. There was a sizzling noise and smell of burning wood and sulfur near her left ear. She could smell burning hair but wasn't sure if it was hers or the monsters.

It seemed to be frustrated for a moment, relaxing its grip as it began convulsing again. This time, she took the opportunity to roll it onto it's back and punched it several times with all her might until it's face was bloodied and bruised. Its bony childlike frame pinned beneath the muscularly feminine form of Celeste. With each blow, she could feel the bones in its face move in a sickening way and slide back into place like puzzle pieces. It was unnerving and gave her an ill feeling in the pit of her stomach.

'What is this thing?' she thought, as she continued her assault.

It made a sound, like a small child screaming and bit into her, its needle-like teeth digging deeply into her right forearm. She screamed in agony. She wanted to rip her arm from between its jaws but knew it would take a chunk of flesh from her. Instead, she took her left thumb and gouged at one of its large silvery eyes. It opened its mouth and began to cry out. As soon as she was free, Celeste rolled off of it, getting to her feet at once, manifesting a razor-sharp double-edged sword with a gilded handle. As the creature came at her again, she took one long swipe and felt the blade move through flesh as easily as if she'd just sliced through butter. She watched as its large eyes widened in shock before its head slid off of its bat-like shoulders and landed on the floor with a stomach curling wet smack. It took a few seconds before its body, which still hung in the air with its arms outstretched in the attack, followed. She looked down at the decimated creature, its red-black blood oozing across her rich hardwood floors, staining and singeing the carpets. Splatters had sprinkled across her sofa and table and dripped from the glimmering blade of her sword. The sword began to sizzle where the blood-stained the shimmering steel, and Celeste let it drop to the floor with a clatter. She stared at the body, her breath settling.

As her adrenaline began to ebb, the pain in her arm became excruciating, and she began to shake as she watched the holes being burned into her floor, the wood disintegrating and the hard, grey cement underneath showing through. She found herself running to the kitchen to throw up in the sink. It had been a long time since she'd had to fight for her life, not since the Kents had given her back her humanity, and her nerves had got the best of her. With her arm throbbing and pain in her head and back that she hadn't noticed before, she made it to the telephone and redialed Eli's cell phone number. Again, it went directly to voicemail. She started to say something after the beep, but all she could do was cry until the phone beeped again and the call was disconnected. Sniffing, she cursed herself for being such a girl and quickly dialed another number. He picked up on the first ring with a gruff, "Elo"

"Adrian put your pants on. I need the cleaners," she said sharply before hanging up the phone before he could protest. Being a demon prince, he could clean this mess in the blink of an eye. Being a lust demon, chances were, he had been in a post-coital haze when she'd called. She hesitated for a moment before dialing another number. When he picked up, she couldn't control the sobbing.

"Remy," she choked. "I need you."

* * *

Ricky's was a hole-in-the-wall bar on St. Charles Avenue not too far from Riley's apartment. It was opened twenty-four hours and acted as a laundromat, game room, and bar and grill. He found Riley sitting in a booth in the shadows at the back of the room. A couple of Tulane University students played the dilapidated jukebox and shooting pool, there were a couple of strays at the bar nursing cheap beers, but that was it.

Without a word, Eli slipped into the booth with Riley and signaled the waitress for a beer. Eli remained silent as he waited for his beer, his eyes downcast. He glanced at the stack of books Riley had piled in the booth beside him, each with a myriad of rainbow-colored tabs marking pages. He swallowed the first beer in one gulp them ordered three more before he finally spoke to Riley.

"What's all that?" He asked, and Riley seemed to hesitate. "Spit it out, Ri." Eli sighed through clenched teeth.

"What happened to you?" Riley asked in a low voice. "You don't look -well." Eli snorted and shook his head.

"I'm fine," he assured.

"You don't look fine," Riley said.

"I'm fine, Riley. What's all that shit?" He motioned to the books, and Riley exhaled.

"Well, I was doing some research on your–hobbit. When I came across this-" He opened one of the books to a marked page. Eli exhaled and stared but remained silent. There was an artist's rendering of *Caelestis et Nemesis et Anhur. Dea regina Amazonum*. She wore her waist-long hair in intricate braids that cascaded over her bare shoulders. Instead of the long sheer white gown he'd seen her in, she wore dark pants and leather cuffs on her wrists, her chest, and shins protected by silver armor. On her hip was a sword, and she brandished a silver bow, poised for attack. She was no more than a pre-teen in that painting, but the ferocity in her eyes made her seemed older and wiser. She looked every bit the warrior queen.

"Do you see it? The resemblance is uncanny. There are all of these stories of this woman-"

"The Celestial daughter of Nemesis and Anhur, Goddess Queen of the Amazons. I know." Eli muttered as Riley opened book after book showing different renderings of her.

"Look at this, Eli. It's Celeste. Well, it can't be Celeste but-"

"It is her," Eli said, as he ran a finger over etching of her face. Those eyes and mouth, there was no mistaking that face. Riley laughed nervously and shook his head, but as he studied Eli's rather somber expression, his smile faded. When the waitress came to remove Eli's empty beer bottles, he ordered a whiskey, straight.

"Just bring the bottle," he grumbled, and Riley stared at him in confusion.

"Remember when I told you that Doc was hiding something from me?" He pointed to the painting in the first book. "This is what she was hiding. Celeste Kent is not human."

Again, Riley attempted to laugh, only it died in his throat. "And guess what? Neither am I. But unlike our friendly neighborhood Goddess, here, I'm something else entirely. I, my good friend, am what is known as *The Nephilim*. Not just any spawn of a fallen angel, mind you; I am the son of Heaven and Earth. You know the creation story from Sunday school, well; when God separated the heavens from the earth, guess who first fell to earth?" He pointed to himself with a sad smile. "I drink blood and have no human blood coursing through my extraordinary and very ancient veins. I'm what is known as a breeder. And you know how I know this?" Riley shook his head, dumbly.

"Because," Eli choked out a laugh. "I have a kid...a grown kid...a daughter, a real beauty with a gentle soul and a kind heart, just a lovely girl. She lucked up, though, because she's part human, and it's Grace. How do you like that? My daughter has spent centuries protecting me, sacrificing her own life to make sure her hot head of a father didn't get himself killed. She magically altered her appearance and gave up everything for me, and you know how she did that? She erased my memory every few years." He looked at Riley, a maniacal smile plastered on his face. Riley shook his head and burst into nervous laughter, which quickly dissolved into hysterics.

"What?" Riley finally calmed himself enough to look at Eli through the tears in his eyes. Eli was not amused. He sat stone-faced, his eyes on the amber liquid floating in his glass. "Are you serious? Really, E? Really? How many drinks have you had?"

Rather than explain, Eli opened his mouth and showed him. Riley backpedaled to the opposite side of the booth at the sight of his silvery white fangs, his eyes wide. He let out a yelp of surprise that caused several of the patrons to glance in their direction. If he could have, he would have burrowed into the cracked red leather upholstery. Eli retracted the teeth and sipped his drink as if nothing had ever happened.

"What the total *fuck*?" Riley squeaked.

"Don't worry, my thirst for blood hasn't completely come back to me. Not that I'd drink from you anyway. My tastes are specific to a blue-eyed brunette with a cute laugh and tight ass."

"Mine too," Riley joked, laughing like a hyena.

"Okay, okay, okay. Do that again?" He asked, just to make sure he was seeing what he thought he was seeing. Eli obliged, knowing this would take some time, but Riley seemed to calm down after a second glance and tentative touch.

"Fuck." He whispered, "Did the Doc do this to you? Did she turn you all Vampy?" He asked, staring at Eli with a mixture of fear and awe. His best friend was a freaking vampire. He didn't know if he should be thrilled or terrified.

"Not a freaking vampire, freaking *Nephilim*, there's a distinct difference. I am a living, breathing being. Vampires are not." Eli corrected. "And no, she didn't. I was born this way apparently; exactly when I was born is still a question. It was either at the dawn of time or sometime shortly after that, or as Grace put it, eons ago. Can you believe that? I was born before Jesus, before people, before-time."

Riley sat slack-jawed; he was dumbfounded. He'd always known that there was something different, almost otherworldly, about Eli, but he'd always thought it was just his good looks. There was an aura of power around him that had always drawn people in, but he'd never thought he wasn't human. The eyes, those had been the only truly magical thing about him, the way they changed color with his moods. He stared at Eli's profile for a long time, contemplating the reality of the situation. Eli wasn't human. He wasn't a man, not really.

Yet, he'd been the best friend he'd ever had. He'd also trusted him enough to tell him the truth, so that meant something. He could run from this place screaming and shun Eli the way most of the police force did. The way most people did, now that he thought about it. Eli only had Grace, Boogie, and him, his only family. He trusted him to be there, to be his friend, his brother. Even though he was this ancient mystical being, Eli could easily be broken. Wasn't that the reason Grace had hidden him, to keep him safe? Did this change the way he felt about his best friend; Riley wondered. Did this make Elijah Cain less of the man he had known for years just because he happened to be – an Angel? Eli was an angel. This took him out of his image of what an angel was. He'd been taught that angels were soft, wraithlike creatures with delicate features in white gowns with soft melodic voices. Not hulking black men with blue eyes and deep baritone voices that rumbled like thunder when they laughed.

"Not an angel-" Eli mumbled, "More of a ...god."

"Right," Riley sighed. Absently, he reached up to touch Eli's face. Not knowing what to expect, he sighed with relief when he felt the stubble covered cheek of his friend. Eli glanced at him from the corner of his eye.

"What are you doing?" He asked, sounding somewhat

amused. Finally shaking himself out of his daze, he patted Eli's shoulder and loudly gulped down his drink.

"Well, you look good for your age," Riley mumbled, vaguely, staring at Eli the entire time. He reclaimed his seat, took another healthy swallow of his whiskey, and sighed.

"Sammi," Riley called to their waitress, who leaned against the pool table flirting with one of the college boys. "I think we're going to need another bottle of Jack."

She nodded and sauntered behind the bar. Riley exhaled and turned to Eli, an understandably excited smile giving his face a boyish appeal. "This is so cool. I knew you were a fucking superhero. So, let's start at the beginning." He slapped Eli on the back. "Tell me *EVERYTHING*."

* * *

Relief washed over Eli, and all of the tension in his body melted away as he relayed the story that Grace had both gifted and burdened him with only a short time before. It was as if he had the weight lifted from his chest as he explained everything Grace and Celeste had told him. He relayed Grace's story of his late wife, of his violent nature. He vaguely recalled the events of the night at Jinxie's, his eventual meeting of Remy and Gaston, and of course, sex with Celeste. "It's like she's a part of me."

He was grateful to Riley, who sat and listened, nodding and asking questions at the appropriate times, allowing him to share his burden, at least for a while.

"This explains so much," Riley mumbled at one point.

"What kinds of things can you do, other than the mind-reading?" Riley asked, his eyes alight with curiosity.

"I'm strong, super strong; I have this crazy speed, acute senses, of course, the telepathy, precognition, post-cognition. Grace called me an Oneiroi or Dream Walker, the way I can recall other people's memories and emotions. My hearing is crazy sharp. I can hear a whisper from twenty feet away. There are some other things that Grace says will come. Apparently, those are things from my angelic side. For some reason, preternatural beings are attracted to each other. That's why I'm so drawn to Doc. We share a link just being who we are. We're living breathing myths." He snorted and took another drink.

It was after midnight when all was said and done. Eli was nursing his final glass of whiskey, and Riley had gone through several beers of his own. As the story wound down, Eli's phone jumped and buzzed to life. He looked at the display and pocketed the phone, ignoring it.

"Who was that?" Riley rose, stretching his legs.

"Celeste. Again. I just can't talk to her right now. I don't know what to say. I'm still trying to wrap my head around all of this, and I hurt her- Riley, I called her a monster."

"Tell me this, do you care about this girl?" Eli nodded. "Why?"

"You've met her. She's incredible. She's smart, funny, beautiful, and sexy-"

"And that has changed because of what? She can turn into a ball of light. She gets a little bitey during sex. Who doesn't? I once dated a guy who likes you to punch him in the face during sex. And Adam once slept with a guy who liked to have straight pins stuck into his balls. Even regular people are into some kinky shit. But has that changed who she is? Have you changed?" Riley could sometimes be too smart for his own good, making Eli feel like an even bigger asshole.

"She lied to me-"

"She didn't lie. It seems to me she tried to tell you a bunch of times. From the moment you two laid eyes on each other, you've been drawn together. Hell, even before you met face to face, you had been dreaming about her. That has to count for something, Eli. How would you have felt if I'd have bolted when you sprouted fangs? And we've known each other for years. I know you better than I know anyone else. Imagine how she feels. She loves you. Do you know how lucky you are to have found your perfect match?"

"Maybe," Eli grumbled, even though he knew that she cared deeply for him. He stared at the half-empty bottle in front of him, not daring to look at Riley. Even though Riley wasn't a telepath or psychic, he was smart, and could read Eli, almost as well as Grace.

"Don't give me that maybe bullshit. She trusted you enough to show you what she is, even though it weakened her to the point of collapse. You are the first man she's given herself to in every possible way, all of her, completely. And she's called you how many times?"

"That makes sixteen."

"Sixteen? You call the woman a monster, break her heart, and she's called you sixteen times! She wants you, you jack ass. She loves your stupid ass! And you're sitting here pouting because you just found out you're a fucking Superman? You two share more than most married couples, blood bound as you put it. How often do you find that? My advice to you is to man-up, quit being a whiny dick, and find the woman before she gets tired of chasing you. I guaran-fucking-tee men are lining up to take your place, fangs or not."

"Grace basically said the same thing." He mumbled under his breath.

"Imagine that. So why are you still sitting here looking at my drunk ass? Go and find her before it's too late, Eli. Women like her only come around once in a lifetime. For you, that can be a pretty long fucking time."

He'd had to carry Riley from his car to his front door. Even though they had shared two bottles of whiskey, Eli had had the lion's share, Riley was completely white boy wasted. He tossed Riley onto the bed. As he turned to leave, Riley grabbed his arm.

"You may have been born a god, but you have spent most of your life as just a man. And the greatest gift a man could ever receive is the open heart of another. Remember that." He'd slurred before his eyes drifted shut. "Please don't fuck it up, E."

"You know, for someone completely wasted; you make a lot of sense." Eli laughed.

"Drunk, don't mean stupid." Riley burped.

✻ ✻ ✻

This, among the many other revelations of the night, swirled through his head as the rain began to come down harder. He finally slipped out of the car and headed to his back-door. He hadn't turned on the security lights before he'd gone out, leaving the driveway cloaked in darkness.

He paused. The key was barely in the door when he felt someone else was there. Through the smell of the late November rain, he could smell something else, not quite human. He backed away from the steps and moved toward the front porch, his fingertips itching. He paused only for a second when he felt his fangs. But he continued his guarded stalking toward the front yard. The smell assaulted him as he rounded the corner, but beneath the putrid stench was the light scent of lavender.

"Elijah,"

# CHAPTER FOURTEEN

The voice that came from the shadows of the porch sounded far away until she slowly emerged from the darkness. The rain beat down on her as she inched closer, dripping wet, her hair slicked to her scalp, her eyes wide. She was in jeans and a sweater, both ripped and covered in blood, her expensive boots scuffed. Blood ran down her side in rivulets, pooling at her feet; on the rain-slicked porch, she stood cradling her right arm close to her body, her face battered and bruised. Even though her face was dripping wet, he knew that she had been crying, her eyes were red and swollen, she looked a mess, and he wanted to hold her.

"It was in my apartment. I called you- I killed it." She moved closer, swiftly in the dark, her feet barely touching the ground, but she stopped just out of his reach. He took a step forward, and she took two cautious steps back. He paused only for a moment, and then before she saw him move, he had her face in his hands, his mouth on hers. The kiss was cautious and tender and the most wonderful feeling in the world.

"Come inside." He breathed against her cheek; before ushering her through the front door, then into the living room. He raced up the stairs, leaving her dripping on the rug in the dark, cold room, her arm clutched to her chest. It wasn't healing the way it should, she realized, and it hurt like a son of a bitch.

"Take off your clothes." He came down the stairs, dropping a robe and a towel on the sofa, before hustling into the kitchen to put on the tea kettle. He disappeared upstairs again, returning with a first aid kit, some aspirin, and blankets. When he rushed back into the room, he began starting a fire. Even though there was central heat and air, he preferred using the fireplace on nights like this, and it would warm the chill that set into her bones. She began unzipping the black leather boots she wore, still shivering in her sopping wet clothes, blood running down her arm and onto the floor.

She pulled the ripped sweater off, taking care of her injured arm, exposing a white lacey bra, soaked and clinging to her, her right arm bleeding from dozens of tiny needle-like marks. Eli turned to look at her as the flames in the fireplace grew. He watched as she began peeling her skintight jeans down with some difficulty. Frustrated, she cursed, and the pants slipped down on their own, pooling at her feet. Kicking them aside, she could feel his eyes on her. He couldn't turn away.

In the blush of the firelight, her caramel skin glowed golden, the thin lace of her panties and bra slick to her skin, her nipples straining the thin material. She looked magnificent, like something out of a dream, which she was, after all. He motioned for her to sit beside him on the rug in front of the fire. He was gingerly holding her arm to get a better look at it. The dozens of tiny holds looked painful, and her arm was swelling and bruising in the dim light. He cringed at the sight of it.

Carefully, he reached for the first aid kit and began cleaning the wound. "What happened?" He asked. Quietly and through clenched teeth, she told him of her battle with the demon. Guilt and anger played across his face in tandem, ripping through him as she spoke.

"I tried to call, but you didn't answer. Why won't you look at me?" She inhaled sharply as he began patting her arm dry, pain rocketing through her body in waves. He couldn't face her; instead, he focused on wrapping a bandage around her forearm, securing it. When he was done, he turned away, not able to meet her gaze. Instead, he focused on the crackling fire.

"Eli, look at me." She touched his cheek, turning him to face her. He kept his eyes averted, staring at her lips, her earlobe, anywhere except her eyes. He was ashamed of himself.

"I can't. You need to take everything off. I'll put them in the dryer." He said, referring to her underwear, his voice thick and low.

She stood slowly, willing him to look at her as she slowly released the clasp of her bra and let the material slip off her arms and to the floor. He turned to watch her out of sheer need. Unable to explain it, he was compelled to look at her. When she touched the elastic of her panties, she could hear him inhale sharply in anticipation. She took her time, pushing one side from her hips, then the other, her injured arm held close to her chest as she moved to get the robe, her entire body covered in gooseflesh. He'd never seen anything so sexy in his life.

"Wait," He said through clenched teeth as he rose. He moved closer to her, his eyes downcast, his body rigid.

He reached up and took the band from her hair, letting it fall in drying curls past her shoulders, singed chunks falling to the floor. She looked at him with heavy-lidded eyes, her moist lips slightly parted. He grazed her lips with his, a touch so light it could have been a thought, no other parts of them touching. She closed her eyes and leaned forward, aching for him to touch her. She felt him move behind her, where he took the towel and began drying her hair from the top of her head, gently moving down.

"Your hair is burned," he whispered close to her ear before he took his time, separating the tangled waves with his fingers, his lips on one bruised shoulder blade, and then the other.

Finally, the towel dropped to her feet, his lips touching each of the bruises on her back, then he was still and silent. Turning to face him, not saying a word, her eyes searched his face. He kept his eyes downcast as she kissed him softly on the cheek, trying to get some reaction, something from him other than silence. Instead, he reached for the robe, wrapping her in the thick terrycloth that smelled so strongly of him, she inhaled and snuggled into its warmth. He opened his mouth to say something but stopped.

"It's okay. I'm okay." She whispered against his lips; her warm salty tears mingled with the sweetness of her mouth on his. She moved closer until he embraced her, holding her tighter and tighter. He buried his face in her neck, dropping gentle kisses on her cold skin.

Again, his lips brushed hers, "I'm sorry. I was so stupid. You are not a monster; I didn't mean that. I didn't mean to hurt you. I never wanted to hurt you." Before kissing her again, a real kiss that she felt from the top of her head to her toenails.

"I'm sorry. I should have been there. It was just so much-" She pulled away to look at him, searching his eyes.

"Grace told me the truth, the whole truth." He kissed her neck and shoulders, his hands moving inside of the robe.

"You're soaking wet." She said, running her hands under his shirt, pushing it up until he could tug it over his head.

"I'm sorry," He lifted her off the floor, holding her so tightly she could barely breathe. Her bruised and battered body sang with pain as he held her, but she remained silent, reveling in the feel of his body so warm and hard against her own. She wrapped her legs around his waist, the robe falling to the floor. His large hands spanned her back; he rested his head on her breast, listening to her heartbeat. As his grip tightened, she let out an involuntary whimper of pain. He looked at her bruised and battered body.

"Broken rib," She hissed. "Almost healed." She assured.

"I'm sorry. I'm so sorry." He mumbled and carried her up the stairs to his bedroom where he laid her on the bed. She sank into the comforter, watching as he started a fire in the fireplace that mirrored the one in the living room below. He seemed to be taking his time, calming himself as he stoked the fire to life until an amber glow was cast. The smell of burning wood filled the room, the rain outside falling sharply against the windows in a disjointed rhythm. He turned to look at her in the soft glow of the firelight. He slowly and deliberately undid his belt buckle, kicked off his shoes, and slowly unfastened his jeans, kicking the damp denim off before advancing toward the bed.

He lay on the comforter with her holding her close. He kissed her urgently, his fingers sinking into her damp hair. He pushed her back onto the bed, his eyes boring into her.

"I was stupid and scared, and you were – you could have been killed. I would never forgive myself if anything happened to you. I love you. I'm in love with you, Doc. I think I've been in love with you since the day we met. Maybe even before. I will never hurt you again." She wrapped her legs around his waist and pressed against him. He hovered over her, his heart swelled, and he was suddenly filled with a burning need for her. He kissed her hard, his hands barely touching her taut nipples. Her body arched into him, her fangs extended, her eyes glowing in the firelight. She reached up and touched his teeth in wonder and relieved amazement, a sexy smile on her lips.

"Gorgeous." She breathed, and he was inside of her, their bodies rising and falling in a frantic rhythm, until she shook uncontrollably, a deep moan escaping her, but Eli's frenetic pace continued. He couldn't stop. He wanted more, he needed more. In the darkness, their eyes met, and she could see the question in his eyes. She smiled and turned her head, pulling her hair away to expose the delicate skin of her long bare neck. He could smell the blood pumping through her, feel her pulse race, and leaned closer, his lips barely brushing her skin.

"Do it. It's okay. You won't hurt me." She urged, gently pushing his head down. He tasted the tender skin of her shoulder for a second. She tasted faintly of vanilla; he thought just before his teeth sank in, and he began to drink of her. She gasped excitedly, her heart-stopping for a second, as waves of delight assaulted her. She gripped the sides of the mattress and writhed beneath him.

In that first bite, he knew her life, he could feel her coursing through him, and they were utterly one being, and he was overcome with the heady feelings of love, peace, and joy. It was like a drug that opened him to every bit of her world, every emotion, every fear, every dream. She was entirely his.

Her taste was familiar to him; sweet and warm, and full of life. The flavor was unmistakably Celeste, a heady combination of sweetness and light, purity and sex. The more of her he took, the more he needed, the more he wanted, he wanted all of her, every piece of her, and tears flowed from his eyes. He felt as if he were drowning in the pure essence of her soul, and from that moment on, they would be irrevocably connected. At that moment, she was his, only his, forever.

His body reacted, moving faster and harder as his mouth worked on her shoulder. She squirmed against him, her body convulsing, her nails digging into the flesh of his backside, leaving long bloody scratches. He continued to drink, filling himself with her until she felt herself going weak. "Not too much." She whispered, and with mammoth effort, he released her.

When he released, so did everything else. And he came long and hard until he collapsed on top of her still trembling body, still comfortably inside of her. She looked at him, blood dripping from the corners of his mouth, and she kissed him. The combination of her blood and the taste of her tongue made him weak. He held her, his body shivering, teeth chattering.

"Are you cold?" She asked, breathlessly, wrapping the covers around them in the fire-lit room.

"No." His teeth chattered, a smile on his face, his eyes alight with a new kind of elation. He felt lightheaded and slightly dizzy as if he were floating in a thick cloud of contentment. Every worry, fear, and everything disappeared until there were just the two of them and his overwhelming euphoria.

"No." He brushed the hair out of her face and kissed her, the taste of her still in his mouth; he wanted her again.

"Did I hurt you? How are your ribs?" He ran a finger over her rib cage.

"Better, sore, but better." She assured.

The whistling of the tea kettle drew his attention. Slowly, he stood and padded down to the kitchen completely naked. He returned with two steaming mugs of tea. Handing one to her, settling next to her under the covers, they stared silently into the fire.

* * *

"Finish telling me what happened. How did you get here?" He finally asked. She looked up at him and wiggled her nose like Samantha from *Bewitched,* and he smiled. "Cute."

"I didn't know what else to do. I had to leave before the cleaners came, and the smell of it-" She shivered at the memory of that sickening wet smacking sound as its head landed with a thud. "But you know what? I don't think it was the same thing that killed Nicky. I mean, it was- bigger," she muttered before sipping her tea. "And its breast- it seemed more male this time. It was still nasty, but there was something different. Everything happened so quickly-" She tried to remember why she'd felt that this creature was different, but she couldn't put her finger on it right away. "It smelled different." She mumbled into her mug.

"Are you sure?" Eli asked. She nodded as it dawned on her.

"It smelled different. It still stank to high heaven, but it wasn't the same. And it spoke in a deeper voice. The one that killed Remy's friend at Jonas's was smaller, almost the size of an eight or nine-year-old. This one was taller, stronger. It moved differently," she said. "Didn't you say you saw it that same night? How did it look?"

Now that he thought about it, it was larger, leaner. "Is it possible that there are two of them?" She asked in a low voice, her lips still on the rim of her cup.

"That's it. You're moving in with me until we figure this out."

"Excuse me," She placed her mug on the nightstand before turning a wary eye to him.

"I will not have you alone in that apartment. If one got in, then so could the other. I mean, what if it's more than two. Who knows how many of those things are out there? You're staying with me until we get this sorted out, and that's all there is to it." She backed away to look at him full in the face. He had to be kidding. Was he seriously trying to tell her what to do?

"No, I'm not." She said.

"Yes, you are."

"So, the mighty Elijah Cain has spoken, and I'm just supposed to cow to your will? Are you forgetting who you're talking to?" She asked, now on her knees, her arms folded across her bare breasts. He stifled a smile.

"I know exactly who I'm talking to. Do you forget who you're talking to, *Caelestis*?"

She lifted a brow as a smirk teased the corner of his mouth that damned dimple making a surprise appearance.

"Oh, really? So, am I supposed to bow down to the great and powerful Fallen one? Should I kiss the feet of the First to Fall?" She asked in a mocking tone. "Don't believe your hype, Detective. I can still kick your ass."

Without speaking, he placed his cup on the table, his eyes on her face. Slowly, he moved closer, deliberately running a warm hand up her inner thigh. She chewed her lip to stifle the sigh that was threatening to escape. She couldn't let him win this argument. If he won this one, he would think he had the upper hand, and that was not true, by any means. "Like it or not, you are very important to me, lady. If anything else happened to you, I couldn't live with myself. Baby, I need you..."

She was taken aback by his intensity and distracted by his roaming fingers. She licked her lips. A tiny high-pitched sigh escaping her, and he pulled her down to lay beneath him. The weight of him on her always clouded her judgment.

"You need me to what?" Her voice broke, and she closed her eyes, relaxing into his touch, sinking deeper into the pillows. When she opened her eyes again, he was lying on his side staring at her, his expression unreadable, his eyes studying her face as if he were burning her into his brain. His fingers stopped their slow creep.

"I need *you*." He said simply. She reached for him, holding him close, kissing him with a fervor that he hadn't experienced before. He touched his forehead to hers and smiled.

"Are you ever going to say it back?" A slow cheeky smile played across her lips, and her face lit up. The apprehension seeped out of her and was replaced by a mischievous glint in her eyes. He watched in fascination as they brightened to a blinding shade of cerulean.

"Say what?" She teased.

"I told you that I'm in love with you. I love you."

"Yeah, I caught that." She stretched and faked a yawn.

"And?" He waited. She looked at him from the corner of her eyes and feigned disinterest.

"And it was very nice of you-" He began tickling her sides, and she squirmed, laughing that delectable chuckle of hers. It reminded him of something magical, which he assumed was just about right. He couldn't decide if it reminded him of wind chimes or Christmas bells, but it made him love her even more. She finally relented when tears flowed down her cheeks.

"Say it," He kissed her cheek and brushed away a stray tear.

"I love you, Elijah." She ran her hand over the soft low-cut dark curls on his head; they felt like silk beneath her fingertips. A current of electricity ran down his spine, and he kissed her.

"Say it again." He hovered above her, his face inches from hers, his breath against her lips.

"I love you," she whispered. He entered her slowly, his eyes on her face. She made a low gasping noise and seductively bit her lip.

"Again." He kissed her, moving his body against her.

"I love you," she gasped.

"Again," he choked and repeated the motion. She repeated it again and again, each time he pushed into her until she could no longer speak.

* * *

"Do you want to talk about it?" She asked cautiously. She lay on her back, her head on his shoulder as she stared at the fire. It was the wee hours of the morning, and they lay silently for a while, too drained to move. She was too sore from her fight and Eli's decathlon of lovemaking that she didn't even want to try.

"How did you know?" He asked, finally.

"I had a feeling when we met the first time that you were preternatural, but there was something different about you, that you weren't strictly one thing. You weren't like anyone I had met before. I felt drawn to you. It's magnetic. I knew for sure when we went to Jinxie's because after you drank the nectar, you became very-"

"Horny." He finished, and she nodded. "But I think I was horny before we got there." He ran a hand up her leg.

"I know." She turned to face him, moving to share his pillow, resting her still tender arm on his chest. She looked so young, her caramel skin lineless, her eyes dancing in the firelight, and any vestige of make-up completely absent. She could easily pass for her late teens, he thought.

"How *old* are you?" He asked cautiously.

"I'm legal. But if you need a number, I think I am about 3,460 years old, give or take a century," she said. He whistled and stared at the ceiling, trying to wrap his mind around that little fact.

"According to Grace, I have no age," he sighed, still astounded by that little revelation.

"I always wanted to date an older man," she teased, nipping his chin with her teeth.

"Tell me, honestly, Doc, are you okay?" He tilted her chin up so that she looked into his eyes. She was still bruised, but they were fading fast to the yellowish-green hue of healing wounds. He brushed her hair away from her face, letting his fingers linger over the bruise at her cheek, a haunted look in his eyes.

"I'm doing better than the other guy," she yawned, and he gave her a light shake.

"I'm serious, Celeste." She kissed him lightly on the lips.

"I'm fine, I promise. I'm a war goddess and Amazon, after all. A little bite won't hurt me." She assured him.

Eli let the tips of his fingers skim her skin, barely stroking the fine hairs on her arms. She had never realized such a small motion could be so sexy. It raised gooseflesh on her warmed skin and sent a chill down her spine. They lay silently, cuddled together under the warmth of the blankets, the occasional crackle of the fire the only sound in the room, the rain falling softly outside. She stretched and yawned, her body molding to fit his, their limbs entangled.

"How'd you get the bruise here?" He asked, absently stroking the sore spot on her breast.

"Fucker hit me in the titty," she grumbled sleepily, and Eli burst into a sudden fit of unbridled laughter.

\* \* \*

Remy and Gaston stood silently by as Adrian stared at the gory scene before them. The room was in complete shambles, furniture overturned and broken, blood splattered on walls, floors, and ceiling. The entire scene looked like something out of a slasher movie. Walls and furniture smoldered from an acid that filled the room with a sulfuric stench that burned their nostrils and eyes. A once gleaming sword was corroded and eaten through from tip to hilt on the floor near the foyer, the handle still shining a pure gold. In the center of the macabre landscape was the decapitated and rather rapidly decomposing body of the demon. It lay in a pool of the black acidic blood that had eaten through the surrounding rug and hardwood floor, exposing the cement underfloor.

"Well?" Gaston asked in his French-accented English.

"Well," Adrian said with a heavy sigh, his hands shoved deep into the pockets of his jeans. "It's human. It started as human anyway." Adrian took a step closer but made sure that his expensive leather loafers stayed clear of the corrosive blood. Squatting, he picked up the discarded Bō staff and jabbed at the head.

"Stop poking and get on with it." Gaston admonished and kicked the staff out of Adrian's hands.

"Really, is that necessary? Honestly." Adrian sighed and rose to his full six foot three. Though he was born a demon, Adrian was a delicately pretty Asian man with smooth tanned skin and dark almond eyes. He dressed impeccably, even at this ungodly hour.

Gaston gave him an insolent look before turning his back on the demon to answer his cell phone. "I love it when you're mean to me, daddy." Adrian purred, and Remy couldn't suppress the smile that quirked at his lips. Gaston rolled his eyes and walked further into the foyer, ignoring the jab.

"Ok, what is it?" Remy asked, folding his arms across his chest. Adrian's sighed and turned his attention to the creature.

"It's nothing I've ever seen before. Not one of mine," he assured. "It looks like some sort of combination of human and Gallu demon, but it smells like a basilisk, maybe. But there are some other things in there I can't make out. It's some sort of super-hybrid." He griped. "Honestly, Remy, I have no idea what or who this thing is; or where it came from." He glanced back at the monster on the floor and shook his head.

"I think Lilith needs to see this. She's older than I am. She may have seen this bugger before." Adrian ran a hand over his face and sighed. "I don't even think the eaters will touch this one."

Remy shuddered at the mention of The Dead Eaters. Though he'd never seen one without its head to toe dark shroud, he'd heard them eat, a gluttonous noise of smacking toothless hungry mouths. Again, he shuddered. "Good. Those fuckers creep me out. Let's move it before the cleaners come."

"It's almost dawn. They should be here soon." Adrian agreed and turned to look at the disembodied head once more and gasped. Remy turned to see what had elicited such a reaction from the unflappable demon. The dead demon's face had returned to its human state, and it was Remy's turn to gasp in shock.

"I know him." He said, leaning closer. The dark curly hair and muddy eyes were so familiar, but it took him a moment to connect the face with a name and location. "I know him." He repeated, and Adrian watched him, waiting.

"This is CeCe's research assistant-Xander something." He said, his eyes wide. "This can't be the one that killed Nicky. CeCe said it was-smaller. This isn't the demon we're looking for. It's still out there." Adrian ran a hand over his mouth. Remy rose slowly, his mouth suddenly dry.

"What does this mean?" Adrian asked.

"It's hunting her," Remy whispered. The words were barely out of his mouth when Gaston spun on them, his face pale and tense with fear.

"Gaston? What's wrong?" Remy was beside his brother in a second.

"Where is Celeste?" Gaston grabbed Remy's arm with such force that he was momentarily thrown off balance. The sheer panic in his eyes did nothing to ebb Remy's rapidly overwhelming feeling of dread.

"Who was on the phone, Gaston?" Remy asked, grasping his older brother's shoulders. They stood staring at each other, not saying a word.

"Gaston!" Remy yelled and seemed to break the trance his brother had fallen under.

"What's going on?" Adrian asked, a cold chill running down his spine. He had never seen Gaston Kent look anything other than the cold businessman. But now, his usually calm demeanor was shattered as he shook silently, tears pooling in his dark brown eyes.

"Did it bite her, Remy? Do you know if it bit her?" He gave Remy a shake, his brow peppered with sweat, his eyes large, almost manic. Remy shrugged as he tried to think. He'd only spoken to her on the phone. He hadn't actually seen her. She had been sobbing, her voice was high and cracked.

"I think she said it did. Yes. It bit her arm, she said. Why?" Remy's voice rose an octave as his stomach seemed to sink lower. "Who was on the phone, Gaston?"

"Silver Wolf, she said that Briar is turning. That thing bit him, and he's turning, and he's out. He's looking for her." Remy felt his blood run cold. "Where is she, Remy?"

"With the cop," Remy gasped. "I told her to go to the cop."

"Why would you do that? He can't protect her." Gaston asked, a bit taken aback. "We have to get her to the Collective's chamber so that they can help her. She will be shielded and protected-"

"He can protect her, Gaston." Remy said, "I've seen his true face. He's *Nephilim, the God Destroyer.*" Gaston dropped his hands from Remy's shoulders, and Adrian gasped. "He is *The Fallen One.*"

# CHAPTER FIFTEEN

Someone, no, something was coming. Eli could feel the anger and pain rising in the creature and sat up with a jolt. Beside him, Celeste slept, her body relaxed, her bandaged arm propped up on a pillow. She looked pale to him, her forehead beading with a light sheen of sweat. Tucking the covers up around her, he kissed her warm cheek. Rising slowly as not to disturb her, he slipped on a pair of sweats and gingerly removed his Glock from the drawer in his bedside table. He glanced back at her one last time before silently slinking downstairs to greet his guest.

The first floor was quiet, save a slow creaking coming from the kitchen. Eli paused and listened. His eyes closed, he moved closer. The creature was in the kitchen, pouring something into a mug.

"Tea?" He asked and opened his eyes. Lowering his gun, Eli padded into the kitchen to find him sitting at the kitchen table, rocking back and forth in his chair, a warm cup of herbal tea on the table before him. He didn't look up when Eli entered the room. He simply sighed.

For some reason, Eli wasn't surprised to see him sitting there in his skintight leather pants and stylishly ragged t-shirt. His leather jacket was well worn but costly. He wore no jewelry except small gold hoop earrings in each of his ears. He leaned forward, his elbows on the table as he inhaled the sweetly floral aroma of the herbal tea.

"Celeste always told me that I should drink chamomile tea. She said it would help me sleep better." He said. Eli didn't respond.

"She's still asleep then? Good. I came to talk to you." He

looked up, and Eli was taken aback by his appearance. The once golden skin was pale, almost ashen. His bright blue eyes were obsidian and hollow, his cheeks sunken, and the platinum hair was tinged black at the roots.

Eli took the seat across from him, placing the gun on the table before him. That garnered a raised eyebrow from his guest.

"Planning on shooting me, Detective Cain?" He asked with a crooked smirk. His smiled was the only thing that remained of the golden rock star.

"Won't work. I've tried." To illustrate his point, he lifted his chin to expose a scarred over a bullet wound. "But I'm always willing to give you a shot at it. Pardon my pun." He sipped the tea and grimaced. "What's the point of having eternal life if you can't enjoy it?" He signed and ran a hand over his spiky hair. "You know your senses are heightened to the point of pain. Every sense is magnified to the point of insanity. I guess that's why we mostly come out at night. Fewer people on the streets, less activity, less noise. But it's so lonely." He whispered.

"Did you come here to tell me that, Nicky?" Eli asked. He wanted a beer, he thought, and it appeared before him, a tall cold bottle of beer, cap off and waiting. It surprised him, but then, it was something he thought he could get used to.

"Nice trick. I'll bet you're learning all sorts of things about yourself." He teased, sipping his tea carefully. Eli rolled his eyes.

"Are you going to tell me why you're here? It's late."

"Yes," Nicky conceded. "It is, and he's coming, the giant." He said remorsefully. "I came here tonight to warn you." He said after a while. This time Eli lifted a brow. "Something is coming for you. And it's not just the Assiri."

"Assiri?"

"The little demon hobbit who did this to me; it's called Assiri. I think it may be as old as you are. Yes. I know who you are. I know because it knows. When it changes you, you become connected; it's like a symbiotic relationship. I know what it knows. I see what it sees. And what it sees is a way to take down the Council … with you. The Assiri is about to set off a chain of events that will bring about a war in the otherworld. The Dark Fae are counting on it. You and Celeste together are the key to stopping it. So, the goal of the Dark Sisters and the Dark Queen is to use the Assiri to bring out the Fallen One."

"You mean me?" said Eli. Nicky put his finger to his nose and smiled ruefully.

"I'm not a demon. I'm an angel, at least that's what I was told." He grunted and swallowed the remainder of his beer.

"You're a god, but that's beside the point. Demons and Angels are not that different. In fact, they are one and the same. All angels have demonic blood and vice versa. The king of all demons, Satan himself, was born an angel. Anyway, getting you to go, rogue, as it were, that's where the Assiri comes in. Since you are a ghost, you have no alliance with either side. In football terms, you're a free agent and can sign with anyone you want. You're not obligated, but you are involved with one of the highest-ranked members of the Collective." He gave Eli a wink.

"Broke the maidenhead, have we?" Eli gave him a warning look, and Nicky laughed, holding his hands up in surrender. "Don't get upset. I'm just saying I know that she cares for you, loves you. I get it. And so do The Dark Fae. Those damn sisters planned on that happening once they discovered you. They managed a deal with the devil, so to speak. It was to get close to her. The idea was to use your love for Celeste to release the beast, but something about the Assiri that the sisters didn't understand when they set it loose. That fucker is insane. You can't control insanity, and that is where they lost it. You see, the Assiri likes what it calls pretty things, hence, my initiation into the land of the undead. I guess I was a little too sparkly to resist. The same thing with CeCe. She's a little too dazzling to resist. The only problem is she didn't do what the Assiri thought she would, and she killed one of us them. Whatever."

"And they thought killing her would bring me to their side?" Eli asked, manifesting another beer. Nicky nodded.

"By killing Celeste, you would become their weapon against the Collective. The Collective who were supposed to be protecting the *Caelestis*. They would use your pain to take down the entire otherworld government, then the Council of the Gods. After all, who better to kill a God than a God? And you, my gorgeous friend, are one of the oldest and most powerful. Don't get me wrong; the Collective isn't completely innocent either. Some of them have motives regarding you that are purely selfish. They want you in their service just for the intimidation factor and the bragging rights, and because you're a breeder. They would keep you two and use you for breeding an army of super-soldiers, breeding Nephilim, an army of indestructible killing machines."

"Why are you telling me this? How are you telling me this?" He finally asked.

"The Assiri is asleep. It's like it dies when it goes to sleep. It can't see me then. And I'm telling you this because I love her. I love her, but I can't protect her. I couldn't even protect myself. Look at me, Eli. I'm dying. This- thing is taking over, and soon, there will be no more Nicky, no more humans left. Soon I will be just another symbiote to the Assiri, like the half a dozen or so other pretty things it's collected unless it dies permanently. You are my only hope of killing it. You need to get her out of here. She's going to need help now because it's trying to take her as well. The Assiri has very different ideas for her than the Dark Fae or even the Council could ever imagine." He reached across the table and grasped Eli's hand in both of his. "Promise you will not let this happen to her." Tears filled his eyes, making them look like wells of ink.

"Promise."

Eli nodded, his own eyes wide. The emotion that poured from Nicky filled him, making him want to weep for the man. He was rapidly losing his battle with the Assiri, but he fought with all he had to protect his friend, no his family. Celeste was Nicky's family.

"I promise," Eli choked.

There was a thud coming from the front porch. The sound grew louder and louder until it sounded as if someone were ripping the streets outside. The walls shook, rattling the dishes in the cupboard. Something that sounded like a freight train made the entire house shake. Nicky sighed heavily and rose to his feet.

"He's here," Nicky groaned. There was a booming crash, and the floor shook, knocking pictures off of the walls. Cold November air rushed into the kitchen in a gale, blowing the curtains and debris from the shattered door into the room. The lights flickered, and the entire house seemed to vibrate every time whatever was approaching took another thundering step closer.

Nicky looked pained every time another footfall echoed from the blackness in the hallway. Whatever was coming was large enough to block out the moonlight. It looked like a mountain moving forward, large dark eyes glittered, and the harsh sound of labored breathing preceded the moving mammoth.

"Just remember this, Eli, those that seem friend may, in fact, be your enemy. Those that seem enemy maybe your greatest ally. The Dark Sisters are not what you would expect, so be careful. They are not what they seem; they are greed, betrayal, lust, and envy wrapped in pretty packages. Watch your back because they will do whatever they can to tear you apart. Be wary of pretty little birds who whisper in your ear. You have the gift of truth. Use it. Never let your guard down. Never let your emotions get out of control because the moment you do, they will have you. You are the only thing standing between them and the destruction of the human race as we know it. Beware Ragnarök."

It happened so quickly that Eli wasn't even sure it had happened at all. As he rose to stand beside Nicky, who stood near the archway to the hallway, Nicky turned on him. The barrel of his Glock was aimed at his chest. Nicky smirked and pulled the trigger. The bullet hit Eli in the center of the chest. He looked down to see the hole and the blood coursing down his bare skin. He took a step back, stumbled, and found himself looking up at the ceiling. He heard a scream somewhere and turned to see the giant Briar grasp Celeste and toss her over his shoulder. Tears coursed down his cheeks as the pain rocketed through his body. He couldn't breathe, he couldn't move. He felt as if something were holding him down, pinning him to the cold tile floor. He gasped and heard a harsh whistling as air escaped through the hole in his chest. The bullet had pierced a lung, and he could no longer breathe.

"Celeste," he choked, the pain burning him as the last vestiges of air escaped his torn lungs. He realized then that he was dying.

Nicky knelt beside Eli. The gun still grasped in his hand. "Remember what I have told you. Remember your promise and beware of the Dark Sisters and Ragnarök. Now, time to wake up." He placed the still hot barrel against Eli's temple and pulled the trigger again. The room went dark.

# CHAPTER SIXTEEN

He awoke with a start, his body drenched in a cold sweat. He touched his chest, expecting to find a gaping bullet hole. Instead he found himself perfectly intact. Calming, he noticed the dim light coming from the bathroom and the sounds of Celeste being sick.

He rose from the bed, not bothering to cover his nakedness, to find her sitting naked on the floor beside the toilet. She looked pale, her body covered in sweat. He knelt beside her and tucked a damp curl behind her ear.

"You're burning up. How long have you been in here?" He asked.

"I didn't want to wake you." She croaked through dry, cracked lips.

"You should have. Is it your arm?" She nodded tiredly and held up her arm. Panic immediately set in when he saw it, but he kept his face calm. Black vines of infection were growing from beneath the bandage and wrapping around her elbow. He removed the soiled bandage, and she managed a sickening groan as she stared at it. The tiny holes were festering with something thick, black, and sticky. Pus oozed from the dozens of holes, and something dark moved beneath her skin. The skin between the holes was a thin net of broken flesh that strained to its breaking point. Her arm was red and swollen to nearly twice its normal size, turning yellow in some spots. The smell was that of rotting meat and filled the room, turning her already sick stomach.

"Oh, my God." She leaned over the toilet and threw up again.

"I have to get you to the hospital," Eli said.

"No. Call Jonas or--Grace. We have to find a preternatural doctor who can fix this," She leaned over again and threw up more.

The tinny sound of a car alarm somewhere down the block caught his attention, and Nicky's words came back to him in a rush.

"I need to get you out of here." He slipped on his jeans before searching for something to cover Celeste. The thudding of footsteps was coming closer, and he could hear cats screeching and dogs barking. He looked out of the window and saw the shadow moving slowly up the street towards his house, and his blood ran cold. He found a pair of gym shorts and a t-shirt, and as quickly and carefully as he could, he dressed her before lifting her limp body into his arms.

\* \* \*

They were halfway down the stairs when the front door was ripped from its hinges and tossed across the yard. He paused and suddenly felt hands on his mouth. He turned to see Remy, whose eyes were glowing amber, and Gaston huddled with him on the narrow staircase. Remy pointed up, indicating that they go back upstairs, then placed a finger over his lips. Swiftly and quietly, they moved back into the bedroom, the four of them listening as Briar tore through the downstairs.

"How did you get in here?" Eli asked, confused, "I thought vampires had to be invited in?"

"Really? Is that what you're worried about right now?" Remy snapped and searched the room for some sort of exit. "Is there a back way out of here?"

"No," Eli said. Remy and Gaston shared a look before turning back to Eli, who cradled Celeste close to his chest. Remy moved to the window, estimating the drop.

"You can jump," Remy said. "You'll be fine, big guy."

"I can't risk hurting Celeste. She's already in pretty bad shape." Gaston was touching her face, his eyes on the mangled arm that peeked from beneath the sleeve of the shirt. Nodding, Gaston looked at Remy, and they seemed to communicate something before they spoke again.

"This is what's going to happen," Gaston was saying, "Remy and I are going to run the defense. When you see an opening, you break for the door and get her out of here." He said. Eli found it a little disconcerting that the Frenchman in an Armani business suit was using football analogies.

They eased out of the room and moved with lightning speed down the narrow staircase. The brothers stood at the foot of the stairs, looking down the narrow hallway before signaling to Eli to follow and move into the living room. Eli sprinted down the stairs on silent feet past the two brothers standing shoulder to shoulder in preparation for battle. He'd just stepped into the destroyed living room when he saw a shadow barrel into Gaston's back, slamming his elegantly clad form into a wall. Gaston grunted as the wall cracked open under his weight by the sheer force of the man. A human would have been knocked unconscious by such a hit. Gaston, Eli reminded himself, was not human.

"We've got this," Remy smirked and ran at the mountain full speed. He launched himself into the air, landing on Briar's leather-clad back, and pulled at his neck with all of his strength, giving Gaston time to recover. He wiped the blood from the corner of his mouth and smiled before he charged at the giant's midsection, forcing him back into the hallway.

To keep from being pushed, Briar dug in his heels and grasped the wooden railing. Gaston's surprising strength moved the mountain whose boot-clad heels pulled up the floorboards. There was a ripping crack as the railing was pulled from its wooden spindles, and the three went down into a tangled heap.

In the moonlight, Eli caught of glimpse of Briar's face, and his heart jumped. The angelic smiling man he'd met was gone.

In his place was a snarling black-eyed monster. His hands were claws with dark ragged nails, and his pleasant smile was ruined by rows of silver-grey needle-like teeth. He snarled and bit at Remy's arms and neck but failed to connect. Remy had a firm chokehold on him, his arms wrapped like steel bands around Briar's thick neck. The entire scene was alarming. The fact that Remy was laughing manically made it all the more surreal.

* * *

Eli didn't see anymore. He was heading through the remains of his front door to his car. He opened the back seat and gingerly lay Celeste down, covering her with a blanket he'd kept in the trunk for some reason he couldn't quite remember at the moment. As he rounded the car to get into the driver's seat, he saw something fly through the living room window and across the yard. It carved a large divot in the lawn, coming to a stop in a flower bed. It stood shaking clumps of mud and rocks from its jeans and face before he realized it was Remy.

"Get out of here!" He screamed at them before wiping blood from his nose and mouth with the back of his hand. Eli moved closer to make sure he was okay when something in the house exploded. They both ducked and covered their heads as glass and wood and metal rained down on them. Eli's kitchen was no more than a hole at the back of the house. Inside, Gaston and Briar sparred like gladiators. Eli watched, in amazement, the surreal sight of the biker clad in leather and chains scrapping with a main in a tailored Armani business suit, a modern-day David and Goliath. The image would have been comical if he hadn't been terrified.

"Go." Remy gave Eli a shove towards the car. "We've got this." As he spoke, Gaston was slammed to the ground like a rag doll. Briar was on him in a second, repeatedly pounding his face and body with a fist the size of a ham.

Eli gave Remy a worried look.

"Get CeCe out of here. We have it. This is the kind of shit that gets my dick hard." He gave Eli a shove towards the car before launching himself back into the fray. He landed on the giant's back again, his arms tight around his neck, and he bucked like a wild bull. Remy held on, laughing and screaming something incoherently cheerful.

"Your brothers are fucking lunatics," he said to Celeste as he climbed behind the wheel.

"You haven't seen the half of it," she moaned before falling silent. He looked back at her, and she looked pale and tiny curled up on the back seat. His panic rose again, and he reached for the ignition before he realized what he'd forgotten.

"Keys," he groaned and cursed through clenched teeth. His keys had been on a peg in the kitchen, a kitchen that was no more than a hole at the rear of his house. He growled and gave the steering wheel a fierce punch and realized that his skin had turned a glossy smooth black. He watched in horror as bright blue symbols etched into his hands and arms, moving upward in a beautifully elegant scrollwork that seemed to be on fire. He glanced at his reflection in the review mirror, and the face that stared back made his breath catch. His skin and face were shining onyx. His eyes glowed bright neon blue in the chiseled look of the *Fallen One*. He absently touched the glowing mark on his chest and stared at his own eyes in wonder. This was his true face, this stone man.

He was staring when something dark and heavy landed on the hood of the car, shaking the entire vehicle. Before he could register what the thing was, it struck the windshield, raining shards of glass across Eli's bare chest and face. It reached in with clawing fingers and slashed at his face and neck, hissing in the most repulsive way.

He needed to get it away from the car, he thought and reached out, unsure if he wanted to grab the Assiri or hit it. But neither of those things happened. He held up his hand and felt an electric current move from his shoulders down his arm to his fingers, where it released with an explosion of white-blue light that hit the demon in its chest and sent it reeling. The force of the bolt sent it head over ass until it slammed with a crack through the second floor of the house, shattering the few remaining windows.

There was a pause in the fighting in the ruins that had once been Eli's kitchen as the sonic boom echoed through the night.

"Fuck," Remy laughed, both shocked and impressed, before Briar's meaty fist connected with his delicate jaw and knocked him across the room. Car alarms sang to life for blocks and in rapid succession. The streetlights exploded, casting the narrow street and the surrounding homes into darkness. Remy and Gaston looked at him, eyes wide in shock for a moment before Remy screamed for him to go, and their grappling began again in earnest.

Eli touched the steering wheel, and the engine roared to life. He leaned back so that he could get his feet up over the dashboard and kicked out the shattered windshield so that he could see where he was going. It took two hard kicks of his bare feet on the tempered glass before it gave way. He held onto the steering wheel, trying to catch his breath and wrap his mind around everything that had just happened, before backing out of the driveway. Before he tore off down the darkened street, he saw the Assiri rocket up into the darkness, just as another explosion rocked the street. In the distance, he could hear approaching sirens before glass and wood rained on his car, the force shattering the driver's side window as he roared away, tires squealing as he disappeared into the night.

❋ ❋ ❋

"God Damn it," Boogie cursed as she made her way to the front door. "Damn it, Elijah-" She stared as she flung the heavy door open. This was the second time tonight he'd leaned on the doorbell like a crazy person. The sight of him standing barefoot ceased her rant and bloody, covered in dirt, grass, and wood chips with Celeste's limp body in his arms. Her right forearm hung limply and was a disturbing tangle of black tinged veins that disappeared under the sleeve of the three sizes too big t-shirt. They reemerged at her neck, twisting around her throat and creeping up her cheek. She was sweaty, her skin a sickly gray. She seemed so small and delicate cradled in his arms.

Behind them, garbage trucks rattled down the street, noisily picking up cans. The sun was just peeking over the clouds, and street sweepers were whirling in the early dawn cleaning the French Quarter sidewalks as Eli and Celeste disappeared behind the door of the house on Ursulines Avenue.

"Boogie, I need help." Eli choked. "I think she's dying."

"Oh my God," she gasped and moved aside so that they could enter. "Take her to the guest room."

Eli mounted the steps two at a time. He was at the landing when Grace stepped out of her bedroom, no longer holding her glamour; she looked no older than Celeste in pink pajamas with bright green frogs all over them, her thick mahogany hair pulled back into a sloppy bun.

She gasped and covered her mouth with a hand as they moved past.

"What happened?" She trailed behind Boogie on her heels. Eli laid Celeste across the bed.

"We need a doctor. She was attacked, bitten by something called Assiri." He stood nervously, running a hand over his face as he spoke, tears making two clean streaks down his soot-covered cheeks. "I need a doctor. Can we get a doctor?" His voice was thick and hoarse with panic and fear; it was heartbreaking. Grace touched his arm. "We need someone....she stopped talking, Grace-"

As he spoke, his skin changed from deep chocolate to mottled blue then glossy black. The deeply etched scrolls rolled down his shoulders, blue flames rising as his fear and panic and anger grew. Grace could feel the anger rolling off of him in waves, and she caught her breath.

"Shit," she mumbled under her breath, placing a hand on his chest. "Calm down," she said, forcing him to focus those neon eyes on her. Almost as quickly as it started, the transformation stopped.

"Okay, okay, we'll get help. You come with me, and I'll clean up that cut," she said and began leading him from the room. Grace looked back at Boogie and nodded before taking him into the hall bathroom.

He hadn't even realized he'd been hurt until he stared at himself in the mirror. He had a long cut along his forehead that was healing but was still caked with blood and dirt. She sat him on the side of the tub and began to clean his wound gently.

"How did this happen?" Grace asked, wiping the dirt from his cheeks.

"Um, must have happened when the kitchen blew up." He whispered, near tears. "Or when the demon punched out the windshield." Grace raised a brow but said nothing.

"Is the doctor coming?" He asked, grabbing her hand and looked at her with wide worried eyes. "Yes." She nodded and kissed his cheek gently. "We'll get the best preternatural doctor in the region," she promised.

❊ ❊ ❊

"I thought you were bringing a doctor." Eli snapped as Boogie and Grace reentered the bedroom sometime later. Grace wore a pale blue tracksuit and sneakers, her hair still in a messy bun. Boogie, on the other hand, wore pale green hospital scrubs. She clutched a large patchwork bag in her hands that rattled strangely when she moved.

"I did. Boogie. She's a Silver Witch. She practices white magic but knows how to fight black magic as well. Actually, she knows how to fight any magic. I told you we'd get the best, and she is one of the best. If she can't help her-" She drifted off.

"I'll make coffee and some breakfast. You keep CeCe comfortable. She's going to need you." She patted his arm before leaving the room.

Boogie turned the dresser into a medieval pharmacy. She unloaded several brown glass bottles with names or descriptions scribbled on them in fading ancient scrawl. Eli sat on the edge of the bed, and instinctively, Celeste put her head on his lap. She was drenched in sweat, her mouth dry, and her hair sticking to her forehead. The tangles of black veins creeping up her arm had spread across the right side of her face and chest. He stroked her sweat-soaked hair and watched as Boogie took a closer look at Celeste's mangled arm.

"Why'd it spread so quickly? She was fine a few hours ago?" He asked

"Vigorous exercise – got the blood pumping – moved it faster through the body." Boogie stifled a grin. "You nearly fucked yourself to death, CeCe," Boogie laughed at her morose humor.

"Boy, whatever it was, sure did a number on you. I've never heard of Assiri. Yuck, smells like Gallu and-something else." She said, putting on a pair of bifocals that resembled a jeweler's lens, leaning closer, a cotton swab in her hands. Celeste screamed loud enough to shake the windows as Boogie took a sample of the infection oozing from her arm.

"Some sort of serpent venom." She said curiously. "Huh, parasites-I haven't seen this since-" She looked at Celeste with questioning, worried eyes. "It's Basilisk."

"What? How is that even possible? They're extinct." Celeste breathed, and Boogie lifted her shoulders in an awkward shrug.

"What's a Basilisk?" Eli asked, his face twisted with disgust and worry.

"It's an ancient serpentine creature, poisonous and extremely deadly, but they've been extinct for thousands of years. There is nothing recorded that has Basilisk venom or anything remotely similar that still exists. But this-this is definitely Basilisk venom."

"Can you help her?" Eli asked, his hand absently stroking Celeste's shoulders.

"Yea, but it's going to hurt like a motherfucker. You're going to have to hold her still." Boogie went to the dresser and began mixing ingredients from the little brown bottles.

"Get some towels," she said as she completed the mixture. "I also need warm water, clean gauze, bandages, and you might want to get a trash can because she's going to be puking a lot more."

When he returned from the bathroom, Boogie laid out all of the supplies he'd given her as he stood by and watched anxiously. Celeste drifted in and out of consciousness; she was completely soaked in sweat and lay in the tangled sheets. She looked so frail and lifeless. Eli had never been so scared in his life. He took a nervous step forward but wanted to stay out of Boogie's way. Finally, he made his way to the bed, sitting beside Celeste, who turned to face him, a dazed smile on her lips.

"Hey baby," she whispered, her lids drifting closed.

Boogie, finally, had two mixtures complete; one a clear sweet-smelling liquid, the other a thick purple black paste.

"Did you drink from her after this?" Boogie asked, and then looked at Celeste lying in the damp, crumpled sheets wearing Eli's t-shirt and shorts, before taking in Eli in his current state of dress, pants on inside out, shirt backward, and shook her head.

"Of course, you did," she grumbled. Shaking her head in exasperation, she quickly made another mixture of the clear liquid and handed it to him. "Drink this, just in case you managed to ingest some of the poison. I don't want to have to do this again tomorrow because you couldn't keep your teeth out of her." He willingly obliged and gagged a little as it went down. It was thick, sweet, and tasted of almond and licorice.

"What is this?" He choked.

"Anise, cyanide, wormwood, some other herbs you've never heard of." He began coughing.

"You gave me poison?" He screeched. Boogie rolled her eyes.

"Calm down. It won't kill you, but it will counteract the Basilisk venom, you big baby. Could she be pregnant?" Boogie asked. His eyes widened in shock.

"Boogie-"

"Did you wear a condom?" She asked, turning to face him, one hand on her hip.

"Not the first few times." He mumbled, a bit embarrassed. Boogie gave him a withering look, and he averted his gaze. She added something pink to the mixture she'd prepared for Celeste, shaking her head and mumbling under her breath.

"I taught you better, Eli." She slapped him on the back of the head. He winced, watching her from the corner of his eye warily but said nothing else as she continued to work.

"Okay, I need you to get behind her, sit her up and wrap yourself around her. I'm going to need her to keep as still as possible, which will be hard because she's strong. That may work to her advantage in fighting this. This is going to hurt a lot, and she may lose consciousness. But I need you to keep her as still as possible. Okay?"

He nodded numbly and did as he was told. He sat with his long, lean legs wrapped around Celeste's, his arms wrapped around her chest, pinning her left arm to her side and held steady. Her right arm, swollen and discolored, was propped on a pillow awaiting Boogie. Boogie reached for the liquid first.

"Celeste, sweetie," She gave Celeste's cheek a light slap, rousing her. "I need you to drink this." She held the bottle to Celeste's lips and slowly allowed her to drink. Celeste obliged, her eyes drifting closed as she finished. "This will help to keep it from spreading anymore. It's kind of an antibiotic, but with a little kick. It'll purge the poison from her system." She explained to Eli as she helped Celeste drink.

"Okay," Boogie exhaled and nodded to Eli. Celeste moaned,

and her head fell to the side, her body limp.

"I love you, baby," Celeste whispered.

"I know. I love you back." He kissed her cheek and exhaled.

"Here we go." Boogie's shoulders tensed as she took Celeste's limp arm and used a gloved finger to slather the thick purple paste onto her wounds.

As soon as it touched her, Celeste screamed blue murder, instinctively trying to jerk out of Boogie's grasp. Her body bucked against Eli, who held her tight to him. The pain was devastatingly intense; her mind was a tangle of red and black as the agony seemed to touch every frayed nerve in her body. Her anguish was heartbreaking, and he could feel the tears dropping onto his forearm as she continued to bellow. Her voice broke as Boogie continued, her head down, her hands moving as quickly as possible.

Celeste sobbed and kicked, her body tensing anew with each new torture. Each shriek tore at him, and he felt his tears fall. If he could, he would take the pain for her, he told her over and over in hushed tones whispered into her ear. At one point, he could have sworn he saw smoke lifting from her skin as more and more of the black pus oozed out of her and onto the towels that Boogie had laid across the bed; the smell was like death and burning flesh.

Boogie stopped for a moment, exhaling sharply before she began to press on the wounds, drawing out more of the infection and poison. Celeste bellowed like a wounded animal, digging her heels into the mattress, she pushed back until Eli's back bounced against the headboard. The wall shook, and a framed picture fell to the floor with a crash. Her body seemed to levitate for a moment, her mouth open, but no sound would come. When it did, it was hoarse and raw and spent.

At one point, Celeste dug her fangs into his arm, and Eli cursed under his breath. She did not have the gentle touch she did during lovemaking. He assumed this was what it must feel like to be food. Warm blood dropped onto the bed, staining the sheets bright red, but he held her steady.

He whispered words of encouragement into her ear. Unable to use her voice anymore, she sobbed quietly for a while, relenting to the torturous pain, and then she was out. She was unconscious by the time Boogie slathered on the last of the paste, the poisonous infection snaking out of the holes in her flesh sickeningly, sizzling as it hit the air. He held her still until Boogie stripped off her gloves. She was sweating, tears in her vivid eyes. Her bright green scrubs were splattered with blood and other more worrying things. She wiped her forehead with the back of her hand and looked at a wilted Celeste with sorrowful eyes.

"Okay, give it a few minutes, and then we have to clean the wounds and bandage them." As she spoke, Celeste rolled to the edge of the bed, and Boogie, instinctively, held the trash can as a flood of black sticky bile poured from her, her body shaking violently as it rushed past her lips. All Eli could do was to hold her hair as she wretched.

After her second use of the can, Eli suggested that they just toss the whole thing. He kissed Celeste's sweat-soaked forehead and cradled her. He didn't even mind when she threw up all over him and the bed. Instead, he ran a warm bath, filling it with the sweet-smelling bath bubbles Grace kept for guests. He lifted her gently and took her into the other room. He sat on the edge of the tub; Celeste cradled against him like a child.

Boogie came in as he was preparing to undress her and placed a plastic wrap around her arm.

"I need to use a special mixture to clean it. Try not to get it too wet. Go on. I'll wait downstairs. Clean me up a bit. Grace went out and bought a few things for you two to wear. They're on the bed. I think she'll be fine. She's strong." Then Boogie did something that surprised Eli, as well as herself, she gave him a gentle kiss on the cheek and walked away, softly closing the door behind her.

* * *

He undressed Celeste and slipped her into the bath before stripping off his blood and vomit stained clothing and slipped into the water behind her. He began to bathe her gently. She sighed and leaned forward as he soaped her back and arms, the bruises from the night before were all but gone.

"No funny business. I don't have the energy to say no." She teased lightly. He kissed her shoulder and smiled.

"When have you ever said no to me, Doc? How do you feel?" He asked, and she granted him a tired chuckle.

"Like I've been hit by a train, my arm is on fire. My head is throbbing. I'm exhausted, I can barely hold my head up or my eyes open, and I must look a hot mess." She groaned, "And I threw up in my hair." She closed her eyes and manifested a bottle of shampoo. He took it from her and gently washed her hair, filling the bathroom with her scent, jasmine, and lavender, with a hint of vanilla. She moaned and leaned against him, relaxing as he cleaned her with his gentle touch.

"You have the best hands," she whispered drowsily.

Once their bath was complete, he wrapped a towel around his waist and wrapped her in a bath sheet before sitting her on a chair in the corner of the room. Boogie had changed the bed linens and was on her way out, the soiled bundle in her arms. He dressed Celeste in a pair of pink and yellow flannel pajama pants with cartoon monkeys all over them and a pale pink tank top. He smiled and shook his head. Grace had the funniest taste in clothes when she didn't have to pretend to be his grandmother. Celeste sat limply as he brushed her hair and pulled it into a clumsy but effective ponytail, and placed her on the fresh sheets.

He'd just slipped on his drawstring pajama pants and t-shirt when Boogie knocked softly on the door. He called for her to come in and watched as she placed another towel under Celeste's arm and began to cleanse the wound gently. As the purple-black goop was rinsed away, Eli could see that the ugly creeping vines of infection had started to fade, and the tiny holes in her arms were purged of all of the foul black pus. She was already starting to heal.

"Why don't you go get something to eat? This is going to take a minute; the worst of it is over," Boogie suggested. And too tired to argue, he half stumbled down to the kitchen. The doorbell rang as he made his way down. He found it odd that it was the front door instead of the back gate where most people came, people who knew Grace anyway. Groggily, he opened the door to see two uniformed policemen standing before him. One was tall, dark with a pinched birdlike face, the other short and round. Eli rubbed his tired eyes and sighed, "Yes?"

"Good Morning, Detective Cain?" He nodded at the officer, "We're responding to several calls about a woman screaming at this location." The taller of the two said. The other was looking past Eli as Grace peered at them from the kitchen, a platter of food in her hands.

"Eli?"

"It's okay, Gracie." He yawned. "They must have heard the television upstairs. I fell asleep with it on. "

"Ma'am, are you okay?" The stout officer breathed as if he couldn't catch his breath. He stared suspiciously at Grace, who smiled radiantly and waved. "Fine, Officer. Would you like a sandwich?" They both apologized and said no thank you. Grace shrugged but stayed, watching as they spoke to Eli.

"As you can see, we're in perfect health, and it is early-" He motioned to close the door; the tall cop stopped it.

"Are there any other women in the house?" The taller man's name was Wilson, and he was nervous. Not about a being on a domestic call to a cop's house. He was nervous because he was at the home of the infamous Cain's. Eli was also known throughout the force as being somewhat creepy. Standing there before him, in his pajamas and barefoot, he just looked tired and exasperated. Still, something was ominous about the man, something in his eyes.

"My girlfriend is upstairs asleep; she has the flu. I can wake her if you'd like, but that won't be necessary." He asserted, his eyes locking with the muddy brown eyes of Carter.

"No," Carter agreed. His voice was small and seemed to come from a far-off place.

Eli caught the eyes of both men in succession, as Carter continued to stare at him sleepily. Wilson seemed to sway slightly, his eyes suddenly heavy. Then as if on autopilot Eli's voice took on a low deep monotone.

"We're fine. There is nothing to report here. I fell asleep with the television on. My–sister," He said, trying to remember Grace no longer fit the role of grandmother, "is fine. My girlfriend is asleep. Nothing more." They nodded dumbly and smiled.

"Sorry to have disturbed you, sir. You have a good day." Wilson mumbled. They turned and walked away. Carter looked at Eli as if he had just laid eyes on him. Eli smiled and closed the door, his head swimming. That was the first time he had glamoured someone. The first time he could remember any way.

Glamouring, Eli came to realize, was a handy little tool, and easier than he thought it would be, and surprisingly guilt-free

❋ ❋ ❋

He found Grace sitting at the kitchen's center island with a pretty woman with honey-colored hair and skin. She looked at Eli with warm brown eyes, and he gave her a tired smile. She wore blue jeans and looked to Eli like a man's sweater, which hung loosely past her knees, her short blond hair disheveled. She was quite pretty, he thought.

"Lisette?" He asked. She rose and embraced him.

"How is she?' She was shaking. He figured she'd heard her sister's cries of pain, and she had been as terrified as whoever had called the police. He had been up there with her, and he had been disturbed.

"Better. Go on up. She'll be glad to see you. Boogie's just

finishing up. Third door on the left." He pointed up, and she rushed off. Eli sat heavily across from Grace, his face tired and worn. Grace slid a sandwich over to him and got up to pour him a cup of coffee.

"I called Jonas. He said the boys took down the giant. He's locked up in the Collective's chamber." Grace said, and he couldn't help but smile.

"Remy did seem to get off on that," he chuckled. "They are as crazy as shit-house rats." He sipped his coffee, relishing the warm richness as it went down.

"She's going to be okay," Grace assured him. "Boogie said that if you had waited any later, it could have been much worse." She patted his back and gently rubbed his head as he sipped the coffee.

"Is Boogie the witch who bound me?" He asked absently, rubbing his tired eyes.

"Yes. Boogie is very old and very strong." She answered his next question before he'd even thought to ask it. He gave his daughter a weak smile and pushed the sandwich away. He held the coffee mug, the warmth seeping into his fingers, and stared down into the dark liquid.

"I love her, Grace. And I love you. I need you and Boogie to make me a promise. If anything were to happen to you, Riley included any of you, I want you to bind me. You tell Boogie that I want her to bind me before it gets bad again completely." He spoke in a voice so low and even that it scared her.

"I know you love her, love us, but isn't that a bit extreme-" He clutched her hands, his eyes dark and intense.

"I need you to promise. There are people out there who are waiting for me to break, and if anything happened to any of you, I would be destroyed. And I think it would be the worst possible thing that could ever happen. I think it would be worse than before. Worse than when your mother-" She nodded, her own eyes filling with tears.

"Okay, Okay. I promise. And Boogie promises. Okay? But we'll be fine." He kissed her knuckles before releasing her hands. Slowly, he moved to stand near the patio doors. He stared blindly at the garden, inhaling the sweet smell of her winter annuals.

"I don't remember your mother, Gracie. Was it like this with her?"

"No. No, she's special. I don't doubt you loved my mother, but Celeste, I think, is your soul mate. You and my mother were so different. She was soft,-spoken and very agreeable, delicate. You loved her, but not like this, not like her. " She moved quietly to him and lovingly stroked his cheek, a wistful smile playing at the corners of her mouth.

"Don't look so worried. I have had a long time to deal with my mother's death. I'm not going to get all evil step-daughter on, Doc. I like her. I think you've met your match." He was silent for a moment, taking in her words and contemplating his next question.

"I saw Nicky Sky last night. I was dreaming, I think, and he said that the Dark Fae are planning on releasing the beast. Truthfully, Grace, was I that much of a monster?"

"You were so different back then, Elijah. We all were."

"That wasn't an answer," he said.

"Sure, it was." She winked and sipped her coffee. "Oh, don't pout. You aren't an evil or malicious man, Eli. Death is sometimes the only viable option." She said without emotion. Eli stared at her for a long time, a smile starting to form on his lips.

"Tell me," he said, "What are we going to do about you?" She lifted a brow.

"What about me? I'm great. Look at me. I'm fabulous. I have excellent genetics," she said.

"I mean, how are we going to explain to you and the absence of grandmother Grace? No one is going to believe you're my daughter. We look to close in age." He sipped his coffee and bit into his sandwich, suddenly aware of how hungry he was. He couldn't remember the last time he'd eaten. She waved a hand dismissively.

"It's already handled." She sighed, obviously proud of herself.

"Really?" He asked around a mouth of bread, ham, and cheese.

"You see, I am Gracie Cain, little sister. Grace Babineaux, the grandmother, passed away peacefully in her sleep last night after a long battle with cancer the night of her annual Thanksgiving dinner. I returned home from New York to help my big brother grieve. I was sent to live with relatives when our parents died, and after burying Grandma Grace, in two days, I will decide to stay. The obituary runs tomorrow." He was duly impressed, and it showed on his face.

"As I said, it's been handled. Boogie and I have been at this for a very long time. I'll get Boogie to put a protection spell on the house. You get some sleep. I have a feeling that it will get a little difficult in the next few days." She kissed his cheek before rising to remove their dishes.

Difficult, he thought, that was the understatement of the century.

\* \* \*

"Hey baby," Celeste said dreamily as Eli eased into the room. "Boogie gave me pain killers." She slurred as Boogie chanted something low and rhythmic, casting the room into dim darkness.

"She's a little punch drunk, but she'll be fine after some rest. She'll need to sleep for a few days. Her body has to recoup. No strenuous activities, Elijah." Boogie leveled him with a stare that spoke volumes. "Make sure she drinks lots of water; blood will help her heal faster, your blood. That's all you give her, Elijah. You keep that snake in your pants." Boogie gave him a quick hug and kissed Celeste's cheek before she left.

Lisette had moved a chair to the side of the bed and held Celeste's hand. It was evident that she'd brushed her sister's hair because now it hung past her shoulders in a neat braid. Lisette smiled tiredly at Eli.

"I should get going, too." She stood, stretching her tired limbs, her eyes on him the entire time. She watched with great interest as he leaned over Celeste and kissed her feverish forehead. Celeste managed a tired smile before drifting off to sleep. It amazed Lisette, the ease in which they fell into a comfortable pattern. He wanted Celeste with him, and for the first time, her sister was comfortable sleeping in a man's bed. They belonged, and she couldn't help but feel a pang of jealousy.

Eli felt it all.

"You're welcome to stay. I can sleep in my old bedroom; you're more than welcome to sleep in here with-" She raised a hand to stop him.

"It's just enough that you offered. I will be staying with Gaston at the St. Charles house. He really wants to know that's she's okay. I can't say the same for your house." She smiled apologetically. "My brothers do love a fight."

"So, I saw," Eli agreed as he walked her down to the front door. Boogie and Grace peered at him from the kitchen door. When he looked at them, they scurried away like little mice tittering with laughter.

"Thank Grace for calling us, Eli. Even though she's older than us, she's still our baby sister. And after meeting your family, I know you'll take care of her. I can see why she loves you so much." She stood on tiptoe and kissed his cheek.

When she pulled away, Eli received a spark of sexual energy from Lisette. She openly stared at him, her mind racing through scenarios in which she would see him again. There was something about him she wanted; she wanted to be alone with him. She wanted to belong to him.

Seemingly embarrassed by her thoughts, she averted her gaze, and her cheeks flushed. There was something about him she found irresistible, and she was ashamed of herself for lusting, albeit briefly, after her sister's boyfriend. She glanced at him again, and he could see that she really didn't care that he was with Celeste or that she was engaged. She wanted him. He stared at her uncomfortably, and she gave him a weak smile, remembering that he could read her mind.

"So, I will see you again soon? Both of you, I mean." She smiled nervously, taking a step away from him. Eli thought that Lisette was more than pretty. In that moment, she was beautiful and deceitful, a dangerous combination. He had an uneasy feeling about Lisette. Even though she exuded lust, there was something else, something beneath the surface that made his skin crawl. She wasn't what she portrayed herself to be, he realized. He waved goodbye as she backed down the front steps and stumbled to her car.

*Be wary of pretty little birds*, he thought.

He watched her car turn a corner before he went back inside, securing all of the locks and turning on the security system. He knew that it was an exercise in futility. The house was protected. Grace had assured him; they would be safe here for as long as Boogie's protection spell was in place. Knowing Boogie as well as he did, he knew that would be for a very long time. Finally, he trudged upstairs, too exhausted to think anymore.

Celeste was half asleep, her freshly bandaged arm on a pillow. She lay on her back, her eyes closed, and her chest was rising and falling gently in sleep. He smiled at her for a moment before sliding beneath the covers next to her. She moaned and turned to nestle her head on his chest.

"Boogie says you should drink from me." He put his wrist near her mouth, and she managed to bite, sucking weakly for a moment before she had no energy to continue. His reaction was instant; his body had a mind of its own.

"Drink," he growled, his erection pushed into her lower belly, his fangs brushing her neck.

"Too tired," she whispered and drifted off, her head snuggled into the crook of his arm. He sighed, letting his heavy lids close.

In a matter of days, his whole world had turned inside out

and upside down. He had a feeling that in the days to come, things would only become more challenging. Battles were being waged, and wars being planned, something that had been set into motion from the moment Nicky Sky had taken his last breath.

Celeste stirred, nuzzling closer to him, her bandaged arm resting on his chest. He kissed the top of her head and listened as Boogie and Grace spoke in hushed tones. Boogie was chanting a protection spell, the scent of burning herbs filling the house. He drew Celeste closer, after a few minutes; he too drifted off into an exhausted sleep.

Tonight, he yawned, they would rest. Tomorrow's battles would come soon enough.

&#42; &#42; &#42;

# OTHER BOOKS IN
## *The Fallen Series*

### *Mark of the Fallen*

**Long ago, he abandoned her breaking her heart. Years later, he**

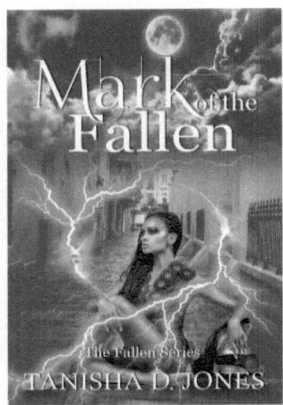

**and re-ignites a long-dormant passion. Can she forgive his betrayal and open her heart to him again?**

Karim, Vampire Prince of Tyre, once rescued Celeste from a watery grave. Bound by his words, he abandons her with dire consequences. Years later, he comes face to face with the woman who has haunted his dreams, but she is already promised to another

Celeste is drawn to the dark and noble Karim. He ignites passion and anger that has burned for eons. Torn apart by his betrayal, she still longs for the only love she's ever known. But she's been promised to a man she doesn't even remember.

Unbeknownst to either, a plot's been set into motion to push Celeste toward a destiny that could lead to the destruction of their entire world. Should she remain faithful to a man she has never met or succumb to a passion that she cannot deny?

**Mark of the Fallen is book two in the sexy and exciting Fallen Series. It's an erotic, action-packed story of a goddess finding her humanity and a human finding his divinity during their ascent to love**

## *Unbound*

**Someone's trying to kill her. He wants to protect her, but her secrets won't let him.**

**They must work through their past or lose everything.**

### *Elijah Cain*

*Eli is still trying to come to grips with who he is. He's overwhelmed about coming into his powers and trying to figure out if what he has with Celeste is real. Everything is*

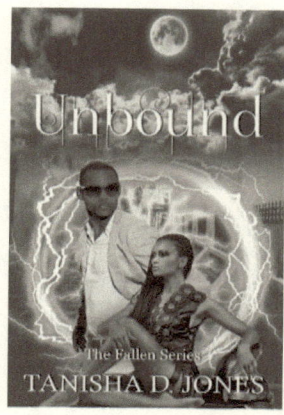

in question. If he doesn't make the right choice, he could be the catalyst to ending humanity.

### Celeste Kent

Celeste and Eli are finally in a good place. She's ready to reveal her past when her ex-boyfriend pops-up on her patio. He claims he's there to help but only causes strife between her and Eli.

As two worlds prepare for war, can Eli and Celeste forgive old betrayals to save humanity?

**Unbound is book three of the Fallen series set in a world of gods and angels. It's an erotic, action-packed story of a goddess finding her humanity and a human finding his divinity during their ascent to love.**